Praise for #1 *New York Times* bestselling author

LISA JACKSON

"[B]estselling Jackson cranks up the suspense to almost unbearable heights in her latest tautly written thriller."
—*Booklist* on *Malice*

"When it comes to providing gritty and sexy stories, Ms. Jackson certainly knows how to deliver."
—*RT Book Reviews* on *Unspoken*

"Provocative prose, an irresistible plot and finely crafted characters make up Jackson's latest contemporary sizzler."
—*Publishers Weekly* on *Wishes*

"Lisa Jackson takes my breath away."
—*New York Times* bestselling author Linda Lael Miller

**Also available from
Lisa Jackson
and HQN Books**

LISA JACKSON

ILLICIT

HQN™

ISBN-13: 978-0-373-77914-7

Illicit

Copyright © 2015 by Harlequin Books S.A.

Recycling programs
for this product may
not exist in your area.

The publisher acknowledges the copyright holders
of the individual works as follows:

Midnight Sun
Copyright © 1985 by Lisa Jackson

In Honor's Shadow
Copyright © 1988 by Lisa Jackson

This edition published by arrangement with Harlequin Books S.A.

For questions and comments about the quality of this book,
please contact us at CustomerService@Harlequin.com.

® and TM are trademarks of Harlequin Enterprises Limited or its
corporate affiliates. Trademarks indicated with ® are registered in the
United States Patent and Trademark Office, the Canadian Intellectual
Property Office and in other countries.

Printed in U.S.A.

HQN™

CONTENTS

MIDNIGHT SUN

CHAPTER ONE

HOLDING HER HEAD PROUDLY, Ashley walked into the room and gave no outward sign of her flagging confidence. Her elegant features were emotionless and the regal tilt of her chin didn't falter. The only signs of the emotional turmoil which stole her sleep were the deep blue smudges beneath her eyes.

She was reminded of vultures circling over carrion as she stepped into the law offices of McMichaels and Lee. Alan McMichaels held the chair for her, and as she took her seat between her cousin Claud and Aunt Beatrice, Ashley could feel the cool disdain in the pinched, white faces of the five people seated near the oiled oak desk.

Claud's rust-colored eyebrows had raised in mild surprise when she entered the room, but he said nothing. Aunt Beatrice nodded stiffly and then turned her pale gold eyes back on the attorney.

The family had never been particularly close. Or, at least, Ashley had never felt the kinship with her father's relatives that some families share.

Today was no exception. Her father's death hadn't brought the family together. If anything, the family, whose members each owned a small piece of Stephens Timber Corporation, seemed more fragmented than ever.

Though the room was spacious and decorated in opulent tones of cobalt blue and brown, the atmosphere within the brushed plaster walls was awkward and confining. Tension, like an invisible electric current, charged the air.

Alan McMichaels took a seat at the modern desk. Behind his chair, through a large, plate glass window, was an expansive view of the West Hills of Portland. The fir-laden slopes, still a rich forest green in winter, were covered with expensive, turn-of-the-century homes that overlooked the city. In the distance, spanning two high ridges, was the Vista Bridge. Its elegant gray arch was just visible in the gentle morning fog that had settled upon the city.

The lean attorney with the silver hair and black eyebrows cleared his throat and caught everyone's attention. "As you know, we're here for the reading of Lazarus Stephens's will. Please hold your comments until I've read the entire document. When I'm finished, I'll answer all of your questions."

McMichaels adjusted his reading glasses and picked up the neatly typed document. A claustrophobic feeling took hold of Ashley and wouldn't let go. The tears she had shed for her father were dry and the only thing she felt was a deep, inexplicable loneliness. She and her father had never been close, but she felt as if a part of her had died with him.

Despite the unspoken accusations of the other people in the room, Ashley met each questioning gaze with the cool serenity of her intelligent green eyes. Her blue-black hair was coiled neatly at the nape of her neck in a tight knot of ebony silk, and she was dressed expensively in a dark blue suit of understated elegance.

Ashley understood the condemning looks from her father's family. With very few exceptions the relatives of Lazarus Stephens didn't approve of Ashley and made no bones about it. Ashley imagined that they had all been secretly pleased when they had learned of the falling-out between Lazarus and his headstrong, spoiled daughter. Aunts, uncles and cousins alike treated her like an outsider.

Ignoring the surreptitious glances being cast in her direction, Ashley folded her hands in her lap and stared calmly at the silver-haired, bespectacled man sitting directly across the desk from her. Alan McMichaels was addressing everyone in the room, but Ashley was left with the distinct impression that he was singling her out.

"I, Lazarus J. Stephens of Portland, Oregon, do make, publish and declare my Last Will and Testament, revoking all previous Wills and Codicils…." Ashley listened to her father's attorney, and her wide green eyes showed no sign of emotion as the reading of the will progressed. Though she remained outwardly calm, her stomach was tied into several painful knots while the small bequests were made to each of Lazarus Stephens's closest friends and relatives.

McMichaels had insisted that Ashley attend the reading of her father's will, although she didn't understand why. Unless, of course, it was her father's wish that she listen in humiliation while Lazarus publicly announced for the last time that he had disinherited his only child.

She paled at the memory of the violent scene that had resulted in the rift separating them. Vividly she could recall the rage that had colored his cheeks, the vicious accusations that had claimed she had "sold out" and betrayed him, and the look of utter disdain and disappointment in his faded blue eyes.

Over the years, the gap between father and daughter had narrowed, but never had that one, horrible scene been forgotten. Though Ashley had chosen to ignore the rumors about her father and his business practices, she hadn't been immune to the malicious gossip that seemed to spread like wildfire whenever his name was mentioned in private conversation.

Alan McMichaels cleared his throat and his dark eyes locked with Ashley's for an instant. "…my nephew Claud," McMichaels continued. In her peripheral vision Ashley saw Claud lean forward and noticed that his anxious fingers ran nervously along the edge of the polished desk as he stared expectantly at the attorney. "...I bequeath the sum of one hundred thousand dollars."

Claud's self-assured smile, hidden partially by a thick, rust-colored mustache, wavered slightly as McMichaels paused. Claud's nervous eyes darted from McMichaels to Ashley and back again.

"I give, devise and bequeath all of the residue of my estate unto my only child, Ashley Stephens Jennings, to be hers absolutely."

Ashley's heart dropped and her face drained of all color. She was forced to close her eyes for a second as she digested the intent of her father's will. *He had forgiven her.* But his stubborn pride hadn't allowed Lazarus to confront his daughter. Her fingers clenched together. Hot tears of grief burned in her eyes as she accepted her father's final forgiveness.

McMichaels had continued reading, but the words were a muffled sound in Ashley's private world of grief. She couldn't look into the eyes of the startled family members.

"Wait a minute—" Claud started to interrupt, but a killing stare from Alan McMichaels forestalled any further comment from Ashley's cousin. Claud sent Ashley a stricken look bordering on hatred.

McMichaels's voice droned on for a few minutes until he finally tapped the neatly typed sheets of white paper on the tabletop and smiled. "That's it. If you have any questions—"

The voices around the table started to buzz, and Ashley felt the eyes of distant relatives bore into her. Pieces of the whispered conversation drifted to her ears.

"I never suspected..."

"Didn't Uncle Laz cut her off?"

"I thought so. Something about an affair with that Trevor Daniels, you know, the one running for the senatorial seat this fall."

"How could she? And with that man! He was accused of taking a bribe last summer sometime. The charges didn't stick, but if you ask me, he paid somebody off to save his neck! Trevor Daniels isn't a man to trust or get involved with!"

"Daniels swore he'd break Lazarus, you know. He always blamed Lazarus for his father's disappearance. If you ask me, Trevor Daniels's father...what was his name? Robert—that's right. I'll bet that Robert Daniels just took off with another woman...."

Ashley lifted her chin fractionally and leveled cool green eyes on the members of her father's family. She was accustomed to the pain of gossip and she managed to let her poise lift her above the insulting speculation being whispered just loud enough for her to hear. Pushing her chair away from the desk, Ashley stood and started toward the door.

Claud was leaning over McMichaels's desk, his ruddy complexion redder than usual. Though he was whispering, Ashley was well aware of what he was threatening. Claud considered himself next in line for control of the Stephens timber empire. No doubt cousin Claud was already devising ways of contesting the will.

Alan McMichaels noticed that Ashley was leaving, and he broke off his conversation with Claud in order to talk to her. He held up his palm to get her attention. "Ms. Jennings—please. If you could stay for a few more minutes. There are a few matters I'd like to discuss with you."

Managing a frail smile, Ashley nodded before smoothing her skirt and walking across the room to stand near the windows. She felt, rather than saw, the hateful glances cast at her back.

Though Ashley's gaze studied the view from the eighth floor of the building, she didn't notice the tall spire of a Gothic church steeple in the foreground or the fact that the fog had begun to lift, promising a cold, but clear, November day. Her thoughts rested on her father and the horrible fight that had torn them apart.

It had taken place in the spacious library of Lazarus's Tudor home on Palatine Hill. "How could you?" Lazarus had shouted, his shock and rage white-hot when he had discovered that the man Ashley had been seeing all summer was the son of Robert Daniels, the man who had been Lazarus's rival before his mysterious disappearance not two years earlier. Lazarus's faded blue eyes had sparked vengeful fire, and his shoulders had slumped in defeat. Nothing Ashley could have done would have wounded him more.

When she had tried to explain that she loved Trevor and planned to marry him, her father had laughed. "Marry a Daniels? Damn it, Ashley, I thought you had more brains than that!" Lazarus had shaken his graying head. "What do you think he wants from you? Love?" When Lazarus read the expectant light in her eyes, he had spit angrily into the fire. "He's using you, don't you see? He's after the timber company, for Christ's sake! He's on some personal vendetta against me. Wake up girl. Trevor Daniels doesn't care a damn about you."

When Ashley had staunchly refused to stop seeing Trevor, Lazarus had slapped his open palm on the table and threatened to disinherit her. Angrily, she had told him to do just that and had stomped out of the room, out of his house and out of her father's life. Determined that she was right, Ashley had been hell-bent to prove him wrong.

It had been an impossible task. Lazarus had been correct about Trevor and his motives all along. At the vividly painful memory, Ashley sighed and ran her fingers along the cool window ledge. One again tears, bitter and deceitful, threatened to spill.

"Ashley, could I have a word with you? It will only take a few minutes."

She turned to face her father's attorney and noticed that the room was empty. "First, let me tell you I'm sorry about your father." She nodded, accepting his condolences and somehow holding on to her frail composure. "And that I hope you'll continue to retain the services of McMichaels and Lee for yourself as well as the business." Once again she nodded, encouraging him to get to the point.

"You must realize that, with your father's bequest, you own a large majority of the stock of Stephens Timber. It's within your power to run the company or hire someone else—"

"Mr. McMichaels," Ashley interrupted, finally able to collect her scattered thoughts. "Right now, I don't think I'm qualified to run the company myself."

"But your father thought you could. Don't you have a degree in business administration?"

"A master's—"

"And didn't you work for the corporation?"

"Years ago—during the summers between school terms. But the industry has changed a lot in the last eight years," she protested.

"Your father seemed to think that you had a real knack for handling the executive end of Stephens Timber."

"Did he?" Ashley shook her head in confusion. Why hadn't her father been able to tell her what McMichaels was repeating? "I think we should leave things just as they are for the time being. It was my understanding that Claud had been managing the day-to-day transactions for all practical purposes. My father was in semiretirement."

"That's right."

Ashley forced herself to think clearly. The strain of the past few days had been exhausting, but she couldn't ignore her responsibilities. "So, until I know a little more about the business, and until my teaching contract is fulfilled, I'll have to rely on Claud. The only thing I'll require for the present is an audit of the company books and monthly financial statements. I'll talk to Claud and ask him to continue to stay on as general manager of the corporation, at least temporarily."

McMichaels stuffed his hands into his pockets and appeared uneasy.

"Is there a problem with that?"

The attorney frowned, seemed about to say something and thought better of it. "No, I suppose not. You can do whatever you like."

"I know about the company's reputation," she assured the surprised lawyer. "I haven't lived my life with my head in the sand. I expect that Claud will see to it that anything Stephens Timber does is strictly legal. Advising him will be your job."

McMichaels smiled. Relief was evident on his tanned features. "Good."

Ashley managed a thin smile. It was the first since the news of her father's heart attack. "Whether I like it or not, I've got a teaching contract that doesn't expire until June fifteenth. I'll talk to the administration and explain the situation, and if the community college can find a substitute for next term, I'll consider moving back to Portland and working with Claud."

"I think that would be wise," McMichaels agreed. He touched her shoulder in a consoling gesture. "You're a very wealthy woman, now, Ashley. You'll have to be careful. People will be out to take advantage of you."

"Only if I give them the chance," she replied. Ashley spoke a few more minutes with her father's attorney and left his office with the disturbing feeling that something was on Alan McMichaels's mind. She shook off the uncomfortable sensation and reasoned that the lawyer wanted to give her a little more time to deal with her grief before hoisting any corporate problems onto her shoulders.

Once in the elevator, Ashley was alone. She closed her eyes and moved her head from side to side, hoping to relieve some of the tension in her shoulders.

Pushing through the glass doors of the building housing the firm of McMichaels and Lee, Ashley stepped into the subdued winter sunlight. A slight breeze caught in her hair and chilled her to the bone. She had just started down the short flight of steps to the street when Claud accosted her. Ashley braced herself for the confrontation that was sure to come. Ever since her falling out with her father, Claud had been groomed to inherit the presidency of Stephens Timber. No doubt his feathers were more than slightly ruffled.

"You knew about the change in the will, didn't you?" he charged, falling into step with her.

"Of course not."

"I don't understand it—"

"Neither do I. Not really, but the fact is that father left the company to me." When she reached her car, she turned to face her cousin. "Look, Claud, I know this must be a shock and disappointment to you. The thing of it is that I'd like you to continue to run the corporation just as you did for Dad, but you'll have to report to me. I've told Alan exactly what I expect from you."

Claud tugged uneasily on his mustache. His dark eyes bored into hers. "You won't interfere?"

"Of course I will—*if* I think you're doing an inadequate job. The next few days I'll be at the corporate offices, looking over your shoulder. We can get any of the more pressing problems ironed out then. I want to know everything that happens to Stephens Timber Corporation."

"Then you're moving to Portland?" Claud asked, shifting from one foot to the other. He pulled at the knotted silk tie and found it difficult to look Ashley in the eye.

"Maybe after spring break, if the school administration can replace me. I expect you to send me reports and call me if you have a problem."

"I think I will handle everything," Claud stated with his cocky self-assurance. "Your old man didn't bother to oversee what I was doing."

"Well I am," Ashley stated, her eyes glittering with determination. "Because now it's my reputation on the line."

"Don't tell me you believed all those rumors."

"Gossip is a cheap sort of entertainment for idle minds. What I believe happened in the past doesn't matter. But, from here on in, we keep our corporate nose clean. Stephens Timber can't afford any more bad press." She added emphasis to her words by tapping her fingers on the hood of her car.

Claud grinned broadly. He reassessed his first cousin and his eyes slid appreciatively down her slender body. Ashley Jennings was a woman with class. It was too damn bad she just happened to be Lazarus Stephens's daughter. "We do have one particular problem," Claud speculated aloud.

"What's that?" Ashley had pulled the keys from her purse and her hand was poised over the handle of the car door. She and Claud had never gotten along, but because of the situation, she was forced to trust him, if only temporarily.

"Trevor Daniels."

"Why is he a problem?" Ashley looked unperturbed and gave no indication of her suddenly racing pulse. After eight years of living with the truth, she was able to react calmly whenever Trevor's name was mentioned.

"If he gets the senatorial seat in the fall, he'll put us out of business."

"I don't see how that's possible, Claud." She turned to face her cousin. Her green eyes were still clear and hid the fact that her heart was pounding erratically.

"He's always been out to get the family. You, as well as anyone, should know that," Claud stated.

Ashley felt her body stiffen, but she promised herself not to let Claud's insensitive remarks affect her.

She straightened before crossing her arms over her chest and leaning on her sporty BMW. "Trevor's family, as well as ours, is involved in the timber business. We're competitors—that's all. There's no way he would be able to 'put us out of business.'"

Claud's hands were spread open at his sides. "But you know how he is—he's trying to get the government to make all the forests into designated wilderness areas. If he gets elected—"

"He'll try harder." Ashley's small hands pushed her away from the car. "But not to the point that it would destroy the timber industry. If he did that, Claud, he'd not only thwart his own family's business, but he'd also put a lot of his constituents back in the unemployment lines. He's too smart to do anything of the sort."

"I can't figure it out," Claud said, his eyes narrowing suspiciously.

"What?"

"Why the hell you still stick up for that bastard!"

Ashley raised an elegant eyebrow and smiled confidently. "What happened between Trevor and me has nothing to do with Stephens Timber."

"Like hell! When are you going to face the fact that the bastard used you, Ashley? And all for a chance at the timber company. He thought you would inherit it all, didn't he? And then, when your father cut you off, he split! Swell guy."

"There's no reason to discuss this any further," Ashley replied, her cheeks beginning to burn.

"Just remember that he's out to get Stephens Timber," Claud warned. "He still thinks Lazarus had something to do with his father's disappearance."

Ashley managed to smile sweetly despite the fact that her blood had turned cold. "And just remember who signs your paycheck."

"You need me," Claud reminded her.

"Of course I do, and I'd hate to lose your expertise at managing the company. But that's all I expect from you, and I don't need any lectures about my personal life." Her dark brows arched over determined green eyes.

At that moment Claud understood that tangling with his beautiful cousin would be more difficult than he had imagined. It looked as if, after all, Ashley had inherited more than the timber fortune; she also had received some of her father's resolve. Claud raised his hands in mock surrender. "All right. Just be careful, Ashley. It wouldn't surprise me a bit if Trevor Daniels suddenly started paying a lot of attention to you. You can't trust him."

"I think I can deal with Trevor," Ashley responded with more confidence than she felt. When Claud finally left her alone, she slid into the car, placed her hands on the steering wheel and let the bitter tears of pain slide down her face.

Trevor opened a weary eye. As he lifted his head the weight of the hangover hit him like a ton of bricks. He was still seated in the leather recliner by the fireplace, and his muscles were cramped from the awkward position and the cold morning air. A half-full glass of Scotch, now stale, sat on the small table near his chair next to the newspaper article that had been the impetus for his uncharacteristic binge. The bold headlines were still visible, but the rest of the article was smeared from the liquor that had slopped over the rim of the glass and spilled onto the newsprint.

Running a tired hand over the stubble on his chin, Trevor stretched and cursed himself for his own lack of control. How many drinks had he consumed while locked in memories of the past—four, five? He couldn't remember. The last time he had been so drunk was the night of Ashley's betrayal....

Of their own accord, his vibrant blue eyes returned to the headline: TIMBER BARON DEAD AT 70. The paper was three days old.

"You bastard," Trevor murmured before wadding the newspaper and tossing it into the smoldering remains of the fire. The paper ignited and was instantly consumed by hungry flames.

The first gray light of dawn was already shadowing the spacious den with the promise of another cold November morning. With an effort, Trevor pulled himself out of the chair and ran his fingers through his thick chestnut hair. His mouth tasted rancid and he wondered if it was from too much liquor, too little sleep or the painful memories of Ashley. The article about the death of Ashley's father, Lazarus Stephens, had conjured up all the old pain again— the pain Trevor had promised to put behind him.

Maybe it was impossible. Perhaps Ashley's life and his were entwined irrevocably by the sins of their fathers. Whatever the reason, Trevor had difficulty dismissing the image of her shining black hair and intriguing sea-green eyes.

Trevor rubbed his temple as he walked to the window and let his eyes wander outside the house, past the landscaped lawns and through the denuded trees of the estate his father had purchased. He leaned against the windowsill and considered the unlikely course of events that would never allow him to be free of her.

The feud between the two timber families had been long, ruthless and bloody. Rumor had it that sometime before the Korean War, the partners, who owned a small Oregon logging firm, had become embroiled in such a vicious argument that they had parted ways, each vowing to destroy the other. The stories varied slightly but all seemed to agree that the cause of the dispute was graft. Robert Daniels had supposedly caught Lazarus Stephens skimming off company profits for personal use.

The result of the breakup was that Stephens Timber Corporation and Daniels Logging Company became bitter enemies within the Oregon timber industry.

Trevor didn't know how many of the rumors that had circulated scandalously over the past forty years were true and how many were fictitious. But he was certain of one thing: Lazarus Stephens had been involved in the disappearance of Trevor's father, Robert Daniels.

Ten years before, when Robert had disappeared, Trevor had sworn that not only would he avenge his father, but he would personally see to it that the people responsible for the crime would be punished. But he had been deterred by his feelings for Ashley.

What had happened to Robert Daniels, after he was last seen leaving the dinner meeting with a lobbyist from Washington, D.C., remained a mystery. And now Lazarus Stephens, Ashley's father, the one man who knew the answer, was dead.

Ashley. Just the thought of her innocent eyes and enigmatic smile touched a traitorous part of Trevor's soul. He squeezed his eyes tightly shut, as if he could physically deny the vivid image of her elegant face surrounded by glossy ebony curls.

Thinking of Ashley and her betrayal still made him clench his teeth together in frustration, and he silently cursed himself for caring. Hadn't she shown her true colors? Hadn't she tossed him out of her life and married another man?

Trevor had been blind to her faults and had let his feelings for her manipulate him. But now the tables had turned; if the senatorial race ended in his favor, he would personally see to it that all the suspicious dealings of Stephens Timber were investigated and halted.

His blue eyes narrowed as he stared past the leafless trees to the silvery waters of the Willamette River. A soft morning fog clung tenaciously to the shoreline.

What if Ashley inherited Lazarus's share of Stephens Timber Corporation? What if all those rumors that her father disinherited her were only idle speculation? What if Ashley was now the woman in charge of the corporation Trevor had vowed to destroy?

His headache began to pound furiously just as the telephone rang. Trevor Daniels was jerked back to the present and the most pressing problem of the day: winning the election in the fall.

CHAPTER TWO

DURING THE NEXT few weeks, Ashley's impatience with her cousin mounted with the passing of each day, and her concern for Stephens Timber drew her attention away from Trevor and his candidacy in the May primary. Trevor's face was continually in the news and Ashley was glad for the distraction of the timber company. It helped her keep the memories of the love she had shared with him pushed into a dark corner of her mind.

Between studying the reports that Claud had grudgingly begun to send her and instructing her classes, Ashley barely had a moment to herself. When she was able to find a few minutes to relax, her thoughts would invariably return to Trevor and the few blissful months they had shared together nearly eight years ago.

Now she owned the lion's share of the company Trevor had vowed to destroy.

"Oh, stop it," she admonished as she sat at the cluttered kitchen table in her small apartment near the campus. "You're beginning to sound as paranoid as Claud." At the mention of her shifty cousin's name, Ashley frowned. It didn't take a supersleuth to realize that Claud was up to something, but Ashley didn't know exactly what. The information he had been sending concerning the timber company was sketchy at best. Ashley had the uneasy feeling that Claud was deliberately trying to hide something from her.

The first report from Claud hadn't been as encompassing as Ashley had hoped, but when she had asked her cousin for a more lengthy audit of the books of Stephens Timber, Claud had been reluctant to send it to her.

"Don't worry yourself," he had soothed when she had called him and demanded more complete information. "You've got more than you can handle with your teaching job. Besides which, I've got everything under control up here."

"That's not the issue, Claud. I need the reports," Ashley had insisted.

"Then you'd better come up and look at them," Claud had growled, losing his veneer of civility. "I don't like sending out that kind of information. Right now we've got a shortage of personnel in the bookkeeping department, and I wouldn't want to trust the post office to get the reports to you, even if we were able to put them together."

"You're stalling, Claud," she had responded. "Get the reports together and send them in tomorrow's mail, or I just might take you up on your offer and come up to Portland to see for myself just how well you've 'got everything under control.'"

"Look, Ashley, I don't need a keeper!"

Ashley had begun to worry in earnest.

"And Claud?"

"What?"

"For God's sake, hire the help you need in accounting!"

Claud's reply had been a disgusted snort, indicating all too well what he thought about Ashley's interference in what he considered his domain.

Claud's reluctance had been all the reason she needed to talk to the school administration about getting out of her teaching contract. Within a week, the administration had found a suitable replacement to take over her classes for the rest of the school year. All she had to do was finish the term, and that task was nearly accomplished. Christmas vacation started next week.

At that thought, Ashley quit thinking about her cousin and let her gaze return to the untidy stack of papers sitting on the table. As she started grading the tests, she listened to a local news channel on the television.

She was frowning at a particularly bad answer to one of her questions and sipping coffee when news of an accident involving Trevor was announced by the even-featured anchorman.

Ashley almost spilled her coffee, her throat constricted in fear and her eyes snapped upward to stare at the small television situated on the kitchen counter. She had left it on for background noise, but at the sound of Trevor's name, all of her attention became riveted to the set.

"…Trevor Daniels was rushed to Andrews Hospital in Salem when the car he was driving slid off the road, broke through the guardrail and rolled down an embankment.…" The screen flashed from the earnest reporter to the site of the accident and the twisted wreckage of Trevor's car.

Ashley's stomach knotted and nausea rose in her throat. "Dear God," she whispered, placing her hand protectively over her heart. Her blood ran as cold as the clear December night. The pencil she had been holding over a stack of papers dropped unobserved onto the table as she concentrated on what the wavy-haired reporter was saying.

"Reports have varied as to the cause of the accident," the reporter, once again on the screen, told the viewing audience. "Police are investigating the site, but as yet have not confirmed the rumors of foul play. Mr. Daniels remains in serious, but stable condition."

"No," Ashley murmured, at the fleeting thoughts of Trevor and the love they had shared. Absently, she removed her reading glasses, rubbed her temples and stared at the screen. When she found the strength to move, she pushed her chair away from the table and some coffee spilled onto the tests. She didn't notice.

Without considering her motives, she dialed operator assistance and was given the number of Andrews Hospital. Her fingers were trembling when she punched out the number for the hospital in Salem. After several rings, a member of the staff answered and told her politely, but firmly, that Mr. Daniels was taking no calls and seeing no visitors.

Ashley replaced the receiver and slumped against the wall. What was happening? Within the course of three weeks her father had suffered a fatal heart attack, she had inherited the company and now, Trevor Daniels, the only man she had ever loved, had nearly been killed. The reporter had glossed over the mention of foul play; certainly no one would want to harm Trevor....

Get a hold of yourself, she warned. *He doesn't care for you—never did. Nothing will ever change that.*

She continued to listen to the news program, hoping that a later bulletin would give her an update on Trevor's condition. After wiping the table, she poured herself a fresh cup of coffee and tried to concentrate on the test papers she had been grading. The task was impossible.

Teasing thoughts of Trevor, provocative images of a younger, more carefree time, continued to assail her. She remembered the first time she had seen him more than eight years before. She had been immediately attracted by his flash of a rakish smile, and his lean, well-muscled body. But it was his eyes that had caught her attention and captured her heart. They were a brilliant shade of blue and challenged her silently. The hint of amusement in their clear depths had touched a very intimate part of her—and had never let go. Those damned blue eyes seemed to look through her sophisticated facade and bore into her soul and they had dared her to seduce him....

With a start, she dragged herself back to the present. "Don't brood about what might have been," she told herself, though her stomach had knotted painfully.

If she could just get through the next few days, she would have time to herself and by that time she would know more about Trevor's accident.

"No one is allowed to visit Mr. Daniels," the rotund nurse insisted upon Ashley's inquiry. The large woman was standing behind the glass enclosure of the hospital reception area and had only looked up from her paperwork when Ashley had inquired about Trevor.

"But I'm a personal friend," Ashley stated with a patient smile. She hadn't spent the last two hours in the car to be thwarted by hospital politics.

"It wouldn't matter if you were his mother," the strict nurse replied, glancing up from the chart she had been studying. In the past two days she had dismissed five reporters, seven photographers and about fifteen "personal friends" of the famous man lying in room 214. Security in the hospital had been increased due to the celebrity of Trevor Daniels. The sooner Mr. Daniels was out of the hospital, the better, for staff and patient alike.

The nurse, whose name tag indicated that she was Janelle Wilkes, smiled warmly. "I'm sorry, Ms.—"

"Jennings. Ashley Jennings," Ashley supplied.

"I'll tell Mr. Daniels that you were by."

"I'd appreciate it," Ashley retorted, sneaking a longing look down the corridors of the building. If she could only have a quick glimpse of Trevor—just enough to ease her mind, so that she would be convinced that he was indeed recuperating and on the road to recovery.

She left the hospital in frustration, after giving the nurse her name and telephone number.

Ashley didn't really expect Trevor to call, and she

wasn't disappointed. In the next few days, while school was ending for the holidays, Ashley had been in and out of her apartment, but either Trevor hadn't called, or she had missed him. She suspected that the would-be senator had received her message and promptly tossed it in the trash.

She told herself that she would never try to contact him again.

HIS WOUND HAD healed to the point where he could take charge of his life again, and Trevor Daniels intended to start this morning. Ignoring the warnings from his concerned campaign manager, Trevor hoisted his suitcase from the closet and tossed it carelessly onto the bed.

He couldn't wait to break away from Portland. His plan was simple. All he needed was a few hours alone with Ashley.

Hiding a grimace of pain, Trevor withdrew a faded pair of jeans from the closet and stuffed them into the open canvas bag. Determination was evident in the knit of his thick, dark brows and the hard angle of his jaw.

Everett Woodward, wearing an expression of disapproval on his round face, walked into the room and silently observed Trevor's deliberate movements. He sipped his second drink patiently while he watched Trevor fill the bag with casual clothes. It was obvious that Trevor had a purpose in mind, a purpose he hadn't confided to his campaign manager. Everett took a chair near the window in the master suite of Trevor's home. The would-be senator had noticed his entrance, but chose to ignore it. Everett frowned into his drink, silently plotting his line of reasoning to deter Trevor from making the worst political decision of his life. The damned thing of it was that Trevor had never thought rationally whenever Ashley Stephens was involved. And this time, Ashley was involved. Everett knew it.

"You know that I think you're making a big mistake," Everett ventured, stealing a quick glance through the window at the threatening sky. The chill of December seeped through the panes. There was the promise of snow in the air.

"So what else is new?" Trevor retorted with no trace of humor. He threw a bulky ski sweater into the bag before zipping it closed and eyeing his uneasy companion. "You always think I'm making mistakes."

"You're a gambler," Everett pointed out with a frown. "Gambling and politics don't mix."

"I can't argue with that." Trevor reached for his jacket and tried to change the course of the conversation. "I thought you were downstairs going over political strategy or something of the sort."

Everett avoided the trap and concentrated on the subject at hand. "We're not talking about some obscure issue here," Everett reminded the lean, angry man staring at him from across the room. "Your entire political future is on the line—everything you've worked for. The way I see it, this is too big a risk to take."

Trevor's square jaw tightened and the thin lines around his eyes became more distinct as his gaze hardened. "The way *I* see it, I don't have much of a choice." The small red scar on his cheek seemed to emphasize his words.

"You're not thinking clearly."

"What's that supposed to mean?" Trevor demanded. He paced restlessly in the confining room before looking pointedly at his watch. Through the window, he could see gray storm clouds gathering, their somber reflection darkening the clear waters of the Willamette River. Raindrops fell against the window, blurring his view.

Everett shifted uncomfortably in his chair and pushed his stocky fingers through his thinning hair. "Ever since the accident you've been obsessed with Stephens Timber."

"It began before the accident."

"Okay, ever since those phony charges last August, then."

Trevor turned to face the short man seated near a small table. "The charge was bribery," Trevor stated, his lips thinning.

"I know. But the important thing is that it was dropped." Everett looked as exasperated as he felt. "Admit it, Trevor, that is what all this—" his upturned palm rotated to indicate the packed bag "—is all about, isn't it?"

"Part of it," Trevor allowed with a grimace. "The bribery was just the latest of Lazarus's tricks. You seem to have conveniently forgotten that Lazarus Stephens was involved with my father's disappearance."

"Ten years ago. Idle speculation. No proof. Look, Trevor, you can't become obsessed with that all over again." Trevor's cold blue eyes didn't waver. Everett pressed his point home. "You can't fight a corporation the size of Stephens Timber, for God's sake! It employs over three thousand people in Oregon alone and Claud Stephens knows just whose palm he has to grease to get what he wants."

"But Claud only works for the company. He doesn't own it, does he?"

Everett changed his tactics when he noticed the dangerous glitter in Trevor's eyes. If there was anything Trevor Daniels enjoyed, it was a challenge.

"Look, Daniels, you've come too far too fast to throw it all away now. Forget what happened in the past, forget the accident, and the bribery scandal last summer, and, for God's sake, leave Stephens Timber alone!" Everett's expression was pleading. "Concentrate on the election in November."

"It's not that easy," Trevor admitted, rubbing his hand over the irritating pain in his abdomen.

"Rise above it."

Trevor's muscles flexed. "That's a little too much to ask, don't you think?"

Everett rolled his eyes upward and let out a frustrated sigh. "What I think is that you should quit brooding about false bribery charges and the accident," Everett explained with a lift of his shoulders. "Besides which, we have to make up for lost time. The days you spent in the hospital are gone; you missed a couple of very important meetings."

"They can be rescheduled," Trevor thought aloud. "Right now I have other things on my mind."

"You should be concentrating on the opposition."

"I am."

"Stephens Timber," Everett guessed, shaking his balding head despondently. "You're going to have to ease up on them."

"And play into Claud's greedy hands? No way."

"If you want to win the election—"

Trevor stopped dead in his tracks and wheeled around to confront his friend. Anger flared in his eyes. "I'm not even sure about that anymore. I had a lot of time to think while I was lying in that hospital. I'm not really sure that being a United States senator is all that it's cracked up to be. It certainly can't be worth the price."

"You're tired—"

"You bet I am!"

Everett held up his soft palms as if to ward off a blow, hoping that the gesture would calm Trevor. It didn't. Trevor had good reason to be upset, but Everett had hoped that the politician in Trevor Daniels would overcome the anger. "You've got to think about your career, Trevor, and you can't afford to take any time off right now. Think of all the hard work you've put into this campaign before you go mouthing off to the press about all of this nonsense concerning the accident. The last thing we need right now is another scandal!"

"Is that all you ever think about?"

"It's what you pay me to think about," Everett reminded his employer before draining the remainder of his warm drink. "My only concern is to get you into that vacant senatorial seat this fall."

"Even if it kills me?" Trevor asked with a sarcastic frown.

"Don't be ridiculous—"

"Then don't ridicule me!"

Everett's light eyes were steady when they clashed with Trevor's angry blue gaze. "I'm the guy who takes care of your security, remember? If I thought, I mean really thought that someone was out to get you, then I'd be the first one to suggest that you pull out of the race. But face it, if someone wanted to nail you, they would have done it before now. And, believe me, it wouldn't be some two-bit job on your car. Even the police didn't buy that one. For Christ's sake, don't turn paranoid on me now!" Everett muttered.

The words sunk into Trevor's weary mind. He let out his breath and his broad shoulders sagged. "Maybe you're right," he conceded, though his voice still sounded skeptical.

"Of course I am."

A crooked smile tugged at the hard corners of Trevor's rigid mouth. "I can think of a few times when you've been wrong."

"All in the past," Everett assured him with a knowing grin. "I don't claim to be infallible…just the nearest thing to it." The rotund campaign manager walked across the room and poured three stiff fingers of bourbon from a bottle sitting on the bar in the corner of the room. "Here, have a drink," he offered. "We both could use one."

After Trevor took the glass and swallowed some of the bourbon, Everett continued with his never-ending advice.

"Now, whatever you do, try to forget about the accident and the scandal. Avoid the press at all costs until some of the noise dies down.

"Don't go spouting off about your car being sabotaged or you'll end up on the front page of the *Morning Surveyor* all over again. The last time was bad enough. Publicity from that rag, we don't need." Everett took a calming sip of liquor. He was somewhat satisfied that he had finally gotten through to Trevor, though it had taken a hell of a lot of talking. Trevor Daniels had a good chance of winning the primary in May, not to mention the election in November, if he didn't blow it by letting his hot temper control him. It was Everett's job to protect and mollify the would-be senator. That task might prove difficult if Trevor was hell-bent on seeing Ashley Stephens again.

Trevor set his empty glass on the bureau. He had tossed the campaign manager's words over in his mind, but despite Everett's warnings, the gleam of determination resurfaced in Trevor's hard gaze. Trevor wasn't the kind of man to take things lying down, and never had been. His roguish charm and country-boy smile had won him many votes in the past, but it was his fierce determination that had brought him to the forefront of the political race for senator. Everett Woodward knew it as well as anyone. No amount of logic or smooth talk from Everett would change Trevor's mind once it was set.

"I want you to cancel all of my appointments for the next couple of days," Trevor said.

Everett sighed audibly. "Why?"

"I'm taking a little time off."

"Now?" Everett rose from the chair and eyed his employer suspiciously. "But you can't, Trevor. Not now. It's just not possible."

"Anything's possible. You're the one who gave me that advice when I first considered running."

"Exactly why you can't take a vacation now. Your schedule's a mess as it is. All that time you were recuperating—"

"From the accident," Trevor interjected. Everett opened his mouth to argue, but thought better of it. He knew just how far to push Trevor Daniels, and when to stop. "Think of my leave of absence as following doctor's orders for rest, if it will make you feel better," Trevor suggested.

"Is that what you want me to tell the press?"

The skin tightened over Trevor's cheekbones. "I don't give a damn what you tell them. Say whatever you want."

"You're not being very reasonable about this," Everett cautioned.

"That's because I don't feel very reasonable at the moment." Trevor hoisted the canvas bag off the bed and slung his jacket over his shoulder before turning toward the door.

"So, where are you going?"

"Away…alone."

"Alone?" Trevor's remark sounded dangerous to Everett and very much like the lie it was. Everett hesitated only slightly before playing his trump card. "I just hope you use your head, Daniels. And I hope that you're not going out on some personal vendetta against Stephens Timber Corporation. That wouldn't be wise—politically or personally."

Trevor's hand paused over the doorknob. He turned to face his concerned friend. "What's that supposed to mean?"

"It means that Ashley Stephens can't help you now," Everett said kindly. He noticed the stiffening of Trevor's spine and the sudden chilling of his gaze.

"Her name isn't Stephens anymore," Trevor stated. The tanned skin strained over Trevor's rugged features.

"But you and I both know that she and Richard Jennings were divorced several years ago. We also know that she owns the majority interest in Stephens Timber. Claud could be replaced in a minute, if Ashley decided to let him go."

The curse on Trevor's tongue was restrained. "You've done your homework," he observed, his voice cold.

Everett rubbed the tension from the back of his neck. "You pay me for that, too. Look, Trevor, I don't want to step out of line. What you do with your personal life is your business. I'm only worried when it begins to affect your career."

"So what are you suggesting?"

Genuine concern registered in the younger man's gaze. "Just be careful. Don't do anything, or get involved with anyone if you think there's a chance you might regret it later."

Trevor's voice was calm. "I'm not about to forget what's important in my life, if that's what you mean."

"The right woman sometimes can change a man's way of thinking."

Trevor frowned and turned the doorknob. "Then we really don't have much of a problem, do we? I think that you and I both agree that Ashley Jennings is definitely not 'the right woman.'"

With his final angry statement, Trevor jerked open the door and left his campaign manager to contemplate the half-empty bottle of bourbon.

CHAPTER THREE

ASHLEY SQUINTED INTO the darkness, watching warily as the snow piled around the edges of her windshield wipers. The mountain storm had come without warning and caught her off guard.

She had come to her father's Cascade Mountain retreat seeking solace. More than anything right now, she needed time alone to think things out. Now that her teaching obligations at the college had been fulfilled, she would be able to devote all of her energy to the timber company.

For the past week she had been in Portland, trying to sort through the books of Stephens Timber Corporation. As each day had passed it had become increasingly clear that Ashley couldn't trust her cousin Claud as far as she could throw him. There was little doubt in her mind that she would have to give him his walking papers as soon as she returned to Portland.

Armed with her briefcase full of financial reports concerning the operation of the vast timber empire, Ashley had spent the last two nights at the cabin poring over the accountant's figures concerning profit and loss, assets and liabilities and projected timber sales for the next two years.

Earlier in the afternoon she had pushed the neat computer printouts aside and decided to make a quick trip into Bend to replenish her dwindling grocery supply. On the way back to the cabin, the wind had picked up and within minutes powdery snow was falling from the heavens in a near-blizzard. The main highway was still clear, but the side roads, which already had an accumulation of snow, were quickly becoming impassable.

Her fingers tightened around the steering wheel and her thoughts wandered precariously to Trevor. In the short time since his accident, it seemed that there was no escaping him.

His engaging, slightly off-center smile had been photographed repeatedly and his rugged face had become incredibly newsworthy. Even last summer's scandal concerning alleged bribery charges hadn't tarnished his reputation; he was still considered by the local papers to have a lead in the primary election. Right now, Trevor Daniels was Oregon's favorite son, or soon would be, if the latest polls proved accurate.

According to Claud, Trevor's senatorial bid was sure to be a disaster for the company. Ashley disagreed. Trevor Daniels was too shrewd a politician to let personal rivalry interfere with his campaign. Besides which, Ashley was convinced that she couldn't trust Claud or his motives. What she had once considered a slight grudge against her because of Lazarus's will, Ashley now realized was a very deep flaw in Claud's character. For a fleeting moment she wondered if Trevor's accusations, which she had previously considered unlikely and vindictive, might be true.

Shifting gears as the Jeep started to climb the rugged terrain, Ashley thought about the events leading up to Trevor's sudden prominence and fame. Senator Higgins's fatal heart attack had left a vacant seat in Washington, D.C., and public opinion seemed to think that Trevor would be elected to fill the void.

Well, at least he got what he wanted, Ashley chided herself, feeling a trace of the old bitterness return. *That's a lot more than you can say for yourself.*

The tires slid on the snow-packed mountain road before

holding the vehicle steady on the slippery gravel. "Just a little farther," Ashley coaxed.

Slowly she turned the steering wheel toward the narrow lane angling up the steep hillside. She frowned as she noticed ruts in the newly fallen snow. There were only two other pieces of property bordering hers and the mountain retreats that occupied those adjacent parcels were used for summer homes. Or at least they had been.

But this was her first visit to the cabin in several years. Perhaps the neighboring houses were being used over the Christmas holidays. She found the thought that she wasn't completely alone in the remote section of the mountains comforting. Though she had come seeking solitude, she now appreciated the knowledge that there was someone nearby in case the storm became more violent.

Once again Ashley's thoughts turned to Trevor and his recent accident. Though it had occurred only a week ago, she still couldn't forget about it and found herself wondering how he was doing. Her telephone calls to the hospital had never been returned and when she had tried to see him again, she had been thwarted by a determined security guard. Ashley got the message: Trevor didn't want to see her.

She couldn't blame him. For all practical purposes, she owned Stephens Timber Corporation, a corporation that in the past had represented everything in the timber industry Trevor opposed. Though she was forcing changes within the company it would still be a long time before some of the old techniques could be abandoned for safer, more environmentally sound modes of timber harvest.

"You're a fool," she admonished, and caught her lower lip with her teeth. She tried to concentrate while crossing the remaining distance to the cabin, but couldn't help hoping that Trevor had recovered from the injuries he'd sustained in the accident. How had the accident affected his career—*his damned career?* Were his eyes still as incredibly blue and erotic as they once had been?

"Damn it, Ashley," she swore, her knuckles whitening over the steering wheel, "why can't you forget that man? He never loved you—he just used you...."

THE PAIN IN his side hadn't subsided. With each passing minute it throbbed more sharply, growing until a dull headache pounded mercilessly behind his eyes. Trevor had overexerted himself and he was paying dearly for it.

The long drive had fatigued him and set his nerves on edge. Just the thought of seeing Ashley again disturbed him more than he would like to admit.

After fumbling in the pocket of his jeans he extracted a small vial of pills. He was chilled to the bone and the raw ache under his shirt throbbed mercilessly. Disgusted with himself and seeing the prescribed medication as a sign of weakness, he dropped the small brown bottle on the table and ignored it.

"Damn it!" Trevor cursed to himself as he reached for his neglected glass of Scotch. The liquor was warm and did little to relieve the dull ache in his abdomen.

Though his muscles were cramped from the cold, he could feel the warm trickle of sweat running down the back of his neck. He absently rubbed his forehead and wondered how much longer he would have to wait for Ashley to return. Leaning back in the chair, he closed his eyes and listened to the sounds of the night. Presently, the liquor started to take effect. The ache in his head was beginning to subside and the razor-sharp edge of his mind dulled slightly, sacrificed for the freedom from pain. He sat rigidly in the leather chair, his wet jeans clinging stiffly to his legs, while he sipped the remains of his distasteful drink.

The rumble of an approaching vehicle's engine caught his attention. Headlights flashed against the far wall, illuminating the rustic room. It was a place Trevor remembered well, a room where he had spent many lazy afternoons in years past. It was the very spot where he had first felt Ashley's trembling surrender. It had been early spring. They had run into the cabin to escape the sudden shower. He could still smell the fresh, damp scent of her black hair, taste the raindrops that had run down her cheeks. It seemed like a lifetime ago. How long had it been? Seven years? Eight? His mind was too cloudy to recall and it really didn't matter. He didn't give a damn about Ashley…at least not anymore.

The engine was killed and a car door slammed. Trevor had to force himself to remain patient. All of his senses were alert, his raw nerves stretched paper-thin. It had taken the better part of three days to track Ashley down and when he had finally found her, he had been pleased in a perverse sort of way. He found it ironic that Ashley had chosen to return to the cabin. It seemed to justify his reason for being here.

The key turned in the lock. Trevor heard the sound of cold metal resisting intrusion. Though he sat in another room, he could clearly see the entrance of the cabin from his vantage point in the darkness.

As the door was pushed open, Trevor narrowed his eyes. It was too dark to see clearly, but Trevor quickly determined that the small form brushing snow off her jacket and stamping her boots on the hall carpet was Ashley. As he watched her voyeuristically, the sour taste of deception rose in his throat.

He had hoped that he would feel loathing when he saw her again, but the contempt he had cultivated had refused to grow. His fingers tensed around the arm of the chair when her gaze swept past the door of the den. She pulled off her stocking cap and let her long, dark hair tumble free. Trevor's lips compressed into an unforgiving line of disgust; she was more beautiful than he had remembered.

ASHLEY HESITATED A MOMENT, thinking that the cabin felt different somehow, and then with a frown shrugged off the disturbing feeling and set the bag of groceries on an antique sideboard while she removed her boots and jacket. After hanging the ski jacket on the curved arm of the hall tree, she picked up the groceries, walked into the kitchen and put on a pot of tea as she replenished her cupboards.

The teapot had just begun to whistle when an unexpected noise made her heart miss a beat. "Ashley." The sound of her name made her gasp. It came from a male voice that was darkly familiar. She rotated quickly to confront the intruder.

The man was standing in the doorway to the den. "Oh my God," Ashley whispered, barely believing the apparition. Her eyes were captured in the shadowy depths of his blue gaze.

"Ashley," he repeated slowly, as if he knew how much of a shock he had imposed upon her. His voice caught on her name and it carried her backward to a past in which she had shared her life, her love with him. "I didn't mean to frighten you," he said softly.

Her throat was suddenly desert-dry, and she felt the sting of wistful tears burn against her eyelids. Her step forward was hesitant, as if she expected him to vanish as quickly as he had appeared. "What are you doing here? How did you get in?" Her voice was a muted whisper and her sea-green eyes were filled with a thousand questions spanning eight years.

"I hope I didn't startle you," he stated. "I...wanted to make sure that you were alone."

Though her smile was fragile, her round eyes never wavered. "Why are you here, Trevor?" she asked, finding her voice. "Why now?" All of Claud's warnings caused a painful wrenching of her heart.

The small light of defiance in her gaze bothered him. He felt the need to apologize but ignored it. He had planned this night for nearly two weeks and had never once considered that he might feel compelled to explain himself to her. His lips thinned as he reminded himself that she was the one who had to account for what was happening to him. His blue eyes held her transfixed.

"I got your message at the hospital."

"But you didn't call."

"I wanted to see you in person—"

"I came by the hospital."

"—alone."

Ashley's heart missed a beat but she forced herself to appear calm. She couldn't—wouldn't—let Trevor use her again. If he was here, it was for a reason, and she couldn't delude herself into thinking that it was just to be with her once more.

Trevor frowned at his own admission. "I thought it would be better for everyone concerned if we talked in private." He seemed sincere. But then, he had once before. She felt the old bitterness return.

"Are you sure that would be wise, Senator? What if your constituents found out that you were talking to the owner of Stephens Timber Corporation? Wouldn't that ruin your credibility?"

For a breathless instant anger sparked in his eyes. "We can start this by going for each other's throats, Ashley, but I don't think that would accomplish much, do you?"

"I suppose not." She walked past him and flipped the switch on a brass table lamp. The room was instantly illuminated in a bath of dim light. Ashley's smile trembled as she looked at him. Trevor appeared to have aged five years in the past month. Yet he was still the most intriguing man she had ever met. His cold blue eyes were just as enigmatic as she remembered.

It took a few moments for the shock of seeing him again to wear off. "I'm having a little trouble understanding why you're here," she stated, still trying to hold on to her shattered poise. It was obvious that he had been sitting in the leather chair near the fire. Ashley took a seat on the edge of an overstuffed couch and tucked one foot beneath her. The fabric of her jeans stretched over her leg muscles, and Trevor was forced to shift his gaze back to the concerned expression on her elegant face.

It was still unlined, a perfect oval of alabaster skin with large, even features, lofty cheekbones and a sparkle of innocence that danced in her eyes when she laughed. Tonight her eyes were sober and suspicious. Her skin was flushed slightly from the cold, and her dark, finely arched brows drew downward in concentration as she tried to understand the man who was silently regarding her.

"Okay, Trevor, I'm sitting down and I think I'm about as calm as I'm going to get," she said.

"Good." His gaze was stony and cold.

Ashley had always had a powerful effect on him in the past and time hadn't made Trevor immune to the seductive curve of her chin or the trace of sadness in her wistful smile. Trevor had to force himself to remember the reason for coming to the lonely cabin in the remote stretch of mountains. It would be damnably easy to forget the rest of the world tonight. All too easily Ashley could entrance him and he would fall victim to the subtle allure of her slow smile.

Ashley shook her dark curls, as if to clear her mind. *Dear God, what was Trevor doing here?* "This is quite a shock, you know. I thought that…"

"You thought that I was recuperating from an accident."

"Yes."

"I was," he admitted in a rough whisper. Though he sat away from the light, Ashley could see his sharply defined features. His strong face no longer held the warmth she remembered, and deep lines of worry webbed from the corners of his eyes.

"And now that you feel up to it, you decided to break into my cabin. Right? That's against the law, Senator."

"I've been charged with worse." There was a viciousness in his words that she didn't understand until she remembered the bribery charges. She studied his face. His chin was still bold and square, but his cheeks had hollowed, probably because of the accident. A tiny scar, still an angry red line, cut across his jaw. Beneath his eyes were dark shadows, evidence of too many sleepless nights. When he stared at her she saw no trace of emotion on the rugged contours of his face, but she read something in the chill of his gaze. He looked haunted. "Trevor...what's going on?"

"I want to know just how desperate Stephens Timber is to get me out of the senatorial race."

"*I* have nothing against your politics, you know that."

A disdainful black brow cocked. "What I know is that for all practical purposes, you own Stephens Timber, right?"

The brutal glare in his eyes forced the truth from her lips. "Except for a few shares—"

"But your cousin, Claud, he's the general manager—the guy who's responsible for the day-to-day operations?"

"Claud reports to me. Look, Trevor, I don't know what you're getting at, and I really don't see that I'm obligated to tell you anything. Just what the devil is going on?" Her mysterious green eyes pleaded with him.

Light from the antique lamp diffused into the far corners of the room, making the shadows dangerously intimate. Scarlet embers smoldered in the fire, just as they did on the first night she and Trevor had made love. Time might have hurried past them, but Ashley knew she would never love another man with the reckless, unbound passion she had felt for Trevor.

Trevor's eyes darkened, as if his thoughts had taken the same precarious path as hers. Passion flickered in their midnight depths before he jerked his gaze away from her to study the fire. It was as if, in that one hesitant moment, he had inadvertently divulged too much of himself to her.

Ashley reached over and brushed the back of his hand with hers. With a jolt, his head snapped backward and his eyes drove into hers. Gone was any trace of desire. In its stead lurked cruel suspicion, lingering just below the surface of his gaze, silently accusing her of a crime she couldn't begin to comprehend.

She withdrew her hand. Her fingers trembled as she pushed her hair out of her eyes. Dread crawled up her spine. "This has something to do with your accident, doesn't it?"

"I'm not sure it was an accident."

Ashley was stunned. Perhaps she hadn't heard him correctly. "But the papers said—"

"I know what they said. I know what the police report said. But I'm not convinced."

"Wait a minute." She closed her eyes in order to clear her mind. There had been too many emotional shocks tonight and her tangled feelings were interfering with her logic. Stretching her fingers outward in a supplicating gesture, she begged for his patience. The rumors of foul play entered her mind and she shuddered. "Let's start over.…"

His frown became a poignant smile. "A little late for that, wouldn't you say?" The sarcasm in his words sliced into her heart.

She bit back the hot retort forming on her tongue. She folded her hands over one knee and forced herself to remain as calm as possible. "I think it's about time you leveled with me. You owe me that much."

"I owe you nothing."

Her frayed nerves got the better of her and her thin patience snapped. "That's where you're wrong, Trevor," she contradicted. "First, you broke into my place after trudging God only knows how long in the snow—just to hide your truck. Next, you sat in the dark in order to scare the living daylights out of me, which, by the way, you did. Then, you end up making vague accusations and ridiculous insinuations that don't mean a damned thing to me! I keep getting the impression that you're waiting for me to say something...or fall into some kind of trap, but I can't for the life of me figure out what it is! What happened to you, Trevor? Just what the hell happened to you and what's all this nonsense about your accident—"

"I've told you before, I don't think it was an accident."

She lifted her arm as if to ward off another verbal assault. "Yeah, I know," she mumbled while placing her hand on the arm of the chair and pushing herself out of it. She stretched before bending over and examining the contents of the basket of wood sitting near the fireplace. She needed an excuse for time to gather her scattered thoughts.

Tossing a large piece of oak onto the coals, Ashley slid a secretive glance in Trevor's direction. The crackle of flames shattered the silence as the fire began to consume the new log. Returning her gaze to her task, Ashley spread her palms open to the warmth of the flames and didn't bother to turn her head or look at Trevor when she spoke. With practiced calm she asked, "I've known you for a long time, haven't I?"

"Eight years," he supplied, eyeing her backside as she kneeled before the ravenous flames. He couldn't help but consider her supple curves. Her jeans were stretched tightly over her buttocks, leaving little room for his imagination.

For a fleeting moment he wondered if her skin was still as soft as it once had been.

"Eight years, that's right," she agreed. "In those eight years I've called you a lot of things." His dark brows raised inquisitively when she paused. "But I've never accused you of being a lunatic." She dusted her hands on her jeans and smiled to herself as she stood. She was content to run her fingers over the rough wood of the oak mantel as she continued. "So you see, you're going to have a difficult time convincing me that you drove over a thirty-foot embankment intentionally."

"Of course not."

The first cold feelings of doubt had already taken hold of her. What was it Claud had said? That Trevor was still convinced that Stephens Timber had something to do with his father's disappearance?

He studied her quietly, watching the gentle curve of her neck as she laid her head against the mantel. Her ebony hair brushed against her white skin when she pushed it over her shoulder. Her round eyes were filled with concern and worry for him.

When Trevor rose from the chair too quickly, a dizzying sensation swept over him in a sickening wave. The pain in his side was once again beginning to throb. Grimacing against the dull ache, he made his way over to the fireplace and propped his shoulder against the warm stones. He pressed his hand against his abdomen until the ache subsided.

Holding her transfixed with his sober gaze, he spoke. When he did, the skin tightened over the rugged planes of his face and his eyes glinted with renewed determination. "Look, Ashley. I didn't intend to lose control of the car, you know that as well as I do."

Ashley's heart was thudding with dread. In her anxiety, she ran her fingers through the thick strands of her blue-black hair. Letting her forehead drop to her palm, she gently massaged her temple. Her voice was ragged, barely a whisper. "Then what you're suggesting is that someone tried to kill you."

"Not just someone, Ashley." His eyes drove into hers. "I think Claud hired someone to tamper with my car." Trevor's hand reached out and took hold of her wrist.

Ashley's breath caught in her throat. "That's preposterous!"

"I don't think so," he retorted. She tried to pull away from him, but he wouldn't release her arm. Dark blue eyes, the color of midnight, impaled her. "I think you'd better tell me everything you know about your cousin."

"This is insane," she managed to say, though her throat was constricting her breath. "I'm the first one to admit that Claud isn't a saint, but you can't go around accusing him of trying to kill you, for God's sake."

"Not until I have proof."

"Which you don't?"

"Not yet."

"Then how can you even suggest that he's involved?"

"Gut feeling."

"That won't hold up in court, Senator. But you know that, don't you? Or at least you should since you're a lawyer."

"Ashley, look, I know that I'm right."

She read the determination in his angry blue gaze. "And you want me to help you prove that Claud was trying to kill you, right? Trevor, you've got to be joking."

"I'm dead serious. I know that Claud and your father paid that mill owner in Molalla to file those bribery charges!"

"How?" Her green eyes sparked with indignant fury. "How do you know that? Did the man tell you?" Her lips turned downward in repressed rage and she pulled her hand free of his grasp.

"The police were convinced that the charges were false. They dropped the case."

"But what proof do you have that my father was behind it?"

"That mill, which had been on the verge of bankruptcy, was suddenly operational again."

"Circumstantial evidence, counselor." She waved her hand frantically in the air. "And even if your suspicions are right, who are you to say that my father was behind it?"

"I checked. Who do you think supplies that mill with rough timber?"

"I couldn't hazard a guess," she lied, knowing what he was insinuating. Her heart was like a trip-hammer in her rib cage.

"Then you're not doing your job, Ashley. The primary customer for Watkins Mill in Molalla is Stephens Timber." Trevor began to pace the floor in long, agitated strides.

"I don't understand you, Trevor," Ashley said, her voice beginning to tremble. "My father and Claud both warned me that you had some sort of personal vendetta against the timber company but I never believed them—"

"Until now?"

She nodded her head. Hot tears of frustration burned in her eyes as she stared at the only man whom she had ever loved. "Is it because of me?"

His pacing halted. He stood with his back to her and she could see the muscles of his shoulders tensing beneath the soft cotton fabric of his shirt. "No, Ashley, this started long before I knew you—"

"Because of your father's disappearance."

He turned on his heel and when he looked at her his eyes were filled with the torture he had suffered for nearly ten years. He didn't need to answer.

"Then Claud was right. You have a grudge." She closed her eyes against the truth. "You really don't think much of me, do you?"

"It's your family I wonder about."

"To the point that you would go out of your way to prove them guilty of anything." She shook her head in confusion and light from the fire caught in the ebony strands of her hair. "I own the company now. You know that I wouldn't be involved in anything illegal—"

"And I also know that you weren't in control of the corporation when my father disappeared, or when those phony charges were filed, or when my car was sabotaged."

"If it was."

"I have a mechanic who will back me up."

She ran her fingers nervously through her hair, but her eyes never left his. "Why did you come here, Trevor? What is it exactly that you expect of me?"

His blue eyes never left her face and he pinched his lower lip between his thumb and forefinger pensively. "I want you to go through all of the company records and look for anything that might prove my theories."

"Wait a minute—you want my help in proving that Stephens Timber and my family were involved in something illegal?" She was incredulous.

His voice was low and steady. It sent a shiver as cold as the black night down her spine. "What I want from you, Ashley, is the truth."

Ashley's mouth was suddenly desert-dry. Her voice was barely a whisper. "And when I go through all the company records and I find nothing, what then?"

"All I want is the truth."

She weighed the alternatives in her mind as she reached her decision. "Okay, Trevor, I'll look through everything. But I want something in return."

"I wouldn't expect anything else from Lazarus Stephens's daughter."

"When I check all the records and clear my father's name, I expect you to make a public statement." His dark brows rose inquisitively. "A statement that ends once and for all the bitterness between our two families and a statement that absolves my father of all the charges you've attributed to him."

Trevor considered her request. "How do I know that you'll be honest with me?"

Her chin inched upward defiantly. "I guess you'll just have to trust me," she murmured. "I realize that might be difficult for you, but I don't see that you have much of a choice."

His eyes darkened. "I'll need proof, Ashley. I'll give you my public announcement, if you can prove to me that your family hasn't been involved in the accident, the bribery or my father's disappearance."

Her confidence wavered. "I'll let you know."

Trevor reached for his coat and Ashley's heart dropped. He had reappeared so suddenly in her life; she couldn't let go of him—not yet. There were so many memories they had shared, so much time that had separated them. Desperately she clung to the thread of hope that he still cared for her. "You can't leave," she whispered, her heart in her throat. He paused, one arm thrust into the suede jacket.

"Why not?"

"The storm—it's nearly a blizzard."

His eyes darkened ominously. "What are you suggesting, Ms. Jennings? That I spend the night, here, alone with you?"

CHAPTER FOUR

EIGHT YEARS SEEMED to roll backward as she stared into Trevor's smoldering blue eyes. His gaze touched the most feminine part of her soul and made her voice husky.

"You can't leave in this storm," Ashley repeated. "You'll have to wait until it dies down."

His eyes darted to the frosted windowpanes before returning to search her worried face. "That might not be until morning." Trevor slowly advanced upon her, his eyes lingering thoughtfully on the concerned knit of her brow. His voice was dangerously low. "Do you really think it would be wise for me to stay?" he asked as he reached her. Slowly, his fingers traced the elegant curve of her jaw.

He noticed the hesitation in her sensual sea-green eyes. "I don't think you have much of a choice."

Trevor's hands stopped their loving exploration and his gaze hardened. "That's where you're wrong, Ms. Jennings." He shoved his arms into the sleeves of his jacket and flashed a smile as bitterly cold as the night. "All I need from you is a lift to the Lamberts'."

Her brows quirked. "You're staying at the Lambert place?"

"That's right."

She stepped away from him and eyed him suspiciously. "Just how long have you been planning this?" she asked, tilting her palm upward and making a sweeping gesture to include everything that had transpired within the walls of the intimate room.

"Since my car went out of control and rolled down a thirty-foot embankment."

Her spine stiffened slightly. "You really believe that Claud was behind the accident, don't you?"

"If I didn't, I wouldn't be here." Eyes as cold as glass pierced hers. His voice was devoid of emotion and Ashley realized with a welling sense of disappointment how little he cared for her.

She shook her head and sighed. "I can't believe that anyone, not even Claud, would want you dead."

"I don't think he wanted to kill me, just shake me up a little. Scare me. And that, dear lady, he accomplished."

"But why?" Before he could answer she held up her hand and chewed on her lower lip. "Because of the election. You think that he's so paranoid you might win, that he set up the accident to warn you in hope that you might back out, right?"

"That's the way I have it figured."

Ashley managed a humorless smile. "I think you've been reading too many spy stories lately, Senator. Your entire theory reads like some cheap James Bond rip-off."

"Maybe that's because you can't see the truth when it stares you in the face, Ashley," he suggested with a frown. Deep furrows lined his forehead and surrounded the tense corners of his mouth. "But then you never have been able to sort fact from fiction where your family is concerned. You probably still don't believe that Stephens Timber was responsible for the ecological disaster near Springfield."

"My father denied it," Ashley whispered.

"But you know better, don't you? Your father's company was spraying with a dangerous pesticide, Ashley. Probably because Lazarus recommended it. It was effective and cheap."

"No one knew it was dangerous—"

Trevor's eyes glittered ominously. "There had already

been cases linking that pesticide with health hazards. The FDA was in the process of banning it. But your father didn't listen and the people living near the area that was being sprayed paid for it, didn't they?"

"It was never proven—"

"That's a cop-out, Ashley and you know it. Maybe you just preferred to hide your head in the sand. You didn't have to look into the eyes of the people when they found out that they were dying. The effects of the spray sometimes take months to show up, but when they do, the result is the same—a slow and painful death."

"No one knows if the pesticide was the cause."

"Yet. Researchers are still working on it." The skin stretched tightly over Trevor's harsh features as he remembered the day he had to revise Dennis Lange's will. Dennis was only thirty-three when he had come to Trevor's office, and mentioned that he had some of the symptoms of the pesticide poisoning. Dennis had died six months later, leaving a young widow and three-year-old daughter. Trevor had vowed on his friend's grave that if he ever was in a position of power, he would fight against the indiscriminate use of chemicals on the environment. "Your father knew about the hazards, it was just more convenient to ignore them."

Masking the fact that his words had wounded her heart, Ashley turned, walked out of the room, grabbed her jacket and reached into a downy pocket for the keys to the Jeep. She had already pulled on her boots, zipped the ski jacket to her neck and wound her hair into her stocking cap by the time Trevor joined her in the small foyer. "Let's go," she whispered while purposely avoiding the silent questions in his bold eyes.

THE LAMBERT CABIN was only a little over a mile up the hill, but the drive took nearly ten minutes because of the snow that had drifted over the seldom-used road. The storm wasn't nearly as fierce as it had been, but large flakes still drifted leisurely to the ground and danced in the bright beams of the headlights.

Though it was nearly nine o'clock, it seemed like daylight. The pristine drifts of snow, settled carelessly against the trunks of graceful Ponderosa pines, gave the night a blue-gray illumination. Clumps of pine needles protruded proudly from their winter cloak of white and the shadowy mountains blended into the dark sky.

Ashley had to wipe the windshield with a cloth as condensation collected on the cold glass. The Jeep hit a patch of ice. One tire spun wildly, causing the vehicle to slide on the slippery terrain and roughly tossing the passengers against the dash. Trevor winced in pain when his shoulder was thrust against the door.

"Are you all right?" Ashley asked, when the wheels of the Jeep were securely gripping the gravel once again. Her elegant face was pinched with concern.

"Just great," Trevor replied sarcastically. "Thanks to your cousin Claud."

Ashley pursed her lips together angrily and the remainder of the trip was made in mutual silence.

Lights were glowing in the paned windows of the Lambert cabin. Trevor's pickup was parked near the garage. Nearly three inches of snow had piled on the hood and roof of the truck.

Ashley stopped the Jeep and pulled on the emergency brake, but let the engine idle. She turned to face Trevor and found that he was staring thoughtfully at her. His eyes were deep blue and sensual. They seemed to caress her face.

"You could come in," he invited, tugging gently on her stocking cap and allowing her hair to fall in wisping black curls around her face. Her breath caught in her throat at the intimacy of the gesture.

"I...I don't think so," she whispered, shaking her head and avoiding his probing stare. "It would be best, for both of us, if I left."

When his fingers softly touched her temple, they trembled. Ashley closed her eyes and moved her head away from his persuasive touch. "You'll be okay, won't you... by yourself?" she asked, thinking of his injury. In the close quarters of the Jeep, it was difficult not to feel the urgency of his touch.

"I'll manage," he said, his voice tight.

"You're sure?"

"I'm used to doing things on my own, Ashley," he reminded her. "I can take care of myself."

"And that's why you spent a week in the hospital."

His jaw clenched furiously as he reached for the handle of the door. "You can blame Claud for that one."

Ashley's hand, which had still clung to the steering wheel, reached out to clutch his arm. "Let's not argue," she implored. "It's time to stop this fighting before it gets to the point where it can't be stopped."

For a breathless instant, there was silence. Snowflakes gathered on the windshield, providing a protective curtain from the rest of the world. His eyes searched the innocent wisdom in her gaze.

"Why did I ever let you go?" he asked himself, his blue eyes filled with dark self-mockery.

She swallowed against the dryness in her throat as, slowly, he lowered his head and his lips brushed tenderly against hers. How long had she waited for this moment? She sighed and one hand slid beneath his jacket to touch him gently on the neck. Old emotions, long dormant, began to assail the most intimate parts of her. His kiss was flavored with the hint of Scotch and reminded her of a time, somewhere in the distant past of her carefree youth, when they had made love in a fragrant field of clover.

"I've missed you," he whispered as he reluctantly pulled his lips from hers. "Dear God, Ashley, I've missed you." His strong arms held her close to him and he buried his face in the thick ebony strands of her hair. "Stay with me."

A sob, filled with the raw ache of eight forgotten years, broke from her lips. The warmth and protection of his embrace was all she had ever wanted. She leaned her forehead against his neck and she closed her eyes against the feelings ripping her apart. She had vowed never to let this man touch her again and yet she couldn't let go.

She could hear the sound of his heartbeat, feel the warmth of his breath as it whispered in her hair. Her heart wrenched painfully as she remembered how brutally he had thrust her out of his life and she knew that she could never trust him again.

"I...I have to go," she stated, her voice quaking with the small lie. She couldn't allow her vulnerability for Trevor to overcome her common sense.

"Why?"

"I have things I've got to accomplish."

"Such as?"

"Such as start looking through the company books. At your request."

Gently he released her. His lips were pulled into a thoughtful line of disbelief. "That's just an excuse, Ashley. You're afraid of me, aren't you?"

She let out a ragged breath. "No, Trevor, I'm not afraid of you, as a man or as a senator. But I am afraid of what becoming involved with you might mean."

"I don't understand."

She avoided his gaze and stared out the partially covered windshield. "I've worked a long time to become an independent woman. All my life I've had some man telling me what to do. First Dad, then you and finally Richard."

At the mention of her ex-husband's name, Trevor's muscles tightened. "I don't want to get involved with a man for a while," she murmured. "Not until I'm certain that I can stand on my own two feet."

"Haven't you been doing that?"

She nodded. "For several years. But now I have to prove myself—to myself."

"With the timber company," he guessed. "The last thing I would have expected from you, Ashley, is that you would turn into a latent feminist." He raked frustrated fingers through his chestnut-colored hair. "I thought you liked living in the lap of luxury."

She turned her mysterious eyes back on him. "There are a lot of things you don't know about me," Ashley suggested, smiling wistfully. "Maybe someday we'll talk about them. But…right now, I need time, Trevor. Time to think about you and me, about what we meant to each other and about everything that has happened between your family and mine."

He frowned, his dark brows blunted in vexation, but he seemed to accept what she said. "This is your decision, Ashley," Trevor reminded her. Then, with more dexterity than she thought him capable of, he opened the door of the Jeep, climbed out of the vehicle and walked, head bent, toward the front door. As he opened the door to the rustic Lambert home, he turned toward her. Ashley imagined that he was inviting her inside. She swallowed against the ache in her throat at the sight of him standing in the snow.

Somehow Ashley managed a weak wave before she put the Jeep in reverse, released the brake and headed back to her cabin. The picture of Trevor standing on the small porch in the darkness, with snowflakes clinging to his wavy chestnut hair, stayed with her on the short trip home.

Once back in her own cabin, she brushed the snow off her shoulders, hung the jacket on the hall tree and hurried into the den. After checking her watch and contemplating the wisdom of her actions, she dialed the number of John Ellis, accountant for Stephens Timber Corporation.

The young accountant answered on the third ring. "John, this is Ashley. I know it's late, but I need a favor."

"Anything," was the congenial reply.

"Can you send me a copy of all transactions that have occurred at the company for the last eight months?"

There was a weighty pause on the other end of the line. "What do you mean by 'all the transactions'?"

"I mean everything—general ledger, checkbook, computer entries, expenses, payroll, the works."

"That's a lot of information…I suppose you want to audit the books of every branch—"

"I do. But let's start with Portland."

"You're joking," he said tonelessly while contemplating the magnitude of the task.

"No. Sorry, John, but I'm dead serious."

"Great. I figured as much." Ashley could almost hear the wheels turning in the young accountant's head. Despite his grumbling, John loved to scour the books. "And I suppose you want it tonight?"

"That would be nice, but I'll settle for tomorrow."

"Tomorrow!" John's anxious voice indicated that he thought she had just asked for the moon.

"Look, I realize that everything won't be available, but just start sending things to the Bend office through the computer. I'll pick up the first set of figures around three in the afternoon and then I'll get anything else on Thursday."

"You make it sound so easy—"

"I knew I could count on you. Thanks."

"Don't thank me yet. You might be asking the impossible."

"Don't I always?"

There was an amused chuckle on the other end of the line. "Yep. I suppose you do."

"Then you're going to love this. I'd like all the records for each branch available next week when I'm back in Portland."

"Is that all?" he asked sarcastically.

"Just one more thing. I want you to keep this confidential. Don't tell anyone at the office what I'm doing. Not even Claud."

There was silence on the other end for a moment. "You think someone's embezzling, don't you?" the accountant thought aloud.

"I hope not," Ashley murmured fervently. "God, I hope not." She replaced the receiver carefully and a small shiver of dread ran down her spine. What had she gotten herself into? If she found nothing in the books, Trevor still wouldn't be convinced that she was telling the truth. And, if she did discover that someone in the company was skimming money from the corporation to sabotage Trevor's campaign, she would only prove that all of the rumors that had circulated about Stephens Timber were true. Either way, it was a no-win situation.

ASHLEY OPENED HER eyes against an intruding beam of sunlight, which was flooding the room in the soft silvery hues of winter. The sheets on the small bed were ice cold. Ashley hurriedly reached for her velour robe lying at the foot of the bed. As quickly as her cold fingers could accomplish the task, she pulled the soft blue garment over her shivering body.

Tying the belt under her breasts, she raced down the steps leading from the loft and quickly restarted the fire in the den. Then, intent on putting on a hot pot of coffee and rebuilding the fire in the wood stove, she hurried into the kitchen. She was rubbing her forearms briskly as she entered the kitchen but she stopped dead in her tracks when she viewed the littered kitchen table.

Strewn carelessly over the smooth maple surface were dozens of pieces of paper. Computer printouts, general correspondence and financial statements were piled on the table without any trace of organization.

Ashley pulled an exaggerated frown at the documents as she walked over to the stove and lit the fire. So much for Trevor's theory. Nothing in the documents even remotely hinted at foul play. She had been awake until nearly two in the morning poring over the documents she had brought with her from Portland. True, she had just barely scratched the surface of the company records, but she felt an incredible sense of relief that all the books for the last month seemed in perfect order. "Put that in your mouth and chew on it a while, Senator," she whispered vindictively to herself. Then, without warning, a distant memory of Trevor, which she had locked away in a dark corner of her mind, came vividly back to her. His thick brown hair was rumpled, his muscled torso naked and bronze against pale wintergreen sheets, and as he had reached for her, his sleepy blue eyes had sparked with rekindled passion....

Stop it, Ashley! she demanded. *It's over. When are you going to accept the fact that he never loved you?* But the thought of last night and his tender embrace nagged at her and contradicted her angry words. Last night, she had felt his need, witnessed his restraint and known that he still cared for her, if only just a little.

Forcing herself to ignore the traitorous yearnings which had begun to flow within her veins just at the thought of his kiss, Ashley went through the motions of brewing coffee. She couldn't afford to feel anything for Trevor—not now, not ever. The pain of the past had left her too vulnerable and scarred and she had vowed never to be trapped by his erotic eyes again.

When the kitchen began to warm up and the coffee was perking, Ashley straightened the corporate reports and put them into her briefcase before she went back to the loft, discarded her robe and headed for a hot shower. The warm water was invigorating as it splashed against her skin and hair. Softly, she began to hum.

By the time she had towel-dried and slipped into a clean pair of jeans and sweater, she could smell the inviting aroma of coffee wafting through the small cabin. Without bothering to put on her shoes, Ashley made her way down the stairs and padded over the scattered throw rugs and oak floors to the kitchen.

"Good morning," Trevor remarked as she raced through the open archway separating the den from the kitchen. Ashley's heart jumped to her throat.

She hesitated slightly at the shock of seeing him again. In the daylight he seemed more real than he had in the shadowy night. His eyes were as clear and blue as the mountain sky and the enigmatic smile that had trapped her in the past was neatly in place. Her heart hammered excitedly for a moment, but then reality returned to her. Indignant fire sizzled in her sea-green eyes. "Don't you know how to knock, for God's sake? Or do you just get a kick out of breaking in and scaring the living daylights out of me?"

His easy smile was self-assured and his blue eyes twinkled in amusement as he took a sip of his coffee.

"Help yourself," she mocked with a severe frown.

"Still have a sweet disposition in the morning, I see," he remarked before lifting his cup. "Join me?"

"Don't you have anything better to do than a bad impression of a cat burglar?"

He raised his hands in protest. "I haven't stolen anything—"

"Yet." She took a chair opposite him at the table and accepted the coffee he had already poured for her. It was laced with sugar and cream. Just the way she liked it. "I drink it black—"

"Since when?"

"Since I got a little older and have to watch my weight."

Again his blue eyes sparked with humor. He cocked his head in the direction of her cup. "Go ahead," he suggested, "indulge yourself. Sin a little."

Her dark brows raised fractionally but she managed a smile.

"By the way, I did knock," Trevor announced, "but no one answered."

"I must have been—"

"In the shower," Trevor finished for her. Ashley nodded and smiled into her cup. "When you didn't answer, I got worried. After I came into the cabin, I realized you were in the bathroom, but it didn't seem to make much sense to go back outside and wait in the cold while you took your sweet time upstairs. I think we know each other well enough not to worry about formalities."

She was forced to smile, but the familiar caress of his eyes encouraged her to shift her gaze out the window to stare at the soft accumulation of snow. "How did you get in?"

He reached into his pocket, withdrew a dull piece of metal, and tossed it onto the table.

Ashley's heart missed a beat as she turned her attention to the object and touched the cold metal. "The key— how?" she began to ask, but her voice caught and faded. She had given the key to Trevor eight years ago, during Indian summer when they had met in secret tryst at the cabin. Tears, unwanted and filled with silent agony, stung the backs of her eyelids. Silently she dropped the key back onto the table.

"I never threw it away," he said solemnly. There was a wistful sadness in his gaze.

"You kept it all these years?" Her voice had grown husky.

He nodded and frowned thoughtfully into the black depths of his coffee.

The telephone rang shrilly and disrupted the intimate atmosphere which had surrounded them. Ashley was glad for an excuse to leave the table and avoid the unasked questions in Trevor's bold eyes.

"Hello?" she called into the receiver as she brushed the hot tears aside.

"Ashley. It's John."

Ashley managed a smile at the familiar voice. "Good morning."

"If you say so," he replied. "Look, I've got a start on the Portland records and I'll send them to Bend. I called Eileen Hanna at the Bend office so she'll be expecting them. She didn't ask any questions when I said they were just some financial projections that you asked for."

"Good."

"However, she might get a little suspicious when she sees the volume of paper involved," John warned.

"Don't worry about it. I'm sure Eileen won't question anything that I want." Eileen was one of the few employees in the vast timber empire who didn't begrudge Ashley her inheritance. The quiet, fiftyish woman was a feminist to the end and perceived that any advance of women in the timber industry was a major step in the right direction.

"I'm still working on the rest of it. I'm afraid it will take a couple of weeks to pull all the records together."

"That's fine. I'm not as concerned with how long it takes as much as I am that we do a thorough job." When she replaced the receiver, she found that Trevor had entered the room and was leaning against the arch separating the kitchen from the den. He studied her lazily, sipping his coffee.

The thought that he was listening in on her telephone conversation with John made her bristle. "Are you trying to add eavesdropping to your skills of crime, Senator?" she asked scathingly. Her ragged emotions took hold of her in an uncharacteristic burst of anger. "First we have breaking and entering and now we can add eavesdropping. If you don't watch out, I might be inclined to believe that last summer's bribery charge wasn't phony after all."

The gentle smile that had curved his lips disappeared, replaced by a grim line of determination. The glint in his steely blue eyes became deadly and his jaw was tight with the restraint he placed upon himself.

"I came over here this morning because I thought that we could settle a few things between us," he stated flatly. "But obviously that's impossible."

Regret washed over her. "Look, I didn't mean—"

"It doesn't matter." He set his cup on the bookcase and stared at her with condemning eyes. "You never have trusted me and I doubt that you ever will. All your well-rehearsed speeches about being your own woman are a lot of garbage, Ashley. What it all boils down to is that you're afraid of men and me. You can't let yourself feel anymore."

His vehement words hit her like a blast of arctic air, chilling the kind feelings she had felt for him. She ignored the tears pooling in her eyes and leveled her disdainful sea-green gaze in his direction. "I was talking to John Ellis, the accountant for the timber company. He's doing some work for me—work that I requested because of you. In a couple of hours I can pick up the reports in Bend."

His smile was forced and cynical. "Good. Then maybe you can find out just how misplaced your loyalties have been." He walked to the door and put his hand on the knob. "Call me when you find out whom Claud paid to do his dirty work!"

"If I do—"

Every muscle in his body tensed and his hand whitened over the doorknob. "Just remember that we have a deal, lady. I expect you to hold up your end."

A gust of cold air filled the room as he opened the door. He walked out and slammed the wooden door behind him. The tears that had been pooling in Ashley's eyes began to flow. "Damn you, Trevor Daniels," she whispered, her small fists clenching. "Why can't I just forget you?"

Managing to pull herself together, she walked across the room and picked up Trevor's empty cup from the shelf on which he had placed it. She started into the kitchen, but stopped, her green eyes focused on the table.

There, shining dully against the polished maple, was Trevor's key to the cabin.

CHAPTER FIVE

THE OFFICE IN Bend wasn't particularly large, but it was run efficiently due to Eileen Hanna's sharp eyes and knack for organization. When Ashley entered the airy offices located on Wall Street, Eileen looked up from her desk and smiled broadly.

"I've been expecting you," the plump, red-haired woman exclaimed as she led Ashley into a private office.

"It's good to see you again," Ashley replied with a good-natured smile. "If all the offices of Stephens Timber were run this efficiently, I'd be out of a job."

"Nonsense!" Eileen replied, but warmed under the compliment. She unlocked a closet, withdrew a neat stack of computer printouts and handed them to Ashley. "John said you wanted to go over some projection figures. Looks like he got a little carried away."

"I told him to send me anything that might be pertinent," Ashley said, eyeing the reams of paper. "I guess he took me literally."

"He's an accountant, what do you expect?"

Ashley laughed. "What I expect is more printouts."

"You're not serious." Eileen withdrew a cigarette from her purse and tapped it on the corner of the desk.

"John said that he might be sending a few more things to me later today or tomorrow. I'll pick them up on Thursday."

"Maybe you should bring a semi," Eileen suggested as she lit her cigarette and blew a thin stream of smoke toward the ceiling.

"I'll keep that in mind." Ashley hoisted the neatly bound papers under her arm and smiled fondly at the industrious woman.

"Next time you're here, I'll buy you lunch."

"It's a date, but I'll buy," Ashley promised as she walked out of the room and winked broadly. "It's time I got some use out of my expense account." When Ashley left the building, she could still hear Eileen chuckling.

IT HAD BEEN difficult to keep thoughts of Trevor from interfering with her work. The harsh words of their final argument kept flitting through her mind. She had been unnecessarily cruel because of her conflicting emotions and now she regretted the fact that she had blown up at him. It had crossed her mind to call the Lambert house and apologize to Trevor, but she had discarded the idea for now. She wanted to review all the information she had received from John Ellis before talking with Trevor again. Besides, she figured she and Trevor each needed a little time to cool off.

During the following two days, Ashley studied every computer printout that John had sent. She wasn't happy with herself until she had looked over each entry and sifted through the documents with a fine-tooth comb. By the end of the second evening, Ashley had barely made a dent in the volumes of information sitting on the edge of the desk in the den. Her eyes were burning and her muscles ached from her cramped position of leaning over the desk.

The grandfather's clock had just struck eight when Ashley heard the rumble of an engine nearing the cabin. A pleased feeling of exhilaration raced through her body. Waiting, she removed her reading glasses and tapped nervous fingernails on the edge of the desk. The engine was cut and footsteps approached the cabin. Within seconds there was a loud knock.

With a satisfied smile, Ashley answered the door. Trevor stood on the porch wearing his enigmatic smile and tight, worn jeans. Snowflakes had collected in his dark hair and began to melt and catch the reflection of the interior lights. He was carrying a large package under his arms.

"If it isn't Senator Daniels?" Ashley teased.

"Not yet, it isn't," he replied. "Ask me again in November."

"Come in," Ashley requested, standing aside. She viewed him from beneath the sweep of dark lashes, and her green eyes gleamed wickedly. "Isn't it nice to have an invitation for once?"

His broad shoulders slumped, but his dark eyes glittered. "Why do you purposely goad me?" he asked in exasperation. "I came here with a peace offering, but I can see you're not in the mood to settle our differences."

"I doubt that we can do that in one night—"

"You might be surprised," he ventured, his voice lowering suggestively.

Ashley's interest was piqued. She couldn't hide the light of expectation in her round eyes. A pleased blush colored her cheeks. "Just what have you got in mind?"

"You'll see…." Trevor brushed past her and went into the kitchen. Ashley followed in his wake, barely able to conceal her interest.

"What have you got…" Her words died in her throat as he took off his jacket and unwrapped the ungainly package. Stripping the white paper away, he exposed two large Dungeness crabs. With a frown of approval, he placed the orange shellfish in the sink. "Where did you get those?" Ashley asked as she eyed the crabs speculatively.

"Newport."

"You drove clear to the coast and back?"

"It's only a few hours—don't you remember?"

She swallowed against the lump in her throat. "Of

course I remember," she whispered hoarsely before turning away from him to hide the tears that were gathering in her eyes. The last time she had been with him, they had met in secret rendezvous near Neskowin on the rugged Oregon coast. All night long they had watched the stormy sea batter the rocky shoreline from the window of the small beach house. After dining on fresh crab and wine, Trevor had made erotic and endless love to her until the dawn had come and torn them apart.

"Come on, Ashley," he persisted, walking over to her and wrapping his arms around her waist. "Lighten up. Let's just try to forget the bad times and concentrate on the good."

"That might be easier said than done," she murmured.

He pressed a soft kiss into her blue-black hair. "Not if you try. Besides, it's Christmas Eve."

"I know." She had expected to spend the holiday alone for the first time in years and had tried to ignore the loneliness she felt. Now Trevor was with her and her spirits lifted.

"Then let's have a truce—in honor of the holiday."

"Okay, Senator," she said bravely, despite the churning emotions battling in her throat. "I'll give it a shot." Blocking out the storm of feeling raging within her, Ashley forced all of her attention on the simple tasks of heating French bread, tossing together a green salad and pouring the wine while Trevor cleaned and cracked the crabs. They worked in silence and Ashley was caught in memories of the past.

The light meal was enjoyable. Side by side, they sat by the fire in the den and laughed about the good times they had shared. Trevor was as charming as he had ever been and Ashley knew that if she let herself, she could fall hopelessly in love with him all over again. The rich sound of his laughter, the merry twinkle in his bright blue eyes and the sensual feel of his fingers when he would lightly touch her shoulder reminded her of the happiest time in her life—when she had been desperately in love with him. Even without all of the traditional trimmings, the evening became the warmest and happiest Christmas Eve she could remember. Relaxing with Trevor was perfect and natural.

Several hours had passed before Trevor cocked his head in the direction of the desk. "You've been looking over the records of Stephens Timber," he deduced.

"That's right. But I'm afraid you'll be disappointed. So far, everything looks fine. Nothing to prove that anyone in the family is the criminal you suspect."

"You're sure?" She felt him stiffen. He was sitting behind her on the floor, his strong arms folded securely over her shoulders. She was leaning against him as she stared into the glowing red embers of the fire.

She shook her head and her hair brushed against his chest. "I've barely started. Those reports are just for the last few months. I looked them over quickly and they seemed okay. I couldn't see anything glaringly obvious."

"Claud doesn't make glaring mistakes," Trevor stated. All traces of humor had disappeared from his voice.

"I know, I know. I've started going through the pages again. This time I'm studying each entry individually, but it's going to take weeks."

"Ashley." His fingers pressed urgently against her shoulders and dug into the soft muscles of her upper arm. "I don't have much time."

"Then I'm going to have to recruit help, Senator," she decided with a sigh. "I have other things I have to do. I can't spend the next two months sequestered with computer printouts just to uphold your good name."

"Or yours." He reminded her. "Just make sure your recruit is someone you can trust."

"Of course."

"This is important. Anyone who helps you can't tip Claud off. Can you be sure that the people working for you are loyal to you and not your cousin?"

Ashley didn't hesitate. "There are a few. Give me a break, Trevor. We employ over—"

"That doesn't matter. It's not quantity, but quality that counts."

"I can handle it."

"I hope so," he whispered, touching his lips to her hair. "Sometimes I question your judgment."

"That's the problem, isn't it? You always have."

The air was thick with unspoken memories. Silence weighed heavily on Ashley's slim shoulders as she stared into the bloodred coals of the fire. "I don't know you anymore, Trevor. Not at all," she said in a quiet moment of complete honesty. "And what I remember…what happened between us, turned out very badly." She turned her head and her green eyes looked directly into his.

"A man can change…" he ventured.

"And so can a woman."

His eyes searched the soft contours of her face before she turned away from him to concentrate on the slowly dying fire. "What if I said that I wish I had it all to do over again?" His fingers touched the round of her shoulders and lingered in the black silk of her hair.

The old ache burned savagely in her heart. "I'd say I don't believe you—no matter how much I'd like to. I'm not bitter, Trevor; just wiser than I was. What happened between us was your doing and nothing you can say will alter the past." She felt the warmth of his fingers in her hair and knew that she had to pull away from him and break the seductive spell he was weaving. She couldn't let herself forget the past and the pain. Struggling against reawakened love, she managed to stand and step away from the power of Trevor's touch.

Her voice was firm. "I think it would be better to forget what happened eight years ago and concentrate on what's happening now. For instance, the reason you're here and what you really want from me."

The grandfather's clock in the entry hall ticked off the silent seconds. A chill as cold as a North Pacific gale made Ashley shiver with dread and she rubbed her hands over her arms.

"I thought we could spend some time together. It's Christmas." Trevor's eyes never left her face. He watched even the most subtle of her reactions; the nervous manner in which she clutched the gold chain encircling her throat, and the movement of her tongue as she wet her lips. Desperately she wanted to believe him.

"And you need me to check into the company records to condemn my own family. Isn't that what this is all about? Isn't that the only reason you're here? Aren't you just trying to clear all the dirt surrounding the Daniels family and push it onto the name of Lazarus Stephens in order that you can get elected? That is the most important thing isn't it? Your career."

"And what's important to you, Ashley?" Trevor asked quietly. His face had saddened. "Eight years ago all you wanted to do was settle down, get married, have children. Now you're talking about women's rights and finding yourself! What the hell's that supposed to mean?" His blue eyes were blazing. "And what about your husband—how does he feel about all this new way of thinking? Or is he the reason you've become so liberated?"

Ashley's eyes snapped with indignation. "Richard and I were divorced four years ago."

"I know that."

"Then why do you continue to refer to him as my husband?"

"Because he was!"

"And that still bothers you," she said, understanding a little of his pain.

"Shouldn't it?" His cold blue eyes narrowed and he lifted himself from the floor, trying to relieve the tired muscles supporting his back.

"You were the one who couldn't make a commitment," she reminded him, hoping to hide the trace of wistful regret in her voice.

Trevor's fist opened and closed against his jeans, as if he were physically attempting to regain control of his temper. "Don't twist the truth," he warned. "I was willing to do just about anything to keep you—"

"Except marry me."

"Ha!" The sound of his humorless laughter was as bitter as the night. "How many times did I ask you to marry me? Or have you conveniently forgotten about them?" His voice was low, the sound dangerous. There was a kinetic energy in the air, ready to explode with the repressed passion of the heated argument.

Ashley's dignity wavered for an instant. "That's right, Trevor. You did ask me to marry you, several times." She waved the back of her slim hand in the air as if the number were insignificant. "But asking isn't the same as doing. I was tired of being engaged and tired of having an affair. I wanted to be your wife!"

"Correction," he interjected cruelly, his dark blue eyes burning with accusations. "You wanted to be anyone's wife. Even if it meant running back to the man your father had chosen for you."

"I loved you…." She sighed, tears pooling in her eyes with the painful admission. "Trevor, I loved you so much."

"Until you realized that I wasn't going to become a millionaire overnight. The daughter of Lazarus Stephens wasn't able to live without the comforts of wealth. You couldn't wait for me, could you?"

"Now who's twisting the truth?" she charged.

"Damn it, Ashley, this isn't getting us anywhere." His fist crashed into the warm rocks of the fireplace and then he swore, wincing against a sudden, blinding stab of pain.

Ashley's anger fled and was replaced by concern. "Are you all right?"

"I'm fine."

"Trevor." She touched his arm. For a moment her fingers brushed his wrist and his blue eyes sought hers, unspoken questions in their stormy depths. Her throat tightened. He rubbed his forehead before letting his head fall backward to stare at the open rafters supporting the roof. "Dear God, Ashley, I wish I understood you."

His plea sounded earnest. A lump formed in her throat when she considered what she might have shared with Trevor. Had she waited, as he had asked, would all of the happiness of their youth have blossomed into a deep, self-less love? Could they have shared their lives? Would she have eventually borne his children, comforted him when he needed her, shared his deepest agony?

As if he had read her mind, he asked the one question he had been avoiding for three days. "Why did you come here, to the cabin?"

She withdrew her hand and tears filled her eyes. "There were a lot of reasons—I needed a rest, there was work I could do here, I wanted to get out of the office, but there was something else," she admitted with a wry frown. "I came here because of you." Sea-green eyes met his. "It seemed that every time I turned around, I was reminded of you. Just a few weeks after Senator Higgins's death, your name became a household word. Then there were the bribery charges—the newspapers…television…you were everywhere.

"When Dad died, all I heard about was what damage you would do if you were elected. Now, just lately, your accident hit the front page. I couldn't get away from you." Her voice softened. "I thought that if I came here for a couple of weeks, I could think things out, sort out my feelings."

"And have you?"

Her smile was frail and filled with self-mockery. "I thought I had." Her lips pursed into a thoughtful pout. "Now I'm not so sure." Emotions she had thought long dead were reawakening. She couldn't help but remember the feel of his hands against her skin, or the way his eyes darkened in passion when she smiled suggestively.

The rustic room seemed to shrink and become more intimate. Ashley had to concentrate to keep her thoughts from wandering dangerously to a distant past.

He stared down at her, attempting to look past the innocent allure in her eyes. She had always been a puzzle to him, enigmatic and beguiling; the only woman he had ever let touch his soul. He had vowed never to make that mistake again, and he had been able to keep that silent promise to himself until tonight, when he gazed into the intelligent complexity of her eyes. At this moment he wanted her more desperately than he had ever wanted anything in his life. "Do you want me to stay?"

She didn't avoid his penetrating gaze. "Yes. I've missed you, Trevor." Giving up all the thin pretenses, she faced what she had tried to deny for eight solitary years. "I've missed you so badly."

He forced himself to look past the tears welling in her eyes. "Not badly enough to come back."

"I couldn't." She shook her head and fought the tears. "I think you understand that my pride wouldn't allow it."

"I've never been able to understand anything about you."

Standing, she faced him. "Only because you never really tried."

Slowly his strong arms encircled her waist and pulled

her body gently to his. There was a restraint in his touch
and torment in his gaze.

"I must be out of my mind," he muttered to himself as
his head lowered and his lips brushed hers. The pressure
of the kiss increased. Ashley sighed through parted lips at
the power of his arms and the warmth of his mouth covering hers. The faint taste of wine passed from his lips to
hers and the familiar taste brought back memories as bittersweet as the past they had shared together.

Her knees seemed to melt with the warm persuasion
of his embrace. She touched him lightly on the shoulders
and could feel the tightening of lean, corded muscles beneath her fingertips.

His tongue rimmed her lips before slipping between her
teeth to explore the secrets of her mouth. It touched her familiarly, sliding seductively against the polish of her teeth.

Trembling with a wave of passion, her fingers dug into
the firm flesh of his shoulders. The forgotten ache of womanly need uncoiled wantonly within her, forcing her blood
to race wildly through her veins and pound in her ears.
Her breathing became rapid and shallow. With each flickering touch of his supple tongue against hers, her desire
for him increased and the uncontrollable yearning became
more heated; a throbbing distraction demanding release.

He lifted his head from hers, but continued to press her
body against his, letting her feel the taut rigidity of each of
his muscles straining against his clothing. "I want you," he
whispered hoarsely against her hair. It was a statement as
honest as the cold mountain night. "I want you more than
I've ever wanted a woman."

She swallowed against the dryness that had settled in
her throat. "And I want you," she murmured.

His penetrating eyes studied the mystery of her. "With
you it's more than passion or lust. It always has been."

Her heart nearly missed a beat. If only she could believe that he loved her…just a little. "You've always had a way with words, Trevor. That's why you've done so well in politics, I suppose."

"Are you accusing me of distorting the truth?" His voice was thick and slightly mocking. A hint of laughter danced in his eyes. Ashley was captivated by his smile—the slightly off-center grin she had grown to love that summer eight years before.

"Stretching the truth," she corrected.

"In order to seduce you?"

"To get your way."

"If I'd had my way with you, things would be a lot different between us." His fingers wrapped possessively over her wrist. "Do you have any idea what you do to me?"

"I just want…to be with you," she whispered, rising onto her toes and kissing his cheek. Softly she outlined the shape of his brows with the tip of her finger. Everything she did seemed so natural, just as it had in the past.

Trevor groaned with the frustration tormenting him. He noticed the innocence in her clear green eyes and the heat burning in his loins began to ache. "Ashley," he ground out, "I don't want you to do anything you might regret."

"I won't."

He clenched his teeth together and forcefully willed his passion aside. "What I'm trying to say is that you don't have to feel obligated to me."

"I don't, Trevor," she replied, showing just the hint of a dimple. "Not anymore."

Her hand pressed against his cheek and he could stand the bittersweet torment no longer. With a sensual movement, he turned his head and touched the tip of his tongue to her palm, letting the moist heat from his body flow into hers.

"Trevor…" she moaned, her voice fading into the night. "Oh, Trevor." She shuddered with the pain of ragged emotions, the same feelings she had been denying for eight agonizing years. His tongue created a moist path between her fingers and she felt as if her entire body were ignited by his warm touch. Her throat became dry, her voice a breathless whisper. "I've always loved you," she vowed.

"I want to know that you're mine," he said, steeling himself against the desire running rampant in his veins and the passion dominating his mind.

"I always have been."

"Ashley, don't. Don't lie to me. Not now."

"I'm not—"

"Prove it."

"If only I could," she wished.

"Let me make love to you." It was a simple request. His dark blue eyes bored into her, exposing the depths of his torment. Her feelings for him were dangerous. They entrapped her in the same words of love that had betrayed her in the past. His offer was tempting, yet she hesitated, afraid of losing herself to him as she had once before.

"There's nothing I want more," she admitted.

"But you're afraid."

"There's no future for us…." Her dark brows had pulled into a worried frown. With all of her heart she wanted to lie beside Trevor, to find the exhilaration once again of becoming one with him. But the old fears resurfaced.

"Shhh. Don't think about tomorrow." His fingers caught in the thick strands of her blue-black hair, pulling her head to his. For a delicious moment, his lips brushed over hers, lingering just a fraction of a second. "Let me love you, sweet lady," he whispered.

Her response was to let go of the fear and the pain of the past. Her surrender was complete. "Please," she murmured. Reaching upward she twined her fingers in his hair and turned her lips upward to accept the warm invitation of his mouth.

"It's been so long," he groaned as his lips pressed against hers and conveyed to her his overwhelming masculinity.

Her heart thudded irregularly with the urgency of his kiss. Desire, hot and fluid, crept up her veins as she felt his tongue meet hers. Without breaking the heated kiss, he shifted and lifted her off the floor to cradle her against his chest. Trevor began to carry her up the stairs to the loft.

"I can walk," she protested, thinking of his recent injury.

"Not a chance," he replied. "You might change your mind."

"Never." Tears of happiness welled in her eyes as she looked up at the angular face of the man she loved.

When he reached the top of the stairs, Trevor didn't hesitate. He strode across the small loft and dropped Ashley onto the bed, before lying beside her. The room was shadowed, but in the pale illumination from the skylight, Ashley could make out the masculine angles of his face.

She felt the touch of his hand as he caressed her cheek and she read the desire smoldering in the depths of his eyes. His fingers slid seductively down her throat to linger at the neckline of her sweater.

Closing her eyes, she leaned against him and let out a shuddering sigh when his fingers dipped below the ribbing at her neck to tentatively touch the swell of her breast. Her hands worked at the buttons of his shirt, letting it fall open to expose his solidly muscled chest. The bandage, a swath of white against his dark skin, reminded Ashley of the reasons he had come to the cabin, the reasons he was here with her now. Her fingers gently outlined the white gauze.

Slowly he lifted the sweater over her head. Shivering slightly when the cool air touched her skin, she was only aware that she wanted Trevor as desperately as she ever had. She needed him now, tonight. She was destined to lie in the shelter of his arms, feel the strength of his body straining against hers. And there would be no regrets. Tonight she belonged to Trevor alone.

He watched her silently, his warm hands touching her cool skin. She swallowed against the arid feeling in the back of her mouth when his hand cupped her breast. The ache within her burned more savagely. When his head lowered and he touched the flimsy fabric of her bra with his lips, she thought she would die in the sweet agony ripping through her. Her breasts pushed against the thin barrier of lace and silk as his tongue wet the sheer fabric and the cool night air caressed her skin. He groaned as his mouth captured the hidden nipple straining against the taut lace.

Ashley clutched his head against her, exhilarating in the torment of his lovemaking. Tears ran down her cheeks as he unclasped her bra and her breasts were unbound. His fingers moved in slow rhythmic circles over one nipple while his tongue rimmed the other.

"Oh, God, Trevor," she pleaded. "Make love to me, please make love to me."

His hands found the waistband of her jeans, and his fingers dipped deliciously close to her skin. She was unaware of the precise moment when he removed the rest of her clothes as well as his own. She was only conscious of the sweet torment heating within her, a wild tempest of passion only he could calm.

When at last he moved over her, she was rewarded by the feel of his firm muscles pressed urgently over her body. His bare legs, soft with dark hair, entwined with hers. His hands touched her rib cage as if he were sculpting her, and his lips, hard with passion and warm with desire, molded over hers. "Love me, Trevor," she cried, unashamed of her tears.

"I always have…." He lifted his head and gazed into her soft green eyes. Her dark hair was spread over the white pillow. He knew now what he had always suspected: Ashley Stephens was the most incredibly beautiful and intelligent woman he had ever met.

Burying his head in the soft curve of her neck, he claimed her in a sensuously slow union of his flesh with hers. The warmth within her began slowly to uncoil as he found that part of her he had discovered sometime in a stormy past. He tasted the salty tears of happiness that ran down her cheeks; he felt the heated moment of her submission and stiffened when her fingernails dug into the muscles of his back.

Ashley whispered his name into the night when the final moment of surrender brought them together and bridged the black abyss of eight lost years.

As his body fell against hers, he held her as if he expected her to vanish. The corded muscles of his arms offered the gentle assurance that he did love her and always had. If only Ashley could believe him. If only she could think that Trevor would never leave.

CHAPTER SIX

SUNLIGHT WAS STREAMING through the windows when Ashley opened her eyes on Christmas morning. She snuggled deep beneath the colorful patchwork quilt and felt the warmth of Trevor's body against her own. He made a low sound in the back of his throat and the arm draped possessively across her abdomen tightened before his even breathing resumed.

Ashley watched his dark profile against the stark white sheets. In slumber, some of the harshness had disappeared from his features; the tension that had been with him the last few days had faded with the night. The lines around his eyes had softened and the pinched corners of his mouth were relaxed. His hair fell over his eyebrows. Ashley lovingly brushed it out of his face while she pushed herself up on one elbow and stared down at the only man she had ever loved. Why, Trevor, she thought sadly, why can't we live like this forever? Why do we continually do battle with each other?

The quilt covering Trevor had slipped downward, exposing his chest to the cold morning air. Ashley's eyes followed the rippling lines of his muscular body to rest on the white gauze wrapped tightly over his torso. Gingerly she touched the bandage, frowning thoughtfully. Was it possible that Claud could have been responsible for Trevor's accident? It seemed unlikely, and yet Ashley knew that Claud could be cruel and ruthless if he felt cornered or threatened. And Claud had mentioned to Ashley that he considered Trevor's senatorial bid a direct threat to Stephens Timber. To what lengths would her bitter cousin go?

Her touch disturbed him. Trevor opened a sleepy blue eye and smiled when he saw that Ashley was already awake.

"You're a sight for sore eyes," he murmured. The hand that had been curved over the bend in her waist moved seductively upward until his thumb rubbed against her rib. "God, I could get used to this." He stretched before sitting next to her and looking into the incredible allure of her eyes. "Merry Christmas, Ashley," he whispered before bringing his face next to hers and pressing anxious lips to her mouth.

Slowly, he pushed her back against the mattress and let his weight fall carefully over her. Her breasts flattened with the welcome burden of him and slowly she slid her fingers up the solid muscles of his arms to rest on his shoulders.

When he raised his head, there was a trace of sadness in his gaze. "You don't know how long I've waited to wake up with you beside me," he admitted. A wistful look stole over her refined features. Trevor traced the disbelieving arch of her brow.

Ashley felt as if her heart had swollen in her throat. "You only had to ask," she whispered.

Something dangerous flickered in his gaze. "You were married," he reminded her.

"That was a long time ago."

Trevor lay over her, his supple body imprisoning hers against the bed. She didn't move or attempt to escape from the gentle bonds of his muscles flexed possessively over hers. As she gazed into his knowing blue eyes, Ashley realized that she could never love another man. Her marriage to Richard had been a mistake from the start and it was over before it had ever begun.

"I should never have let you go," Trevor whispered into the thick ebony silk of her hair. His body began to move rhythmically over hers, enticing the most delicious responses. Her heartbeat thudded irregularly in her chest. "I should have chased you down and forced you to marry me."

"You wouldn't have had to force me, Trevor. That was the one thing in the world I wanted."

"And the only thing that Lazarus Stephens's money couldn't buy."

She let out a ragged sigh and looked beyond him to the exposed rafters of the ceiling. Her breathing was becoming shallow and rapid. "Must we always argue?"

"I can think of better things to do...."

Her fingers tangled in his hair. "So can I."

Trevor lowered his head, his lips claiming hers in a kiss filled with passion and despair. His hands rubbed against her skin, softly caressing her body and making her blood warm as it ran through her veins.

The magic of his touch evoked the most primitive of responses within her. Liquid heat circulated and swirled upward through her body as she felt the firm muscles of his chest brush erotically across her breasts, teasing the dark nipples to expectant peaks aching with desire.

His lips touched and teased her, inflaming the wanton fires of passion to surge through her veins until she began to move beneath him. Her hands strayed downward, touching the rippling muscles of his back and outlining each tense sinew with her fingertips.

Trevor closed his eyes and groaned in helpless surrender. His hands began to knead her breasts and his knees impatiently parted her legs, testing her willingness by rubbing himself gently against her abdomen.

A soft gasp escaped from her throat, and when he lowered his head to capture her parted lips with his, Ashley thought she would die with wanting him. His tongue explored and plundered the sweet delights of her mouth while he gripped her shoulders firmly with his hands and entered the dark warmth of her womanhood.

Ashley's mind was swirling with erotic images. Her fingers dug into his back as she felt the womanly pressure within her build. Slowly, as if enjoying the torture of denial, he pushed closer to her, touching her most intimate core, closing the space that held her away from him and savoring the sweet agony of her cry.

"Please," she whispered throatily, her glazed eyes looking into his. Her throat was dry, the words a strain. "Take me, Trevor," she begged.

The light of satisfaction glimmered in his eyes as he began to thrust against her. He watched in fascination while she responded in kind, holding on to him in desperate need, as if she expected him to disappear into the cool morning air.

Sweat beaded on his brow and glistened against his naked skin as he restrained himself, waiting until he felt the warmth of her explode in a liquid burst of satiation. Then he, too, let go and felt the sudden rush of blinding fire as he sealed their union of flesh and mind and fell heavily against her with a moan of triumphant release.

"I love you, Ashley," he claimed. "God forgive me, but I've always loved you. Even when you were married to another man."

The lump in Ashley's throat expanded with his words. "Shhh, Trevor—not now." Lovingly, her fingers touched his hair, smoothing the wavy chestnut strands away from his face. His words touched the deepest, most precarious part of her heart and she couldn't allow herself the luxury of believing them. Not now. Not ever.

She had felt the pain of his betrayal once before and had sworn never to live the life of a fool again. It would be too easy to believe him—to trust her heart—to let the pain recapture her in its bittersweet claws.

After a few moments of reflective silence, Ashley attempted to lighten the mood in the cold cabin. "How about breakfast in bed?" she asked.

Trevor smiled knowingly and ran a sensuous finger down the length of her body. "I'm afraid I wouldn't be able to concentrate on food."

She laughed and shook her hair out of her eyes. "Well, I could. I'm hungry enough to eat a horse. Come on." Slapping him playfully on his rump, she hopped out of the bed, grabbed her robe and slipped it on. "I'll make breakfast while you get the fire going in the den."

"And then you'll serve me in bed?"

Ashley was halfway to the bathroom by the time his words hit her. When she turned to look over her shoulder and cast him an intentionally provocative glance, she found him leaning on one elbow, his blue eyes following her every move.

"You are talking about breakfast, aren't you, Senator?"

"Among other things…"

"Um-hmm. I think we'd better eat in the kitchen. It might be safer."

"Spoilsport."

"Look who's talking. You're the one with the important project, or have you forgotten?"

"It's Christmas!"

Ashley smiled despite herself. "That it is. Merry Christmas, darling." She winked at him seductively, turned on her heel and made a big show of going into the bathroom to change. She half expected him to follow her and was more than slightly disappointed when he didn't.

After she had showered and changed, she walked through the loft again and noted that he was still in bed, but far from sleeping.

"Come here," he commanded when she breezed past the four-poster. His delft-blue eyes were smoldering with passion.

"Not on your life," she teased, but when he reached out and took hold of her wrist, she was forced to spin around and face the determined set of his jaw. Her wet hair dangled in glistening ebony ringlets around her flushed face as he roughly pulled her down on the bed.

"You're no gentleman, Senator Daniels," she laughed as she fell against him.

"And you love it." His fingers toyed with the buttons of her sweater. "Someone should teach you a lesson, you know."

"And you're applying for the job?" Her eyebrows rose a skeptical fraction.

"I've got it." One of the pearllike fasteners near her neck was loosened, exposing just a hint of white skin at her shoulder. Her green eyes danced in mock dismay as she clutched at her throat. The love she had harbored for eight long years was unhidden in the even features of her face.

There was something captivating about Trevor's slightly off-center smile, something inviting and dangerous in his midnight-blue eyes. When he leaned over to kiss her shoulder, Ashley shuddered with anticipation.

He buried his face in her neck and drank in the sweet scent of her clean, damp hair. It held the faint fragrance of wildflowers, just as he remembered it. They had been alone in the cabin, and the dewy drops of summer rain had clung to her hair.

"I've never wanted a woman the way I want you," he admitted, touching her throat with his lips.

A thousand emotions made Ashley shiver as he pressed himself against her. She felt the ache of desire begin to flood her veins when he lay atop her and pressed the length of his naked body over hers. Even through her slacks and sweater she could feel the heat of his passion pressed urgently against her skin.

"Forget breakfast," he suggested, running his tongue against her ear. "I have a better idea...."

Without regret, Ashley wound her arms around his neck and brought his head against hers, eager to let the happiness linger and feel the warmth of his lips dispel the chill in hers.

As SHE POURED water for coffee, Ashley could hear Trevor grumbling about the things he had to put up with. She smiled to herself when she remembered her hasty escape from the bed. After making glorious love while the late morning sun infiltrated the room through the skylight, she had dozed quietly in the shelter of Trevor's arms. Then, when she could tell that he wasn't expecting her to leave, she had bolted from the bed, snatched up her clothes from where they had been carelessly tossed and raced down the stairs to the kitchen.

He had sworn roundly, which had only caused her to laugh at his frustration. It felt so right, so natural being alone with him. It was almost as if what had separated them in the past was beginning to disappear.

While Trevor attended to the fire in the den, Ashley started preparing what she could for a festive brunch. The cupboards were pretty bare, but she prided herself on the end result of broiled grapefruit, blueberry muffins, sausage and poached eggs.

"Not too bad for a novice," she decided as she dusted her hands on the apron she had tied over her clothes.

Trevor must have heard her. "It's Christmas, you know. I'm expecting baked ham, cinnamon rolls, eggs Benedict...." He poked his head into the kitchen.

"Keep it up, Senator, and you'll be lucky if you get cornflakes."

He studied the floor for a minute before his eyes came back to rest on her. "It wouldn't matter what we ate, you know."

She returned his grin. "I suppose not. But since I put out the effort, I expect you to do the meal justice."

They ate in the kitchen and Trevor, for all his protests earlier, ate with relish. A surprised glint surfaced in his blue eyes. "I didn't think Lazarus Stephens's daughter knew how to boil water, let alone cook."

"I'm learning," she joked, before adding more seriously, "There are a lot of things you don't know about me, Trevor. I've grown up in the last eight years." He lifted his dark brows appreciatively, as if in mute agreement, and took a long swallow of his coffee.

The intimate conversation made Ashley bold. "So why haven't you ever married?" she asked before her courage escaped her.

He set his cup down and stared out the window for what seemed an eternity. "I'd like to give you the old cliché about never finding the right woman," he replied, rubbing his chin in the process and continuing to stare at the frosty panes. "But then, we both know it would be a lie."

Ashley stared at him, her breath caught in her throat. She shook her head sadly. "I just told you that I've grown up. I'm not as naïve as I was, Trevor, nor as—"

"Trusting?"

"That, too, I suppose. I'd like to think that you and I were just star-crossed lovers and that our time hadn't come yet. Now that we've found each other again, everything will be fine." She ran one finger around the rim of her cup and stared at the murky coffee. Her voice had grown hoarse. "But that's not the way it is. You're not Prince Charming, and I'm certainly no Sleeping Beauty, waiting for a man to change my life." Her sea-green eyes held his calmly. "Too much has happened between us. And," she added pointedly, "it's my guess that the reason you haven't married is that you haven't found the perfect mate."

"Is there such a thing?"

"I doubt it." She shook her head. "You want too much in a wife, Trevor. A strong woman, who will support you and your damned career. A woman who will do what you want without question, but still has a mind of her own. A woman who will give up everything to be at your side—if and when you want her. And a woman who will wait with the home fires burning until you decide to come home. That's too much to expect from anyone."

"Including you."

She smiled sadly. "Especially me."

"And what do you want in a husband?"

Love, she thought to herself, but couldn't force the word from her lips. Instead, her lips puckered into a secretive frown and she started picking up the dishes. "I don't want a husband," she replied.

"You did once. Very badly, as I recall."

"That was a long time ago."

He scowled darkly and his fingers drummed angrily on the table. "And you managed to get yourself one, didn't you?"

"It didn't last."

"Why not?"

She shrugged her shoulders to indicate that it really didn't matter, but Trevor's fingers gripped her forearm and restricted her movements. "Richard and I weren't suited—"

"That's a lie! The man was hand-picked by your father."

"Maybe that was the problem." She looked pointedly at her wrist and the tanned fingers restraining it.

With obvious reluctance Trevor let go of her arm. "This isn't getting us anywhere," he muttered, pushing back his chair before fiercely striding out of the room. Ashley heard his footsteps echo in the hall before the front door of the cabin opened, only to slam shut with a resounding thud that rattled the timbers of the rustic mountain retreat.

Knowing that it would be best to let him cool off, Ashley finished clearing the table and set the dishes in the sink to soak before grabbing her jacket from the hall tree, slipping on her boots and going outside.

Trevor's footprints left deep impressions in the snow. She followed the powdery prints and forced her hands deep into her pockets. She loved Trevor with a passion that was achingly evident every time she was near him, and yet, try as she would, she could find no way of resolving those problems that held them apart.

When she found Trevor he was standing near the edge of a sharp ravine, his back to her. He was staring past the snow-covered abyss to the majestic peaks beyond. The sky was a brilliant blue and the snow-laden mountains stood proudly in the distance, their treeless upper slopes reflecting the icy radiance of the winter sun's rays.

Trevor hadn't heard her approach and when Ashley put a reproachful hand against his sleeve, he stiffened. "I didn't mean to pick a fight, you know," she whispered, her breath misting in the cold mountain air.

His smile was cynical, and a muscle worked beneath his clean-shaven jaw. "Seems like you and I can't avoid arguing."

"It's hard to clear the air."

"Especially when so many lies cloud it." He thrust his fists deep into his pockets and leaned against the denuded white trunk of a birch tree. Thoughtfully he pursed his lips and his dark brows drew together in careful consideration over intense blue eyes.

"I never have lied to you," she replied.

He looked as if he didn't believe her. "But your family. First Lazarus, now Claud—"

"My family would never have come between us," she

replied, "if you weren't so hell-bent to ruin Stephens Timber Corporation."

A sound of disgust formed in his throat. His eyes had turned as frosty as the winter day. "You can't convince me that Claud isn't out to get me."

"I know. I've tried."

"He's out to ruin me politically, Ashley."

"I think you're jumping to conclusions."

"The right ones. Claud is scared spitless that if I win I'll be able to lobby for wilderness protection and somehow cut off his supply of timber. Your father was opposed to any new wilderness protection acts. He didn't give a damn about the environment, and it seems as if Claud was tutored well."

"But Claud doesn't own the company."

"No, he just runs it. And he won't rest until he's ruined me politically."

"That's ridiculous!" Ashley retorted. She brushed the snow from a boulder and sat on it, holding her knees with her arms and huddling for warmth. Try as she might, she couldn't believe that Claud would be so murderous. It was true that Trevor's campaign included a firm stand on wilderness protection, which, in the past, Stephens Timber had vehemently opposed. The issue was a delicate one, pitting the economy against the environment. In lean times, when unemployment was high, jobs and the timber industry won over the environment. But right now, unemployment was down and public sentiment seemed to support Trevor's position.

"Senator Higgins was an efficient lobbyist for the timber industry," Trevor said. His broad shoulders slumped as if he were bone-tired.

"And you won't be?"

"Right. Higgins was in your father's pocket and I suspect that Claud is hoping that another candidate will fill

Higgins's shoes." Trevor's voice was without inflection, but his face was a study in grim resolve. "He can look somewhere else because it sure as hell won't be me."

Ashley smiled bitterly. "I don't see where you get off acting so sanctimonious. Your family is still a very viable force in the timber industry."

"But my brother keeps his nose clean."

"What's that supposed to mean?" Ashley demanded.

"Just that Jeremy has managed to follow pretty closely in my father's footsteps. Daniels Logging Company has always worked within the law."

"And my father didn't? Is that what you're implying?"

"I'm just stating the facts," he replied coldly. "Jeremy has seen to it that Daniels Logging has been ahead of its time. We've never clear-cut, always participated in reforestation, even before it was fashionable, and always left a buffer zone near streams, to protect the rivers." Trevor's square jaw hardened. "And to my knowledge, the use of pesticides by Daniels Logging has been kept to a minimum, in order to protect the public."

Ashley's elegant brows raised scathingly. "You've implied some pretty heavy charges, Senator."

"I've always called 'em as I see 'em."

"Or so your campaign manager would like the public to think."

Trevor scowled angrily, but didn't offer a rebuttal. He noticed the bluish tint to Ashley's lips and reluctantly he stood. After brushing the wet snow from his jeans, he said, "I think we'd better go back inside before you freeze to death."

"Are you worried about me—or the scandal my demise would cause?"

Trevor's admonishing stare was stern. "I wish for once, just once, you'd give me a break."

"That works two ways, you know."

They walked back to the cabin in silence, each wrapped in secret thoughts of the past that linked them, bound them together, and always kept them at sword's length from each other.

In some respects, Trevor was right, Ashley decided. Daniels Logging had always had an untarnished reputation for working with the government, its employees and the environmentalists, instead of opposing them. While Stephens Timber was forever being gossiped about for being ruthless and unsympathetic to both employees and the public, Daniels Logging was considered a cornerstone of Oregon industry.

Ashley gritted her teeth in determination. All that was about to change. Then both Trevor Daniels and Claud Stephens would understand what it meant to deal with her. She intended to make Stephens Timber a model company, come hell or high water.

Ashley's thoughts were grim, but she had trouble believing that Claud would actually try to force Trevor out of the campaign, either by the phony bribery charges or this last, unbelievable mishap with Trevor's car. Claud was too much of a coward to do anything so bold. It wasn't his style to take unnecessary risks. And none of the records indicated foul play, at least she hadn't found anything out of the ordinary.

Ashley breathed a silent prayer begging that her instincts about her cousin were right.

ONCE BACK IN the cabin, she managed to steer the conversation in any direction but on Trevor's career or the past. Trevor seemed to be taking pains to avoid another argument as well. The afternoon faded slowly into nightfall.

It wasn't a traditional Christmas by any standards. No candles, roast goose, lighted tree or carolers gave the holy day the special traditions Ashley had observed in the past.

However, being alone in the mountains, wrapped in the strong arms of the one man who had ever meant anything to her, made this Christmas more special and intimate than any she could remember celebrating. What better way to observe the holiday than to share it with the man she loved with all her heart?

That night, lying in the security of Trevor's embrace, listening to the regular beating of his heart as he slept, Ashley cried soft tears of quiet happiness and whispered a silent prayer of gratitude for the special moments she had shared with him.

The cabin was illuminated only by the glowing, blood-red embers of the fire and the pale moonglow reflecting on the soft blanket of snow outdoors. The paned windows were frosted from the cold and the only sound breaking the stillness of the night was the occasional hiss of the fire as it encountered pitch.

Ashley closed her eyes and tried not to think that this night might be the last she would ever spend with him.

THE SHARP RING of the telephone brought Ashley out of a deep and trouble-free sleep. Trevor groaned, shifted on the bed and then continued to snore peacefully without even opening an eye. The last few weeks had exhausted him.

Carefully, so as not to disturb him, Ashley slipped from beneath the covers, grabbed her robe and hurried down the stairs to answer the phone in the kitchen. As she picked up the receiver, she pushed the tangled strands of her hair out of her eyes.

"Hello?"

"Ashley!"

With a sinking sensation, Ashley recognized the smug male voice of her cousin. "Good morning, Claud," she replied quietly, careful not to awaken Trevor. After sneaking a careful glance up the stairs, she walked to the far side of the small room, stretching the telephone cord its full length.

"What's going on?" Claud demanded after a few strangling moments of silence.

"What's going on?" she repeated casually, though her heart had seemed to miss a beat. She knew in an instant that Claud was on to her plan to help Trevor. "What do you mean?"

"Knock it off, Ashley. I know that you've been checking up on me."

Ashley's nerves were stretched to the breaking point. She had to support herself by leaning a slim and sagging shoulder against the wall. Somehow, despite the dread constricting her throat, she managed to keep her voice steady.

"Of course I have. You've known that all along. That's why I quit my job. I decided that Stephens Timber needed me."

"So why are all the reports being sent to the Bend office?" Claud asked in a voice filled with gruff indignation. "It looks to me like you're doing a major audit of the books."

"I told you I wanted to check all of the records," she replied evenly.

"There's more to it than that," Claud accused. Ashley could almost hear the wheels turning in his mind.

"Just a simple, all-encompassing audit."

"We have accountants to do that."

"I prefer to look over everything myself."

"You can stop whitewashing, Ashley. I know you're up to something. I just want to know what it is."

"Nothing all that mysterious, Claud. I just want to personally examine the books."

"In Bend? Over Christmas? Give me a break, for Christ's sake. You're supposed to be on a vacation."

"I am."

"With the company records?" He was clearly dubious.

"Right."

"You sure know how to have a good time," he mocked, openly challenging her.

Ashley smiled grimly to herself. "I'm not the kind of person to shirk my responsibilities, Claud. You may as well face that fact right now. Either you can work with me or against me, but we both know who makes the ultimate decisions regarding the company."

"And you just love to rub my nose in it, don't you?" Claud said disgustedly.

"Only when I'm forced to." She let out a weary sigh of frustration and tried to assuage her cousin's growing suspicions. "Look, Claud, what I'm doing is merely routine. Now that my job with the college is over, I think I should spend as much time as possible acquainting myself with the company books. Otherwise I won't be all that effective, will I?

"I intend to be more than just a figurehead with this corporation. It's my duty to learn everything there is to know about Stephens Timber."

"So you called John Ellis? Why didn't you get in touch with me?"

Nervously she twisted the phone cord, but she forced her voice to remain determined. "I did. Remember? You were the one who balked at sending me the information I needed."

"So you went behind my back."

"I did what I had to do."

Claud was still angry, but his suspicions seemed to be placated, at least for the moment. "So when will you be in Portland?" he asked, changing the subject.

"Soon. I don't have a precise date, but sometime before the first of the year." Ashley wanted to end the conversation as quickly as possible, before Trevor woke up. "I've got things to do right now, but I'll talk to you when I'm back in town. I'm sure you'll be interested to know how the books look."

"I already do," Claud muttered before hanging up.

When Ashley replaced the receiver, she let out a long sigh of relief and turned toward the stairs. She found herself face-to-face with Trevor. His expression was murderous.

"So someone at Stephens Timber tipped Claud off," he charged.

Ashley stood her ground, refusing to back down to the anger in the set of his jaw. "Claud's suspicious, if that's what you mean."

"What I mean, dear lady," Trevor spat out, "is that no one in that damned timber company of yours can keep his mouth shut." A deadly gleam of anger sparked in his eyes. "Or else you were just stringing me along all the time. This entire meeting was just a charade."

"I didn't come knocking on your door," Ashley pointed out, her eyes widening in disbelief.

"But you didn't exactly fight me off, did you?" he threw back at her, his angry glare burning through to her soul.

A small part of Ashley wanted to wither and die. Could this be the same man she loved with all of her heart? Did he really believe that she had sold him out? The fists rammed against his hips and the tense muscles straining beneath his shirt indicated that he was barely holding on to his temper, as if he really thought she had betrayed him.

"I wanted to be with you, Trevor."

"Why?" he demanded, taking a step nearer to her and gripping her shoulders with his tense fingers. "Why? So that you could get close to me? Are you just like the rest of your family, Ashley? Would you do anything to protect your name?" he asked, his words slicing through her heart as easily as a razor.

"Of course not!"

"No?" Disbelief contorted his rugged features. His eyes narrowed in unspoken accusation. "You didn't believe a word I said, did you? And you had no intention of holding up your end of the bargain."

"You know better than that," she insisted, her words trembling as they passed her lips. Dread slowly inched up her spine.

"What I know is that you used me, lady. You slept with me just so you could get close—see how I planned my campaign—so that you could protect your timber empire."

Ashley was too numb to speak. The fingers pushing into her flesh were painful, but not nearly as agonizing as the words coming from Trevor's lips.

"You missed your calling, lady," he stated. "You should have been an actress. That performance you gave me last night was damned near convincing!"

Without thinking, she raised her hand as if to slap him, but the fingers tightening on her shoulders prevented the blow from landing.

"You bastard," she hissed, tears beginning to run down her face.

"Like I said before—I call 'em as I see 'em."

"Then you're a blind man!" She pulled herself free of his grasp, lifting her head above the treachery of his insults. "You never could believe that all I ever wanted was you. You never could trust me and you never will."

A muscle worked at the corner of his jaw. For a moment the anger on his face was replaced by raw and naked pain. But just as quickly as it had appeared, his misery was hidden and Trevor's blue eyes became as cold as the midnight sun.

"Just remember that you and I have a bargain, lady. I expect you to keep your end."

She took in a shuddering breath. "And if I don't? What will you do, Trevor?"

"I swear to you that I'll destroy Stephens Timber Corporation and drag your family's name through the mud until it will never come clean."

"So much for the image of the kind and just politician," she threw back at him. "You'd better watch out, Senator, that gilded reputation you work so hard to keep in the public view might just become tarnished."

"I don't give a damn about my reputation, Ashley, and you know it."

"What I know is that nothing matters to you—nothing other than your damned career. That's all it's ever been with you, Trevor." His head snapped upward, as if she'd struck him. "I was foolish enough to think that you cared for me once," she continued, unable to stop the words from tumbling from her lips. "But now I'm a little older and wiser."

He looked as if he was about to protest. His broad shoulders sagged and he shook his head, as if he couldn't stand to hear another word. "If only you knew," he whispered.

"I'll keep up my end of the bargain," she stated wearily, "just to prove you wrong."

He managed a bitter smile before he turned toward the door. She stood in the hallway, unable to move, her arms cradled protectively over her breasts, and watched in miserable silence as Trevor slowly pulled on his boots, buttoned his jacket and placed an unsteady hand on the door.

"Goodbye, Ashley," he whispered, casting one last glance over his shoulder in her direction.

She couldn't even murmur his name. Her throat was hot and swollen with the grief of losing him again. In an instant he was gone, leaving her cold and bereft, just as he had done nearly eight years ago....

She slumped to the floor totally alone and surveyed the

cabin with new eyes. Was this the place, the very spot, where her love for Trevor had begun?

The tears ran down her face in earnest as she remembered the first time she had ever laid eyes upon the ruggedly handsome face of Trevor Daniels.

CHAPTER SEVEN

EIGHT YEARS AGO, at the age of twenty-four, Ashley had been aware of the vicious rivalry between Stephens Timber and Daniels Logging. The rumors surrounding her father and some of his business practices couldn't be completely ignored, although Ashley chalked most of the gossip up to envy. Lazarus Stephens was a man of wealth and power. That was enough to start the eager fires of gossip running wild throughout the Oregon timber industry.

After she had graduated from a university in Paris, Ashley had taken a job with her father's company. In the year since she had started with the firm, she had held several positions; it had been apparent from the start that Lazarus was grooming his only child for the presidency of Stephens Timber, if—and when—he decided to retire. Ashley had been only too willing to follow in her father's footsteps. The only person who'd seemed to mind at all was her cousin Claud, who had been with Stephens Timber for several years and was jealous of his younger cousin.

Though she didn't like to admit it, Ashley realized that she had been spoiled beyond reproach by her overly indulgent father. Lazarus had lavished Ashley with anything she wanted after her mother's death. Expensive schooling abroad, flashy European sports cars, exotic vacations anywhere in the world; nothing had been too good for Lazarus's only child.

The end result was that Ashley had grown up pampered and expected to be treated like a princess. In a word, she was spoiled. And at twenty-four, it had begun to bother her. Her conscience had begun to twinge, if only slightly.

On her first vacation since starting to work with the company, Ashley decided to cancel her planned Mediterranean cruise, and instead, she spent her free time at her father's rustic cabin in the Cascade Mountains not far from Bend. For the first time in her life, Ashley began to recognize that the world didn't revolve around her or Stephens Timber. The glamorous life she had heretofore led began to lose its luster and appeal.

Even the image of her father was beginning to dim. She told herself that she had overheard too many idle tongues wagging, but she couldn't shake the feeling that something wasn't quite right with all of Lazarus's business dealings. Though she was loath to admit it, Ashley was beginning to wonder about the truth in the rumor surrounding Robert Daniels's disappearance. It was one subject her father avoided like the plague. He would never discuss anything to do with Robert Daniels or what had come between Lazarus and the man who had once been his business partner. Not even with Ashley. At the mention of Robert Daniels's name, Lazarus would visibly pale and then gruffly dismiss the subject. For the past year, ever since she had left the security of school abroad, Lazarus's animosity toward Robert Daniels had begun to make Ashley uneasy. She needed time to think things out and reevaluate her pampered life. And so, at the first opportunity, Ashley took off for the mountains.

The solitude of the rustic retreat made her depend solely upon herself for the first time in her life. The cabin hadn't been used since the summer before and smelled musty. As soon as she had changed into faded jeans, Ashley opened the windows, aired the rooms, washed the linen and scrubbed floors feverishly. No job was too difficult. She stacked wood in the garage and washed windows inside and out. At night her muscles ached, but she fell into a restless sleep with a feeling of vast accomplishment.

For the first week, she spent all of her time at the cabin either cleaning, experimenting in the rustic kitchen, reading or riding the horses that her father kept on the place. Zach Lambert usually took care of the two geldings, but while Ashley was staying at the cabin, she looked after the horses, much to Zach's obvious disapproval.

It was the second weekend since she had come to the mountains when the trouble began. Zach's daughter, Sara, who had been a childhood friend of Ashley's, insisted that Ashley come to a party Sara was hostessing for some of her friends from college. Ashley wasn't in the mood for a party and didn't want to attend, but found the prospect of spending another afternoon by herself just as dull. Besides, Ashley rationalized, there wasn't a polite way of declining. The Lambert place was just up the lane, and both Sara and her parents knew that Ashley was alone. There was no choice but to attend the party and hope for the best.

Ashley walked into the Lambert cabin knowing she had made a big mistake. The only person she recognized was Sara, and as hostess, Sara was dashing in and out, from one knot of jeans-clad guests to another. She smiled and waved to Ashley before hurrying into the kitchen to replenish a tray of hors d'oeuvres.

Ashley wandered through the modern cedar cabin and captured the attention of more than one pair of appreciative male eyes. In her backless apricot sundress, with her long black hair flowing loosely past her shoulders, she looked the part of a rich man's daughter.

Her green eyes moved over the other guests with cool disinterest, the smile on her face well practiced but vague. She wondered why she had accepted the invitation to the party at all and hoped she could find a viable excuse to leave the festivities early and return to the solitude of her father's cabin. She needed time alone to think about her life, her father and the business.

She accepted a glass of wine before edging toward the sliding glass door leading to the back of the cabin. Feeling the need to escape from the laughter and thick cigarette smoke, Ashley slipped out of the cabin and away from the crowd.

When she stepped onto the deck, a tall, broad-shouldered man approached her. He was older than she, but probably not yet thirty. His face was handsome, if somewhat angular, and his eyes were the deepest shade of blue she had ever seen.

He studied her intently, not bothering to hide his interest. Ashley experienced the disturbing feeling that she should recognize him. There was something familiar about him that made her uneasy.

The set of his mouth was slightly cynical for so young a man, and a few soft lines etched his forehead, giving him a wiser, more worldly appearance than could be expected for a man his age. His thick hair ruffled slightly in the wind and Ashley noticed that the chestnut color was streaked with gold—as if this man spent many hours in the sun.

Probably a cowboy, she thought to herself, glancing at his worn jeans and boots.

He stopped a few feet from her and leaned against the railing of the deck, supporting himself with his elbows as he stared brazenly at her.

"Is there something I can do for you?" she asked, tossing her wavy black hair behind her shoulders.

His thoughtful eyes narrowed. "Do I know you?"

"There's an original line," she retorted.

"It's not a line."

"Then, I doubt it." Ashley was sure that she would remember such a proud, defiant face.

A glimmer of recognition flashed in his eyes. "You're

Ashley Stephens," he stated, as if the name meant something to him.

"And you're…" She lifted her dark brows expressively, begging his indulgence.

"Trevor Daniels."

Ashley's smile fell from her face. The name hit her like a ton of bricks. She was standing face-to-face with Robert Daniels's son. Though she had never met him, she had seen pictures that had been taken years ago. All the whispered innuendos she had heard about her father flitted through her mind. She swallowed back the sickening feeling rising from her stomach.

"I think it's about time we got to know each other," Trevor stated, his calm belied by an angry muscle working overtime near the back of his jaw.

"Why?"

"Because we have so much in common, you and I."

She looked disdainfully up at him. "I doubt that."

"Sure we do. Let's start with our fathers. Weren't they in business together once?"

"If you'll excuse me," Ashley whispered, taking a step away from this formidable man.

"I don't think so." A hand, large, powerful and surprisingly warm, reached out and took hold of her arm, spinning her back to face him. "I want to talk to you."

"About what?"

His face drew into a vindictive scowl. "Let's start with what you know about my father."

Other guests had joined them on the deck and were showing more than casual interest in the confrontation between Trevor Daniels and the attractive, raven-haired woman. Ashley's gaze flickered to the unfamiliar faces before returning to Robert Daniels's angry son. "I don't know anything about him," she whispered.

"But your father does."

Her eyes turned frigid. "I'm not interested in causing a scene, Mr. Daniels."

"I'll bet not."

"Then maybe we could drop this discussion."

"Not on your life."

"I have no idea what my father does or doesn't know about your family."

"Tell me about it."

Once again she glanced at the interested eyes trained upon her. "Not here!" She jerked her arm away from his grasp with as much pride as she could muster.

"Where then?"

He crossed his arms over his chest and eyed her speculatively. That intense, midnight-blue gaze started at her feet and inched up her body, appraising her. By the time his eyes had returned to hers, Ashley felt the stain of unwanted embarrassment burn her cheeks. "Let's talk about this in private."

"Anywhere you suggest," he agreed with a sarcastic curve of his sensual lips.

She had to think quickly. Guests had crowded the small Lambert cabin. Ashley was sure that there was no privacy anywhere in the house. "My father has a cabin…not far from here. After the party…"

"Now!"

She was about to protest but the hardening of his jaw convinced her that he meant business. After hasty apologies given to a slightly confused Sara, Ashley left the Lambert cabin with Trevor Daniels, his boots crunching ominously on the gravel, striding behind her.

Without an invitation, or so much as a look in her direction, Trevor got into the passenger seat of her sporty Mercedes convertible and for the first time in her life, Ashley was embarrassed by the ostentatious display of wealth.

The short drive was accomplished in stilted silence.

Only the dull whine of the engine and the tires spinning on loose gravel disturbed the quiet of the mountains.

Ashley roared to a stop near the garage, pulled on the emergency brake and shut off the engine. "We can talk here," she suggested, but Trevor was already getting out of the car.

Damn the man! He intended to go inside. Just the thought of being alone with him made Ashley's pulse quicken. She chalked it up to the fact that he was Robert Daniels's son. That alone made her nervous.

Her hands were shaking when she unlocked the door, opened it and silently invited him inside.

Once in the den, Trevor looked at the less-than-opulent surroundings with a cynical arch of his brow. "Spending a quiet vacation in the mountains?" he mocked, his skeptical gaze taking in the interior before returning to her.

"I was."

"A change of pace from your usual style," he observed as he walked across the rustic room and stood near the window, pretending interest in the view of the craggy slopes of Mount Washington. He placed a boot on a footstool and leaned on one elbow as he studied the view. His jeans stretched tightly over his hips and thighs and Ashley had to look away from the erotic pose. Was it intentional? For a moment she wondered if he intended to seduce her, but pushed the rash thought aside. He seemed like a rational man, not one who might seek revenge against her father by compromising her.

But if he did, how would she react? The thought quickened her heartbeat. Trevor turned to look at her and Ashley realized he expected her to reply to his comment.

"How would you know what my usual style is?" she asked, her throat uncommonly dry.

Trevor grinned cryptically before moving away from the window and settling into one of the worn leather chairs near the empty fireplace. "There's a lot I know about you," he admitted, watching the slightly confused knit of her brow. "I know that you studied art in Marseilles before switching majors and universities, that you prefer BMWs to Chevys, that you would rather shop in San Francisco than L.A., and that you don't, for the most part, spend time alone in the Cascades."

Ashley listened to his observations with her breath catching in her throat. Either he was incredibly lucky at first impressions or he had spent a lot of time studying her. It occurred to her that their meeting at the Lamberts' wasn't by chance.

She gambled. "So why did you come looking for me?"

He didn't deny it. "I wanted your help."

She was wary. Her elegant brow puckered suspiciously. "But why?"

"I want to find out what happened to my father."

"I have no idea where he is," she replied honestly.

He thought for a minute, but seemed to believe her. His broad shoulders slumped slightly and he changed the subject, convinced that he would get no further with Lazarus Stephens's stubborn child. "So what are you doing up here, anyway?" Once again his merciless eyes traveled over the interior of the room, lingering for just a moment on the book Ashley had been reading. He picked it up and frowned. It was written in French. *"Les Misérables."* He looked at her sharply. "What're you trying to do—see how the other half lives?"

"Improve my mind," was her pert retort. Suddenly she wanted him out of the cabin and out of her life. There was something enigmatic and dangerous about him, something that touched her and wouldn't let go....

"Why did you come here?" he demanded, blue eyes seeking hers.

"I needed a vacation."

"You work for your father."

"That's right." How much did he know about her? Why did he care?

Trevor glanced from her to the loft, and back again. His fingers were tight with tension when he pushed them through the coarse strands of his hair. "It just doesn't fit," he muttered.

"What doesn't?"

"You…this…" He held up the book, making a sweeping gesture to include everything in the cabin. Finally, somewhat defeated, he returned his gaze to her. "You're not exactly what I expected."

"Sorry to disappoint you," she replied, noticing the hardening of his angular jaw. "Maybe you should have done your homework a little better."

He slowly rose from the chair and walked back to the middle of the room where she was standing. "I hate to admit it, lady," he whispered, "but you haven't disappointed me at all." He reached out. The tips of his fingers trailed the length of her bare arm, sending chills of anticipation through her veins, before lingering at her wrist.

"I haven't been much help to you."

"Yet." He stepped closer, and his gentle fingers didn't release her wrist. He tugged on her arm, bringing her body next to his. Ashley knew that he was about to kiss her and that it was madness, but the thrill of it all—the excitement of his touch—made it difficult to resist.

For a heart-stopping moment, she felt his hesitation, as if he, too, was unsure. "This can't happen," he whispered just before his lips pressed urgently against hers.

Ashley closed her eyes and swallowed against the persuasive warmth his kiss inspired. His fingers caught in the strands of her hair, holding her close, brushing against the exposed muscles of her back, begging for more intimacy. She felt her body, as if ripe with need, respond to him.

His fingers splayed against her naked back, forcing her closer to him. The gentle pressure of his chest crushing against her breasts created a savage fire that burned bright in the deepest part of her.

Her breasts ached for his touch and when an exploratory hand cupped the restrained fullness, she lifted her arms upward and wound them around his neck, thus offering more of herself to him. *This is crazy,* her mind screamed from somewhere in the dim reaches of her rational thoughts, but she couldn't stop the torrid fires beginning to consume her.

His head lowered and his lips nuzzled the exposed length of her throat, leaving in their wake a dewy path of desire. He kissed the hollow of her throat, his lips hovering over the sensitive pulse in soft warm breaths. Ashley responded, her heartbeat quickening convulsively.

Slowly, he pressed on her shoulders, forcing her to kneel with him. Then, when she was positioned to his liking, he lifted his head from her neck and gazed steadily into her eyes, watching her reaction as he leisurely slipped the thin strap of her halter dress over her left shoulder. She shuddered in anticipation, but continued to hold his gaze.

The dress fell open and one breast spilled out of the soft apricot fabric. Ashley felt an embarrassed blush rise upward through her body as Trevor gazed at her, his blue eyes fierce with desire. Tenderly his fingers came forward and traced the straining dark peak.

Ashley inhaled deeply, closing her eyes against the warm sensations swirling within her. How could one man make her feel as if she would do anything he commanded? She told herself that she was being reckless, playing with fire, but she didn't care. All she could think about was wanting him, a wild lust that was traveling in wicked circles within her body, aching for release.

"I've wanted you for a long time," he admitted, his

voice rough. He was half lying now, and the warmth of his breath fanned her breast.

"You...you don't even know me...."

"That's where you're wrong, sweet lady. I've known you for so long, so very long."

"Just because I'm Lazarus Stephens's daughter."

His blue eyes were wicked when he looked up at her. "Just because you're Lazarus Stephens's beautiful daughter." Gingerly, his lips closed over the rosy tip of her breast. The denial that had been forming on her lips was never spoken. She could think of nothing other than letting him touch her, assuaging the bittersweet ache that was beginning to throb within her.

His tongue teased her gently and she moaned for more of the savage pleasure. Her fingers twined in his hair, forcing him closer. He took more of her into the warm cavern of his mouth. One hand splayed against her naked back, while the other softly kneaded her breast as he suckled and drew out the sweetness she offered.

Slowly, his lips moved from the naked breast to the delicious mound covered in soft apricot fabric. The nipple was taut and straining against the dress and Trevor placed his mouth over the covered tip, suckling and wetting the fabric with his mouth.

Ashley's head was spinning crazily and she knew that if she didn't stop his masterful lovemaking now, she wouldn't be able to break the magical spell of love he was weaving.

"Touch me," he whispered as he lifted his head and wound his fingers in the ebony silk of her tangled hair and tugged on it, forcing her head backward so that he could nuzzle her exposed throat. Gently he guided her hand to the evidence of his desire.

Ashley let her fingers linger slightly on his straining jeans. The low moan from the back of his throat convinced her that he wanted her as much as she wanted him.

"Oh, God," she whispered. Slowly, she withdrew her hand. "I…I can't." Tears of frustration stung her eyes.

"Shhh…Ashley," he said. He kissed her eyelids and tasted the salt of her tears. "Just let me love you."

"I don't know you, Trevor," she said, trying desperately to rise above the lustful urges of her body. Never before had she been so tempted by a man, so ravaged by desire. Never had the ache within her throbbed for a release only he could offer.

"You will," he promised, gently rising on one elbow. His eyes took in the tangled disarray of her blue-black hair, the mystic allure of her green eyes and the swelling invitation of her firm breasts. "I've waited a long time for you," he vowed, as one long finger traced the column of her throat, past the hill of her naked breast, to probe beneath the apricot dress draped over her waist. "I can wait a few more days."

"And what makes you think that I'll agree?"

He smiled despite the strangling ache in his loins. "Because you want me as badly as I want you."

"You're so damned sure of yourself, aren't you?" she asked, her breath still ragged.

"When I have to be." His finger traced the definition of her lowest rib. "You and I have so much in common, you see."

"So you think it's fate. Right?"

"Most definitely not."

"What then?"

His eyes drove into hers as if he were searching for the darkest part of her soul. "It's a case of a man being obsessed with a woman."

She laughed at the absurdity of the situation, holding the bodice of her dress over her breast. "Obsession? You can't be serious!"

His eyes darkened dangerously. "Just wait and see how

serious I am." With that, he hoisted himself from the floor and offered a hand to Ashley, who accepted his help.

When she straightened and managed to slip her shoulder strap back into place, he took hold of her arms and roughly pulled her against him. His lips moved suggestively over hers. "I'll see you tomorrow."

Her breath caught in her throat. "I have plans," she offered lamely.

"Cancel them." With his final words, he left her and walked out of the door.

"Bastard," she muttered under her breath, determined never to see him again.

ASHLEY SPENT A sleepless night dreaming of making wild and wanton love to Trevor and in the morning she admonished herself for her immature lust. She told herself that some of the fascination she felt was because he was the adversary—the one thing in life she had to deny herself.

"He'll use you," she warned herself whenever she caught herself thinking about him that morning, but she couldn't help but look out the window in anticipation whenever she heard a vehicle rumble down the lane.

At ten o'clock there was a knock on the door. Ashley's heart was racing when she answered it and discovered Trevor, his cynical smile in place, standing on the small porch.

"I thought you were going to be busy today," he mocked. His blue eyes twinkled devilishly as they raked possessively over her body.

The anger she wanted to feel refused to surface. "It wasn't anything important." She moved out of the doorway, allowing him to enter. "I thought you might like to go on a picnic."

"That's not exactly what I had in mind—"

"I'll bet not. But I've already saddled the horses and

thrown together a lunch," she replied, trying to overlook the hint of seduction in his intense gaze. "It'll be fun."

"Promise?"

"Guaranteed."

He smiled before laughing out loud. "You're full of surprises, aren't you?" he asked with a pleased expression softening his face. "The daughter of Lazarus Stephens saddling horses and making sandwiches—it just doesn't fit."

"Maybe what doesn't fit is your stereotype of spoiled little rich girls who refuse to get their hands dirty."

"Maybe." He shrugged his shoulders and followed her into the kitchen. Ashley pulled a bottle of wine out of the refrigerator and shoved it into the already bulging leather bag, which was slung over the back of one of the kitchen chairs.

Trevor watched her pack. "Saddlebags?"

"How else are we going to carry all this food? What did you expect? A picnic basket?"

"I suppose."

Ashley smiled to herself. "Then I guess my first impression of you was wrong."

"Oh?"

"You're not a cowboy?"

"Far from it." Trevor chuckled to himself at the thought. "I'm working at a law firm in Bend for the summer."

"A lawyer?"

"Not yet. But soon, I hope."

"You're still in school?"

"Willamette University," he replied, taking the bulging leather pouch and slinging it over his shoulder. "I hope to take the bar exam in January."

"And what then, counselor?" she teased, her green eyes dancing merrily. Strange as it seemed, she hadn't felt this happy in years. She was comfortable with this man; the fact that he was her father's rival's son added just a little bit of daring to the relationship.

He hesitated for a moment, sizing her up, and decided there was no reason to hide the truth. "Politics."

There was something in the way he said the word that gave Ashley pause. "Whatever for?"

He grinned cryptically. "To change things, of course." He held the back door for her and then waited somewhat impatiently while she locked it.

They walked together down the short path that led to the stables. Diablo and Gustave were tied to the fence and nickered softly when Ashley approached.

"Looks like rain," Trevor remarked, eyeing the cloudy sky.

"You're not going to weasel out of this," Ashley stated. "I worked all morning planning this thing, and we're going on a picnic come hell or high water."

"Whatever you say, ma'am," he drawled with a bad western affectation.

"You do know how to ride?"

Trevor positioned the saddlebag on Diablo's broad, black back. "A little." Diablo stamped a dark hoof and tossed his head, jingling the bridle in contempt.

"It's all right." Ashley soothed the agitated horse with a soft pat on the neck before taking the reins of the smaller horse and swinging into the saddle.

They rode together in silence, Ashley leading the way on Gustave, a fiery bay quarter horse who had the bad habit of shying away from any noise. "Don't be such a scaredy-cat," Ashley admonished as she rubbed Gustave's thick neck.

The dusty path led uphill through sagebrush and pine trees. After traveling for three miles, they reached the spot Ashley remembered from her childhood. It was a barren ridge with an enthralling view of the snow-covered Cascades.

When she stopped, Trevor pulled up next to her and cast an approving eye at the view. "Worth the ride," he muttered as he studied the mountainous horizon. The blue sky had filled with gray clouds that gathered around the highest peaks. "Could be in for some rain," he reminded her.

"Then we'd better eat now," Ashley stated as she swung out of the saddle. "I'm starved."

While Ashley spread a blanket and arranged the food, Trevor tethered the horses. Ashley smiled as she watched him work. "Not bad for a tenderfoot," she teased.

Trevor smiled and took a seat next to her on the blanket.

The first drops of rain started to fall just as Ashley poured the wine. As quickly as possible, they drank the wine and feasted on cold chicken, cheese, grapes and French bread. Even with the threat of rain, the meal was perfect. Ashley, as she laughed at Trevor's witticisms, wondered vaguely if she was falling in love.

Because the storm looked as if it would worsen, Trevor repacked the saddlebags and they started back to the cabin much earlier than Ashley had planned. She had envisioned a warm, lazy afternoon with Trevor, learning more about him.

The summer shower began in earnest about halfway back to the cabin and Ashley was forced to urge Gustave into a trot. Once back on familiar soil, the quarter horse sprinted for the barn with Diablo on his tail.

Ashley was breathless by the time they were back in the stables and her long black hair was tangled from the fast ride.

Trevor unsaddled and cooled the horses while Ashley returned to the cabin, started a fire and unpacked the saddlebags. The wind picked up and the sky grew overcast, darkening the interior of the cabin. Rain pelted against the windows.

The fire had just caught and Ashley was sitting on the hearth attempting to brush the knots from her hair, when Trevor came back into the cabin. Raindrops lingered in his dark hair and reflected the warmth of the crackling flames. The interior of the cabin was filled with the scent of burning wood and hot coffee.

"I…I made some coffee," Ashley stated, straightening and setting the brush aside.

Trevor walked across the short distance separating them and his magnetic blue eyes never released hers. Ashley's pulse quickened at the nearness of him. When his cold lips pressed hungrily against hers, she knew that she would never find the strength to deny him again. His strong, muscular body was tense. She could feel his want in his restraint.

His tongue tested and probed and her lips parted willingly for him. She would offer everything to this exciting, mysterious man, hoping that he would care for her… if only a little.

A rush of liquid heat began to build within her, sending pulsating messages throughout her body. She couldn't think or move when his warm, persuasive lips lingered on her neck and nibbled at the sensitive skin near her ear.

"Tell me you want me," he whispered, his demand gentle.

"You know—"

"Say it!"

"I want you," she admitted hoarsely.

"Why?"

"I don't know—"

"Why, damn it!" He gave her shoulders a shake and forced her to look in his eyes. "Tell me it's not just a game with you. That you're interested in more than a quick one-night stand with the son of Robert Daniels."

The words stung, but she bravely returned his gaze. "Oh, Trevor, it's not because you're a Daniels," she whispered. "I know that I want you and not just for the rest of the afternoon."

His relief seemed genuine and the lines of frustration marring his brow relaxed as his lips found hers in a kiss that was as tender as it was urgent.

His fingers slowly unbuttoned her blouse and he paused only to kiss her downy white skin when the fabric began to gap. Her breasts strained against the wet cotton and tingled in swollen anticipation when his tongue probed near the lace edging of her flimsy bra.

"No more excuses," he whispered against the ripeness of her aching nipples.

Ashley swallowed against the dryness settling in her throat. "I only want to be with you," she murmured, sucking in her breath as he unhooked the front clasp of her bra and pushed both it and her blouse over her shoulders to be discarded in a wrinkled heap on the floor.

Then, gently, using his weight, he forced her to the floor and let his hands run in sensual circles over her smooth, white skin. Though the ache in his loins burned uncomfortably, he forced himself to go slowly, to give as much pleasure as he would extract from the voluptuous daughter of Lazarus Stephens.

She was lying next to him, and her damp, black hair fell over the white mounds of her delicious breasts, brushing over the taut, protruding nipples when she moved her head.

Slowly he descended, and when his mouth covered one rosy point, she moaned in pleasure, running her fingers through the thick, damp strands of his hair. Never had she felt such ecstasy and torment. Without considering her actions, she began to unbutton his shirt, forcing it off his shoulders and letting her fingers run over the tight muscles, the mat of curly black hair and the hard male nipples. His breathing became as ragged as her own and Ashley knew that there was no going back. Tonight she would give herself willingly, gloriously to this man. The fiery union of their bodies would be equaled only by the blending of their souls.

When his fingers toyed with the waistband of her jeans she didn't resist. She belonged to Trevor and she felt an overwhelming sense of relief when his strong hands forced the denim fabric to slide easily over her hips, down her legs and past her ankles to find the same fate as her crumpled blouse.

His fingers lingered on her legs and the warmth within her grew. His eyes held hers as he slowly unzipped his jeans and kicked them off. She saw the reflection of the fire in the passion of his gaze. They were naked together, one man and one woman, high in the privacy of the proud Cascades. The smell of coffee and pitchy wood mingled with the scents of rainwater and sweat to blend together in a sensual aroma.

When he came to her, it was the most natural act she had ever experienced. Slowly he lowered his body over hers, positioning himself so that he could read the expression on her face, withholding the urge to take her in a quick eruption of desire.

At first he had planned to bed her quickly and forget her, but he knew now that he was forever lost to her. He wanted Ashley to feel the exquisite pleasure of their mating.

His face was tight, the lines of strain evident when his head lowered and his lips touched hers at the very moment that she felt his desire touch her soul.

"Trevor," she moaned in resplendent agony as he slowly moved within her. "Please...please..." Her words were fuel to the fire of his white-hot desire. The rhythm quickened until, at last, he could hold back no longer. With a rush of unbound passion, he let go, and Ashley felt the shudder of his release as he collapsed upon her. His weight was a welcome burden. She wrapped her arms around his torso and closed her eyes against the tears of joy threatening to overtake her.

Was it love she felt for this man or merely lust?

THE AFFAIR HAD run a torrid course through the rest of the summer. Whenever Ashley would get the chance, she would leave the Willamette Valley and meet Trevor in a private tryst of love in the Cascades. After that first moment of triumph and uncertainty, Ashley knew that she loved Trevor Daniels, not because his father was a rival to Stephens Timber Corporation, but because he was the most exciting and wonderful man she had ever met.

It was a glorious summer filled with dreams and promises, laughter and love. For the first time in her life, Ashley learned how to care for someone other than herself. It felt wonderful. She wanted to shout her love for Trevor from the mountaintops.

Somehow—Ashley suspected that Claud was the source—Lazarus found out that she was having an affair with Trevor. Her father was livid.

"How could you do this to me?" he had raged. Seated at the scarred wooden desk in his den, he seemed suddenly old.

"It just happened, Dad," she had tried to explain.

"Just happened! Don't tell me you're that naïve, for God's sake! All that schooling in France—didn't you learn a damned thing! I'll bet Daniels planned this affair all along."

"That's preposterous," Ashley replied indignantly, but a niggling doubt entered her mind. Hadn't Trevor as much as admitted that he had been looking for her, that he had wanted her for years? Was their affair just a way to seek revenge against her father?

"You're so blinded by love that you can't see the truth when it stares you in the face," Lazarus charged, his complexion turning scarlet. His hands raised into the air in a gesture of defeat and supplication for divine intervention. "That son of Robert Daniels is just using you as a weapon against me! He's obviously trying to dig up some dirt on our family and find some way—no matter how obscure— to blame me for his father's disappearance!"

"This has nothing to do with Robert Daniels," Ashley insisted, but she couldn't forget her first heated conversation with Trevor at Sara Lambert's party.

"The hell it doesn't!" Lazarus's fist crashed onto the desk, rattling the drawers.

"Dad, I love him!" Ashley cried.

"Oh, for crying out loud!" Lazarus braced himself against the desk in his office. His eyes slid from Ashley to the view of the Portland city lights before returning, condemningly, to his only child. "Can't you see that he's using you? If that bastard can't find a way to ruin my reputation, he'll settle for you and yours. He knows that by seducing you, he's wounding me." He ran agitated fingers through his thinning hair and his large shoulders slumped in defeat.

Though Ashley's heart went out to him, she couldn't deny the love she felt for Trevor. "You'd better get used to this, Dad," Ashley warned rebelliously, though her faith in Trevor was beginning to waver.

"And why's that?"

"Because I'm going to marry him."

"Out of the question!" Lazarus's watery blue eyes flamed in indignation. "The man isn't even your social equal, for Christ's sake!" He tapped his fingers restlessly on the desk. "If I were you, I wouldn't get my hopes up. Trevor Daniels has no intention of marrying you. To him, you're nothing more than a quick affair. Take my advice and get rid of him. If you want to get married, why not someone with a little class, like Richard Jennings?"

Ashley stormed out of her father's estate, intent on proving him wrong. Trevor was waiting for her at Neskowin on the coast and she was sure, with just the right amount of persuasion, she could coax him into marrying her now, before he finished law school.

She was sadly mistaken.

The weekend at the beach was wonderful and she kept the fight with her father a secret. They spent the days walking on the rain-drenched sand, and during the nights they lay together, sipping imported wine, warming their feet on the bricks of the fireplace and staring out at the black waves crashing furiously in the winter's storm before making incredible love and promising their lives to each other.

It was heavenly and it ended.

When Ashley finally explained that she wanted to get married right away, Trevor was adamant. He wanted to finish law school and establish his career before taking on the added responsibilities of a family.

"Then what am I supposed to do, sit around and wait while you decide whether you want to run for the presidency?" she replied caustically, the pain of his rejection cutting her to the bone.

His features hardened at the mention of his politics. "Of course not—"

"Then you still want me to wait for you."

"Only a few years."

"A few years." It sounded like the end of the world. All of her fears and her father's prophecies were coming true. For the first time in three months, Ashley doubted Trevor's love.

"Look, Ashley," he whispered, gently running his fin-

gers through the silken strands of her hair. "I love you—
I'm just asking you to be patient."

"Patience isn't my long suit."

"It's not forever."

"You're sure about that?"

"Of course." His eyes were clear blue and honest. For
a moment she was tempted to believe him.

"Then what about the reason you got to know me in
the first place—to try to get me to admit that my family
was involved in your father's disappearance. The reason
you took the time to get to know me at all was just so that
you could get some information from me, information to
discredit my father."

"That's not the only reason."

Ashley could tell that he was lying through his straight
white teeth. The veiled hatred in his eyes at the mention
of Lazarus convinced her that the love she thought they
had been sharing was all based on a lie.

"I think it's over for us," she stated, tears stinging her
eyes.

"Only if you want it to be."

"There's no other way," she murmured, slowly gathering
her things and throwing them into her suitcase. Silently,
she prayed that he would back down and apologize, that
he would beg her to stay. But it didn't happen.

She left the cottage in the middle of the storm, regretting that she had ever laid eyes on Trevor Daniels.

CHAPTER EIGHT

THE THOUGHTS OF the past took their toll on Ashley and she had to remind herself that what had happened didn't matter. She and Trevor had a bargain and she was going to do her damnedest to prove that all of his accusations about her father, Claud and the timber company were unjust. If he had given her nothing else, Trevor had granted her the chance to clear her family's name. For that much, she supposed bitterly, she should be grateful.

She placed her hands on the floor and straightened from the position she had assumed when Trevor had left her. The cabin was cold. She managed to light a fire in the wood stove in the kitchen to give her a little heat as she packed her things and secured the cabin against the winter weather. She worked without really thinking about what she was doing. Her thoughts, still filled with pain, continued to revolve around the past.

Disgusted with herself for being so maudlin, she walked to the window and looked out at the snow- covered ground. Winter birds, dark against the backdrop of white snow, flitted through the pine needles, chirping out lonely cries as they landed on the ground and foraged in the powdery snow.

"You really can't blame Trevor," she whispered to herself as she saw a bird find the seeds she had placed on the deck. Ashley's breath condensed on the window, clouding the clear panes. "You only got what was coming to you."

Most of the agony she had endured was her own fault.

If she had just forgotten Trevor, as she had promised herself that stormy night in Neskowin, the following events never would have occurred. But as it was, blinded by fury and disgrace, Ashley had stormed out of the beach cottage and had returned to Portland.

In the following few weeks after the breakup with Trevor, Ashley had resumed working for her father and had secretly hoped that she might be pregnant. She wanted desperately to have Trevor's baby, a lasting memory of the love affair that wasn't quite strong enough to survive. At the time, she had been sure that a child, Trevor's child, was all she needed to heal the pain.

It hadn't happened. Ashley cried bitter tears of anguish when her monthly cycle resumed and all her hopes of bearing Trevor's child were destroyed. Her dreams of the future had been shattered as easily as if they had been delicate sea shells crushed by the tireless anger of the sea.

Ashley had married Richard out of spite. Richard Jennings was the man she had been dating before she met Trevor. Richard worked for Stephens Timber and was the only son of rich, socialite parents. It hadn't taken long for him to propose to the beautiful and headstrong daughter of Lazarus Stephens.

For her part, though at the time she had suspected that she might be deluding herself, Ashley had hoped that another man would replace Trevor. It didn't take her long to realize that she had been wrong.

The marriage had been a mistake for both Richard and herself. Richard had expected a doting wife interested only in supporting him in his engineering career, but Ashley had shown more interest in the timber business than in homemaking.

It wasn't all Richard's fault that the marriage had failed, Ashley decided with a grimace. Though Ashley had hoped to purge herself of Trevor, and though she had tried to be everything Richard wanted, she had failed miserably. Even Lazarus hadn't gotten the satisfaction of the grandchild he had expected from the short-lived union.

A divorce was inevitable. Lazarus Stephens went to his grave an unhappy, selfish man who never had suspected that his daughter was incapable of providing an heir to the Stephens Timber fortune.

Perhaps it didn't matter, Ashley thought as she walked up the stairs to the loft and opened her suitcase. When she and Richard had divorced, she had lost all interest in owning any part of the vast timber empire. If she had learned anything from her brief but passionate affair with Trevor, it was how to be her own person and still care for other people. Trevor had helped her mature. By leaving her, he had forced her to rely on herself and become self-sufficient.

Maybe that was why her marriage had failed; she'd been too strong, while Richard was weak. It hadn't been Richard's obvious affairs that had finally gotten to her; it had been his lack of character and strength.

What's the point of dredging it up all over again? she asked herself as she folded her clothes and placed them in the open suitcase on the bed. The sheets were still rumpled in disturbing evidence of her recent lovemaking with Trevor. She swallowed the urge to cry and hastily straightened the bedclothes.

Working swiftly, she managed to clean the cabin, pack her bags and bundle up all the reports from the Bend office. As she took out the garbage she noticed an empty champagne bottle and remembered how she had shared a glass of the sparkling wine with Trevor in front of the fire the night before. It seemed like weeks ago, when it had only been hours. Could so much have happened in so short a time?

When she finally had packed everything into her Jeep, she returned to make sure the fire was no longer smoldering and to cast one last, searching glance around the interior of the rustic home. Her heart ached painfully. She wondered if Trevor was still at the Lambert cabin just a few minutes away. She pushed the nagging question aside and frowned. She couldn't run to him—not yet. Until she had cleared her father's name, she had nothing to offer Trevor.

"That's life," she muttered to herself, climbing into the Jeep. "Merry Christmas, Ashley," she chided with a self-effacing frown. She turned the key in the ignition and the trustworthy engine sparked to life. Ashley drove away from the snow-covered cabin without once looking back.

IT HAD GROWN dark by the time Ashley made it back to the Willamette Valley. The blackened skies were moist and the city streets of Portland were slick with rain. Most of the large homes in the West Hills were illuminated with colorful Christmas lights that twinkled in the gathering darkness and were reflected in the raindrops collecting on the Jeep's windshield before the wipers slapped them aside.

Her father's home was a huge, Tudor structure with seven bedrooms and five baths. Why he had ever purchased so large an estate was beyond Ashley, as Lazarus had never remarried and had no children other than herself. Most of the bedrooms had never been occupied. It seemed an incredible waste.

As Ashley turned up the cedar-lined drive, she noticed that the interior lights of the house were glowing warmly.

Ashley smiled to herself, knowing that Mrs. Deveraux, a fussy French lady who had been Lazarus's housekeeper ever since Enora's death and was still in charge of the house and grounds, must have guessed that Ashley would return tonight.

"Wouldn't you know," Ashley said to herself, pleased that Mrs. Deveraux had thought about her. The kindly old woman still treated her like a child. Tonight it would be appreciated. What Ashley needed right now was a warm meal and a hot bath. Once refreshed, she was sure that she could tackle the mountain of computer printouts once again.

No one answered her call when she entered. Ashley left her bags at the foot of the grand, oiled-oak staircase and walked into the kitchen, where she found a note from Mrs. Deveraux tacked to the refrigerater door. The message was simple: Mrs. Deveraux had gone out to the movies, would be back around ten and had left a crock of soup in the refrigerater. Also, as a postscript, there was a message from John Ellis, the accountant for Stephens Timber, requesting that Ashley call him the minute she was back in town.

The note made Ashley uneasy. There was no telling what Claud had done after calling Ashley this morning. She couldn't help but wonder if her cousin had pumped John for information after getting no satisfaction from her.

After heating the homemade chowder in the microwave, Ashley dialed John's number at home and let the soup cool.

"Hello?"

"John? This is Ashley."

There was a sigh of relief on the other end of the connection. "Are you back in town?" John's voice sounded anxious, almost fearful.

"Just got in."

"At your father's house?"

"Yes. Why—"

"Good! I'll be there in about half an hour."

"Slow down," Ashley demanded, unnerved by the calm man's uncharacteristic impatience. Her palms were beginning to sweat. There was something about the conversation that made her more than slightly uneasy. "What's going on?"

"I'll talk to you when I get there." With that, he hung up the phone and Ashley was left to consider the unusual conversation.

"What the devil?" she wondered, as she sat down at the kitchen table. Her mind was racing when she tested the soup with the tip of her tongue, decided it was the right temperature and began eating the delicious meal of hot chowder and warm biscuits.

Had John discovered something out of the ordinary in the financial reports? What was it that made him sound so worried and concerned? It was almost as if he were frightened of something...or someone.

"You're beginning to sound as paranoid as Trevor," she admonished herself, smiling slightly at the rugged image her willing mind conjured.

Ashley finished her soup and placed the bowl in the dishwasher just as the doorbell rang. She walked to the front door, opened it and ushered in a very agitated John Ellis.

"What's going on?" she asked as he shed his coat and tossed it carelessly over a bent arm of the wooden hall tree near the door.

"That's what I want to know."

They walked into the formal living room and John stalked from one end of the elegantly furnished room to the other.

"Did you find something suspicious in the books?" Ashley asked, her throat beginning to constrict. Something was wrong—very wrong. John was usually a calm individual known for his attention to detail and sound judgment.

Tonight his face was flushed and his eyes darted nervously from Ashley to the door, the window and back to Ashley again. Several times he rotated his head, as if to relieve the tension in his neck.

"I don't know—" He held his hands, palms up, in her direction. He seemed genuinely confused.

"Take your time," Ashley insisted. "Have a seat and let me get you a cup of coffee, or brandy?"

"Anything." He looked as if he didn't care one way or the other. He was restless and uneasy.

She combined the two drinks and gave him a black cup of coffee laced with brandy. He took the mug, drank a long swallow, and then settled back in one of the stiff chairs near the windows.

Ashley took a seat on the corner of the couch and sipped her coffee. "Okay, so tell me what's happening?"

"I don't know, but I don't like it. Claud is suspicious."

"About the reports I requested to be sent to Bend?" Ashley guessed, knowing the calculating nature of her cousin. It was too bad Claud was so well qualified for his job; his sharp mind and legal background made him indispensable.

"Right. For the last few days he's been questioning me—make that grilling me."

Ashley nodded. Her features showed none of her inner distress. "What'd you tell him?"

John rolled his myopic eyes toward the ceiling. "Nothing, I think. He asked why there were so many printouts and I said that you wanted to go over the books and get a feel for running the company. Claud told me that you could never possibly need that much paper, and I told him that I was just sending you what you requested. He didn't like it much, especially when I said that I would do the same thing, if I had inherited a company the size of Stephens Timber and it had been several years since I'd actually worked in the business."

Ashley let out a long, ragged breath. "Did Claud buy your story?"

Shrugging his shoulders, John shook his head. "Who knows? I told him that I was working on this special audit with you and Claud told me that I was to report directly to him. If there were any discrepancies in the books, he wanted to know about them—pronto."

Ashley frowned and tossed her hair over her shoulder as she rubbed her chin. "Did you—report to him?"

John seemed genuinely disappointed. "Of course not."

"Good." The tension in Ashley's muscles relaxed slightly. "So what did you find?"

"Most everything is pretty cut-and-dried," he replied, smiling at his own unintentional pun.

"Except?"

"Except for a couple of things." John drained his cup, reached for his briefcase and snapped it open. He handed a few crisp sheets of paper to Ashley. They were copies of invoices to the Watkins Mill in Molalla.

Ashley's heart nearly stopped beating when she saw the price Claud had charged for the timber and the date on the invoice. "This...this happened last June?" she asked, her throat constricting. The transaction occurred only a few weeks before the bribery charges were made against Trevor.

"Right. And the price of the timber is way off—ridiculously low. At first I thought it had to be a computer error. We were selling rough timber at three times that much."

"But you changed your mind?" Ashley prodded, barely daring to breathe. Something in John's mannerisms told her to brace herself.

John adjusted his glasses and scowled. "Yes. It just didn't make any sense to me."

"But now it does?" Ashley was almost afraid to ask.

"No. I know how it happened, I just don't understand why."

"What do you mean?"

He seemed to hesitate before he reached into his briefcase and extracted some gray photocopies of invoices, which he handed to Ashley. "I did some more checking. Claud was the one who gave the mill the price break, but he had your father's approval."

Ashley let out a shuddering sigh. "You're sure about that?"

"Got the memo right here." He handed the next incriminating piece of paper to her. Ashley accepted it with trembling fingers.

"Dear Lord," she whispered as she recognized her father's bold scrawl.

"What's this all about?" John asked.

"I'm not really sure," she replied. "But I'm afraid it means trouble—big trouble."

"I thought so." The young accountant rose and paced around the room. "I'm not too crazy about being in the middle of this," John admitted, "whatever the hell it is." He regarded his employer intently. "I thought at first that this might just be a power struggle between you and Claud. But there's more to it than that, isn't there?"

"I think so."

"Does any part of it have to do with Trevor Daniels?" The question sent a cold shock wave through Ashley.

"Why would you think that?"

"I just put two and two together." John's mouth slanted into a sarcastic grin. "That's my job."

"And did you end up getting four?"

"I think so." John held up one finger. "Claud's been furious ever since you took over." Another finger was raised. "You ask me for all of these reports. The only discrepancy concerns the Watkins Mill. Beau Watkins, the owner, was the one who was involved in that bribery mess with Daniels last summer, wasn't he?"

Silently, Ashley nodded.

"Right." He held up a third finger. "Claud's been storming around the office ranting about Daniels's bid for the Senate. It's really a sore spot with him. Therefore—"

"You deduced that Trevor was involved."

"Bingo." The fourth finger straightened.

Ashley couldn't lie. She was asking too much of John to expect him to follow her blindly. "Trevor's convinced that there are shady dealings within the company."

"That's hardly today's news."

"I know." Ashley sighed. "But he thinks that Claud would go to any lengths to ruin his chances in the senatorial race."

"What lengths?" John's expression was grim.

Ashley shrugged indifferently, though the skin was stretched tightly over her cheekbones and her stomach was knotting painfully. "Bribery, sabotage…"

"Attempted murder?"

"He implied as much," Ashley admitted.

John ran unsteady hands over his chin. "I can't believe that Claud would be involved in anything like that."

"Not only Claud, but my father as well."

"No way!" But the pale accountant didn't seem convinced.

"I have to prove that they're innocent."

John looked at the incriminating memo and invoices. "I only hope we can."

"If we can't, then we'll have to face up to the problem, won't we?" Ashley asked the stricken young man.

"Nothing else to do."

"Good. Then we're both of the same opinion." She strode across the room and stared out at the black drizzly night. The city lights of downtown Portland twinkled in the distance. "What I want you to do is request a leave of absence. Use any excuse you want to, maybe a medical reason, too much stress on the job, that sort of thing. Then you can come here and work. You'll be paid just the same, and you can work without Claud staring over your shoulder."

"Just in case we find something incriminating."

"Exactly."

John took in a deep breath before cracking a nervous smile. "All right," he agreed.

Ashley smiled. "You don't have to do this, you know."

"Why not? Because it might get dangerous?"

She sobered. "I don't think so. At least I hope not. If I really thought there were any danger involved, I wouldn't ask you to be a part of this. It's just that there aren't many people I can trust at the company."

"I know. And I like being one of the few."

"I do appreciate it, John."

The accountant smiled. "Then keep it in mind the next time I'm up for a raise."

Ashley laughed. "It's a deal."

John gathered his coat and briefcase and left a few minutes later.

A thousand questions filled Ashley's mind. Was Claud involved in a plan, as Trevor had claimed, to keep him out of the primary in May? And what about the accident and bribery charges? Could Claud or Lazarus have been part of such a deadly scheme?

Ashley picked up her suitcases and began to trudge up the stairs. What about the disappearance of Robert Daniels? All these years Trevor had maintained that Lazarus had been involved in a plot which had led to Robert's... Ashley shuddered. If Robert Daniels wasn't dead, why had he abandoned his family? And where was he now?

"I'm too tired to think about any of this," she told herself as she reached the upper floor, deposited her bags in her room and went into the adjoining bath. She turned on the water to the sunken tub and began removing her clothes.

Could all of the wicked rumors be true? Had she hidden her head in the sand to avoid facing the truth about her father? She stared at her image in the mirror. She was a mature woman today, worldly wise, slightly cynical, and she wasn't afraid to face up to the truth. She only wished that she had been wiser when she was younger and hadn't been so blindly trusting of her father or Trevor.

After peeling off her clothes and pinning her hair loosely on her head, she settled into the hot tub and moaned as the water covered her body. "Dear Lord, what a mess," she whispered to herself. Closing her eyes, she wondered vaguely where Trevor was, and with whom.

TREVOR PACED BETWEEN the cedar walls of the Lambert cabin like a caged animal. He alternately stared out the window and glanced at the telephone. The argument with Ashley this morning had been a mistake and all day long he had half expected Ashley to call or drive over seeking amends.

Maybe that was asking too much of her. If he knew anything about that woman it was that she had inherited her father's stubborn pride.

His hands clenched and relaxed at his sides as he swore, walked across the room and picked up the telephone. He dialed the number of Ashley's cabin angrily and waited with impatience as the flat rings indicated that Ashley wasn't there.

"Answer it," he ground out, desperation taking hold of him. All day he had tried to convince himself that what he had overheard this morning had been innocent. If Ashley had wanted to deceive him, she wouldn't have taken the chance to speak with Claud.

But Claud had called her.

"You're making a mountain out of a molehill," he told himself as he replaced the receiver and took a long drink from his warm bourbon.

Then why had she left? It wasn't like Ashley to run away. She'd only done it once before and that was because he had asked her to wait for him. That time she had run to another man and married him. His fingers clenched around the short glass and the cold taste of deception rose in his throat.

He finished his drink and set the empty glass on the table. His lips had tightened over his teeth when he dialed the phone again. This time there was an answer.

"Hello?"

"I'm on my way back to the valley."

"About time," Everett replied. "You missed a couple of Christmas parties that could have been feathers in your cap."

"Give the governor my regrets."

"Already done." There was a slight hesitation in Everett's voice. "Did you accomplish what you set out to?"

Trevor's smile was grim and filled with self-mockery. "No."

The statement should have put Everett's worried mind at ease. It didn't. The campaign manager came directly to the point. "So what are you going to do about Stephens Timber?"

"I'm not sure."

"And Ashley?"

"I wish I knew."

"I hope you come up with some better answers before you start campaigning in earnest, my friend."

"I will."

"Then you didn't find anything out about your accident or the bribery charges?"

"No—not yet."

The reply sounded ominous to Everett. "Then, forget them. At least for now."

"A little difficult to do," Trevor stated, rubbing the bandage over his abdomen with his free hand.

"Concentrate on the election."

"I am."

"Good." Everett let out a relieved sigh.

"You worry too much."

"With you, it's a full-time job. When will you be back?"

Trevor's eyes narrowed as he stared out the window at the darkness. "Tonight."

"Call me when you get in. I'll meet you at the house."

"See you then." Trevor hung up feeling suddenly very old and incredibly tired. He raked his fingers through his coarse hair and sat on the edge of a recliner positioned near the windows. What if Ashley was coming back to the cabin? What if she had only gone out for the day—shopping, or to clear her head. What if she was, now, at this very moment, returning?

"You're a fool," he muttered under his breath, "a damned fool!" Once again he reached for the phone.

EVERYTHING WAS GOING as planned. John Ellis had requested a three-week medical leave, which Ashley had granted. Claud had muttered unhappily when he heard that the head of the accounting department was taking an unscheduled leave of absence, but hadn't made too big a deal about it.

"Why now?" Claud had grumbled.

"Because he's ill—stomach problems. Probably too much stress on the job," Ashley had answered with a patient smile, though her throat constricted with the lie.

"Lousy timing, if you ask me," Claud had pointed out. "Year-end is always a bitch for the accounting department. Ellis couldn't have picked a worse time if he'd tried."

"Give the man a break, for crying out loud. He'll be back soon. I'm sure that the rest of the staff is perfectly capable of pulling his weight, at least for a couple of weeks."

Claud had glared unhappily at Ashley for a few uncomfortable minutes. Then, with a sound of disgust, he had snapped open the morning edition of his favorite financial journal and turned his attention back to an article dealing with mining rights.

Ashley, displaying professional aplomb despite the fact that her knees were shaking, turned on an elevated heel and walked briskly out of Claud's office. Deception had always been difficult for her, even with her slightly underhanded cousin. It had been difficult hiding the fact that John Ellis was working at her house in the West Hills. So far, no one knew that he was there other than Ashley, John's wife and Mrs. Deveraux, who were all sworn to secrecy.

This cloak-and-dagger business will be my undoing, she thought ruefully as she entered her own suite of offices. *I'm just not cut out to be a spy.*

She sat down wearily in the chair her father had occupied for so many years, closed her eyes and rubbed her forehead. The nagging headache behind her eyelids began to throb.

In the last week, neither she nor John had found any other incriminating evidence against either Claud or Lazarus. Even if her father had been involved with Beau Watkins of the Watkins Lumber Mill in Molalla, that didn't necessarily mean that he instigated the bribery charges. So far, the evidence was only circumstantial at best.

But the invoices represented the first set of concrete facts indicating that Trevor's charges against her family might be more than the idle speculation of a wronged son.

Thoughts of Trevor, his eyes narrowed suspiciously and his chin set in ruthless determination, invaded her mind. His charges against her father and Claud couldn't be ignored. What about the spraying of the pesticide near Springfield? Did Lazarus understand the health hazards involved and then just go ahead with the spraying, neglecting the welfare of the public? Ashley couldn't find it in her heart to believe that her father would do anything so cruel. Though not a particularly warm individual, her father had taken care of her when Enora, Ashley's mother, had died.

Ashley didn't hear Claud open the door. She was so

wrapped up in her own morbid thoughts that Claud had advanced upon the desk before she realized he was in the room.

He slapped a magazine down on the polished walnut desk. The glossy periodical was open to the current events section. Accompanying a short article on politics in Oregon was a snapshot of Trevor. Ashley's heart nearly skipped a beat as she looked at Trevor's intense expression and the glitter of determination in his eyes. The bold letters of the headline were a question: TREVOR DANIELS, OREGON'S NEXT SENATOR?

"We've got to stop this before it turns into popular opinion," Claud stated. One of his short fingers poked at the snapshot of Trevor.

"Stop what?"

"Daniels, for God's sake." Claud dropped into a chair near the desk. His dark eyes were clouded in disgust. "Read the article. The reporter acts as if Daniels is a shoo-in in the primary!"

"The latest polls show that—"

"The hell with the polls. It's the election that counts."

"And you're afraid that Trevor will win."

Claud let out an angry gust of air. "Damn right. If he does, we may as well close down."

Ashley's arched brows pulled together as she studied her cousin. Her heart was pounding warily in her chest. "Why?"

"He's out to crucify us."

"By us, do you mean you and me, or the company?"

"Same thing."

Ashley gathered her courage and met her cousin's furious glare. "Why does Trevor Daniels threaten you?"

Claud looked at her as if she were insane. "You still don't understand, do you?"

"Understand what?"

"The man's sworn that he'll get us one way or the other. He still blames your father and the timber company for the fact that his old man ran off with another woman— or whatever. Not only that, he thinks that someone here was involved in the bribery charges leveled against him last summer."

Ashley held her breath, watching, waiting, while Claud confided in her. Claud paused, rose from the chair and, after ramming his hands into his pockets, walked over to the window.

"Were we?" she asked softly.

Claud braced himself on the window ledge and smiled cynically. "Of course not, Ash! What would be the point?"

"To discredit a political adversary—"

"Bah!"

"You just stated that we had to do something about him."

"We do." Claud's fingers drummed nervously on the windowsill. "But something legal."

"Such as?" Ashley held her chin in her hand and her wide sea-green eyes noted all of Claud's aggravated movements.

"Back the other candidate."

"Orson?"

"Right. Bill Orson is Trevor's biggest competition in the primary. He was also pretty tight with your dad. He's the logical choice." Claud frowned thoughtfully.

"I'm not sure—"

"Look, Ashley, we're running out of time. Daniels is beginning to get a lot of press." He pointed a condemning finger toward the magazine. "National publicity. We've got to do what we can to protect our interests."

"Don't you think you're jumping off the deep end?" Ashley asked. "We're only talking about the primary and it's still several months away. Even if Trevor wins in May, he'll still face the other party's candidate in November."

"If he gets the chance."

"Which you want to thwart."

Claud pulled at the edge of his mustache. "That's putting it a little bluntly, but sure, let's call a spade a spade. If Daniels somehow managed to get himself elected, it would be a disaster!"

"His own family is in the logging business," Ashley replied. "Don't you think you're overreacting?"

A cruel smile touched Claud's thin lips. "What I think is that you're still carrying a torch for that bastard! God, Ashley, when will you ever grow up? He used you!"

Ashley crossed her arms over her chest. "And I think you're boxing with shadows."

Claud laughed out loud. "You still think you have a chance with him, don't you?" Ashley had to bite back the hot retort forming on her tongue. Angering Claud any further wouldn't accomplish anything. "Well, I'm inclined to agree. I wouldn't be a bit surprised if Trevor came sniffing around you, at least until after the election. That way he could stop the opposition before it began. All the easier for him."

Ashley swallowed back her indignation. "If you think you can get me to go along with whatever it is you want by insulting me, Claud, you're wrong."

Claud shrugged his bulky shoulders. "I wouldn't want to do that, cousin dear. After all, you're my boss."

"And that still sticks in your craw."

"A little." Claud frowned to himself. "But what concerns me more is the upcoming primary. You may as well reconcile yourself to the fact that we've got to do all we can to stop Daniels before all hell breaks loose."

With his final words, Claud walked past the desk, took one last look at the magazine article and left the office.

"You're wrong," Ashley whispered as the door closed behind her cousin, but his accusations had hit their mark. Had Trevor pretended interest in her just to get what he wanted from her?

The long nights of lovemaking came to her mind and Ashley remembered the honesty in Trevor's clear blue eyes. "If anyone's being deceptive," she thought aloud, "I'm willing to bet it's you, dear cousin," she mimicked. "And I'm not about to back a bastard like Bill Orson!"

Finding new resolve, she reached for the phone, intent on calling John Ellis. The sooner she found answers to Trevor's questions, the better.

CHAPTER NINE

"THAT'S IT," JOHN ANNOUNCED, his weary voice filled with relief.

"You're sure?" Ashley couldn't believe that the task that had seemed so monumental a few weeks ago was now finished.

"There's nothing else." John's expression was one of certainty. Other than the incriminating invoices and memo from Lazarus, John had found nothing to substantiate Trevor's accusations against Stephens Timber.

Ashley should have been jubilant, but she wasn't. "You've checked through everything?" Her fingers tapped nervously against her chin as she sat in the chair facing the desk. John was sitting behind mounds of computer print-outs, each carefully labeled and banded together on the top of Lazarus's desk in the den of the stately old manor.

"I've gone over every piece of paper you've brought me." John leaned back in the chair and propped his boots on the desk in a gesture of satisfaction. He stretched and even from where she was sitting, Ashley could hear his vertebrae crack. How many hours had the poor accountant sat at her father's desk, poring over black-and-white figures?

Ashley tried to accept John's audit as final, but during the last couple of weeks with Claud at the office, she had begun to doubt her earlier convictions about her family's innocence. Working with Claud on a daily basis had forced her to face up to the fact that the man had no sense of moral responsibility. Dollars and cents were his only motivation.

Abruptly she got out of her chair and paced anxiously between the desk and the window. The city lights of Portland winked seductively in the clear, black night.

"I thought you would be relieved," John remarked.

"I am—sort of."

"But?"

"These reports are all recent—all in the last six months."

"What're you getting at?"

She stopped near the window and stared at the cloudless night. "I want to clear the family name once and for all. There are a couple of things I want to check out, but it will have to be done at the office. If I take home the reports I need, Claud will become suspicious."

"Why?"

"Because they're old. Some of the documents won't even be on the computer," she thought aloud, her eyes piercing the blackness of the still night.

"What will you be looking for?"

Ashley smiled cryptically and faced him. "I don't know. I won't until I see it. But I want to check the records about the time of the Springfield spraying." She saw the look of protest in the accountant's eyes and she continued. "I want to see the books from day one—when Dad started the company—"

"Because of Robert Daniels's disappearance?"

Ashley let out a long sigh. "Right."

"I don't think you'll find anything," John offered, hoping to give some comfort to her worried mind.

"Let's just pray that you're right."

Later, after John had left for home, Ashley sat in her father's desk chair, worrying about the future. Several times she considered calling Trevor and once she had even gone so far as to reach for the phone. But she hadn't. Her pride forbade it. She sighed and let her hand fall to her side.

Ashley felt that she couldn't go to Trevor until she was certain of all the facts. The small piece of evidence against Claud and Lazarus would only add fuel to Trevor's inquisitive nature and Ashley wanted to be prepared with all the answers to his accusations before she saw him again.

If she saw him again. The argument between them was still unresolved and Ashley doubted if there would ever be a time when they could feel the freedom and love they had shared while alone in the mountains. *It was all just a lie,* she tried to convince herself, but the memory of Trevor's intense blue eyes, filled with honesty and raw passion, still touched a very vital part of her. She found herself hoping that he still cared, if only a little.

For the last two weeks, each time she had picked up a newspaper, Trevor's face had been plastered all over it. Claud was no longer worried about Trevor's bid for the Senate, he was downright furious that the polls showed Trevor Daniels leading the race.

Just the previous week Ashley had walked into Claud's office and overheard the tail end of a telephone conversation.

"I don't care what we have to do," Claud had stated emphatically, his lips white with rage, just as Ashley had walked into the room, "we can't let that son of a bitch win!"

Ashley had known instinctively that Claud was referring to Trevor, but she pretended that she hadn't understood the conversation.

Claud had glanced in her direction, paled slightly and then changed the course of the discussion, as if he were talking to an advertising executive about a future ad campaign.

Ashley's step faltered sightly and her heart filled with dread, but she didn't call Claud on the lie, knowing that it would be better for everyone concerned if Claud didn't think she was suspicious of him.

At that point, she had become convinced that Trevor's accusations about her family weren't completely idle speculation on his part. The look of pure hatred and ruthlessness that had crossed Claud's face while he was on the phone had been blood-chilling.

Just a few more weeks, she had thought to herself. *Just until John and I have all the evidence available. Then, when I know what really happened in the past, I'll confront Claud and give him his walking papers.* No matter how valuable he was to the timber company, Ashley knew that Claud was power-hungry and dangerous. Just like her father.

IN THE DAYS that followed, John had returned to the office and when Claud would go out for an afternoon, John and Ashley would go over the old records of the timber company. There never seemed to be enough time to sort through all the handwritten documents, but at least Ashley felt certain that Claud wasn't suspicious, not yet anyway.

Ashley's industrious work at the office seemed to convince Claud that she was interested only in the timber company. If he had any earlier thoughts about her relationship with Trevor, he didn't voice them.

Even though she ached to see Trevor, she had made a point of avoiding him for two reasons. The first was that she couldn't face him without being certain of the facts. The argument with him still cut her to the bone and she knew that she could never confront him until she had uncovered all of the truth and had solid facts to present to him.

The other reason was Claud. If anyone saw Ashley with Trevor, or overheard a telephone conversation between them and reported it to Claud, the results would be disastrous. For, as each day passed, Ashley was beginning to believe that Claud might have been involved in the planning of Trevor's accident. But she didn't have any proof. Not yet. She was working on gut instinct alone and that wouldn't hold up in court, which was exactly where she supposed her snaky cousin would wind up facing criminal charges.

CLAUD HAD BUSINESS in Seattle. For the first time since Ashley had returned from the mountain cabin and her tryst with Trevor, Claud had been called out of town. Ashley, as president of the timber company, insisted that he go; the matter in Seattle was pressing and Claud's legal expertise was desperately needed. Or at least she managed to convince Claud that his business acumen was without compare. Though his ego was stroked, he boarded the plane to Seattle reluctantly, casting Ashley a final glance that made her shiver with inward dread.

Once back in the office, she forgot Claud's cruel, cautionary stare. For the first time in several weeks, Ashley felt free. There were things she had to accomplish, one of which was to contact Trevor. Her heart raced at the thought and she wondered what kind of a reception she would receive.

He didn't answer when she tried contacting him at home, and when she called his campaign headquarters an efficient but cold voice told her that Mr. Daniels would get back to her. Ashley waited impatiently all afternoon, busying herself in the office, studying the old ledgers for the company, but Trevor didn't return her call.

At seven o'clock, she went home, helpless to shake the uneasiness beginning to settle on her shoulders. She told herself that he was busy, and for him not to call her wasn't out of the ordinary. Maybe he wanted to wait until he was sure that she was alone. Perhaps he would call tonight.

Frustrated from waiting, Ashley changed her clothes and tried, once again, to reach Trevor at home. There was still no answer and her nerves were frayed as she tried the campaign headquarters. The phone was answered by a recording machine, which played a message about the hours of business.

Ashley slammed the receiver back into the cradle and stalked downstairs. Was Trevor purposely avoiding her? It wasn't unlikely considering the circumstances, except that he had been so damned interested in the records of the timber company. Maybe that was because his accident had been so recent, and now, nearly six weeks later, his attention was focused on the future rather than the past.

A past which included Ashley, and a future which couldn't.

As outspoken as he had been against the Stephens Timber Corporation, Trevor couldn't risk a clandestine relationship with Ashley even if he wanted to, which Ashley seriously doubted.

"Hard day at the office?" Mrs. Deveraux asked when Ashley finally went downstairs and into the kitchen. The housekeeper had prepared Ashley her favorite dinner of pot roast and potatoes. The table was set for one.

"A little rough," Ashley admitted.

The lady with the perfectly coiled white hair pursed her thin lips together thoughtfully as she placed the steaming serving bowls onto the table. "You don't have to go around killing yourself, you know."

"Pardon me?" Ashley was taken aback. Mrs. Deveraux had never made personal comments to her, not since she had moved out of the house at eighteen.

"Just because your father left you the company, doesn't mean that you have to run it."

"But I enjoy it—"

"Bah! It doesn't take a genius to see that you're miserable. How much weight have you lost since you moved back here?"

"Only about five pounds." Ashley set a platter of beef onto the table.

"And on my cooking!"

"I haven't been particularly hungry," Ashley said with a shrug.

"Why?"

"I don't know, no appetite, I guess."

"Hmph! It's the timber company," Mrs. Deveraux pointed out. "It killed your father and it's doing the same with you. Either that, or you're pining for some man you left back at the college."

Ashley felt an uncomfortable lump form in her throat. Because Mrs. Deveraux was the only mother Ashley had known since she was in her early teens, the kindly old woman had a way of making Ashley feel like a contrite child. "I wasn't seeing anyone there."

"Well, sit…sit." Francine pointed a plump finger toward the table.

"You're not eating?"

A twinkle lighted the elderly woman's blue eyes. "Not tonight. I'm going out."

"With George again?" Ashley accused and clucked her tongue. "Another hot date? My, my, this is getting serious."

Mrs. Deveraux chuckled but the smile curving her lips at the mention of her beau quickly faded. "You should be the one going out. You're young and single."

"Divorced."

"Makes no difference. So am I."

Ashley forced a grin she didn't feel. "When I find the right man—"

"Well, you certainly won't find him here." The doorbell chimed and Francine Deveraux smiled. "You're too young and pretty to be losing weight over that damned company.

Sell it to your cousin, he would like to own it. Then you'll be a wealthy lady without all these worries."

"And afterward what would I do?"

"Marry a duke, an earl...."

A senator, Ashley thought wistfully to herself.

The doorbell chimed again.

"I must go. You think about what I've said."

"I will. And you have a wonderful time."

"Okay. End of lecture." Mrs. Deveraux kissed Ashley lightly on the cheek and hurried out of the kitchen. As Ashley pierced a piece of the roast with her fork, she heard the door open and the sound of laughter as Mrs. Deveraux greeted George. Within a minute, the door was closed and the great house seemed incredibly empty.

"If only everything were so simple," she said to herself, forcing the delicious food down her throat. Try as she would, she couldn't eat half of what Mrs. Deveraux had served.

With a groan, she got up from the table and tossed the remains of her dinner down the garbage disposal. "What a waste," she muttered before cleaning the dishes and trudging upstairs.

After a leisurely bath, she settled into bed and turned on the television for background noise as she sifted through the pages of a glossy magazine. When the local news came on, Ashley set the magazine aside and turned her attention to the smartly dressed anchorwoman who smiled into the camera.

"Rumor has it that one of the candidates for the senatorial seat vacated by Senator Higgins may be out of the race," the dark-haired woman stated evenly. Every muscle in Ashley's body tensed. "Trevor Daniels, a popular, proenvironmentalist candidate and lawyer originally from the Springfield area who later practiced law in Portland, will neither confirm nor deny the rumor that he is considering dropping out of the race."

"No!" Ashley screamed, bolting upright in the bed.

"Mr. Daniels was leading in the most current polls," the anchorwoman was stating, "and so his alleged withdrawal from the race before the May primary comes as somewhat of a shock to the community and the state."

Footage of Trevor, taken very recently at a campaign rally at Oregon State University, showed him talking with the students in the quad under threatening skies. The would-be senator was smiling broadly and shaking hands, looking for the life of him as if he were born to be a politician. Trevor's chestnut hair ruffled in the breeze and his face was robust-looking and healthy.

Ashley's heart contracted at the sight of him, and she noticed more than she was supposed to see. There was something different about him; a foreign wariness in his eyes, and a slight droop to the broad shoulders supporting the casual tweed jacket. Tanned skin stretched tautly across his high cheekbones and the set of his thrusting jaw somehow lacked conviction. What Ashley noticed were the slightest nuances, which had apparently eluded the press.

"Dear God, what happened?" she whispered while the anchorwoman listed Trevor's accomplishments and the pitfalls of his campaign.

"...not only was Mr. Daniels able to fend off false charges of bribery, which occurred last summer, but just recently he sustained an injury in a single-car accident that nearly took his life...." The anchorwoman continued, giving a little background on Trevor's life, including the fact that his father had disappeared ten years ago and though his brother, Jeremy, ran the family business of Daniels Logging Company, Trevor had been known for his tough stands on fair timber-cutting practices and wilderness preservation.

"Again," the woman was saying, "we can neither confirm nor deny this rumor, but if anything further develops on the story, we'll report it to you later in the program. Mr. Daniels is scheduled to speak at a rally in Pioneer Square tomorrow at noon. Perhaps we'll all know more at that time."

When the news turned away from the May primary, Ashley snapped off the set and fell back against the pillows while uttering a tremulous sigh. *Why would Trevor be planning to drop out of the race?* All of his life he had had political aspirations, and he was currently leading Bill Orson in the polls for the primary. Pulling out now just didn't make a lot of sense.

Just then Claud's words of a few days earlier rang in her ears. "We can't let that son of a bitch win!" he had stated to an unknown caller. Could Claud be somehow responsible for the rumor? And was it even true? KPSC wasn't a station to report sensational rumors just to gain viewer attention. Most of the stories reported by the Portland station were purely factual, very seldom conjecture. And yet, the rumor was unconfirmed.

Though it was nearly eleven, Ashley reached for the bedside phone and with quaking fingers punched out the number of Trevor's home. There was still no answer in the grand house on the Willamette, and Ashley wondered if Trevor had moved. He'd never felt completely comfortable in his father's stately home. The vestiges of wealth were too harsh a reminder of the price his father had paid to make Daniels Logging Company successful.

With a sigh, Ashley hung up the phone and settled into the pillows, hoping for sleep. If nothing else, she would be at Pioneer Square the next afternoon to see Trevor, if only from a distance. It seemed like years since she had set eyes on him.

Fortunately Claud was still out of town, so there would

be no one looking over her shoulder. *Tomorrow,* she promised herself, come hell or high water, she would find Trevor. Maybe, just maybe, she would force a confrontation with him.

PIONEER SQUARE WAS a mass of cold, disenchanted citizens. People from all walks of life milled around the red brick amphitheater with frowns. Elderly couples rubbed their hands together for warmth as they stood next to men and women dressed smartly for work in the business offices flanking the city block designated for the square. Gaudily costumed young people with punk hairdos and glittery clothes were joined by a disenchanted group of street people. Joggers paused on their daily run through the city streets on the way to Waterfront Park and young mothers pushing strollers braved the cold February air to hear Trevor Daniels speak.

Ashley stood on the edge of the crowd, her stomach tied in knots. Pieces of angry conversation filtered to her ears.

"You really don't think he'll show?" a jeans-clad student with a scruffy beard asked his friend.

"Nah—politicians, they're all alike—say one thing and do another."

"This guy—he's supposed to be different."

"Sure, he is. Then why isn't he here?"

"Beats me."

"They're all alike, I tell you. They just want you to think that they're something special." The shorter of the two paused to cup his fingers around the end of a cigarette before lighting it. He blew out an angry stream of smoke as he shook his blond head. "I'll tell ya one thing, I'm not votin' for this clown, Daniels. Hell, he can't even show up for his own goddamn rally."

"Maybe his plane was delayed—"

"His plane? Gimme a break. He's supposed to be in town."

"Okay, okay, so the guy's a jerk. Who're you gonna vote for? Orson? That son of a bitch would sell his own mother's soul if there was a dime in it."

"God damn!" The short man ground out his cigarette and frowned. "I was hoping this guy would do something—"

"Meaningful?"

"Give me a break!" His gruff laughter drifted off as the two young men walked toward the podium.

Ashley's anxious eyes skimmed the crowd. Nowhere was there any trace of Trevor. The rally was supposed to begin at twelve and it was nearly twelve-fifteen. Worried lines creased Ashley's forehead as she blew on her cold hands. It was cold, but fortunately dry, and the wind blowing down the Columbia Gorge cut through her coat and chilled her bones.

"Come on, Trevor," she whispered, and her breath misted in the clear air. "If you want to lose this election, you're certainly going about it the right way."

Finally there was a flurry of activity near the podium. Ashley's anxious eyes were riveted to the small stage that had been prepared for the event. The crowd murmured gratefully as a small, round man stepped up to the microphone.

It had been many years since Ashley had seen Everett Woodward, but she recognized Trevor's campaign manager, whose high-pitched voice was echoing in the square. He introduced himself to Trevor's restless public and then politely explained that Trevor had been detained in Salem and that the rally would be rescheduled for another, undisclosed date.

No one was pleased at the news. While some of the

would-be Daniels supporters began to disband, a group of hecklers standing near Ashley began to taunt Everett.

"So where is he?" one demanded gruffly. "I don't buy your story that he's in Salem. He was supposed to be here today."

"Yeah, right. And what's all the rumors about him pulling out of the race? What happened? Did he get caught with his hand in the till or something?"

Everett, in his seemingly unflappable manner, ignored the jibes, but his brow was puckered with worry.

The hecklers continued their conversation in private. "If you ask me, Daniels was probably caught with his pants down—in bed with somebody's wife."

"Oh yeah?" The other youth chuckled obscenely and Ashley started to walk away. She was concerned about Trevor, and wasn't interested in any gossip about him.

"Sure, why not? The way I hear it, he was involved with a daughter of some hotshot timber guy—a rival or something—and she was married to someone else."

"Hey, I've got new respect for this guy...tell me about it...."

A protest leaped to Ashley's tongue when she realized the hecklers were discussing her. She had to physically restrain herself from causing a scene and telling the two men that her love affair, that beautiful and fleeting part of her life, had been long over before she married Richard. An unwanted blush flooded her neck and her steps faltered slightly, but she clamped her teeth together, lowered her head against the wind and walked resolutely toward the object of her quest: Trevor's campaign manager.

Everett noticed her approach and a flicker of recognition registered on his placid face. The corners of his mouth twitched downward.

When she was close enough to be heard, Ashley didn't mince words. "I want to talk to Trevor."

Everett smiled coldly. "You and the rest of the voters in this state."

"It's important. I telephoned the campaign headquarters yesterday and a receptionist promised to have Trevor return the call."

"Which he didn't?"

"Right."

Everett was about to make a hasty retort, but changed his mind.

"I don't think he got the message," Ashley informed the round campaign manager.

"Or maybe you didn't. Did it ever cross your mind that maybe Trevor didn't want to talk to you?"

The muscles in Ashley's back stiffened and for a moment she considered letting the subject drop. But too much was at stake. In the past few weeks she had learned that her love for Trevor would never die and that at least some of the pain in the past was her fault for not trusting him. It was imperative that she see Trevor again. With newfound strength she swallowed her pride.

"Which is it?" she demanded, her muscles rigid. She braced herself for the rejection she was sure would follow. "You're his campaign manager, and from what I understand, very good at what you do. Certainly Trevor would confide in you, let you know if he didn't want to see me again."

Everett considered the woman standing before him. The pride and determination in the lift of her chin were compelling. Ashley Stephens Jennings was a far cry from the spoiled timber brat she had once been.

He fingered the handle of his umbrella and his gaze left her to study the architecture of the buildings surrounding the square. "I think it would be best if you forgot about Trevor Daniels," he ventured. "It would be political dynamite if the press found out that you were seeing him again."

"That's ducking the issue, Everett. Has Trevor told you that he doesn't want to see me?"

Everett gazed into the quiet fury of her blue-green eyes. There was a new dignity and spirit in her stare. He found it impossible to lie to her. "Right now, Trevor isn't really sure what he wants," the campaign manager admitted.

"Including his ambitions for the Senate?"

The portly man's eyes glittered dangerously. He knew he'd given too much away to the becoming daughter of Lazarus Stephens. "Leave him alone, Ashley," he warned. "Before Trevor saw you again, he knew what he wanted. And now...oh, hell!" A fleshy fist balled in frustration.

"And now what?" Ashley whispered, her throat constricting.

Everett laughed feebly. "I guess you and your father got what you wanted all along," he said in disgust. "Single-handedly you seem to have convinced the best goddamn man in Oregon to back down from his one shot at making it. Do you know what you've done? Have you any idea what you alone have cost this state?" His face reddened with conviction and his hands gestured helplessly in the air. "He would have been good, Ashley, damned good."

With his angry remark, he turned toward his car, and then cast another warning over his shoulder. "Give up, Ashley, you've gotten what you wanted. It's over for him. Now, for God's sake, leave the poor bastard alone!"

After grinding out his final, gut-wrenching advice, Everett slipped into the dark interior of a waiting cab. The battered car roared to life, melding into the traffic heading east toward the Willamette River.

Ashley was left standing alone in the wintry air. She felt more naked and raw than she had since the last time she had seen Trevor walk out the door of the mountain cabin. Shivering from the frigid wind, she wrapped her arms under her breasts.

An ache, deep and throbbing, cut through her heart and pounded in her pulse. "Dear Lord, Trevor," she whispered, "what happened to us?" She looked up at the cold gray sky and tears gathered in the corners of her eyes. How had she been so blind for so long? Why had she let other people, other things, unnecessary obstacles separate her from him? Was it pride, or was it fear of the truth that had kept her from facing the fact that she loved him more desperately than any sane woman should love a man?

Her fingers were clenched tightly around her abdomen when she heard her name.

"Ms. Jennings?"

Unaware that anyone had been watching her, Ashley whirled and faced a young man, no more than twenty-five, who was staring intently at her. His clean features gave no hint of what he wanted.

"Pardon me?" she whispered, carefully disguising the huskiness in her throat with poise.

"You are Ashley Jennings, aren't you—Ashley Stephens Jennings?"

"Yes." She was instantly wary. The last twenty-four hours had been a roller coaster of conflicts and emotions and something in this man's studious gaze warned her to tread carefully.

The young man flashed a triumphant smile. "I thought so. Elwin Douglass." He stretched out his hand and reluctantly Ashley accepted his larger palm in her icy fingers.

"Is there something I can do for you?"

"I hope so. I'm a freelance reporter." Ashley's heart froze in her throat. "I'm doing a series of articles about the politicians in the primary…and, well, I'm starting with Trevor Daniels."

"Mr. Daniels wasn't here today," Ashley replied, sensing that she didn't want to become embroiled with this young man. "You should be talking to him and I have to get back to work—"

"I'll walk with you. This won't take long," he reassured her. "You're in charge of Stephens Timber, aren't you?" He was writing in a notebook, glancing at her and refusing to be put off.

"Yes. I'm the president. Several people help me handle the management. I couldn't do it alone." Involuntarily she thought of Claud and cold dread stiffened her spine.

A traffic signal on Fifth made her pause. Douglass grabbed the opportunity. "I know. But your company, at least in the past, has been very vocal in condemning environmental candidates such as Daniels."

The signal changed and Ashley stepped off the red-brick curb and onto the wet pavement. "Look, Mr. Douglass. I really don't want to give an impromptu interview right now. Perhaps if you called the office, we could arrange a time that would be convenient for both of us."

The bold reporter refused to take the hint. "Well, there's just a couple of questions."

"Really, I don't think—"

"You're Lazarus Stephens's daughter, right?"

"Of course, but—"

"His only child, the one who got involved with Trevor Daniels several years ago."

"If you'll excuse me," Ashley stated, increasing the length of her stride. The offices of Stephens Timber Corporation were now in view. Ashley was never more glad to see the renovated, turn-of-the-century hotel sitting proudly on Front Avenue.

"Wait a minute. What do you know about this rumor that Daniels is withdrawing from the race?"

That's an easy one, and safe, too, Ashley thought to herself. "Absolutely nothing," she answered honestly. Her smile was well practiced and cool. "Now, seriously, if you'd like to continue this interview, at another time, just give the office a call." She fished in her purse, found a business card and extended it to him. "Right now I have work to do."

Grudgingly Elwin Douglass accepted the small white card and slipped it into his wallet.

Ashley pushed open the wide glass door of the building and effectively ended the interview. Her chin was held proudly, her strides determined. Despite the warnings from Everett Woodward, and the unspoken insinuations from the reporter, she knew that she had to see Trevor again.

Tonight.

CHAPTER TEN

TWILIGHT HAD FALLEN by the time Ashley arrived at Trevor's stately home. Despite the gathering darkness, Ashley could see that the grand two-story structure hadn't changed much in the past eight years. Built of cedar timbers and bluestone, the English manor stood proudly on the banks of the silvery Willamette River.

Sharp gables angled against the steep roofline, and ancient fir trees guarded the estate. Leaded windows winked in the harsh glare of security lights, which illuminated the rambling structure and cast ghostly shadows over the dormers.

Gathering her purse and her composure, Ashley got out of her car and walked up the rough stone path to the front door. Though she had entered that door dozens of times in the past, her heart began to thud anxiously as she ascended the steps of the stone porch and braced herself for Trevor's inevitable rejection.

Everett's warning echoed dully in her mind—*Leave the poor bastard alone.* What did that mean? It was more than a threat; the campaign manager's words sounded like a plea, as if Everett was attempting to protect Trevor. The thought sent cold desperation racing through Ashley's bloodstream. Why did Trevor need protecting? He had always been a strong, proud man, capable of taking care of himself and finding a way of getting what he wanted in life. He had always stood alone, fighting whatever battles he had to without anyone's help.

Unable to dispel the overwhelming sense of dread settling upon her, she rang the doorbell and waited impatiently. The melodic chimes sounded through the solid wood door, but there was no evidence of life from within the huge house. Fear for the man she loved took a stranglehold on her throat.

The scent of burning wood drifted in the air, indicating that a fire was burning in one of the massive fireplaces within the manor.

She stood alone on the porch and the only sound that interrupted the stillness of the night was her own irregular breathing. Nervously, she stretched upward on the toes of her shoes and peered into the closest window. The room into which she was looking was dark, but there were soft lights glowing in the far doorway, as if illumination from another room was filtering down the corridor. Apparently whoever it was within the manor preferred his privacy.

After a few quiet minutes of indecision, Ashley tossed her hair over her shoulders and rapped sharply on the dark wood door. She had come to see Trevor and she was bound and determined to find him, even if it took her all night. Whoever was in the house would just damned well have to get off his duff and answer the door. After eight years, she was sick and tired of waiting.

Her heart was beating wildly when she heard footsteps approaching the door.

It opened with a moan and she found herself staring into the anxious blue eyes of the man she loved with all her heart. He looked older than she remembered; his hair was unkempt, his eyes dull. *He looks as if he's been to hell and back,* she thought to herself. He was a far cry from the strong, unbeaten man with the flash of determination in his eyes that she remembered so well. Her heart twisted in silent agony for him and the pain he bore.

"Ashley?" Trevor asked, leaning between the door and

the frame, as if he were too tired to stand unaided. The scent of Scotch lingered in the air.

His voice was surprisingly indecisive and the thrusting determination of his jaw was undermined by the painful questions clouding his eyes. A stubble of beard darkened his chin and his skin was stretched tightly over gaunt facial features. His clothes consisted of worn jeans and an unbuttoned flannel shirt, which was faded and rumpled, with the sleeves rolled over his elbows as if he hadn't wasted the time or the effort to change in several days. When he looked into her eyes, the rigid lines near his mouth softened slightly and the tension in his shoulder muscles slackened.

"Ashley...dear God, woman, is it really you?"

She hesitated. Nothing could have prepared her for the tired and broken man she was facing. A faint smile touched the corners of his mouth, but even that seemed an effort. Tears of misunderstanding filled her eyes.

"Oh, Trevor, what's happened to you?" she whispered, her voice catching in the dark night.

"Nothing that matters. At least not now." He closed his eyes as if to push aside the demons playing with his mind. "I've missed you, lady," he admitted roughly, and he opened the door a little wider.

It was all the encouragement she needed. With a strangling sob, she ran to him and wrapped her arms securely around his neck to hold on to him in quiet desperation. All the old barriers that had held them apart for so many years seemed to crumble and fall. His arms held her securely, crushing her body with the power of his, as if he, too, were afraid that she was only a figment of his imagination and would vanish into the night as quickly as she had appeared.

Silvery tears streamed down her face and she drank in the familiar scent of him, all male and warm. There was the lingering trace of Scotch on his breath. When he pressed his lips to hers, she felt as if she would melt into the polished oak floors of the grand entry hall.

"I thought I'd lost you," he rasped, and for the first time Ashley noticed the tears gathering in his eyes. Never before had she seen Trevor cry and there was something endearing in the knowledge that this proud man cared enough to let her see his weakness.

"Shhh…I'm here now. That's all that matters," she murmured, smoothing the disheveled chestnut hair from his eyes and kissing his tear-stained cheeks.

"I won't let you leave me again," he vowed, recovering his composure and kicking the door closed with his foot.

"If I remember correctly, Senator, it was you who left me."

"Not eight years ago, lady. That's when I made my mistake with you. I should never have let you walk out of my life."

"And I shouldn't have walked—"

"Amen."

With a quick movement, he bent and slipped one arm under the crook of her knees, lifting her lithely off her feet.

"What are you doing?" she murmured into his neck as he started to carry her to the back of the house.

"What I should have done a long time ago," he returned. "I'm going to make love to you until you promise that you'll stay with me forever." His words pierced her heart like silver needles, reminding her of a past that held them together only to push them apart. "I've made more than my share of mistakes in my life, but not tonight. I've waited too long for you to show up on my doorstep."

"And what if I hadn't? How long would you have waited?" The warmth of his body seemed to flow into hers, and his rock-hard muscles rippled slightly when he walked. Despite the unspoken questions lingering between them, Ashley felt her body responding to Trevor's captive embrace and the sparks of possession in his eyes.

"I don't know," he replied darkly.

"You could have called."

Shame tightened his jaw. "I was afraid."

"Of me?"

He let out a disgusted sigh. "For you. Whatever it was that I was up against, I didn't want you involved."

"But you asked me to check the company records—"

He placed a silencing finger to her lips. "After our argument, I realized that it had been a mistake to ask you for your help in the first place and then, later..."

"Wait a minute—slow down. What the devil are you talking about?" she asked, her arms still encircling his neck. When she pulled her head away from his shoulder in order to study the anxious lines of his face, she could read nothing but worry in his gaze.

Trevor noticed the confusion in the mysterious sea-green depths of her eyes as he carried her into the den. He shook his head as if to knock out the cobwebs that had gathered in his mind from too many nights without sleep and too many bottles of alcohol to deaden his nerves.

"Not now," he whispered as he placed her on the plushly carpeted floor before the fire. Passion darkened his eyes as he brushed a strand of dark hair from her face and gazed down upon her. His finger traced the length of her jaw, pausing slightly at the pout on her lips. "Tonight you and I are going to forget about all the craziness between our families, all the lies, and all the betrayals. Tonight, we're going to concentrate on each other, just as if the slate were clean."

Her fingers grabbed hold of his wrist, effectively halting the assault on her senses from the sensual touch of his hands. Her words came out in a ragged whisper. "You act as if you expected me to show up here tonight."

His shoulders drooped from an invisible burden and he looked away from the elegant contours of her face to stare into the fire. Drawing his bent legs to his chest, he placed his folded arms over his knees and stared at the scarlet embers of the dying fire. "I didn't think I'd ever see you again," he admitted reluctantly. "I thought you were lost to me forever."

"But why?"

"I almost lost you once before when you married another man."

Ashley felt the burn of her betrayal in her chest. "You know that was a mistake, I told you so. Even Richard would admit it." She touched Trevor gently on his arm, forcing him to turn and face her again. "Don't you know I've never loved another man, not with the passion I've felt with you? I only married Richard because I didn't think you wanted me, and I'll never make that mistake again. It wasn't fair to anyone. Not you, or Richard, or myself. In the past eight years I've learned a lot; one thing is that if you find something you want, I mean really want, you've got to hold on and never let go. I learned that from you, Trevor. That and so much more."

Trevor buried his face in his hands. "I hope you know that I would never do anything to hurt you," he said.

"I do." She didn't question him for a moment. She had come to him and found him raw and naked and vulnerable. For the first time in her life she knew that he cared, that he had always cared as much as he could allow himself.

"And the last thing I would want would be for you to be subjected to any kind of danger."

"Of course—Trevor, why are you talking like this?"

He turned to study her worried expression. Her fingers on his forearm moved slowly, soothingly against his skin. He swallowed against the uncomfortable lump which had formed in his throat and made speech impossible. "I love you," he admitted, his eyes boring into hers.

The movement against his arm stopped abruptly and a sad smile touched the corners of Ashley's mouth. How many years had she waited to hear just those words?

Trevor took her small fingers in his and touched each one to his lips. The moist warmth of his tongue as it slid seductively against her skin forced a tremor of longing to shake her body.

Blue eyes held her fast as his hands pushed her coat off her shoulder before straying to the top button of her blouse.

"I'm not going to let you go," he promised as the first pearl fastener slid through sea-blue silk. "I'm going to keep you here, protect you, and you'll never be able to get away from me again." Another button was soon freed of its bond by the warm insistence of his finger.

Ashley's breathing was rapid, coming in short little gasps, and her heartbeat thundered in her ears. Her breasts rose and fell as his hand slid lower, to the third button. "I've never wanted to get away from you, Trevor," she rasped when her blouse parted and the firelight displayed the French lace of the camisole covering her breasts. His hands touched the silken fabric, and Ashley's fingers wrapped around his wrist to forestall the attack on her senses. There were things she needed to know. Questions that had no answers.

"Why didn't you call or come to me?" She looked up at the strained angles of the face, shadowed now in the fire's glow. There was a weariness about him and the smile he rained on her was bitter, filled with agonized defeat.

"It's better this way. I couldn't take a chance of placing you in danger."

Regardless of the passion smoldering in his midnight-blue gaze, the set of his jaw was grim and rigid. His shirt hung open and as he leaned over her, she noticed that the muscles of his chest were tense and strained. There was no bandage to swath his abdomen, but a jagged red scar sliced across the tanned skin, reminding her of the reason he had sought her out in the lonely mountains.

Lightly, her fingers traced the scar. Trevor sucked in his breath and closed his eyes, as if in pain.

"What's with all this talk about danger?"

He paused a long moment and stared down at the vulnerable and beautiful woman lying on the carpet. Her mysterious eyes were heavy with seduction and the fine lace of her camisole couldn't hide the twin points of her nipples straining against the flimsy cloth. "There's nothing to worry about now," he whispered, lowering his head to the inviting cleft between her breasts. "I'll take care of you...."

She felt the heat of his tongue slide against the lacy fabric as a slumbering desire began to awaken within her. She was lost in her love for this man. Seeing some of his pain and worry only intensified her yearning to be a part of him...and his life.

His fingers twined in the ebony strands of her hair. He whispered words of love against the sensitive shell of her ear before his lips pressed against hers with the fire of too many nights of lonely restraint.

Passion parted her lips and she eagerly accepted the touch of his tongue against hers. Her hands pushed his shirt off his shoulders, lingering over the smooth, hard muscles of his upper arms as the cotton garment slid silently to the floor.

"Make love to me," he murmured when her hands touched his belt and hesitated at the buckle. He rubbed against her, making her achingly aware of the urgency of his desire stretching the faded denim of his jeans.

She moaned in response and slowly removed his pants, letting her fingers slide in a familiar caress down the length of his lean thighs and calves. The corded muscles tensed at her gentle touch, and when her fingers slid against the tender arch of his foot, he began to shake from the restraint he placed upon himself.

Passion glazed his eyes. When at last he was freed of his clothing, he stretched out beside her and gently pushed a satiny strap off her shoulder. The result was that one of her breasts was bared to him. He studied the delicious, ripe mound, before cupping its swollen weight with his palm.

"I love you," he whispered again, lowering his head and taking the taut nipple into his mouth. His tongue circled the straining dark peak, moistening and teasing the ripe bud until Ashley moaned in bittersweet ecstasy.

At last he placed his lips around her breast and began to suckle, drawing out the sweetness within her until she thought she would go mad with desire. She cradled his head in her hands, holding him closer, wishing that she could offer more to him than just her body.

When Trevor finally lifted his head to gaze into her eyes, Ashley's heart felt like a bird trapped in a gilded cage as it fluttered wildly against the prison of her ribs. The shadowed corners of the room seemed distant. All she could see were the bold features of Trevor's face as he slowly lifted her camisole over her head.

After discarding the unwanted garment, his fingers trailed slowly up her stockinged legs.

"Trevor…please," she murmured tremulously before feeling him pulling her skirt and underthings down her hips. Soon she was lying naked with him.

Perspiration dampened his torso and gleamed like oil in the fire glow. He kissed her softly on the lips and rubbed his body against hers, all the while watching for the subtle changes in her expression.

"I want you," she whispered to the unspoken questions in his knowing eyes.

"That's not enough."

She swallowed the hot lump in her throat, understanding the words he yearned to hear. A coaxing hand rubbed against her breast in gentle circles, breaking her concentration and causing the liquid fire within her to pulse through her veins.

She was incapable of thinking of anything but this man lying atop her, teasing her gently by rubbing his rigid length over the soft slopes of her body.

"I love you, Trevor," she said again, her heartbeat echoing in the dark room. "I always have."

A sheen of perspiration covered her body and trickled between her breasts. Slowly, Trevor's head lowered to catch the salty droplet with his tongue. "And I love you, Ashley...." His head lifted and his eyes held hers with all the passion of eight lost years. "I never stopped."

With his traitorous admission, he closed his eyes and gently forced her knees apart, surrendering at last to the fire in his loins and the seduction in Ashley's sea-green eyes. He entered her slowly, but with a determined thrust that claimed her as his own. For too many years he had ached for another man's woman, and in the rush of heat building within him, he attempted to expunge forever the mark of Richard Jennings from Ashley's soul. She was his woman now and forever. If he'd learned anything in the past few weeks it was that nothing else in life was worth a damn.

Trevor's torment was evident in the strain on his face and the unleashed power of his lovemaking. Never had their coupling been more bittersweet than now, and Ashley gave herself to the authority of his touch. The sweet fury within her began to rage, hotter and hotter, demanding release until, at last, she convulsed in a passion born of years of denial.

"Trevor," she cried as she felt his answering shudder, and his weight fell against her. Tears glistened in her eyes and when his breathing slowed, he rolled off her before tenderly cradling her head against his shoulder.

"Nothing will ever come between us again," he vowed, his voice rough with emotion and his breath ruffling her hair.

"How can you be so certain?"

"Because for the first time in weeks, I feel like the master of my own destiny." Softly he kissed the tears from her eyes and fought against his own. "You and I, lady, we're going to get through this and we're going to get through it together."

"If only I could believe—"

"Believe."

She wrapped her arms securely around the man she loved, to drown in the scents mingling in the room—the smell of burning wood, the gentle tang of sweat and the muskiness of stale Scotch.

Tenderly he smoothed her hair away from her face. "I was afraid that you would never come here," he stated, blue eyes regarding her solemnly.

"But I called—"

"And no one answered."

"I left word at the campaign headquarters. The receptionist said you'd call me back."

Trevor stiffened beside her. "When?"

"Yesterday afternoon."

His shoulders relaxed slightly. "I've avoided that place," he admitted, "and I didn't answer the phone when I was here."

"But why?" She touched his shoulder lightly. "What's going on with you? The rumor's out that you're pulling out of the race."

"Is that why you came here tonight?" he demanded, his eyes instantly glittering with smoky blue fire.

"No. But it made me realize I had to see you again… touch you. There are things we need to discuss."

Trevor managed a beguiling smile."We will, after I fix you something to eat."

"I'm not hungry," she began to protest.

"Come on, indulge me, I'm starving."

"What you're doing is avoiding the issue."

"In the manner of a true politician." He stood up and pulled on his jeans before tossing her clothes to her. "If you want to talk, you'd better get dressed. Otherwise, I won't be liable for what happens." His eyes slid seductively down her body and lingered at the swell of her breasts. "You're too damned beautiful for my own good."

Ashley smiled wryly as she stepped into her skirt and slid the camisole over her head. While adjusting the zipper of the slim skirt, she caught Trevor staring at her. He was leaning against the fireplace and his arms were crossed over his chest as he watched her work with the obstinate zipper.

"A lot of help you are," she muttered.

"If I come over there and touch you, you can bet that I would be pulling down instead of up."

Her head snapped upward. "You were the one who wanted me to get dressed."

"You got it all wrong, lady."

"Don't I always?"

He shook his head and laughed. "You wanted to talk and I told you that would be impossible, unless you had some clothes on. Otherwise, I might get distracted."

"Promises, promises," she teased just as the zipper locked into place.

Trevor's eyes flashed ominously. "I'm not through with you yet, you know. And every time you tease me, I'll extract my own kind of punishment on you later."

"Sure of yourself, aren't you?" Ashley cocked her head to the side and her dark hair framed her face in soft curls.

Trevor shrugged, refusing to be baited by her coy mood, though he wondered to himself how one woman could tear his guts out with a coquettish toss of her head. "With you, I'm never sure of anything."

Ashley sobered instantly. Trevor took her hand and led her to the kitchen near the back of the house.

"I don't think there's much here…" he said, beginning to scrounge through the contents of the refrigerator.

"Doesn't matter. I'm not the one who's starved," she pointed out, staring unabashedly at the way his jeans strained over his buttocks as he leaned into the refrigerator.

"Hmph… Here we go. How about an omelet?"

"Anything—would you like me to cook?"

"Not on your life." Then, when he looked up, he smiled disarmingly. "It might be safer if you did."

Ashley was glad for an excuse to keep busy. While whipping the eggs and grating the cheese, she could feel Trevor's eyes on her and for the first time in weeks she was completely relaxed, as if she had come home from a long and tedious journey.

They ate the meal in silence, and Ashley savored each sweet second she shared with Trevor.

"So tell me," she insisted, clearing the plates from the small table in the windowed alcove just off the kitchen,"what's with all this talk about your withdrawal from the race?"

"So far that's what it is: just talk."

"Where there's smoke, there's fire," she observed.

"You should know all about that."

She felt the muscles of her back stiffen, but when her eyes met his, she knew that the old animosity had mellowed and that Trevor hadn't meant to bring up his accusations against her father.

"That reminds me," she said, wiping her hands on a dish towel near the stove. "I have something for you."

His gaze sharpened. "You found some proof?"

"I wish I knew what it was," she admitted. "It's in my purse…in the den."

Once back in the cozy study, Trevor stoked the fire, while Ashley turned on a table lamp and extracted the documents condemning her father and cousin.

When the fire was blazing to his satisfaction, Trevor dusted his hands on his jeans and approached Ashley. She started to hand him the documents, but Trevor shook his head. "I don't want to know what you found, if it's something that will hurt you or your family."

Ashley's eyes narrowed a fraction. "I don't understand. You asked me, no, demanded is a better word, that I look for evidence against my family. For the last six weeks I've worked my fingers to the bone. Now you don't want it?"

"What I don't want is to hurt you—not anymore. If there is something in those pages—" he pointed to the papers she was clutching "—that would be better off hidden, then I think you should burn them. Right now."

He was offering her a way out, a lifeline for her father's reputation, but she couldn't accept it. If she and Trevor had any chance at happiness, it was by destroying all the myths of the past and laying to rest the lies. Any future they might share would have to be founded on truth.

"Here." She put the papers in his hands. "Let's start over—a clean slate. Remember?"

He took the pages from her trembling fingers and sat on the hearth near the fire. "I'll be damned…."

"It's what you wanted, isn't it? Proof that my father and Claud were behind the bribery charges."

His broad shoulders sagged. "Was there anything else?"

"Not that I could find," she said roughly. "John Ellis and I worked day and night with all the company records.

Sure, we could have overlooked something, I suppose, but I doubt it. There was nothing I could find around the date of your accident that would lead me to believe that Claud had any part in it. As for your father's disappearance..." Trevor's eyes sharpened and he watched her face. "...I checked, everything I could think of, as far as ten years back." She shook her head and the firelight caught in her raven-black hair.

"I suppose that may be one mystery that's never solved," Trevor thought aloud. He rubbed the tension from the back of his neck and wondered, for the thousandth time, what had happened to his father. "Now it's my turn to be honest," he stated.

Ashley's heart chilled. Had he been using her? Were all his words of love only to extract what he wanted from her? She couldn't believe it, and yet her heart was filled with dread. "About what?"

"I had a meeting with Claud."

His words settled like lead on the room. "You what?"

"I instigated a private confrontation with Claud—just yesterday. That's why I didn't show up at Pioneer Square. I was in Seattle."

"But Everett said you were in Salem."

"That's where he thought I was. If I had told him that I was flying to Seattle to have it out with Claud Stephens, Everett would have hijacked the plane."

"So what happened?" Ashley asked, almost afraid to hear.

"Claud was his usual friendly self," Trevor replied cynically.

"I'll bet." Claud's words again rang in her ears: *We can't let that son of a bitch win.*

"He wanted, make that insisted, that I pull out of the senatorial race. There had already been some rumors to that effect and Claud wanted to substantiate them."

"But that's ridiculous."

"Precisely what I told your cousin."

"And?"

Trevor rubbed his chin and looked intently at Ashley. "When I refused, Claud got a little nasty. He told me that if I didn't withdraw, he would see to it that not only was my name dragged through the mud, but yours as well. He thought the public would want to be reminded of our past association, and he insinuated that he thought it would make good copy for the local papers, including the *Morning Surveyor.*"

Ashley sagged into a recliner by the window. How far would her cousin go to get what he wanted? Her throat was desert-dry, her knees weak, but her conviction strong. "You can't be bullied by Claud's threats."

"Not as long as I know that you're with me—on my side."

Ashley fought against her tears. "I always have been," she murmured.

He looked as if a terrible weight had been lifted from his shoulders. "Now that you're safe, nothing else matters."

"Except your career."

"Damn my career."

"Trevor, you've worked too long and hard to give up now. It's all within your grasp. Everything you've wanted."

His blue eyes darkened savagely. "What I want, dear lady, is right here."

"Meaning what?"

"You never have understood, have you? I'm asking you to marry me, Ashley, and I'm not about to take no for an answer."

"Are you serious?" Desperately Ashley wanted to believe him, and yet, the entire night seemed like part of a dream.

"I've never been more serious about anything in my

life. Will you marry me?" He strode across the room and pulled her out of the chair, forcing her to meet the sincerity of his gaze.

Tears pooled in her eyes and she managed a weak smile. "Of course I'll marry you, Senator. I just wonder why it took eight years for you to come to your senses?"

"Because I've been a fool, Ashley. A goddamned, self-righteous, egotistical fool."

"Join the club."

Trevor laughed aloud before scooping her off her feet and carrying her through the darkened house and up the stairs to his bedroom.

CHAPTER ELEVEN

WHEN ASHLEY AWOKE the next morning, Trevor was already out of bed. She stretched in the cool sheets and smiled as she remembered making love to Trevor long into the night. They had spent the dark hours passionately entwined in each other's arms, with the only interruption being one telephone call that Trevor had received in the early hours of the morning.

"I thought you weren't taking any calls," Ashley had grumbled groggily when she glanced at the digital display of the clock on the nightstand. The luminous numbers had indicated that it was nearly two in the morning.

"I'm not," had been Trevor's cryptic reply. "Only those that come in on my private line, like this one. Then I know it's important." She felt as if he were holding back something from her but she was too tired to care. After his brief explanation, he had reached for the phone and taken the call, which had been lengthy and very one-sided.

Ashley hadn't been able to decipher Trevor's end of the conversation, and she had been too sleepy to concentrate. Before Trevor had finished talking, she had curled up around him and drifted off to sleep, warm and content as he stroked her hair with one hand while holding the telephone with the other. She had felt the coiled tension in his rigid muscles and had wondered vaguely if there was something seriously the matter, but she had fallen back into a dreamless sleep without any answers to her questions.

This morning the entire incident loomed before her and

bothered her a little, but she shoved her worried thoughts aside.

"Your imagination is working overtime again," she chastised herself with a self-mocking smile.

After taking a quick shower, she put her clothes on and brushed her hair before walking down the curved oak staircase to the main floor of the house. The warm morning smells of hot coffee and burning wood greeted her. Ashley was smiling when she breezed into the kitchen looking for Trevor.

The room was empty. There were signs that Trevor had been there; the coffee had finished dripping through the coffeemaker into the clear glass pot, and the morning newspaper had been brought into the house and torn apart. Several sections were still lying haphazardly on the table near the bay window. Ashley scanned the headlines and noticed that the front page of the paper was missing.

It was then she heard the low, angry rumble of Trevor's voice coming from the direction of the den. With quickening steps, Ashley followed the sound. What could have happened? The sketchy memory of the late-night telephone call entered her mind and her heart began to race.

Trevor sounded furious. His rage shook the stately timbers of the old house. "This is the last straw," he vowed and swore descriptively.

When she approached the door of the study, she paused, not wanting to eavesdrop on a private conversation.

"I want to know who in the hell is responsible," Trevor nearly shouted into the receiver and then waited impatiently for the person on the other end of the phone to respond. "Well it's a hell of a way to run a campaign, if you ask me…. What? Yeah, I'm not going anywhere." He looked pointedly at his watch. "See ya then."

Ashley noticed the lines of strain in the rigid set of his jaw and she remembered his look just the night before when he had seemed so beaten. Her mouth went dry when she realized that he hadn't been honest with her. There was still a secret gnawing at his insides and she knew instinctively that it had something to do with her. He looked as if he were a man possessed.

When he slammed the receiver down, his mouth was drawn into a thin, determined line. Rubbing the tension from the back of his neck and shoulders, he closed his eyes and stretched. "Damn!" he muttered, thinking he was alone.

"What happened?" Ashley asked. His eyes flew open and he turned his head in her direction.

"What hasn't?" His fingers rubbed anxiously against the heel of his hands. "Looks like Claud beat me to the punch...."

"What do you mean?"

Trevor cocked his head in the direction of the front page of the newspaper, which was lying near the phone on his desk. "See for yourself," he invited with a dark scowl.

Ashley crossed the room, reached for the paper and as her eyes scanned the headlines her stomach began to knot painfully. "Oh, my God," she whispered when she found the article about Trevor. The by-line indicated that the story had been written by Elwin Douglass, the young reporter who had accosted her at Pioneer Square just the previous afternoon. Ashley felt her knees beginning to buckle and she had to lean against the bookcase for support.

The article was a scandalous piece of yellow journalism about Trevor and his affair with the daughter of Lazarus Stephens, who was currently president of Stephens Timber Corporation. Slanted in such a manner as to present the worst possible image of Trevor, the story, which had fragmented pieces of the truth woven into a blanket of lies, suggested that Ashley and Trevor had been lovers

for the past eight years, even during her brief marriage to
Richard Jennings.

Ashley swallowed against the nausea rising in her
throat. There were enough facts within the text of the article to make the report appear well researched. It would
be blindingly obvious to any reader that someone close to
the story had been interviewed.

The premise of the article was that since Trevor was so
close to his own family's business, as well as entrapped
in a relationship with Ashley Stephens Jennings, of Stephens Timber, he couldn't possibly support a campaign
of wilderness protection and environmentalism with any
modicum of sincerity in his bid for the senate.

The truth of the matter is, the article concluded, *that our
would-be senator spends more time with people closely
associated with business and industry than with the environmentalists who support him. Trevor Daniels seems to
be able to speak out of both sides of his mouth with great
ease and little conscience.*

Ashley's face had drained of color and she was trembling by the time she finished reading the condemning
article. "This is all a lie," she said, shaking the crumpled
paper in the air indignantly.

"You can thank dear cousin Claud for that," Trevor replied, pacing the floor.

"Dear God, I'm so sorry," Ashley whispered, lowering
her head into her palm.

"For what? Being related to that bastard? You didn't
have much choice in the matter."

"No, you don't understand. I don't think Claud was
behind this. Yesterday, at Pioneer Square—I had gone
there to look for you, and when you didn't show up, I approached Everett…."

Trevor's head snapped up to look in her direction and
his dark gaze hardened. "Go on," he suggested. A cold

feeling of dread was beginning to steal over him. What was Ashley admitting?

She lifted her palms in a supplicating gesture before letting them fall to her sides in defeat. "When Everett left, I began to walk back to the office and this guy, Douglass, started walking with me and began asking questions. You know: Wasn't I Ashley Jennings? Didn't I know Trevor Daniels? Was it true that I was president of Stephens Timber? That sort of thing."

"And you talked to him?" The gleam in Trevor's eye was deadly.

"No! At least I tried not to. But he wouldn't stop walking with me...kept requesting an interview." She shook her head at her own folly. "I refused, of course, only answering his questions as briefly and politely as possible. I guess I didn't want to look like a snob. Anyway, he kept asking about an interview and I told him to talk to the office and make an appointment." She shrugged her slim shoulders. "It was stupid of me."

Trevor squeezed his eyes shut tightly and rubbed his temples. "So how did this guy know you would be there?"

"He couldn't have. I didn't tell anyone."

"Not even Claud?"

"He was out of town, remember, in Seattle talking to you."

"But he must have known. Somehow. Someone at the office must have told him."

"I don't think so. I wouldn't have gone to the rally if I thought he would find out about it."

"So you don't trust him either?" Trevor cocked a questioning black brow in her direction. A guarded secret lurked in his dark gaze.

"Of course not, at least not since we found the evidence against him. And one day I walked into his office and overheard him telling someone that...well, I don't know for sure if he meant you, he never said your name, but he said, 'We can't let that son of a bitch win....' When he saw me he pretended that the conversation was about an ad campaign, but—"

"You didn't believe him?"

"No."

"Unless I miss my guess, Claud's behind all this." The doorbell rang and Trevor frowned. "That must be Everett. Watch out, he's fit to be tied."

"Aren't you going to answer it?"

Trevor shook his head. "He has a key. He just rings the bell to warn me—"

"Why?"

A sly smile slanted across Trevor's handsome face and he trailed a familiar finger along the curve of her jaw. "Just in case I'm in bed with a beautiful woman."

"Give me a break."

"I'll give you more than that." His dark eyes penetrated the sadness in her gaze. "Buck up," he suggested, squeezing her shoulders fondly. She felt the strength and determination of his character in his touch. "We'll rise above all this political dirt."

"I don't see how." As far as Ashley was concerned, everything she'd hoped for, especially a future with Trevor, was slipping away from her. "Maybe you should tell me everything. Trevor, I know that something's bothering you—"

Everett Woodward stormed into the den in a rage. His face was puckered into a belligerent scowl that darkened when he saw Ashley. He tossed his briefcase and a copy of the *Morning Surveyor* onto the couch before glaring pointedly at Trevor.

"Well, that's it—the ball game," Everett announced without the civility of a greeting. "All that work and effort right down the proverbial drain."

"Don't you think you're overreacting?" Trevor interposed with a bitter smile.

"Overreacting? *Overreacting!*" Everett retorted, his round face going beet red. "For God's sake, man, your career is on the line here, and you have the audacity to suggest that I'm—"

"Jumping off the deep end."

Everett let out a long, bewildered breath. "What're you doing here?" he asked Ashley when he turned his attention away from Trevor and trained his furious light eyes on her. "Was this Claud's idea, too?"

"That's enough, Everett," Trevor warned. "Ashley's staying here." There was a fierceness in Trevor's voice that made Ashley shudder. His fingers, which had touched her lightly on the shoulder, gripped her more savagely, as if in proof of his possession.

"You're joking!"

"Not at all. We're going to get married as soon as possible."

"Not on your life! You can't; not now! The press will have a field day with the both of you," Everett exclaimed, stunned, his eyes widening behind thick glasses. He took hold of Trevor's sleeve and looked into the candidate's eyes. "Not now, Trevor. You can't associate with Ashley or anyone else at Stephens Timber without looking like a hypocrite. You've already lost points in the most recent polls. All those rumors about withdrawing from the race really hurt you, and now this." He pointed an outraged, shaking finger at the condemning newspaper on the couch. "The last thing you can do right now is announce an engagement to the president of Stephens Timber, for Christ's sake!"

"I said we're going to get married."

Everett was thinking fast when he turned pleading eyes upon Ashley. "Can't you talk some sense into him? What would waiting another year hurt? The campaign would be over—he'd be comfortable in Washington. You could get married then."

"Forget it, Everett. I've made my decision." Trevor's voice was firm; his determination was registered in the tight muscles surrounding his mouth.

"Oh, Lord," Everett said with a sigh. He sunk into the soft cushions of the couch before swearing roundly. "I need a drink."

"It's only ten in the morning—"

"Make it a double."

Trevor smiled at the campaign manager's pale complexion. "How about champagne? To celebrate?"

"Scotch."

Trevor laughed aloud and poured the portly man a stiff drink. Everett accepted it gratefully, took a long swallow and sighed audibly. "I don't suppose you'll name your first child after me, will you?" He raised his sheepish eyes in Ashley's direction.

"We'll see," she said with a smile, relieved that the tense confrontation had abated.

"You're serious about this, aren't you?" Everett asked Trevor.

Trevor cast a meaningful smile at Ashley. "More serious than I've ever been in my life."

"Even if it means losing the election?"

"No matter what."

Again Everett let out a defeated sigh. "Well, just for the record, I think this is political suicide. You're going to alienate every voter in this state. And if you think today's article was bad, just you wait. The press will cut you to ribbons and make today's story seem like a piece of cake.

"Just for once, it would be nice if you would do things the conventional way." He looked at Trevor's thick, unruly hair, the faded jeans and the cotton shirt with the rolled-up sleeves. "But then you never do, do you?"

Trevor crossed his arms over his chest and frowned at his campaign manager and friend. "Do you want to resign?"

Everett weighed the decision. "No. At least not yet, unless you'd rather have someone else."

"Don't be ridiculous." Trevor forced a smile that was as charming as it was self-effacing. "Who else would put up with me?"

"No one in his right mind."

"Good." Trevor clasped Everett's hand. "Then everything's settled."

"I wouldn't say that." Everett wiped the accumulation of sweat that beaded his balding head. "Oh, hell. Let's go over campaign strategy, what little there is left of it."

The two men discussed politics on the leather couch in the study while Ashley poured them each a cup of coffee. After she had placed the cups on the scarred oak table, Trevor took hold of her wrist and forced her to sit next to him before asking her opinion on several issues.

Never one to withhold her opinions, Ashley pointed out what she considered flaws in the campaign, and even Everett had to grudgingly agree with some of her opinions. More than once, out of the corner of her eye, she caught Everett silently nodding encouragement to her, while she explained her feelings regarding Trevor's campaign and the issues.

Trevor smiled at her continually and attacked Everett's arguments calmly. He explained that he wasn't against the timber industry as a whole. How could he be? Daniels Logging Company was a part of his heritage. He only objected to some of the shady business practices of a few of the companies, a prime example being Stephens Timber.

"I still think you should wait to announce your engagement," Everett offered, a hopeful light showing in his eyes.

"At least until after the primary. Once you're the party's candidate—"

"No dice."

"But with this article and all, it might look as if you're buckling under to bad press."

"I don't care how it looks."

"All right, all right," the campaign manager said in utter defeat. "Have it your way—you always do anyway." He snapped his briefcase closed and sighed. The round man left the house shaking his balding head.

"Maybe you should listen to him," Ashley suggested, once Everett had driven away and Trevor had closed the door to take her into his arms.

"Why start now?"

"I'm serious—"

"So am I." They were standing in the foyer of the large house. Thin shafts of wintry sunlight pierced through the long windows on either side of the door. The strong arms around her tightened.

"Look, lady, you're not weaseling out of this marriage no matter how hard you try."

"But your career—"

"Can go to hell if it means I have to knuckle under to the Claud Stephenses of the world. I'm sick and tired of worrying about how anything I do will reflect on my political image. I like to think that I learn from my mistakes, and I'm not about to repeat them. You're going to be my wife come hell or high water!"

"As if I don't have any say in the matter."

"You said plenty last night," he reminded her, kissing her tenderly on the lips. A warm rush of desire began to flow through her.

Ashley smiled and shook her head. Being in Trevor's arms made concentration on anything but his exciting touch impossible. "So what are we going to do about Claud?"

The smile that spread slowly across Trevor's face was positively sinful. He reached behind her and grabbed two coats from the curved spokes of the brass hall tree. After helping her with her down-filled garment, he slid his arms into a denim jacket.

"I doubt that we'll have to worry about Claud much longer," Trevor stated cryptically as he led her out of the front door and draped his arm over her shoulders.

"What have you done?"

"Something I should have done about six months ago. I hired a private investigator." They walked along a brick path leading around the great house toward the river. "He's been on the case for about a month, I guess."

"And that's who you were talking to last night," Ashley suddenly realized. Perhaps now he would explain everything and drive away the lingering doubts in her mind.

"Right." Trevor winked broadly. "With what this guy has found out on his own and the evidence you and John Ellis supplied, I think we'll have enough proof of Claud's illegal activities to lock him up for a while."

"If he doesn't get to you first."

"I'm not too worried about that." Taking her chilled hand in his, he led her to the banks of the silvery Willamette. The wind on the water was brisk, causing whitecaps to swell on the swiftly flowing current. Trevor leaned against the trunk of a barren maple tree and placed his arms securely around her waist. She leaned against him, feeling the warmth of his body surrounding hers while the chill winter wind blew against her face.

"This isn't going to be easy for you, you know," he suggested. "Claud will make it rough. How will you feel if you have to testify against him?"

She shrugged her shoulders. "I don't know. I guess I'll have to wait and see how involved he is."

"Oh, he's involved all right. Right up to his scrawny mustache."

Ashley closed her eyes and fought against any feelings of sympathy she might harbor for her cousin. "You know there's no love lost between us. I swear that he wanted to kill me when he found out that Dad hadn't disinherited me as the rest of the family had thought. I was hoping that he would learn to live with the fact that I own the majority of shares of the corporation, but…" She sighed and shrugged her slim shoulders. "I doubt if he'll ever really accept that I'm his boss. It's hard for him, but that's no excuse for what he's put you through. I just kept him on the payroll because the company needed his expertise and because I wasn't sure that he had done everything you thought…. Now I know differently."

She felt the strain in Trevor's body and his arms circled her as if to protect her from all the evil and injustice in the world. Once again she had the feeling that there was something bothering him, a secret he was afraid to divulge. His cold lips brushed against the crook of her neck. "I think that you should leave," he cautioned.

The words hit her with the force of an arctic gale. Hadn't he just insisted that she marry him? "Leave—to go where?"

"Maybe you should go out of town, just for a couple of days. Until I get some things ironed out."

"But why?"

"Because the press is going to be all over me. And you. Everett wasn't kidding when he said that they'll put us through hell once they find out that we're going to get married. And when the story about Claud breaks—I doubt if either of us will have a minute's peace." He let out a weary gust of breath that misted in the frigid morning air. "As a matter of fact, I'll bet we get more than our share of visitors this afternoon. Everett said that several reporters had already tried to contact me at campaign headquarters. It's just a matter of time before they show up here."

"That may be true, but I'm not leaving," Ashley decided with a proud toss of her head.

"Haven't you listened to a word I've said?" Was there a thread of desperation in his words?

"And that's why I'm staying." She turned to face him and held his square jaw between her hands. "I'm tired of running from everything, including the truth. If I'm going to marry you, and you can be sure that I am, then I'd better get used to the occupational hazards of being a senator's wife."

"If I win."

"*When* you win."

A slow-spreading smile creeped over Trevor's handsome features and the sun seemed to radiate from the midnight blue of his eyes. "You're an incredible woman," he whispered, his throat feeling uncomfortably swollen. "And I don't want to do anything that would put you in jeopardy. I can't lose you, not again."

"You won't. Hey, I've seen my share of bad press," Ashley stated, thinking of all of the gossip surrounding her father and the family business, "and I think I can handle whatever they dish out."

"I can't talk you into leaving, just for a couple of days?"

"It would be a waste of your breath and my time."

"So you intend to stay."

"Forever," she said with a sigh as his arms crushed her against him.

Trevor pressed his lips against her black hair. "You may as well know that I'm not into long engagements."

"Neither am I." She clung to him and listened to the steady, comforting beat of his heart, knowing she could face anything the future had to offer, as long as she was with the man she loved.

"Then, next month. Or sooner."

She smiled against the coarse denim of his jacket. "We have plenty of time," she whispered as tears of happiness pooled in her eyes.

TWO HOURS LATER, after breakfast, the first reporter called. Trevor took the call, declined an interview, referred the reporter to Everett Woodward and slammed down the receiver.

"Well, it's started," he said, his piercing blue eyes holding her gaze. "If you want out, you better make a hasty exit."

"Not on your life."

Quickly she called Mrs. Deveraux to explain the situation, in case any reporters started looking for her. The fussy old woman burst into tears of happiness when Ashley mentioned that she and Trevor were going to be married.

"And here I was worried about you," Francine exclaimed, clucking her tongue. "I should have guessed that you never got over that man."

"It's not quite like it appears in the papers," Ashley stated, hoping to start rectifying the damage to her reputation that the *Morning Surveyor* had wrought.

"Of course it isn't. Who would believe a story like that?" Francine asked indignantly.

"No one, I hope. Look, I'll come back to the house later in the day and pick up a few of my things."

"Good. Then you can tell me all about it. Oh, I almost forgot," the housekeeper stated as an afterthought. "Your cousin has been calling this morning—"

"Claud?" Ashley asked, and Trevor, overhearing the name, whirled to face her. Every muscle on his face was pulled taut.

"He needs to talk to you."

"Isn't he still in Seattle?"

"Oh, no. He got back into town sometime last night, I think." Ashley was sure that Claud wasn't due back into town until the day after next, and from the deadly look in Trevor's eyes she felt instant dread.

"Did you tell him where I was?"

"Oh, no. I explained that you had gone shopping for the day and that I would give you his message."

"How did he take the news?"

"As usual. Not well."

"So things are normal," Ashley thought aloud, though the darkness in Trevor's eyes warned her that just the opposite was true. "I'll see you later."

After Ashley hung up, Trevor switched on the answering machine and began to pace from room to room like a caged animal, alternately surveying the telephone as if in indecision and then looking carefully out the windows to the long, asphalt drive.

"I take it that Claud's back in town," Trevor said, his hands pushing impatiently through his coarse hair.

"He's looking for me."

Trevor stopped midstride. "Damn! I knew I couldn't trust that bastard!"

Ashley put a hand on Trevor's forearm and found the muscles rigid. "What's going on?"

The telephone rang and the recorder automatically took the call. "You know, it wouldn't surprise me to find out that Claud called all the papers in town," Trevor remarked with an undertone of vengeance.

"You can't blame him for everything," Ashley replied with a frown.

Trevor took her hand and led her to the couch in the study. "I think it's about time you knew what we're up against," he said with obvious regret. "Pete Young, the private investigator I hired, looked into several things: the accident with my car, the bribery charges and—"

"Your father's disappearance," Ashley guessed with a shudder.

"Right. Now that the press is involved, it could get very unpleasant."

She smiled despite the dread inching up her spine. "I know." Settling into the corner cushions, Ashley tucked her feet beneath her and stared up at Trevor as he paced the floor.

"When I talked to Pete last night, he was sure that he had enough evidence to prove that Claud had paid to have my car tampered with. He found someone at the garage where my car was serviced who was willing to talk, for a small fee."

"So Claud paid off a mechanic to tamper with your car." Ashley felt sick inside, as if a part of her were slowly dying. She had thought her cousin capable of deceit, and bribery perhaps, but something this cold-blooded and cruel was beyond those bounds. "Dear God," she whispered, turning cold inside.

The corners around Trevor's mouth pulled downward. "According to Everett, Pete also thinks that Claud planted the story in the paper."

"But the reporter talked to me," Ashley offered tonelessly. Why was she even trying to defend her cousin?

"Because somehow he knew that you would be there, or maybe it was just a lucky guess on his part. It doesn't matter. I'll bet that Claud was involved."

Ashley lowered her forehead into her hands and gave in to the tears threatening her eyes. "I really didn't think it would all come down to this," she whispered. All the lies about her family and her father were really true.

Trevor sat on the couch beside her and kissed away the

lines etching her smooth brow. "We can handle it if we just stick together."

"I thought you wanted me to leave."

He took her hand and his eyes narrowed in concern. "I never want you to leave, but I think that it might be safer for you."

"Safer?" Her face suddenly lost all expression as the meaning of his words became clear and rang dully in her weary mind. "There's something you haven't been telling me, isn't there? A reason why you want me to go. Ever since I got here last night, I've had the feeling that there was something bothering you, as if there is some kind of danger lurking around every corner. It's more than concern about your reputation or even losing the senatorial race, isn't it?

"Trevor, what's going on? And don't give me any double talk about reporters and mudslinging." Her face was grave. "I want the truth. All of it. And I want it now."

Trevor let out a weary sigh and touched her cheek tenderly before lowering his eyes.

"What did Claud say, Trevor? When I came here last night you said something to the effect that you never thought you'd see me again. At the time, I thought you were talking about the scandal, but it's more than that, isn't it?" She noticed him wince and pale and a wave of understanding washed over her in cold rushes of the truth. Everything, all of Trevor's actions, were beginning to make sense. "Oh my God…Claud threatened you, didn't he? *And…the price was my life!*"

CHAPTER TWELVE

TREVOR CLOSED HIS eyes against the cold truth. His lips whitened and he swallowed back the savage rage that had been with him for the better part of two days.

"Yes," he ground out, as if the admission itself were tearing him into small pieces, making him impotent against the injustice of the world. "Claud told me point-blank that if I didn't get out of the race, you would get hurt."

"But he only meant that he would ruin my reputation," Ashley protested weakly.

Trevor's eyes glittered dangerously. "He meant that and more. He'd feed you to the wolves if it would save his skin."

"But surely you couldn't believe—"

"What I couldn't do was take a chance with your life. I know how ruthless your cousin can be. He nearly killed me by having my car tampered with, and I'll lay you odds that he was involved in my father's disappearance."

"But he was only twenty-two."

"And a very ruthless, determined man. He learned his lessons from the master well."

"Meaning my father." Ashley slumped against the cushions of the couch, wishing there was some way to end the pain, the agony, the bitterness and hatred between the families of Stephens and Daniels.

"Are you beginning to understand what we're facing?" he asked. "That's why I think you should go away. Just until Claud is safely behind bars and the press has cooled off a little."

Ashley shook her head. "It won't matter. If I did leave, the minute I'd get back to Portland, someone would hear about it and the reporters would start to track me down. That's how it works. If I left we'd only be putting off the inevitable. As for Claud, I'm not afraid of him. I told you before that violence isn't his style. If there's dirty work to be done, he'd hire someone else to do it, and I can't really believe that he's desperate enough to harm me.

"I'm staying and we're going to fight this thing together," she finished determinedly. A small, proud smile touched Trevor's lips. Having made her decision, she straightened, slipped on her shoes and stood.

Trevor was still considering the options. She noticed that the wariness hadn't left his eyes. "Then you're staying here, with me. That way, I'll know you're safe."

"I can't just sit around here like some fearful hostage. I've got a job—"

"With Claud."

"That will be rectified very shortly."

"Then stay with me for a couple of days—"

"Just that long?"

Trevor smiled despite his fears. "You're welcome forever, you know that. As far as going to work, forget it. You'd be too vulnerable."

"I can't—"

"Let that accountant take care of things."

"For how long?"

"As long as it takes for the private investigator to put the pieces together and convince the police that Claud's dangerous."

"Oh, Trevor, you're jumping at shadows. Claud would never hurt me."

"That's a chance I'm not willing to take."

Seeing that there was no way she could convince him otherwise, she gave in. "In that case, I'd better dash home and pack a few things."

"I think it would be safer if you stayed here."

Ashley smiled indulgently. "I've lived in these clothes for two days. I need to change into something more practical than heels, a silk blouse and a skirt. I feel positively grody."

Trevor's eyes slid down her body. "You look great."

"But I feel sticky. Now, nothing you have here is going to fit, so I'd better go home and pack a few things. I'll be perfectly safe. Mrs. Deveraux is home; I just called her a few minutes ago."

"I don't know—"

"Give me a break, Trevor."

"All right. I'll come with you," he said finally, reaching for his wallet and stuffing it into his back pocket.

"I thought you had to stay here and wait for Everett's call."

"The recorder will take the message. Or, he'll call back."

"But—"

"You're stuck with me, okay? I've worried enough about you and I'm not about to let you out of my sight, not until I'm satisfied that you're not in any danger."

"Worrywart."

Trevor helped her with her coat and his fingers lingered on the back of her neck. "It's just that I can't take any chances," he said roughly, his voice catching on the words. "You're the most important thing in my life." Gently he touched her shoulders, forcing her to turn and face him. "Nothing else matters—my career, this house—" he gestured widely to encompass all of the estate "—nothing. Unless you're with me."

"But for so many years—"

"I was alone. I lived, Ashley, and I thought I could bury

myself in my work. I guess I was somewhat satisfied. But then in December, when I saw you again, I knew that I'd been living a lie and that I could never go back to that empty life again."

"But you didn't call, or write. I didn't hear anything from you."

"Because I knew that it would be no good until we settled what had happened in the past. And that included the truth about your family as well as mine."

Just as Trevor reached for the handle of the door, Ashley heard a car roar down the driveway.

"Damn," Trevor muttered. "Too late. Some reporter must have gotten tired of leaving a message with the recorder." His blue eyes pierced into hers. "Are you ready for this?"

Ashley braced herself and her fingers twined in the strength of his. "As ready as I'll ever be."

The doorbell rang impatiently several times and then a fist pounded furiously on the door.

"Not the most patient guy around," Trevor mumbled. "I've got a bad feeling about this."

He jerked open the door and Claud rushed into the foyer, his face ashen, his eyes dark with accusations when they rested on Ashley.

"Wait a minute," Trevor said, placing his body between that of Ashley and her cousin. "What're you doing here?"

"We had a deal," Claud spat out. Then he straightened, regained a small portion of his dignity and let his cold eyes rest on Ashley. "I thought I'd find you here."

"What do you want, Claud?"

"Call him off!" her cousin blurted furiously.

"Who? What?"

"Him!" Claud pointed an accusatory finger in Trevor's direction and it shook with the rage enveloping him. "That bastard's been hounding me for the last month."

"I think you should calm down—"

"And *I* think you should leave, while you still can." Trevor's eyes snapped.

Claud stopped abruptly. "What's that supposed to mean?"

"Just that we're on to you, Stephens."

Visibly paling, Claud turned to Ashley. "He's been telling you all sorts of lies, I suppose."

Ashley held out her palm, hoping to diffuse the uncomfortable tension. She never really had been afraid of her cousin and she couldn't really fear him now. Despite Trevor's accusations, Claud was too much of a coward to try to do her physical harm. "Why don't we all go into the living room and I'll make some coffee. We can discuss whatever it is we need to, once everyone has calmed down."

"I don't know…." Trevor said, his eyes calculating as he studied his opponent.

"I don't want any coffee—"

"Something stronger?" Ashley asked, watching Claud walk agitatedly back and forth in the foyer. She started toward the living room and Claud followed.

"I need to talk to you alone."

"Not on your life," Trevor boomed, falling into step with Ashley. "I'm not about to forget what you said a couple of days ago, something to the effect that Ashley was expendable and you were willing to do the expending."

"He's lying, Ash! I swear—"

"Don't waste your breath," Trevor suggested, and the look of steely determination in his eyes coupled with his tightly clenched fists convinced Claud to keep quiet.

Claud sank into one of the stiff royal blue chairs near the bay window and had to hold on to his knee to keep it from shaking. "There's been some guy following me, Ashley," he said, avoiding the deadly look on Trevor's face and concentrating on his cousin. "I don't know who or why, but I think that it's someone looking for information about the company. You know, there's kidnappings all the time—families with money."

"Don't flatter yourself," Trevor said with a cynical smile growing from one side of his face to the other. He sat next to Ashley on the couch, one arm curved protectively over her shoulders, the other at his side. He looked coolly disinterested, almost bored with the conversation, but he was tense, all of his muscles coiled. Ashley could feel it. If he had to, Trevor was ready to spring on Claud.

"I think someone might try to kidnap me, for God's sake!"

"Why? Who would pay the ransom?" Trevor demanded, his lips curling bitterly.

"Ashley, please. Can I talk to you alone?" Claud was beginning to sweat. Tiny droplets formed on his forehead and there was a note of desperation in his voice.

"Forget it."

"I can speak for myself," Ashley intervened, but Trevor would hear none of it. He leaned forward, pushing his body closer and more threateningly toward Claud.

"While we're on the subject of kidnappings, why don't we discuss what happened to my father," Trevor suggested, his voice low and demanding. "I have an idea that you know just what went on ten years ago."

Claud lost all his color. His bravado was dismantled and he suddenly looked like a very small and frightened man. Nervously, he toyed with his mustache.

Movement caught Trevor's eye and he looked from the scared face of Ashley's cousin through the window behind Claud. "It looks as if we have more company—"

"What?" Claud's gaze moved to the long drive and he saw the police car driving toward the house. "Oh my God…" Turning frantic eyes on Ashley, he whispered, "You can't let this happen. Daniels is trying to frame me for something that I had no part in. Ashley—for God's sake, you're my cousin, can't you help me?"

Ashley's throat was dry. No matter how miserable Claud was, he was still her own flesh and blood. The doorbell rang impatiently just as she answered. "I'll call Nick Simpson."

"Jesus Christ, Ash, I need more than an attorney!"

"Then I suggest you start talking, and fast," Trevor insisted, "if you want to save your miserable hide."

Trevor was convinced that Claud wouldn't do anything harmful to the one person he felt would save him. "Stay where you are," he warned as he left to answer the door.

Claud nearly leaped across the living room, so that he was close to Ashley. "I need to get out of here. I just want a little time, show me the back way out—"

"You can't escape like they do on TV, Claud. This isn't 'Magnum, P.I.'"

"But I haven't done anything—"

His words were cut off by the entrance of two policemen.

"Claud Stephens?" the taller of the two asked.

Claud made one more appealing look in Ashley's direction before straightening and finally finding his voice. "Yes?"

As Ashley sat in stunned disbelief, the officer read Claud his rights and escorted him outside to the waiting police car. For several minutes she sat on the couch, trying to quell the storm of emotions raging within her.

"Was that really necessary?" she asked, her eyes searching the harsh angles of Trevor's face once he returned to the living room.

"I wish it weren't," he admitted, "but whether you believe it or not, Claud can be dangerous." He noticed that Ashley had paled. She was still wearing her coat, but looked as if she were cold and dead inside.

"I don't think we should go anywhere, not for a while." He came back to the couch and wrapped comforting arms around her. "Come on," he said, squeezing her tightly, "I'll get you a drink."

"I...I don't think I want one."

"It's been a rough couple of days, and it's bound to get worse," he cajoled.

"Then I think I'd better keep my wits about me." She ran her anxious fingers through her blue-black hair. "And there's no reason to put off going back to the house, now that the police have Claud." She forced her uneasiness aside and tried to concentrate on Trevor and her love for him. Regardless of anything that might come between them in the future, she felt secure in his love.

"I don't think it would be wise—"

Ashley placed a steady finger to his lips. "Shhh. If I'm going to be your wife, Senator, I'd better learn to cope with crises, wouldn't you say?"

"It's going to get worse before it gets better."

"But that's what it's all about, isn't it—for better or for worse?"

"You are incredible," he said with a seductive smile.

She slapped him on the thigh and stood up, filled with renewed conviction. "Let's get a move on. I wouldn't want to miss the reporters when they get here."

Trevor groaned, but got off of the couch. "Anything you say." He laughed and kissed her lightly on the forehead.

WHEN THEY RETURNED to Trevor's home, after having tea and a lengthy discussion with Mrs. Deveraux, Trevor checked the messages on the tape recorder. As he had suspected, several reporters had called requesting interviews. There was also a terse message from Everett to call him immediately.

Trevor dialed Everett's number and smiled wickedly as the agitated campaign manager answered.

"I thought you were going to wait for my call," Everett complained. Trevor could picture steam coming out of the campaign manager's ears.

"I had other things on my mind…." Trevor's eyes slid appreciatively up Ashley's body. Dressed in jeans and a red sweater, with her black hair looped into a loose braid wound at the base of her neck, she looked comfortable and at home in Trevor's huge house.

"I'll bet," Everett replied. "Now that you and Ashley are together, you'll never be able to keep your mind on the campaign."

"That would be a shame," Trevor murmured irreverently as his eyes followed Ashley up the polished wooden stairs. She was carrying two suitcases, oblivious to his stare or the fact that her jeans were stretched provocatively over her behind as she mounted each step.

"Listen, there are a couple of things you really should know," Everett commanded. "And they have to do with Ashley and Stephens Timber."

The low tone of Everett's voice and the mention of Ashley's name captured Trevor's attention. "I'm listening."

"You'd better brace yourself," Everett warned. "Claud Stephens has started to talk…."

ASHLEY FELT HIS eyes on her back as she unfolded the last blouse and hung it in the closet. She whirled to face Trevor, a sly smile perched on her lips. "What took you so long?" she asked, but the wicked grin fell from her face when she saw Trevor's expression. He was leaning against the door-frame, watching her silently and fighting the overwhelming urge to break down. "What happened?"

She was beside him in an instant, placing her warm

hands against his face. He managed a bitter smile filled with grief.

"The case against Claud looks pretty solid," Trevor said at length, while gazing into the misty depths of her sea-green eyes. "The private investigator I hired called Everett when he couldn't reach me."

"And?"

"Claud's having a rough time. He can't seem to make up his mind whether he needs an attorney or should plea-bargain on his own. I think he opted for the lawyer."

"I hope so," Ashley said fervently. "Claud's used to doing things his own way, and since he's a lawyer I was afraid he would try to defend himself."

"He's smarter than that." Trevor entered the room and sat down on the edge of the bed. His shoulders sagged and he forced tense fingers through his unruly chestnut hair.

"What else?" Ashley asked as she sat next to him. She felt her throat constrict with dread. Something horrible had happened to Trevor. *What?*

Trevor's midnight-blue eyes pierced into hers and his arms wrapped around her as if in support. "Claud's desperately trying to clear his own name, you realize."

"And?"

"And he's saying that Lazarus is the one who instigated the bribery charges against me last summer as well as having kidnapped my father ten years ago."

Ashley felt as if a hot knife had been driven into her heart. She slumped for a minute, but Trevor's strong arms gripped her. "It's not unexpected," she said, her voice failing her. "It's just that I hoped and prayed that Dad wasn't involved." She let out a long breath of air and realized that she had to know everything before she could start her life with Trevor.

"What happened?"

"Claud's saying that my father had gained information

proving that Lazarus had used the harmful pesticide near Springfield—the one that's subsequently been linked to the deaths."

"I remember." Ashley fought against the sick feeling deep within her. Dennis Lange had been a friend of Trevor's and had died because of her father's neglect. His was just one of several families who had been inadvertently poisoned by the spraying.

"Claud seems to think that Lazarus knew what the impact of the spraying would be and the hazards it would impose on the residents as well as the environment. Lazarus panicked when he found out that my father was meeting with the lobbyist in Washington, and after the meeting, he coerced him into his car. They drove to your father's cabin—"

"No!" Not the place where she and Trevor had made love. "Not the cabin."

Trevor's hold on her shoulders increased. "Lazarus tried to buy my father's silence, and an argument ensued. Dad tried to escape from the cabin and he fell down an embankment, probably breaking his neck. Lazarus was afraid that he would be up on kidnapping, bribery and probably negligent homicide charges, so he buried my father somewhere on his land in the Cascades."

"Oh dear God," Ashley murmured, seeing the bitterness in Trevor's features. "Trevor... I'm so sorry, so sorry," she murmured, releasing the hot tears that had burned behind her eyelids and letting them trickle slowly down her face.

"It's not your fault—"

"But I never believed—I couldn't face it."

Gathering strength from the warmth of her body, Trevor let out a long, trembling sigh. "I knew Dad was dead, you know. I just kept hoping that I'd been wrong, that someday he'd show up again. But deep in my heart, I knew."

The news was too distressing for Ashley. She extricated

herself from Trevor's embrace, walked across the room and stared out the window to the clear, ever-changing waters of the Willamette River.

"I knew that my father wasn't a warm person. And I might have even gone so far as to say that he was unthinking and therefore unkind. But I never thought of him as cruel or ruthless." She shook her head and let the tears of pain slide down her cheeks. "There's not much I can do except make a settlement with those poor victims in Springfield. It won't bring back the dead, but maybe it will help their children." Her shoulders stiffened with newfound pride. "And I'll make sure that Stephens Timber Corporation complies with every government and environmental standard as long as I'm involved," she promised.

When she walked back toward the bed, Trevor was staring at her, admiring her strength. He captured her wrist and pulled her down on the bed with him before offering kisses born of sorrow and grief.

"Don't ever leave me," he begged.

"Never...oh, darling." She kissed him with all the fervor her torn emotions could provide. "It's all behind us now."

The telephone rang and Trevor eyed it with disgust. "Go away," he muttered.

"It's the private line. You'd better answer it."

"It could be more bad news."

She smiled through the sheen of her tears. "Then we'll face it together." Hastily brushing her tears aside, she curled against him, feeling more loved and protected than ever.

He frowned and answered the intrusive instrument.

"You and that damned recording machine!" Everett blasted. "I hate talking to those things. I just thought I'd better warn you, the press has gotten hold of Claud's story."

"I expected as much."

"Bill Orson is in a near-panic. You know he was pretty

tight with Claud and the rest of the timber industry. Orson
has already begun amending his stand on the environment
and it looks to me that despite everything, you still have a
good chance of winning the election. Orson's been in too
tight with Claud Stephens to come out clean on this one."

"Good."

There was a stilted silence in the conversation. "You're
still in the running, aren't you?" Everett asked.

"I'll let you know tomorrow...or maybe next week,"
Trevor replied, looking meaningfully at Ashley. "Right
now I'm busy, Everett."

"What the devil?"

"How would you like to be best man at my wedding?"

"Today?"

Trevor laughed aloud. "Very soon, Everett, very soon."
With his final words, he dropped the phone and took Ashley into his arms.

"Everett's not going to appreciate being treated like
that," she teased.

"I don't give a damn what Everett appreciates." Slowly
he removed the pins holding her hair at the nape of her
neck. "Right now there's only one person I intend to sat-
isfy."

"Your constituents wouldn't like to hear that kind of
talk, Senator," she quipped.

"Oh, I don't know...I think it would improve my image
if I were to become a happily married man."

"So this is just for the sake of the voters?"

"One in particular—she's very independent, you see."
He unclasped the top button of her blouse. "But that may
change once she's saddled with a husband and a family."

"A child?" Ashley asked, her breathing becoming irregular.

"Or two...or three." As he counted, he undid the buttons of her blouse and kissed the white skin at the base

of her throat. Ashley's heart began to swell in her chest at the thought of becoming Trevor's wife and bearing his children.

"You're very persuasive, you know," she whispered.

"Years of practice, darling."

She smiled up at the man she loved. "Do you think this will ever work for us?" she asked. "There's been so much keeping us apart."

"All in the past," he assured her. "I told you I was never going to let go of you again, and I meant it." He touched the soft slope of her cheek. "Believe me when I tell you that I love you."

"Oh, I do, Trevor," she said with a sigh. She wound her arms around his neck, never to let go.

* * * * *

IN HONOR'S SHADOW

PROLOGUE

"HAVE YOU PUT it on yet?" Honor called from the adjacent bath.

"Just about." Frowning a little, Brenna Douglass tied the shoulder strap of the sundress her sister had given her just a half hour before. Made of peach-colored crinkly cotton, the dress hung a little in the bust, nipped in at the waist and billowed past her knees. Brenna adjusted the strap and the gaping material fitting her bust line. "There!"

"Let me see!"

Honor poked her head into the bedroom and her blue eyes gleamed. "You look sensational, Bren!"

"Thanks—and thanks again for the dress."

"Believe me, you're welcome," Honor said with a wink. "It'll knock Craig's socks off!"

Brenna blushed. She didn't want to think about Craig Matthews. Everyone, including Honor, thought she loved him. But she didn't. In fact, if Honor or their father had dared guess what her true feelings were... She swallowed and felt ashamed of herself. "Craig probably won't notice."

"Sure he will. Trust me. I know what men like. And that—" she pointed at the gown "—beats jeans and a T-shirt any day."

"I just hope you didn't spend too much money."

Honor ducked back into the bathroom. "Don't worry about it," she said over the sound of running water. "I'll only be in hock until I'm thirty." Then she laughed and Brenna relaxed a little. She adored the dress and thought Honor must have paid more than she should have for it. That was why Brenna was a little suspicious. Her older sister usually had strings attached to every little gift.

But this was different. The dress was her birthday present.

"Hey, Bren?" Honor called as the faucets creaked off.

Brenna's doubts nagged and she sank onto Honor's bed. "Yeah?"

"Do you think you could do a little favor for me?"

Here it comes. "It depends," she said cautiously. She picked up her old journalism textbook and thumbed through its worn pages. "What do you want?"

"Nothing much," Honor said. "I just want you to tell Warren that I'm with Sally."

Brenna's stupid heart hammered. "What? Where?"

"It doesn't matter. Say the library."

"What're you and Sally planning?"

"Nothing—I'm going out with Jeff."

Brenna wanted to disappear. Caught between the proverbial rock and a hard place, she tossed the book onto the nightstand and stared up at the tattered canopy, her thoughts centered on Warren Stone, dreaming of him as she had all summer long. She knew that he didn't love her, never could. After all, he was in love with her sister, and Brenna realized that she would never be anything more than a pale reflection of the beautiful Honor.

Frowning up at the yellowed canopy, Brenna listened to Honor pleading from the connecting bathroom.

"Come on, Brenna, you can do it for me. I'll pay you back someday. Promise! Besides, it's just a little lie."

Brenna's lips curved down. She had never been a good

2 FREE BOOKS
ABSOLUTELY FREE • GUARANTEED

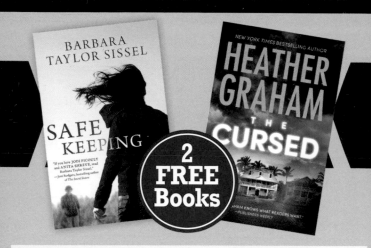

We'd like to send you another 2 excellent reads from the series you're enjoying now **ABSOLUTELY FREE** to say thank you for choosing to read one of our fine books, and to give you a real taste of just how much fun the Harlequin™ reader service really is. There's no catch, and you're under no obligation to buy anything — EVER! Claim your 2 FREE Books today.

Plus you'll get 2 FREE Mystery Gifts (worth about $10)!

Pam Powers
for Harlequin Reader Service

FREE

VALUE:	COMBINED BOOK COVER PRICE:	POSTAGE DUE:
	Over $10 (US) / Over $10 (CAN)	$0

COMPLETE YOUR POSTCARD AND RETURN IT TODAY!

Plus 2 FREE Mystery Gifts!

2 FREE BOOKS

ABSOLUTELY FREE • GUARANTEED

CLAIM YOUR FREE GIFTS

YES! Please send me my **2 FREE BOOKS** and **2 FREE GIFTS.** I understand that, as explained on the back of this card, I am under no obligation to purchase anything!

Affix sticker here

M-8801-0792-MG

191/391 MDL GGCA

FIRST NAME	LAST NAME

ADDRESS

APT.#	CITY

STATE/PROV.	ZIP/POSTAL CODE

♦ HARLEQUIN™ READER SERVICE — Here's How It Works:

BUSINESS REPLY MAIL
FIRST-CLASS MAIL   PERMIT NO. 717   BUFFALO, NY

POSTAGE WILL BE PAID BY ADDRESSEE

HARLEQUIN READER SERVICE
PO BOX 1867
BUFFALO NY 14240-9952

NO POSTAGE
NECESSARY
IF MAILED
IN THE
UNITED STATES

If offer card is missing write to: Harlequin Reader Service, P.O. Box 1867, Buffalo NY 14240-1867 or visit www.ReaderService.com

liar. Any time she tried to tell even the tiniest white lie her cheeks flamed and her words tripped over her tongue. Warren would see right through her.

"I can't do it, Honor," she decided, turning her face to the open bathroom door.

"Why not?" Honor appeared in the doorway. Her glossy blond hair shimmered in the lamp glow and her blue eyes were wide with practiced innocence.

"Because it's not the truth!"

"Come on, Brenna, loosen up. It's no big deal." As she walked out of the bathroom, she lifted her hair off her neck and began braiding her thick locks into a single golden plait. Her lips drew into a knot of vexation, her fingers fumbling as she had trouble adjusting a rubber band near the end of her braid. She noticed Brenna's sandals on the old quilt. "Hey—no shoes on my bed. Listen, help me with this braid, will ya?" Honor perched on the edge of the mattress.

Kicking off her sandals, Brenna sat up and snapped the rubber band into place. "Why lie?"

"Lie?" Honor repeated.

Brenna wanted to scream. *How could Honor do this to Warren? How?* "Yes, lie—to Warren about where you're going."

Honor rolled her large eyes in exasperation and double-checked her hair in the oval mirror perched high over the old mahogany dresser. The mirror was cracked, but Honor's reflection was still radiant. "Because I don't want to hurt his feelings, silly!"

"Warren loves you," Brenna whispered, and the admission tore at her soul.

Smiling to herself, Honor tossed her head, then applied a sheen of gloss to her already-pink lips. "He just thinks he does."

"He wants to marry you," Brenna pointed out stonily.

It hurt her the way Honor treated Warren as if his feelings didn't really matter. In Brenna's opinion, Warren was handsome and clever and nearly perfect. Unfortunately, she'd already lost her heart to him long before he'd started dating Honor. But, of course, she'd never said a word, couldn't admit how she felt.

"Hogwash!" Honor graced her younger sister with her easy grin and a tiny dimple creased her cheek. "I'm not going to marry anybody—at least not until I'm finished with modeling school. Then I'm going to New York or maybe Paris," she added dreamily.

"So why don't you tell Warren?"

"I will…someday."

A horn blared outside and Honor ran to the window, drawing open the blinds. "It's Jeff. He's here!"

Brenna stared at her sister. What could Honor see in the likes of Jeff Prentice—a has-been high-school football star turned mill worker? Jeff was okay. But he was merely ordinary, especially compared with Warren, who was studying law at Lewis and Clark.

"Now, remember, tell Warren I'm at the library or over at Sally's."

"He'll never believe you're studying. You're not even in school anymore. You dropped out of college, remember? Why would you go to the library?"

Honor's smooth forehead puckered thoughtfully and her eyes grew sober. "Well, I don't care what you tell him. Just don't tell him I'm with Jeff. Okay?"

The horn blasted impatiently again and Honor started for the door but turned at the threshold. Her face had lost some of its impish light, her blue eyes turning serious. "Look, Brenna, I know you don't understand, and I know you really like Warren."

Brenna felt crimson heat climb up her neck and stain her cheeks. Had Honor guessed? Gathering her courage, she lifted her chin proudly and met Honor's worried gaze. "Warren's special," she admitted, her voice breathless.

"I know. I like him, too. A lot. And maybe someday I will want to marry him. But not now. I just want some fun in my life!" Her eyes clouded over and her smile faded. "Ever since Mama died—well, you know how dull it's been around here—like a tomb."

Brenna's throat felt thick. She didn't want to think of her mother's death nearly three years before. The old farmhouse seemed lonely and cold without Betsy Douglass's bright smile, mischievous eyes and kind words. Brenna still missed her mother horribly. So did Honor. As older sister, Honor had been forced to shoulder more responsibility than she could handle. Brenna could hardly fault her for wanting to have a little fun. But not at Warren's expense.

"I just want to kick up my heels a little bit, okay?" Leaning against the scarred doorjamb, Honor sighed. "Warren's too serious for me. He's always got his nose in some law book or newspaper, reading about trials and criminals, all that junk. Bor-ing! Besides," she admitted, her eyes crinkling at the corners, "I'm tired of doing everything Dad thinks I should—like marrying stuffy Warren Stone."

Brenna fought down a pang of jealousy. "Warren's not stuffy!" she said quickly, defending him. "He likes to ride horses and go backpacking in the mountains and…"

Honor's golden eyebrows shot up. "Hey, what's this? Are you president of the Warren Stone fan club or something?"

For the first time Brenna realized that Honor didn't really know Warren at all. "'Course not," she said, running her fingers along broken stitches in Honor's old quilt. "I was only pointing out that he likes to have fun, too. He's just ambitious."

"So who needs it?" Honor asked, lifting her palms. "I want to laugh and forget about everything around here.

You should, too. We've been trapped in this dreary house too long."

"I'm okay," Brenna said quietly.

"Are you?"

She seemed genuinely concerned and Brenna felt awful. If only Honor knew how Brenna dreamed of Warren.

Honor glanced out the window, sighed, then took the time to cross the room again and place her hand on Brenna's shoulder. "You should try to be happy, Bren. Mama's not coming back—there's nothing we can do about the fact that she's gone. And she wouldn't want us to be moping around. She'd want you to be happy. You were her favorite, you know."

Brenna's throat was so thick, she could barely whisper, "Like you're Dad's?"

"I guess," she admitted. Brenna sensed Honor had never enjoyed the role of being the apple of her father's eye. "But what I mean is, you need to think about yourself. Go out and have a good time. Call Craig and take in a movie. Forget about all this journalism stuff." She lifted Brenna's textbook from the nightstand and flung it disgustedly on the bed. The pages fluttered open and a note fell to the floor. Brenna's heart nearly stopped. The note was a love letter she'd started to write to Warren.

But Honor didn't notice. As if realizing there was no way she could get through to her younger sister, Honor pushed her bangs out of her eyes and left the room. Her footsteps clattered as she ran down the staircase.

Brenna heard the front door open, then slam shut. The timbers of the old farmhouse shook and windows rattled in their casings.

Releasing a long breath, Brenna stood and gazed out the open window. Lavender shadows stretched long across the dry lawn and weed-choked rose garden. Honor ran to Jeff's black sports car and climbed into the passenger seat.

"About time," he said, his voice loud in the still night air.

"Sorry—I had to sort things out with Bren."

"It's okay." Jeff slung one arm around Honor's shoulders, hugged her fiercely and kissed her hard on the lips. Brenna cringed, but didn't move, watching transfixed as Jeff held Honor close and shoved his new Corvette into gear. The convertible squealed out of the drive, sending a spray of gravel over the brown lawn.

How could Honor do this to Warren? Brenna wondered again, closing the blinds. Turning, she caught sight of her reflection in the cracked oval mirror. Her nose was straight but a little too long and her cheekbones, undefined. Her eyes were wide and hazel, a color that changed from green to gold depending upon the light. Though her features were even, they weren't particularly captivating, and her hair was a wild mass of mahogany curls that couldn't be controlled. The dark waves fell in complete abandon past her bare shoulders.

No, she decided, she'd never be as pretty as Honor—nor as heartless to anyone—especially Warren. She felt a little guilty about Craig. He did care for her. But tonight she intended to set him straight and explain that she wasn't interested in settling down in West Linn. She had plans and dreams and had been accepted at the University of California at Berkeley. Since she couldn't have Warren, she planned on making a career for herself.

Seeing her textbook lying face up on the bed, she started to reach for it, but stopped. She didn't feel like reading—not tonight. Tonight was special. She was eighteen, no longer a high-school girl, but a woman.

Some woman, she thought ruefully, *in love with your sister's boyfriend.* Disgusted with herself, she snatched the half-written love note from the floor and stuffed it into her pocket before snapping out the bedroom light and hurrying downstairs.

Even on the ground floor the air was sticky and hot, though all the windows were open and moths fluttered at the screens.

The TV was blaring from the den, but no light spilled through the doorway. Either her father had fallen asleep or he was watching his favorite programs alone in the dark, a practice he'd started after Mama's death.

A familiar pain cut through Brenna. All too clearly she remembered the day her mother had been stolen away in a screaming ambulance. Brenna had been only fifteen. The past three years had been difficult, but Honor had helped her through that rough period, holding the family together and shouldering responsibility too heavy for most girls her age.

No wonder Honor wanted a good time, Brenna decided. And Brenna owed Honor a lot. But she wasn't sure that debt included lying to Warren.

Barefoot, Brenna padded over the dull patina of the wooden hallway and into the kitchen. Pouring herself a tall glass of lemonade, she sighed. Would she ever stop loving Warren? She pushed open the rusty screen door to the back porch and smiled when she noticed Ulysses, her mother's old lop-eared collie, on his favorite rug near the door. "Hot, isn't it?" she whispered, bending to scratch his ears.

Though October was just around the corner, Indian summer was still in full force. The grass was dry, the ground dusty.

Brenna sat on the edge of her mother's old porch swing, pushing off with her toe until it was rocking gently. She stared past the porch, through a thicket of oak to the Willamette River flowing sluggishly northward. The water was low. Bleached rocks and driftwood reflected ghost-like in the dusky twilight. Drought had claimed the Willamette Valley and there seemed no escape from the heat.

Her thoughts wandered to Warren, as they had for most of the summer and into September. Even though she was about to start college, she felt like a kid, especially around him. Waving off a bothersome mosquito hovering near her ear, she wondered how she could ever lie to Warren and knew in her heart that she couldn't. This time, Honor had asked too much.

Maybe, she thought, she should take Honor's advice and think about herself. Maybe she should risk her pride and admit to Warren just how she felt about him.

Nervously she lifted her glass of lemonade to her lips. Never in her eighteen years had she been impulsive or bold. But tonight she couldn't help herself. She loved Warren Stone so fervently that she could barely think when he was around. And Honor didn't care a whit about him.

Biting down on her lower lip, she glanced through the open kitchen window to the clock mounted over the stove and noticed that he was already late. What if he'd changed his mind and wasn't driving over? Just because Honor had said that Warren would be dropping by didn't necessarily mean he would.

What if she didn't have the nerve to tell him? Or, worse yet, what if she admitted how she cared for him and he laughed in her face?

Her palms were wet and her throat was desert-dry. A thin layer of moisture collected at the base of her throat and she felt it trickle down between her breasts.

The sound of tires crunching in the gravel drive made her heart stop for a second before it began to pound frantically again. Swallowing with difficulty, she listened, hearing the sound of a truck door slam, then footsteps scuffing on the old brick walk.

She could barely look up, but when she did, she saw Warren, tall and lean, his blue eyes as bright as ever, his hands stuffed into the pockets of faded jeans, mounting the two worn wooden steps of the back porch. His face was illuminated by a single, bare bulb over the door.

"Hi, Bren," he said, offering her his off-center smile and warm gaze.

"Hi." Her voice sounded weak.

"Honor around?"

Brenna closed her eyes. Her hands were shaking and she had to clamp them firmly around her glass. Obviously, he thought she was just a dumb little kid and her heart sank painfully at the thought. "No, uh, she's out."

His dark eyebrows rose slightly. "Out?"

Yes, out. Out with Jeff Prentice—the boy she's two-timed you with all along! She tried to say something, *anything,* but couldn't find her voice. It was caught somewhere between her throat and her lungs. His incredible blue eyes were piercing into hers and she couldn't lie. Not even for Honor.

"Out where?" he asked quietly, his jaw working slightly.

"I, uh, don't know."

"Didn't she say?"

Biting her lower lip, Brenna tried to sound convincing. "She said to tell you she'd be at the library—with Sally. That's it!"

"Studying?"

"I guess."

"For what?"

"I don't know!" she snapped, knocking over her glass. Cold lemonade spilled on her sundress, seeping through the soft cotton fabric as her glass clunked to the floor, rolling noisily to Warren's feet.

He grabbed it and placed it on the sill of the open kitchen window. His eyes narrowed a bit and he crossed his arms over his broad chest. "The library," he repeated thoughtfully. "Maybe I could catch her there."

"No!" *Oh, God, now what could she do?*

"Why not?"

Scrambling in her mind for the right words, she said simply, "She might have left by now. I—I don't think she was staying late."

"Then I'll wait," Warren decided, seating himself next to her on the swing. It swayed with his weight.

Brenna thought she would die. He was so close. Her fingers knotted nervously around the chain supporting the swing and she tried not to notice that his long, jeans-clad leg nearly brushed her own. He didn't say a word, just stared past the peeled paint on the railing to the slow-moving river beyond.

She glanced at him furtively, saw that his thick brows were drawn low over his eyes, that his jaw was tight and set, that his gaze was distant. *As if he didn't even know she was sitting next to him.* His features were sharp—no longer boyish, his lashes full and straight, his lips thin but sensual.

Gazing at him, she felt young and foolish. So she was eighteen. Big deal. After all, he was twenty-four—a second-year law student. *And, if her father's plans went right, soon to be Honor's fiancé.*

She had to get away, find some excuse to put some distance between them before she did something she'd regret for the rest of her life. Rising quickly to her feet, she asked, "Would—would you like a glass of lemonade?"

He shrugged. "Sure." But he didn't even look her way.

Disheartened, she walked into the kitchen. She could hear her father in the next room. The television was still blaring but was accompanied by the familiar drone of James Douglass's loud snores.

Her hands shook as she poured icy lemonade into a glass. She would never tell Warren she loved him. She didn't have the nerve. She wasn't as comfortable around boys as Honor was.

He was standing near a post, still gazing distantly across the river, when she walked back through the screen door.

"Here."

"Thanks." He took the glass from her hand, but didn't lift it to his lips. Instead he leaned one hip against the weathered rail and stared directly at her. "Now, Brenna," he said slowly, his voice barely audible, "why don't you tell me why you're lying?"

"L-lying? About what?" She couldn't meet the intensity of his gaze.

"About Honor. Where is she?" When she started to tell him about the library again, he set his glass deliberately on the rail and pressed one strong finger gently to her lips. "And this time you can tell me the truth. She's not at the library—I was just there."

"Maybe...maybe you missed her."

His lips twisted wryly. "I don't think so." His hand dropped to her bare shoulder.

Brenna could hardly breathe. The air was trapped in her lungs and she was hot, her skin flushed in the soft glow of the porch light.

"She's with Jeff Prentice again, isn't she?" he guessed, the skin over his cheeks growing taut.

"I—I don't know." But she lowered her eyes. His thumb was at her chin again, lifting it slightly, forcing her gaze to his.

"You do know."

For a breathless instant, she thought he might kiss her, thought she read a flicker of passion in his eyes, but his desire, if that's what it was, quickly turned to pain. As if suddenly aware of the tension thick between them, he let his hand fall. His shoulders were stiff with pride and he stared across the river. "Damn her," he swore, one fist balling to crash against the side of the house. Paint chips fell onto

the floorboards of the porch. Ulysses growled and somewhere in the surrounding woods, a startled owl hooted.

"You know?" she whispered.

"Of course I know." He glanced at her from the corner
of his eyes. "The whole damned town knows! She's playing me for a fool—has been for months."

"No, I'm sure she really cares—"

"About what?" he demanded, eyes narrowing in the
darkness. "Me?" Before she could answer, he laughed, a
hollow sound that made her cold inside. "Don't bother defending her, Brenna—believe me, I'm smarter than I look.
I guess I've known it all along."

Swearing under his breath, he started down the stairs.

"Warren—wait!" Without thinking, she bunched her
skirt in her fist and ran after him. Her bare feet caught on
the weeds and dry grass poking stubbornly through the
brick path, and her new dress tangled in the thorns of her
mother's overgrown roses. But she didn't care.

When he turned, she nearly collided with him and she
stumbled. But he caught her, breaking her fall by placing his hands firmly over her upper arms. "What is it,
Brenna?" he asked.

Tongue-tied, she was lost in the anger in his gaze.

"Another lie?" he prodded.

"No—please, Warren, just listen." Dear God, could
she go through with it? Her heart was clamoring so loudly
against her ribs he could surely hear it. His face was only
inches from hers as they stood, touching, gazes locked,
beneath the spreading branches of a gnarled old oak tree
and a dusky lavender sky.

"What?" he demanded, his voice nearly gruff.

"I just wanted you to know that…that—" Closing her
eyes, she thought about the love letter hidden deep in her
pocket and she whispered in a rush, "That I love you."

He didn't move a muscle. Just stood there holding her

at arm's length as a soft, rose-scented breeze whispered through the dry leaves overhead. "You what?" he asked softly, in disbelief.

Trembling inside, she lifted her chin defiantly, met his incredulous, night-darkened eyes with her own. "I love you, Warren Stone," she admitted, her voice stronger than before.

"But Craig—"

"He's—he's just a friend."

Warren's face tensed and he looked away. "You don't know what you're saying."

"I do. I—I would have told you sooner, but I couldn't."

"Because of Honor," he guessed, his jaw a tight, white line in the darkness.

"And because I thought you might laugh at me," she said boldly, feeling his fingers flex.

"Oh, Brenna," he murmured, sighing heavily. Warm hands drew her close, encircling her waist possessively. "I'd never laugh at you." His breath tickled her ear. For a second his arms held her tight, forcing her cheek against the hard muscles of his chest. His soft cotton shirt rubbed against her skin.

His chin rested on her crown and she could hear the whisper of his breath in his lungs, feel the irregular beat of his heart.

"What am I going to do with you?" he wondered aloud.

Just love me. Love me as much as I love you!

He tilted up her chin, his gaze lingering in hers and then, before she had a chance to catch her breath, he lowered his head and slanted his warm lips over hers. Her heart took flight. His mouth was hard but gentle and his strong fingers tangled in her hair.

Yielding to a stronger force than she'd ever imagined, she met his kiss eagerly and innocently. She felt heat deep inside—a pulsing liquid fire that was as wondrous as it was hot. It spread through her blood and flushed her skin. She kissed him unashamedly, her arms twining around his neck.

Thoughts of Honor and the fact that in some small way she was betraying her sister's trust fled.

Never had she been kissed so thoroughly, never had her blood raced in wild, glorious abandon.

He groaned her name—a tortured solitary whisper as his lips traveled down the length of her neck to find the fluttering pulse at the base of her throat. "Brenna— Oh, God, no!"

And she felt his passion, rising hot and forbidden as he kissed her, one hand moving slowly against the soft cotton of her dress. Her knees went weak and the tips of her breasts ached for his touch.

"No," he repeated, his voice thick with regret. As swiftly as he had kissed her, he released her and stepped backward, nearly tripping in his haste. "Brenna," he said, disgust evidenced in his angular features, his blue eyes tortured and filled with self-loathing. "This *can't* happen."

"But I love you!" she cried, realizing that he was leaving her. He was walking backward, his eyes still locked with hers, his feet stumbling over rocks and bushes as he made his way to his pickup. Was it her imagination, or did she see longing in his gaze?

"You don't! Believe me, you don't want to. You've got your whole life ahead of you. Remember? You're going to go to college, become a reporter, do all those things you've been talking about for years. Good God, you're just a kid—"

"I'm eighteen," she said staunchly.

"Sweet Jesus," he muttered.

"I love you," she cried desperately.

He hesitated, then swore again. "You don't know the meaning of the word. And what about Craig?"

"But I want you."

He stopped, palms raised when he sensed she might follow. "Listen to me, damn it," he said angrily. "You're too young. This *never* happened!"

"Warren, please—" But her voice was weak, the blush on her cheeks now a wash of embarrassment at the profound and bitter wound of his rejection. She suddenly knew the disgust twisting his features was aimed at her and she realized, much too late, what he was saying—that he didn't want to use her as a convenient replacement for his one true love. *Honor.*

Tears stung her eyes. Why had she thrown herself at him? What had she expected?

"You deserve more than this," he said, half in apology as he climbed into his father's old truck and started the engine.

"I only want you…." But he couldn't hear her quiet plea as his truck roared out of the driveway and sped into the night, red taillights winking behind.

Brenna was left alone and bereft, standing barefoot on the hard gravel drive. Though she fought the urge to cry, tears of shame and regret drizzled slowly down her cheeks to drop onto her bare shoulders—shoulders that had so recently been warm beneath Warren's fingers.

Dashing the stupid tears away, she turned toward the house and noticed a shadow filling the open kitchen window and the red glow of the tip of a cigarette. *No!* Her heart began to pound with dread and she stopped dead in her tracks, her shame magnified a hundred times.

The old lace curtains billowed with the breeze as her father, his face set and stern, stepped into the filmy glow of the porch light. Obviously, James Douglass had witnessed her declaration of love for Warren—the man he hoped would become a husband for her sister.

"Brenna?" he reproached.

"Dad, please. Just listen—"

"Listen?" he repeated, incredulous. "I think I've heard more than I should have. And I pray to almighty God that I'll never hear the likes of *that* again."

"But—"

"Just remember who you are, Brenna. Warren Stone is your sister's!"

"She doesn't want him," Brenna cried.

James Douglass sighed and drew on his cigarette. "That's the problem, ain't it? She doesn't know what she wants," he said. "But she will—just you wait and see. Give her time. And when she finally comes around, you can bet that Warren will be waitin' for her."

Brenna felt hot tears fill her eyes as her father crushed his cigarette onto the porch. "Don't you know that he'll never love you—not the way he loves Honor? That's not what you want, is it? To fill in for your sister?"

Brenna's shoulders began to shake.

"Oh, Brenna, find someone who loves you for who *you* are."

"Like Craig Matthews?" she flung out, trying to wound as she'd been wounded.

"If he suits you," he said kindly.

"He doesn't!"

"Well, neither does Warren Stone, believe me. You've got a scholarship, your whole life—"

"But I love Warren!" she cried, watching her father's face turn ashen. Tears streaming down her face, she dashed up the stairs of the porch, past her father and into the house. Running blindly she took the stairs two at a time, ran into her room and slammed the door. Then, realizing that her father's words were true, she yanked the traitorous love note from her pocket and tore it into a hundred pieces before flinging herself across her bed and burying her head in her pillow.

Her father's words continued to haunt her. "He'll never love you—not the way he loves Honor…."

She knew in her heart that he was right and sobbed quietly, ignoring her father's knock on the bedroom door.

"Brenna?"

"Go away."

"Craig's here."

Why now? "I—I can't see him—not now."

Her father jangled the knob and walked into the room. She could hear him by the door, knew that he felt uncomfortable. He'd never been good at dealing with tears. "He called a while ago," James explained. "I told him it would be all right to stop by. I had no idea—" He cleared his throat. "I had no idea you were caught up with some schoolgirl dreams of Warren Stone."

Her heart squeezed painfully but she sniffed back her tears. She couldn't bear to have her father see her so crushed.

"Anyway, he's here, downstairs waitin'. I think the least you can do is see him."

Brenna blinked rapidly. "I don't know—"

"Come on, Brenna. Don't lay there kickin' yourself over Warren. You'd best just face the fact that he loves Honor."

She gritted her teeth and thought she might throw up. What a fool she'd been! All of her dreams crumbled to dust. Glancing over her shoulder, she saw her father standing stiff and unbending near the door. Even if he'd wanted to, James Douglass was incapable of offering tenderness.

Since his wife's death, he'd never once hugged Brenna or kissed her.

But his eyes had softened. "It's your birthday, and Craig's a good friend," he said. "There's no reason he has to suffer. You could still go out and have a good time."

She sniffed loudly. "Maybe you're right."

His face slackened in relief. "Once in a while, I do know what I'm talkin' about," he muttered.

Brenna forced herself off the bed. She caught a glimpse of her reflection in the mirror and grimaced. Her hair was tangled, her eyes red, her lips swollen, her new dress a disaster. "Tell him—tell him I'll be down in about ten minutes," she said.

As soon as her father was out of the room, she ripped off her sundress and yanked the clips from her hair. She washed her face, touched up her makeup and threw on her favorite faded jeans and T-shirt. Sliding into sandals, she caught her reflection again and was surprised to see that most of her despair had been washed away. If only the hole in her heart would mend so quickly, she thought angrily and flung the strap of her purse over her shoulder.

Craig was waiting in the foyer. Obviously uncomfortable making small talk with her father, he flashed her a grateful grin as she hurried down the stairs.

A tall, lanky boy with sun-streaked blond hair and gold eyes, he was a jock who played basketball and baseball. He'd been Brenna's friend through four years of high school and just this past summer, after graduation, had started dating her seriously.

Unfortunately, Brenna had fallen in love with Warren.

"Let's go," she said brightly, and her father's eyes twinkled. *Just like him,* she thought unkindly. *Dad thinks the scene in the rose garden was all just a big mistake.* Well, she'd prove him right—if it killed her. She linked her arm through Craig's and waltzed through the door as if she hadn't a care in the world, though inside she was shattered.

The hours crept by and her date with Craig was a disaster. He could sense something was wrong, though she wouldn't confide in him, and finally, after a boring movie and brick-hard pizza, Craig drove her home.

In the driveway, he snapped off the ignition, then placed

both his hands on the steering wheel. Staring through the windshield, he let out a long, unhappy sigh. "You're in love with someone else," he said, not even glancing in her direction.

"Wh-what do you mean?" Brenna felt miserable.

"It's obvious, Brenna. It has been for some time." Turning, he faced her and his eyes were filled with sadness. "All summer long I've felt you drifting away."

She couldn't lie to Craig, nor could she tell him the truth. "I—I'm leaving for California next week," she said.

"That's not an answer."

"I know." She slumped down in the seat.

"I love you."

"You don't—"

"Yes, I do, Brenna. I've loved you since we were barely out of grade school." His fingers tightened over the steering wheel, his knuckles showing white. "I always figured that one day, you and I, we'd…oh, hell, it doesn't matter anymore." His face was pale and set. "I just hope whoever this guy is, he knows what a lucky bastard he is."

"It's not like that," she said, then couldn't stop herself. "Believe me, he doesn't know I exist."

"Then he's a fool!" He acted as if he wanted to say more, but his throat worked and he sniffed. Angrily, he flicked on the engine again. "I've got to go."

She started to apologize, but he waved it off. "Just don't tell me 'we'll still be friends,' okay?"

"Won't we?" she asked weakly.

"I don't know, Brenna. I just don't think I can handle it." He gunned the engine, though the car was still parked.

Brenna reached for the door handle and climbed out of his old Chevy. "I'll—I'll see ya around," she whispered, then slammed the door shut. He roared away and Brenna felt more wretched than ever. How could one person ruin their entire life in one night? she wondered dismally.

Wishing she hadn't hurt Craig, she stumbled up the back steps and sat on the porch swing, absently scratching Ulysses behind his ears, and closed her eyes. She couldn't go in the house yet; she had too much to think about.

She didn't even hear Warren's truck in the drive. But his voice, a whisper, caught her attention and she blinked. Ulysses growled, then whined, but Warren didn't seem to notice.

Brenna, from the darkened porch swing, peeked around the corner and immediately regretted her curiosity. Warren and Honor were standing near the back porch, arms entwined, gazing into each other's eyes.

Honor's hair reflected silver in the moon glow and tears glistened in her huge eyes. "I'm sorry," she whispered, her voice sounding strange.

Brenna's heart was thundering in her chest and she felt sick inside.

Honor buried her head in the crook of Warren's neck. "I should never have asked Brenna to lie to you."

He didn't move.

Brenna wanted to die—she couldn't bear to hear them discussing her. Her cheeks flamed. Barely daring to breathe, she drew back into the hidden shelter of the old swing.

"I just wanted to have some fun. If I'd known..."

Her voice drifted away and Brenna imagined Warren was kissing Honor as he had her just hours before. She touched her lips and felt drops of moisture as tears ran from her eyes.

"I'll never let you down again," Honor promised, her voice husky and breathless. Brenna could stand eavesdropping no longer. She had to escape before she mortified herself, her sister and Warren.

Careful not to rock the swing, she stood and slunk along the wall until she reached the door. Then, with her heart hammering at the thought of being discovered, she eased the screen open and slid into the dark kitchen.

Through the window, she could see Honor and Warren. They were no longer hugging or kissing, but it didn't matter. They were together. They always would be.

Brenna's teeth sank painfully into her lower lip. Angrily, she wiped her tears away. She wouldn't cry for Warren Stone. Never again!

Holding back sobs that threatened to erupt from deep inside, she flew up the stairs, vaguely wondering if she would wake her father and finding she really didn't care.

Caught in her own misery, she dashed to her room. Once inside, she took several deep breaths, then kicked off her sandals and hurled her purse onto the bed.

There on the floor was the damning litter—torn scraps of the love letter she'd written to Warren. The ragged pieces seemed to mock her from the worn floorboards.

Through the open window, she heard Honor's laughter.

She wanted to scream but didn't. Throat swollen, she picked up every last torn fragment of paper, ran to the bathroom and flushed the horrid wad of useless scraps down the toilet. Watching the colored paper swirl into oblivion, she brushed her hand over her eyes, sweeping away any trace of tears. Never, she vowed to herself, would she make a fool of herself again. Not for Warren Stone or any man!

CHAPTER ONE

San Francisco, California
Ten Years Later

BRENNA WADDED HER official notice of termination, threw it into a metal basket and smiled grimly as it bounced onto the floor of what had been her office for nearly five years. So much for good luck—not that she'd had much of anything good lately.

She heard a sharp rap on the door of her glass-encased office and watched as Stan Gladstone, editor of the women's section of the *City Weekly*, barged in.

"Come in," she suggested, though he was already draping one knee familiarly over the corner of her desk and staring at the open desk drawers and piles of personal memorabilia cluttering the floor.

She dropped her pen-and-pencil set into her open briefcase.

"I don't like this any more than you do," he said quietly. A solidly built man of fifty, he had bushy eyebrows, thick glasses and a wrinkled face that matched his rumpled shirt and loosened tie.

"I know." She didn't blame Stan for her layoff. It certainly wasn't his fault that the failing *City Weekly* had been bought by a company—some huge conglomerate—headquartered in Chicago.

"Just remember, it's not the quality of your work—

you've done a helluva job in the women's section." He took off his glasses and rubbed his eyes.

"But?"

"No 'buts.' You know that." His eyes pierced into hers. "It's all a case of cutbacks. Each department is being trimmed. Even ours."

"That leaves only one reporter," she pointed out, glancing past the clear glass panes of her office to the desks beyond. Those reporters who had managed to cling tenaciously to their jobs sat in front of glowing computer monitors, typing furiously, smoking and talking all at once.

Stan lifted his hands. "I know. But the new owners don't want to put much emphasis on homemaking news."

"A lot of women read our section," she said defensively.

Yanking on the knot of his tie, he nodded. "I know, I know. But the powers that be have done some marketing research. They figure women of the eighties and nineties aren't interested in what the women of the sixties and seventies cared about. Home canning, granola and yogurt are out. Briefcases, a steady job and crisp business suits are in."

Brenna felt her shoulder muscles tense in self-defense and she glanced guiltily at her own briefcase. "But not for all women. And what about the women who postponed having their families until they were older—or the women who are trying to balance a job with the kids and the household? Or single women who are still trying to cut corners on the food budget?"

"Bill Stinson, he's the new editor—"

"I've heard."

"Stinson wants the paper to have a more 'sophisticated, today' look aimed at the two-income professional couple, the 'yuppies' or 'dinks' or whatever they're called."

"I'm so sick of those words," she muttered.

"Give it a rest, Brenna," he advised, then grinned and winked at her. "If you want to know the truth, so am I."

"Then why? Even yuppies have to eat, keep house and stay abreast of the latest dining trends. Pasta and Chablis, exercise and fashion—the 'right' color of panty hose for the office—that sort of thing," she pointed out as she dropped her pencil holder and stamp pads into her case.

Stan shrugged. "I know, but Stinson seems to think that Janice can handle all that. Besides, she's been with the paper longer than you have."

Brenna wanted to argue, but let out an angry breath instead. The "cut" in the women's department was logical, based on seniority, but unfair. Brenna met Stan's gaze without blinking. "You know, I could be the next Erma Bombeck."

"God help us!"

"I mean it, Stan."

"I know, I know, but every woman columnist thinks she can be the next Bombeck."

"But I really can!"

Stan rubbed his jaw and lifted his shoulders wearily. "Sure, you can. But not on this paper. And does the country need more than one? Look, Brenna, I'm sorry. Really. I tried to talk Stinson out of some of the cutbacks, but the boys in marketing had already convinced him that we don't need so much emphasis on the home and garden."

"Great—just great," she muttered. "What would we do without the boys in marketing?"

"I wouldn't answer that if my life depended on it."

She had to smile. "So would it help if I talked to Stinson myself?"

He shook his head. "I don't think so. But it's up to you." Watching as she stuffed her tape recorder into her briefcase, then snapped the case shut, he shoved his shirtsleeves up his forearms. "I told you I talked to a couple of people I used to work with."

Her heart leaped to her throat. "And?"

"The job in Phoenix has already been filled. But the other one—"

"In Portland," she said, already ahead of him.

"Right. With the *Willamette Examiner*, is still open."

Portland, Oregon. Where Warren Stone was district attorney for Multnomah County.

"I don't want to move back to Oregon," she said firmly, though a picture of Warren, his eyes warm and mischievous, his white smile slashing roguishly across his jaw, filled her mind. "Maybe I can find something here—or maybe they want the next Bombeck in L.A."

Stan rubbed his chin. "Maybe. Given enough time, you'd probably latch on to something."

Brenna's lips twitched. She genuinely liked Stan; hated to leave him. He'd been her mentor when she was still fresh out of college and green as a new twenty-dollar bill. "Thanks for the vote of confidence. You make it sound like you want me to leave."

"Maybe I just don't want you on a rival paper."

Her smile blossomed into a full-fledged grin. "I'm trying to be self-righteous and indignant, you know. Don't make me laugh."

"I'm not trying to." Suddenly serious, he pushed his glasses up his nose. "Isn't your family still up there—somewhere around Portland?"

"Yes." Quickly she grabbed a watercolor painting of migrating geese from the one plaster wall and dropped it onto the desk. She'd never really told Stan about her family and, gratefully, he'd never pried. The little about her background he knew, he'd pieced together himself. "Well, that about does it."

Stan stood, but his face was drawn into a reflective frown. "Look, I didn't mean to bring up a bad subject, Brenna. But it doesn't take a Rhodes scholar to guess that there's some bad blood between you and your dad. And now that your sister's passed away—"

She felt the color drain from her face. After four months, she still couldn't think about the fact that Honor was dead—killed when her car had plunged off a curving coastal highway.

"Maybe you should square things with your old man." Before she could protest, Stan held up his hands. "Look, I don't know what went on in your family, and I'm really not interested, but take it from one who knows: family's important. More important than any job—or your pride."

Brenna's shoulders stiffened. "There are reasons I *can't* go back to Portland."

He snorted with disbelief. "Sure, there are. And not one of them worth a damn. Your father needs you and that brother-in-law of yours, the D.A. or whatever he is, he must be having one helluva time trying to clean up the city and do a decent job of raising two kids."

A familiar lump filled Brenna's throat, but she tried to hide it. "Is that what this push back to Portland is all about?" she demanded, her eyes burning, the old wounds deep and cutting. "You think I should try to pick up the pieces Honor left behind?"

"I've got kids of my own," he explained, then raked his fingers through his silver hair. "Oh, hell, maybe it's none of my business." Frowning so hard that his forehead became a mass of deep furrows, he reached into his jacket pocket and withdrew a small mint-green envelope. "This came in the mail for you," he said, handing the envelope to her. "Looks personal."

He walked to the door, then leaned one hefty shoulder against the frame. "For what it's worth, Brenna, I know you could be the next Erma Bombeck—and the *Willamette Examiner* is looking for someone just like her. They're willing to pay well, and so you'd be in Portland—hell, you could see your old man or not. Distance doesn't matter. Take my advice, you can't hide the rest of your life."

"I'm not hiding—"

But he was already through the door, a fierce-looking man striding through the maze of desks in the newspaper room, his back to her as he wended his way around busy reporters, clanking typewriters and flickering computer screens.

He's right, you know, you are hiding, her mind accused. Pursing her lips, she glanced down at the green envelope Stan had given her and her heart nearly stopped.

She recognized the return address as Warren's. But he hadn't written the letter—his daughter Julie's name appeared in the upper left-hand corner of the envelope. Brenna's hands shook. Julie hadn't written or called since her mother's death. And, of course, Brenna hadn't heard from Warren since the funeral.

Her heart hammered as she opened the envelope and scanned the pencil-written single sheet:

Dear Aunt Bren,

It's almost summer and I'm going to be out of school real soon. Boy, I can't wait!!!

Grandpa said you might be visiting us and I would like it a lot if you did. So would Scotty and Daddy. We all miss Mommy and we were supposed to go on vacation this year. We had a cabin in the mountains and everything, but Daddy said we can't go now. He's real busy with his work.

How is San Francisco? Maybe I should come and visit you—like Mommy did. I want to see Chinatown, but Grandpa says I won't like it.

Please write.

Love,
Julie

Brenna steadied herself by inhaling quickly. Guilt tortured her—a small feeling that had been nagging at her suddenly grew into a huge, ugly monster. How could she have ignored her niece and nephew—Honor's children? Obviously, they were both still hurting, and the little presents Brenna had sent them, as much to appease her guilty conscience for not staying with them in Portland as anything, hadn't helped relieve their grief.

She glanced at the letter again, then folded it and slipped it back into the envelope. "Oh, Julie," she whispered, leaning back in her desk chair and squeezing her eyes shut tight. She felt as if she'd failed. Despite her feelings for Warren, there were children to consider, children she loved.

"Dear God," she whispered, her throat dry. Without thinking, she reached for the phone and flipped through her address book.

"D.A.'s office," a young girl answered over the hum of long distance.

"Yes. I'd like to speak with Warren Stone," Brenna said, nervously twisting the phone cord.

"I'm sorry, Mr. Stone is out. Would you like to leave a message?"

Brenna let out a long sigh. "No—thanks, I'll call later." She hung up and ignored the sweat dampening her palms as she punched out Warren's home number. Five rings later, a young feminine voice answered.

"Hi, honey," Brenna said, her heart squeezing.

"Aunt Bren?"

"I got your letter."

"Good!" Julie's voice crackled with excitement. "Are you coming to visit?"

"Yes."

"When?"

"I'm not sure. Probably this weekend."

Julie whooped with delight.

Brenna's throat became desert-dry. "Is your dad around?" she asked. "Maybe I should clear this with him."

"He's not here."

Brenna bit her lip, but steadfastly stamped down the doubts that loomed in her heart. "How about the baby-sitter?"

"Mrs. Beatty's in the basement doing laundry—do you want me to go get her?" Julie asked.

Brenna imagined Warren's huge house. It would take ten minutes for Julie to retrieve the housekeeper. "No—just tell your Dad that I'll be there—" she glanced at the calendar still sitting on her desk "—probably on Thursday, if I can work things out."

"That'll be great!" Julie said excitedly before hanging up.

Brenna doubted that Warren would agree. For ten years they'd barely seen or spoken to each other. He and Honor had eloped soon after Brenna had taken off for San Francisco. Over the years she'd seen him at family gatherings once or twice a year, but he'd barely spoken to her, avoided being alone with her. That had been just fine.

But at Honor's funeral, she'd tried to comfort Warren. He'd been as cold as the ice that had crusted the ground that bleak December morning.

She tucked the watercolor under her arm, tossed her raincoat over her shoulder, then threaded her way between the desks of the newsroom to Stan's office.

He was sitting in his ratty old chair, the receiver of the phone cradled between his ear and shoulder, his face red with anger. Glancing up when she knocked, he waved her into a side chair. Papers were strewn over his desk and a cigar, long since forgotten and smoldering pungently, lay unattended in a heaping ashtray. Behind him, through a grimy rain-streaked window, Brenna could see the windows of another office building and a sliver of gray sky.

"I don't really give a damn," he growled into the receiver. "You're in the legal department—you tell me what kind of a retraction we need to print!" Slamming down the receiver so hard that his desk shook, he swore again under his breath. "Lawyers! You can have the lot of them!"

She agreed. Warren was a lawyer.

Brenna sat on the edge of a cracked plastic chair as Stan, still muttering furiously about the ineptitude of the legal profession, ground out his cigar.

Brenna couldn't resist needling him. "Good news?" she asked.

Despite his anger, Stan chuckled. "Not unless you think having the commissioner of police screaming up your backside is something to laugh about." He leaned back in his chair and studied her. "What's up?"

"I've decided to take your advice."

"I don't give advice." But his tired eyes glinted.

"Not much, you don't. Anyway, I'd like the name of the editor of the *Willamette Examiner* and a letter of recommendation."

A grin split his face. "Len Patterson runs the *Examiner*. He's an old friend of mine. Believe me, you don't need a letter of recommendation. Your work speaks for itself. I'll give him a call and a sample of your articles."

"And a letter of recommendation."

"Okay—I'll have Maggie type out something."

"Thanks."

"So, what's going on, Brenna?"

"I'm moving back to Oregon." *And Warren Stone could like it or lump it!*

WARREN SLAPPED THE crumpled pages of the *Willamette Examiner* onto his couch and swore loudly. What the hell did

Len Patterson think he was doing? The headlines blazed with the latest gossip about a case he'd been working on for weeks—the abduction of a little boy by his uncle. Now, blast it, with the shoddy reporting of the *Examiner*, the case would probably be thrown out of court.

"Damn!" He raked his fingers through his hair only to see his daughter, Julie, pushing open the door of the den and peering inside.

"Daddy?"

"Hi, sweetheart." He pushed his fury at the damned rag out of his mind, but a headache had begun to pound behind his eyes.

Julie looked decidedly guilty. "This is Thursday, right?"

Warren glanced at the date on the newspaper. "Has been all day," he muttered, frowning. He'd taken the afternoon off, only to be greeted by the shoddy front page of the *Examiner*.

"I, uh, forgot to tell you something."

"No problem. You can tell me now."

"Aunt Brenna called," she said, eyeing the floor.

Warren didn't move a muscle. Brenna hadn't called since Honor's death. "Why?"

"I, uh, sent her a letter and she's coming to visit."

Warren's mind began to spin. "She's visiting us? When?"

"Today, I think," Julie mumbled.

"Today?" What the hell was going on? "Wait a minute—slow down and tell me everything," he said, trying to remain calm. But the thought of seeing Brenna, even for a few short hours, unnerved him. He didn't need her now—not with everything else he had to face.

He reached for the telephone, then quickly dialed Brenna's number in San Francisco. After a series of clicks and a couple of rings, he heard a flat monotone of a voice.

"The number you have just dialed has been changed or discon—"

"Damn!" Warren growled an oath into the receiver, then slammed it down so hard that his entire desk jarred. Why would Brenna have disconnected her phone? It didn't make sense. Even if she were planning a visit, she would still want phone service.

He leaned back in his chair and rubbed his temples. Slowly counting to ten, he shifted his gaze to find his seven-year-old daughter standing in the doorway. Her blue eyes were round and she bit her lower lip nervously.

"Let me get this straight," Warren said, his patience stretched thin, but his voice calm. "What *exactly* did she say?"

"Well, she wanted to talk to you, but you weren't home."

"And Mrs. Beatty?"

"She was busy—doing the wash in the basement, so I took a message. Aunt Bren said that she would be here on Thursday."

"Here?" he asked, his brow furrowing, "In this house?"

Julie shrugged and let her blond hair fall forward, covering her eyes. "I—I guess so."

"But you're not sure?"

"I didn't ask. I'm sorry, Daddy."

"It's okay," he said, the tension in his shoulders knotting painfully. The *Examiner*, page one spread open, taunted him from the couch. "We'll just have to find out what her plans are when she gets here."

Julie smiled a little. "Then you're not mad?"

"Well, maybe just a little, but not at you," he said, one corner of his mouth twisting upward. How Julie reminded him of Honor. "Come here." She ran to him and he gathered her into his arms. Squeezing her until she giggled, he kissed her golden crown. "But next time, you'd better check with me."

"Don't you want to see Aunt Brenna?" Julie asked.

Warren scowled. Yes, a part of him wanted to see her again, but another part warned him that facing his sister-in-law would only spell trouble. "Aunt Brenna's a busy woman," he heard himself saying. "She's got a career to think of, she can't just leave at the drop of a hat, you know."

"She said she was coming and she is," Julie said staunchly as Warren swung her to the ground.

Scotty, in a blast of five-year-old energy, his footsteps clattering noisily, tore into the room. "Come on! We're goin' to the park!" he sang out, his black hair flopping over blue eyes that were round and filled with excitement.

At that moment, Mary Beatty stepped into the den. Mary was a heavyset, no-nonsense woman with a strict code of right and wrong. Warren smiled at the sight of her fists planted firmly on her hips. At the top of her "wrong" list was a father raising two young children on his own. Ever since Honor's death, Mary had paraded a line of potential wives under Warren's nose—from twenty-five-year-old nieces to a friend of a friend of a friend.... Warren hadn't been interested.

"Find your coat," Mary said to Scotty, before her eyes landed on Julie. "You, too."

Both kids scrambled to the front hall where they fought to be the first to the closet.

"I thought they needed to run off some energy," she said, leaning on the doorjamb, her worried eyes scanning Warren's face. "Maybe you do, too. You're invited."

"Thanks, but not tonight."

"Too busy fighting crime and cleaning up the streets of Portland to spend some time with the kids?" she asked, her graying brows arching.

"Just doing my job," he said, catching a fond twinkle in her eyes. "So stop trying to make me feel guilty." He folded his arms over his chest. "Now, tell me about my sister-in-law. What do you know about her 'visit' and this letter Julie wrote?"

Mary shrugged. "I only know what Julie just told you. I found out about the conversation not ten minutes ago."

"Great," Warren muttered.

"I'm ready!" Scotty announced, the buttons of his jacket in the wrong holes, one red mitten and one blue on his hands. His cheeks were flushed as Julie stomped up behind him.

"Scotty pushed!" Julie announced.

Scotty's eyes glittered devilishly. "Did not!" he protested, a little too loudly.

"It's too warm for mittens, stupid," she charged. "And besides, they don't even match!"

"Who cares?" Scotty said, throwing Julie's favorite saying back at her.

"Dad—" she wailed.

"Let's not argue about it, okay?" Warren suggested. He stood and stretched his arms over his head, but the tension that had been with him ever since Julie had mentioned Brenna's name was still lodged deep in his muscles.

"You come with us—please!" Scotty pleaded, running up to Warren and tugging on his sleeve. "You can push me on the swing."

"How about if I join you in—" he glanced at his watch "—about forty-five minutes?" He looked at Mary, who was stuffing her arms through the sleeves of a pink raincoat. "Then you can take off."

Mary zipped her coat. "Fair enough. We'll be looking for you. It's too nice outside to be cooped up in this—" she eyed the den "—prison."

"Is that what it is?"

With a knowing grimace, Mary corralled the kids out of the den and through the front door, leaving Warren standing alone in the marble foyer of the imposing old house his parents had once owned.

So Brenna was determined to visit, he thought, frowning. Julie's letter had probably worked on her guilt. His eyes narrowed and despite his attempts to dismiss Brenna from his mind he felt his heartbeat accelerating. Annoyed, he tried to slow the anxious cadence but couldn't. Nor could he relax. Just knowing that Brenna was in the city at this very moment made him restless.

Why wasn't her phone working? he wondered irritably. Just how long did she intend to stay? He thought about the last time he'd seen her, at Honor's funeral, how she'd offered to help him and how he, in his grief, had lashed out at her.

"I just want you to know," Brenna had whispered, touching his arm gently, "that I'll help you with the children." They had been standing beneath a canopy of black, leafless oak trees in the cemetery. Freezing wind had sliced through the few mourners still lingering at the grave site and sleet had fallen from a leaden sky.

"I don't need any help."

Her hazel eyes had darkened and her cheeks had colored. "It may be difficult. Julie and Scott will need—"

"What? A mother?" he'd cut in, wanting to hurt as he'd been hurt, feeling guilty as hell, hating the fact that his heart still raced at the sight of her. "What is it, Bren? You think you can be Honor? Just step right into her shoes?"

She'd gasped and stepped back and he'd noticed huge tears in the corners of her eyes. "Of course not—I just wanted to help you, that's all."

"They're my kids. I can handle them."

"Fine," she'd said, her back ramrod straight beneath her ebony suit. She'd seemed to want to say more, to wound him back, but she'd snapped her mouth closed and walked stiffly through frozen leaves to her father's car.

He hadn't heard from her since, though the kids had gotten presents and notes at Christmas, Easter and Julie's birthday.

He'd been an ass, he realized now, a first-class, number-one ass. And now he had to face her again. Damn, damn, damn. He just wasn't ready for that emotional gristmill. Shoving his sleeves over his forearms, he strode into the den, poured himself a shot of Scotch and flopped into the soft cushions of a cream-colored leather couch.

Brenna—her image swam before his eyes. Before he could think any of the betraying thoughts that had once tortured him, he swallowed the rest of his drink, then waited, his eyes fastened to the outer hallway where a grandfather clock bonged the half hour.

So where was she? he wondered. Just where the hell was she?

"THIS IS IT," BRENNA said from the backseat of the cab, her heart racing and her palms damp at the sight of Warren's home. Partially hidden in a thicket of fir and oak, the huge house peaked through the branches.

"And he's the D.A.? Maybe our taxes are too high," the cabdriver replied, whistling softly as he glanced at the massive structure.

"He inherited it," Brenna said quickly, defending Warren and wishing she hadn't conversed so freely with the driver.

"Tough life." The cabby accepted his fare and swung open the back door without leaving his seat. "Want me to wait?"

"No thanks." If Warren threw her out, she'd call another cab or insist that he drive her back to her hotel downtown.

"If you say so..."

Brenna stood on the curb until the cab, black smoke spewing behind, made an illegal U-turn and coasted down the narrow street. Then she gazed at Warren's house—the home he'd shared with Honor.

The house was a mansion by today's standards. Built near the turn of the century and constructed of blue stone and clapboard siding, cathedral-like, it rose three stories above the ground to gables and dormers that peaked against a spring-blue sky. Ivy clung tenaciously to the sharp stones of one wall and a clematis stretched across the eaves of the front porch. A turret guarded a winding staircase in one corner. Invisible, beneath the ground, there was a full basement complete with servants' scrub room and a vintage wine cellar. All in all, it was a grand house—a home Honor had loved.

Honor. Brenna's heart constricted. Already, she felt like an intruder.

Hiking the collar of her coat close to her neck, she marched up a curved flagstone path to the front porch. She rapped twice with the brass knocker before the door was flung wide, and Warren, dressed in a white shirt with rolled sleeves and black slacks, stood squarely in the doorway.

His eyes were bluer than she remembered and his face a little more gaunt. The severe angle of his jaw hadn't softened since the funeral, nor had any of the boyish charm she remembered from his youth resurfaced. "Brenna," he drawled, his mouth twisting sardonically. "If this isn't a surprise."

"A surprise?" she repeated. "But I called the other afternoon...."

His gaze didn't flinch. "Julie just told me about an hour ago."

An hour ago? No wonder his jaw was set tight, his eyes cold and humorless.

"I'm sorry—I should have called again. Just to make sure you expected me."

"Water under the bridge," he said, and gave a little push on the door so that it swung completely open. "Since you're here, you may as well come in." His gaze slid down her body to her feet. "Where are your bags?"

"At the hotel," she snapped, trying to remain calm, and failing. Just looking at him again made her heart pound erratically.

"Julie gave me the impression you planned on staying here."

Never, she thought, her stomach fluttering. "I wouldn't dream of it," she said irritably, then instantly regretted her words. There was no point in arguing with him—at least not yet. Where she stayed didn't matter. The children did. "Look, Warren, I don't expect you to roll out the red carpet for me—I just came to visit Julie and Scott."

One black brow rose skeptically. "Come in," he invited, his voice without warmth. "But you'll have to wait. They're at the park."

Great. She hadn't expected a warm reception, but she'd hoped he would have the decency to be civil. And if he thought he could bully her into leaving before she had a chance to talk with Julie and find out just what had prompted her letter, he had another think coming. "Fine," she said, forcing a cool smile. She had the urge to snap back at him, but held her tongue. No reason to start a fight now. Her fingers white over the shoulder strap of her purse, she marched determinedly into the house where Honor had once been mistress.

Nothing much had changed. The furniture was just where it had been before Honor's death. Oriental carpets sprawled in rich weaves of burgundy and blue across golden oak parquet and the vaulted rooms smelled faintly of roses—dried blossoms were visible in ceramic bowls placed strategically on antique tables.

Warren motioned her toward the den and she walked

with him, surveying him through her lashes. He'd aged in the past four months, she decided, though his hair was still glossy black and thick. But the brackets near the corners of his mouth were more defined and the crow's-feet near his eyes firmly etched.

Directing her to a chair, he said, "Julie mentioned she'd written you a letter."

"That's right." Brenna dropped into the soft cushions while he balanced one shoulder against the panes of a leaded-glass window beyond which fir branches danced in a brisk spring breeze.

"So how long are you staying?" he asked, crossing his arms over his chest, the seams of his shirt straining over his broad shoulders.

"I didn't come up here for a visit. I'm moving back to Portland."

"You're *what?*" All of his outward calm dissolved.

"Moving." Brenna realized she couldn't have surprised him more if she had walked into the room stark naked.

"Moving?" he repeated slowly. "Permanently?"

"Yes."

His face slackened. "Hold on a minute. I thought you were here for a visit."

"It's more than that, Warren." She dug into her purse, found Julie's note and handed it to him.

Quickly, he scanned the mint-green page, frowning as he read.

Brenna suddenly felt foolish. "It sounded like she needed me. I guess I should have talked to you—"

His jaw worked. "That would've been a good idea."

"—but I couldn't reach you at the office and when I called here, you were out."

He studied Julie's note, poring over the words as if he, too, were trying to read between the lines. When he glanced up again, all pretense was gone and Brenna recognized pain, as raw as an arctic wind, in his eyes.

"I know you don't want my help," she said shakily, her gaze locked with his. "But I have to."

"Why?"

"Julie's my niece—Honor's daughter."

Warren crumpled the page in his hands. "And I'm her father, Bren. I told you before that I could handle Julie and Scotty. And they've got Mary. She adores them!"

"Mary?" Brenna whispered.

"Their nanny. Mary Beatty. She's a neighbor who takes care of the kids while I'm at work. They're with her now."

Warren pinched the bridge of his nose between his thumb and forefinger. "Look, Brenna," he said quietly, "I didn't mean to be such a jerk when you showed up—it's just been a little bit of a shock. And, really, I appreciate the fact that you flew all the way up here to see the kids. But you don't need to move."

Brenna knew what he was saying and it hurt—it hurt badly. Nonetheless, she had to hear him say the words. "You don't want me here. Is that right?"

"You can stay as long as you like—as long as you have time away from your job. But, really, there's no reason to move back. Unless you think your Dad needs you."

Her mouth tightened derisively. James Douglass had never needed her before—she doubted he wanted her now. She'd called him, of course, and he'd seemed glad to hear from her, even excited that she was moving home, but she'd heard the reservations in his voice. "This has nothing to do with Dad," she said. "Why are you so dead-set against me moving back?" She stared straight into his enigmatic blue eyes and for just an instant she thought she saw a flicker of emotion in his gaze, but he shifted his weight and sat heavily on the sill.

"You were the one who wanted out of here, Bren," he

said. "All those years ago, all you wanted was to become a newspaperwoman—it's all you ever talked about."

"Not all," she said softly, and the muscles beneath his shirt flexed.

"You've got a job in San Francisco—a new life. For God's sake, you're a career woman. What would you do in Portland?" He met her gaze squarely again. "You can't just forget your responsibilities, Brenna."

"I haven't. There have been changes at the *City Weekly*. A Chicago conglomerate has bought the paper, lock, stock and barrel. And there have been cutbacks. You're looking at one right now."

As if he finally understood she was moving to Portland for good, he leaned against the pine-paneled walls. "You *want* to move back?" he asked dazedly.

"Yes." Swallowing hard, she glanced away to the couch, where a copy of the *Willamette Examiner* lay open. "As a matter of fact, tomorrow morning I'm being interviewed for a job at the *Examiner*."

CHAPTER TWO

WARREN FROZE AND his eyes drilled into hers. "You're what?" he demanded, the corners of his mouth drawing into a scowl.

"Being interviewed at the *Examiner*."

His brows blunted over flashing blue eyes and one fist clenched in frustration.

Brenna stared into his stricken face. "The least you could do is wish me luck."

"You're not serious," he said slowly. "This is some sort of a joke, right?"

"No joke—"

"You're not applying for a job at the *Examiner*!" His face darkened with a furious rage.

"Why not?"

"Because the *Examiner* is the cheapest, shoddiest, poorest excuse for a paper in this entire state and probably the entire Pacific Northwest!" He swiped the newspaper from the couch and shook it in his fist. "This is only one step up from those cheap tabloids you see in the checkout stands of the grocery markets!"

Brenna bristled. "Stan Gladstone recommended the job—"

"Who the hell is Stan Gladstone?"

"My editor at the *City Weekly*."

He didn't move, just stared at her. "Does he hate you?" he asked, his voice deathly quiet.

Brenna leaped to her feet. Her own anger igniting, she

stalked straight toward him, stopping so close that the toes of her pumps nearly touched the points of his polished loafers. Though she had to tilt her head, she stared straight into his incredible blue eyes. "That was uncalled for. Stan found me a job, here in Portland, and no matter what your feelings about me or the *Examiner* are, there's nothing you can do about it. I'm moving back, I'm going to do everything in my power to land that job and I'm taking an active interest in my niece and nephew."

Warren inhaled through his teeth. "The *Willamette Examiner* may have just cost me a case against a man who kidnaps children," he grated. "Because of the unprofessional practices at that paper, an airtight case is most likely going to be thrown out of court." He hurled the offending front page into a nearby trash can. "And now you plan to work for the sleazy rag?"

She swallowed hard. "Yes."

His gaze was menacing. "And then, once you're firmly ensconced at the newspaper—and I use the term loosely— what do you expect from me and my family? Do you think you can just march in here and play mother to my children, for God's sake?"

Stunned, she met the fire in his gaze with her own. "You can stop with the lecture, Warren. I'm not eighteen anymore. I don't break quite so easily. Julie and Scotty are Honor's children. I plan to help them, if I can, as their *aunt*. Is that so awful?"

A muscle leaped in his jaw and his fingers clenched only to straighten several times as he tried to control the fury that was so obviously eating at him. "They are *my* children, too." Though quiet, his voice was edged in steel, and his gaze as it delved into hers caused her blood to heat.

"Don't worry, I won't forget it."

"I won't let you." The anger in his expression changed to smoldering fire. For a fleeting instant she thought she read desire in his gaze, but as quickly as it had flared, it died away—or was extinguished.

She told herself she was imagining things.

Warren drew in a shaky breath and glanced away. "Listen, Brenna," he said, wrestling with self-control. "Let's not start out at each other's throats."

"Fair enough. I...I didn't come here looking for a fight. I just thought I should drop by and see the kids. That's all." Good Lord, was that *her* heart thudding so loudly? Being this close to Warren was dangerous and unsettling. She couldn't seem to control the wild thumping in her chest or the crazy fluttering of her pulse.

The front door suddenly burst open with a bang.

Brenna jumped and felt a rush of warm spring air as she heard the clatter of excited footsteps. "Daddy?" Julie called from the foyer.

"In here—"

Brenna took a couple steps backward and as she did Julie saw her and squealed. "Aunt Bren!" Blond hair flying, she raced across the room and hugged Brenna, her small arms circling Brenna's waist.

"How are you, sweetheart?" Brenna asked, surprisingly close to tears.

"Better now—except Scotty's a royal pain in the neck!"

"Am not!" Scotty cried indignantly from the hallway. "You said you'd come to the park!" he accused.

Brenna glanced up to see her nephew clinging to the doorjamb. His face was red from the breeze, his black hair fell across his eyes in wayward disarray and his lower lip protruded stubbornly.

A heavyset older woman, her cheeks rosy, walked past him and started into the den. She stopped short when she saw Brenna.

"You must be Julie and Scotty's aunt," she said, her eyes gleaming as she smiled.

Warren stepped back and gestured between the two women. "Brenna, this is Mary Beatty—Mary, my sister-in-law," he introduced as he strode over to Scotty, then hoisted him high into the air. "Sorry, sport. Aunt Brenna stopped by and I forgot all about the park." Carefully, he let Scotty ride on his broad shoulders.

"Let's go back!" Scotty enthused, clutching Warren's head.

"Nice to meet you," Mary said, a sly smile creeping across her broad face as she shook Brenna's outstretched hand. "I've got to run. Dinner's in the oven. There's enough for everybody and I left a note telling you when it will be done and what to add." With a knowing smile tugging at her lips, she winked at Warren. "I'll see you next week." She gave Julie a quick hug and reached upward to touch the tip of her finger to Scotty's nose before leaving.

"Bye-bye," Scotty called, one hand steadying himself on Warren's head. It was obvious to Brenna that the little boy thought the world of the pink-clad woman. Her heart-strings tugged with envy and fresh guilt. She should have comforted her nephew after Honor's death. She should have offered Scotty and Julie love and reassurance. Despite Warren's objections, Brenna now realized, she should have planted herself firmly into the lives of Honor's children.

"What's for dinner?" Scotty demanded as Warren lifted him high before setting him down.

"Your guess is as good as mine," he said.

"Tacos!" Scotty decided.

"Mary already started something, I don't know what," Julie said. She was still hugging Brenna, her small arms squeezing possessively around Brenna's waist. "You're staying, aren't you?"

"I don't know—"

She felt Warren's gaze narrow on her and color rose on her neck.

"Please—" Julie begged.

"Yes, stay," Warren interjected, his voice flat. She read the unspoken message in his eyes, knew that she was intruding.

"You can help me set the table," Julie insisted.

Brenna had to laugh. "I can? Such an *honor*—" Then, seeing the pain in Julie's rounded eyes, she added quickly, "I mean such a privilege. Come on, let's have a look." As much to put distance between herself and Warren, she grabbed Julie's hand and pulled her toward the kitchen.

The kitchen was in the rear of the house and since the lot sloped away from the street, the main floor was actually two stories above the ground. Sunlight streamed through a long bank of windows, glinting on the hanging copper pans and reflecting in the polished cream-colored tile counters. Potted plants hung from hooks near the windows, green leaves and vines tumbling over the polished edges of brass pots.

The scent of simmering beef and onions wafted throughout the kitchen. Brenna peeked through the glass of the oven door. A huge roasting pot sat within, juices bubbling around the edge of the lid.

"It's been in for hours," Julie said. "Here's the note."

"Beef burgundy," Brenna read, glancing over Mary's instructions. Mary Beatty certainly seemed to be efficient. The house gleamed, dinner smelled delicious, and both Julie and Scotty seemed content and well adjusted.

She should have been happy herself, Brenna supposed, as she found pot holders and lifted the huge pot onto the counter, but deep inside she was disappointed. She hadn't realized how much she wanted Warren's children—and Warren—to need her.

"This looks great," she murmured, lifting the lid and sniffing as a cloud of scented steam rose to the ceiling.

Gravy, onions and carrots still simmered around thick chunks of beef.

"Mary took a class in gourmet cooking last fall," Warren explained. "I guess we're the guinea pigs."

"*I'm* not a pig," Scotty announced, offended. He glanced suspiciously at Brenna, apparently sizing her up. Unfortunately, not one glimmer of recognition flared in his Warren-blue eyes.

"Not a pig, stupid—a guinea pig is a rodent," Julie replied.

"Well, I'm not that, either!" Still grumbling, Scotty stomped out of the kitchen and Brenna heard him clomping upstairs.

"He has a mind of his own, doesn't he?" Brenna murmured, and Warren actually smiled—showing the amused slash of white teeth against his dark skin that she had found so charming ten years before.

"I told you it wouldn't be easy."

"Don't worry about it. Scotty's a dork," Julie announced, setting plates on place mats in an extension of the kitchen that was more sun room than nook.

"That's enough," Warren said.

"Well, he is. Everybody at school thinks so!" She looked up, caught the warning in her father's eyes and snapped her mouth shut.

The meal was tense. Scotty, sitting directly across the round table from Brenna, fastened his wary gaze on her and didn't eat a bite. Julie kept up a constant stream of nervous chatter and insulted Scotty at every possible turn in the conversation. Warren didn't say much, but Brenna read volumes in his eyes when he did glance in her direction.

"Do you like San Francisco?" Julie asked, shoving her plate to the side.

"Yes," Brenna admitted.

"Do you ride the cable cars every day?"

Brenna laughed. "Not *every* day. But once in a while."

Warren leaned back in his chair. His shoulders relaxed for the first time since she'd arrived. "What do you find so fascinating about California?"

"I like all of it," Brenna admitted. "I have a great apartment, on the third floor of an old row house with a view of the bay and—" from the corner of her eye, she saw Warren stiffen "—but I'm moving," she added, "back here."

"You are?" Julie squealed. "Here in this house?"

"Oh, no, honey." Brenna felt her face wash with color. "I'll have to get my own place."

"But we have tons of room," Julie said, turning to her father for support.

"I know," Brenna replied, embarrassed. "But—"

"Sure, Brenna," Warren drawled, a mocking light glimmering in his eyes. "Why not move right in?"

"No!" Scotty cried.

"Shh!" Julie pushed back her chair. "Oh, Aunt Bren, please! We could all be like one family."

Brenna's chest felt tight. "We are a family, honey," she said, feeling Warren's eyes boring into her. "But not that way. I can't live here."

"You don't want to!" Julie charged.

"It's not that—" How had she gotten herself into this no-win conversation? "I just think we all need a little space."

"Why?"

She glanced at Warren, hoping he would help, but his face remained impassive and stony. Only his eyes showed any spark of amusement.

"Where's dessert?" Scotty demanded, and Brenna was grateful for the change of subject.

"Dessert? But you didn't eat your potatoes or meat yet," she replied.

"Mary lets me have dessert," he pointed out, watching her reaction.

Good for Mary, Brenna thought, squirming, though she smiled at her nephew. "But I'm not Mary."

"Too bad," Scotty muttered.

"That's enough," Warren cut in. "You know the rules—you have to eat most of your meal before we even talk about dessert. And even if Mary bends them, I don't."

"I *hate* rules," Scotty announced, shoving his untouched plate across the table and knocking over a bud vase in the process. Water streamed across the table and the two white carnations floated onto the floor. Brenna grabbed a dishtowel from a nearby counter and used it, along with every available napkin, to wipe up the mess.

"Okay, bud, that's it for you." Warren stretched over the table and lifted Scotty deftly out of his chair.

"No!" he screamed.

Warren didn't seem to notice as he hauled his son, kicking and screaming his protests, over his shoulder.

"Not fair!" Scotty yelled. "Not fair!"

"That's right. It's not. Better get used to it," Warren replied, carrying him out of the room and up the stairs.

"He's a pill!" Julie proclaimed as Brenna tried to mop up the mess.

"He's just not used to me."

"Nope—he's a pill! That's what Mama used to say and she was right!"

Brenna tossed the soggy dishtowel into the sink and sat back in her chair. Resting her chin in her hand, she studied her niece.

Julie's golden hair fell to her shoulders in disorderly curls. Her face was still round, but already there were angles where her cheekbones, so like Honor's, would eventually emerge. Julie's eyes, as blue as her father's, were round and dark-lashed and troubled.

"Why don't you tell me why you wrote me the letter?" Brenna suggested.

Julie chewed on her lower lip and avoided her eyes.

"Come on, Julie. Was there a special reason?"

Studying the floor, Julie swallowed. "It's Dad," she said haltingly.

"What about him?"

"He's so—" she shrugged helplessly "—different. Ever since Mama died, he's been real quiet and, I don't know, just *different*."

Brenna felt a deep sadness steal into her heart. "He misses your mother," she said.

"So do I!" Julie cried.

Brenna touched Julie's little shoulder. "We all do."

Julie's face reddened and her chin trembled. Tears gathered in the corners of her eyes. "It wasn't fair!" she said angrily. "Scotty's right. Nothing's fair."

"I know—but maybe, maybe things will be better now."

"Then you *are* staying with us," Julie whispered hopefully, a smile faltering at the corners of her lips, though her eyes were still wet.

"For a while. But not here, sweetheart. I have to get my own place. I have a lot of things."

"But you could store them in the attic or the basement. And you could have your own bedroom and bathroom and—"

A quiet cough caught her in mid-sentence and Julie looked up just as Brenna did. Warren was there. His expression was dark and sober as he stood in the arch between the kitchen and the hallway. "Don't rush your aunt," he advised, ramming his hands into his pockets.

Brenna wondered just how much he'd overheard.

"But she could stay here, couldn't she?" Julie persisted anxiously. "In the room next to mine—I'd share the bathroom if I had to and the connecting closet and—"

"Let's just hold on a minute," Warren cut in, his eyes drilling into Brenna's.

Brenna got the message. "Yes, let's take one step at a time. I haven't even moved to Portland yet."

"But when you do?"

Uncomfortable, Brenna forced a grin. "We'll cross that bridge when we come to it," she said.

"What about tonight?" Julie asked, stubbornly ignoring the warning in her father's eyes. "You have to stay someplace tonight, don't you?"

"That's right. But I have a room in a hotel," Brenna replied, nervous under Warren's scrutinizing stare.

"And tomorrow?" Julie was near tears again, her small face twisting as she battled the urge to break down.

"Tomorrow—maybe," Brenna replied, glancing at Warren for some signal. But his face was blank, his eyes guarded, his expression completely unreadable—almost practiced. "But first I've got to visit Grandpa, then look for an apartment in Portland. After that, we'll talk."

"And then you'll move up here and live around here? Right?"

"Sort of," Brenna hedged. "Probably closer to town."

"That'll be great!" Julie breathed.

Brenna wasn't so sure and Warren's skin tightened over his features.

"There are some apartments right down the street, on the other side of the trees, aren't there, Dad?"

Warren didn't move.

"It wouldn't be the same as you living here, but almost!" she decided.

Brenna was torn. She wanted to help Julie, be as close to her and Scotty as possible, but she couldn't completely ignore Warren's plans for his children. "I'll do what I can," she promised.

"Maybe you should go upstairs and tackle that homework," Warren suggested.

"Oh, Dad, it's only reading—"

"Come on, Julie," he said, his voice rising. "Hop to it."

Grumbling about the injustice of Mrs. Stevens, her second-grade teacher, Julie stomped out of the kitchen.

What have I gotten myself into? Brenna wondered silently as she began stacking dirty dishes to clear the table.

"You don't have to help," Warren said, his voice tight. "I can handle it."

"It's no bother." She balanced several plates on her arm. "I've had lots of training."

"Really, Brenna," he snapped, turning at the same moment she did and accidently hitting her hand.

"Oh! No—" Her feet slipped as she lost her balance. The dirty plates juggled in the air, then, as she clutched after them, fell to the tile floor, smashing into a thousand jagged pieces.

Without thinking, Brenna reached to pick up the one unbroken plate and sliced her finger on a sharp shard of stoneware. Blood oozed around her knuckle.

"Brenna! God, I'm sorry!" White-faced, Warren dropped to his knees, ignoring the broken pottery. He grabbed her wrist. "Are you okay?"

"I—I'm all right."

"Like hell," he muttered, holding her hand high over her head as blood dripped to the floor. "Keep it high," he instructed, reaching into a nearby drawer for a clean dishtowel.

Scrambling footsteps echoed overhead and a few seconds later Julie, her eyes round in horror, raced into the room. "Oh!" she cried. "Oh—oh—"

"Go back upstairs."

"What happened? Aunt Brenna?"

"Just an accident."

"But there's blood!" she whispered, clamping her hands over her mouth.

"Where?" Scotty demanded as he, clad in dinosaur-print pajamas, flew into the room. "Oh, ick!"

Warren still held Brenna's wrist. Calmly, he stared straight into Julie's terrified eyes. "Everything's all right. Trust me. Aunt Brenna just cut herself and I'll take care of it. Now, take your brother upstairs for a few minutes—just until I help Aunt Brenna and clean up this mess. Okay?"

"But—"

"Do it!"

"I—I'm fine," Brenna said shakily. She was more disturbed by Warren's warm scent than her injury. For a moment her head swam. "It doesn't hurt, really."

"But it's so gross!" Scotty said, and Julie, disgusted with her brother, grabbed the back of his pajamas and dragged him screaming toward the stairs.

"I'll be up in a minute," Warren said calmly, then, muttering under his breath, helped Brenna to her feet and into a nearby bathroom where he found a first-aid kit under the sink.

Once the bleeding had stopped, he washed the wound and, frowning, wrapped it with gauze and tape. "You'll live," he predicted, glancing at her, his blue eyes serious as they met hers.

She licked her dry lips. "Thanks," she whispered, conscious of the closeness of the room and the way his fingers were wrapped around her waist. Her pulse was beginning to pound—no doubt he could feel the traitorous beat beneath his fingertips. Time hadn't changed the sorry fact that just being near him caused her errant senses to reel out of control.

"I'm sorry," he said softly. "I overreacted in the kitchen."

"It wasn't your fault."

"Yes it was," he said, sighing, studying the white skin at the back of her wrist. Her heart began to thud. "I was so damned intent on proving that I didn't need your help—"

He shrugged, catching her gaze in the beveled-glass mirror over the sink.

She saw her reflection as he did: dark mahogany hair tousled in a wild cloud surrounding a small face with green-gold eyes, flushed cheeks and full lips. "I didn't mean to force myself on you," she said. "I should have talked to you first. But I'd already lost my job when I received Julie's letter and Stan knew about the position on the *Examiner*."

Warren slowly dropped her wrist. "He didn't do you any favors," he said.

"So you said."

He frowned, his lips thinning, his gaze searching her face. "You don't know what a lion's den you're walking into."

"I haven't even got the job yet."

"Thank God for small favors."

"You really have it in for the *Examiner*, don't you?"

His eyes turned cold. "Maybe it's the other way around. You know, I wouldn't be surprised that if and when you do land this job, Len Patterson, if he doesn't know already, will find out you're related to me and try to use it against me."

"You're paranoid," she accused.

"Tell that to the parents of the boy who was kidnapped by Charlie Saxton," he muttered, his eyes narrowing thoughtfully. "It's a good bet that Len Patterson would hire you just because you're my sister-in-law."

"That's crazy!" She couldn't help the anger in her voice. "I can get the job at the *Examiner* on my own merit, thank you very much. Being related to you has *nothing* to do with it." Her eyes narrowed up at him. "Whether you believe it or not, Warren, I'm a damn good writer. My column was well read."

"So that's why it was cut?"

She felt as if she'd been slapped, and Warren, to his credit, seemed immediately contrite.

"I didn't mean—"

"Sure you did," she hissed, wounded. "You've been trying everything you can to run me out of your house and away from your children. But that was a low blow, and for your information, I know what I'm doing."

"Oh, that's right," he mocked. "Now you're a career woman, a hard-boiled, big-city reporter, right?"

"Close enough."

"Take my word for it, Brenna, you'd better be. Because the *Examiner* plays hardball."

"Dad?" Julie's voice sounded anxious as her small fists rapped against the bathroom door. "Is Aunt Bren okay?"

"See for yourself," Brenna said, hopping off the counter and reaching past Warren to twist the knob. The bathroom door swung open and Julie, still wide-eyed, stood nervously in the hallway. "Your dad patched me up just fine." She held out her bandaged hand and somehow managed to tamp down the anger still blazing hot in her brain. "He missed his calling—he should have been a doctor."

Already shaken, Julie blinked and whispered, "That's what Mama used to say."

Brenna wanted to drop through the floor. "Did she?"

"Something like that," Warren muttered, his lips curving cynically. "Actually she thought I should stick with corporate law—where all the money was—but a doctor— that was a good second."

The phone rang and he walked briskly down the hall to his study, slamming the door shut behind him.

"See what I mean?" Julie asked, tears forming in the corners of her eyes. "Dad's a basket case!"

Brenna stared after Warren, wondering why his last remark made her feel so uneasy.

CHAPTER THREE

BRENNA SHEPHERDED JULIE toward the stairs. "Let's give your dad a break, okay?" she suggested, trying to console her niece. "He's just got a lot on his mind." As they passed the study door, she frowned. Julie was right about one thing—Warren was volatile. "In a few minutes, I'll read you a story—it must be close to bedtime."

Julie pouted. "I suppose so."

"You go up and get ready and I'll clean up the mess in the kitchen—okay?"

Julie shrugged but hurried up the stairs. As quickly as possible, Brenna picked up the broken dishes and wiped the spilled gravy and vegetables from the kitchen floor. "So much for being a whiz in the kitchen," she berated herself as she finished clearing the table and washed the few plates and glasses that hadn't smashed to smithereens.

She wondered about Warren. Though he had tried to convince her that his life with his children was running smoothly, she felt the undercurrents of tension in the house, heard the plea in Julie's voice and noticed the wariness in Scotty's eyes. How could she have been so foolish, she wondered now, as to have let Warren bully her into believing that he could just pick up the pieces of his life without Honor and care for his children with only minor adjustments?

She dropped the dirty dishtowels in the laundry room, then started for the stairs, pausing to knock on the door of

Warren's study. Hearing his gruff, "It's open," she twisted the knob and poked her head inside.

Warren was at his desk, the phone receiver cradled to his ear, his forehead knotted as he listened and wrote furiously on a thick legal pad.

"I'll put the kids to bed, then I'll take off," she mouthed, and he nodded, never missing a beat as he scrawled. But when she tried to duck into the hallway, he motioned her inside.

"I don't care what you have to do," he said into the phone. "Convince the judge that the misprint in the paper won't affect the jurors—that Saxton will still get a fair trial in Portland." He slammed the receiver down, then tiredly rubbed his face. He seemed a million miles away.

"Trouble?" she asked cautiously. "Because of the *Examiner*?"

"Let's just say that I'd like to personally wring Len Patterson's skinny neck." Rising to his feet, Warren stretched. "Now, what were you trying to tell me?"

"Just that I'll read the kids a story, then call a cab to take me back to the hotel."

He hesitated, then fished into his pocket for his keys. Extracting one from his ring, he tossed the key to her. "You can take the Audi," he said.

"Won't you need it in the morning?"

"I'll use my car. The Audi was Honor's."

Brenna's fingers curled over the cold metal. "Why didn't you sell it?" she asked.

He shrugged and his gaze clouded. "Haven't gotten around to it, I guess. After the accident, the insurance company had it repaired."

Her throat went dry. "I—I, uh, thought the car was totaled," she whispered. Her fingers clenched together at the memory of Honor and her horrible death.

"Not quite," he replied quietly. "Anyway, it was fixed and returned and since then it's been parked in the garage."

"Maybe I should just call a cab—"

Warren's smile was tired. "Take the car, Brenna. It's the least I can do." For a second she glimpsed a rare moment of tenderness in his eyes before he glanced quickly back to his legal pad.

Not knowing what to say, she walked to the door.

"Bren," he called softly, "thanks for trying to help with Julie."

"I'll bring the car back tomorrow," she said, pausing at the door.

"Whenever," he replied, as if he didn't care, and Brenna left the room, quietly shutting the door behind her.

As she crossed the foyer, she glanced up the stairs and spied Julie and Scotty on the upper landing. Julie, her arms around a corner post, was leaning over the banister and Scotty peered between the sculpted oak balusters. He held a tattered stuffed dog under one arm and shoved a toy truck through the carved wood. The truck torpedoed to the first floor and landed with a loud crack.

"Not a very good idea," Brenna said, picking up the miniature cement truck and noticing that the dive-bombing had scratched the floor. "If Mary catches you, she'll skin you alive."

"Will not!" Scotty claimed. He placed another toy perilously close to the edge of the landing. Brenna hurried up the stairs and caught the dump truck before it, too, became airborne. "Come on, you two," she said fondly, grabbing the newfound missile, "show me what you want to read."

"Dino-clops and the Robomonsters!" Scotty proclaimed.

"Yuk. That's kid stuff." Julie rolled her eyes. "I want to read *Sherry Williams Makes a New Friend.*"

"I *hate* Sherry Williams!" Scotty ran into his room and

gathered a virtual library of the Dino-clops series. Tucking them under his arm, he raced into Julie's room and jumped onto her canopied bed.

"Hey, watch out. We are *not* going to read about Dino-clops!" Julie insisted.

"Whoa!" Brenna held up her hands, hoping to break up the argument. "Let's try to compromise, okay?" She glanced around the room. The bookcase, bed, dresser and desk were painted a glossy white. The thick rug was ivory colored and stretched to walls papered with a small print of mint green and dusty rose. Clothes, books and toys were scattered over the plush pile of the carpet.

"Dino-clops!" Scotty declared. "Dino-clops, Dino-clops, Dino-clops!" He stomped his pajama-clad foot and threw his books on the floor.

"Hey—slow down."

"Will not! Mommy read Dino-clops!" he said, his face red as he exploded into a full-fledged, kicking and screaming tantrum.

Brenna tried to comfort him by taking him into her arms, but he jerked away and huge crocodile tears ran from his eyes. "Listen, Scotty, how about if I read one chapter from Julie's book and then one of these—" She reached for one of the books he'd flung onto the floor.

"This one!" he said, grabbing a red-bound book with an ogre-like robot on the cover. His tears disappeared as quickly as they'd poured from his eyes and Brenna felt distinctly as if she'd been manipulated by her five-year-old nephew. She decided she didn't like the feeling much as she settled onto Julie's bed and started reading about the escapades in Mrs. Lily Benwick's second-grade class and a precocious, freckle-faced girl by the name of Sherry Williams.

Julie cuddled up close to her, but Scotty hung back,

preferring to suck his thumb and sit in the middle of the room while running a tiny motorcycle across the carpet.

Brenna had just finished the second page when she felt, rather than saw, Warren leaning in the doorway. She glanced up to find him staring at her, his arms crossed over his chest, his eyes fixed heart-stoppingly on her mouth.

"Problems?" he asked, when she finished the first chapter of Julie's book.

"Aunt Brenna didn't want to read about Dino-clops!" Scotty said, his tiny chin thrust forward petulantly.

"Didn't she?" Warren's thick brows rose skeptically.

"That's his side of the story," Brenna contradicted wryly. "We were going to compromise, remember?"

"Scotty's just being a brat," Julie chimed in.

"Am not! Read!" he ordered, standing to his full three feet and pointing emphatically to the cover of *Dino-clops and the Robomonsters*.

"I don't think so," Warren said, his voice stern.

"She promised," Scotty wailed.

"I did—"

"I know, but we're not going to reward him for this kind of behavior. Come on, sport." He took Scotty's hand but the boy refused to budge, dropping to the floor and becoming dead weight.

"I'll be good, Daddy," Scotty wailed. "I'll be good. Please, please, read!"

"Warren, really, I don't mind," Brenna said, wanting desperately to hold and comfort the boy.

Warren's muscles stiffened. "Another time, maybe," he said, harshly.

"Tonight! Tonight! No—!" Again, Warren carried Scotty, kicking and screaming, down the hall to his room and Brenna felt terrible. Rather than help him, she'd only added to Warren's burden with his children.

Julie must have seen the concern in her eyes. "Don't worry about it—that's just the way Scotty is: the pits!"

"I just wish I could help."

"He'll get over it!" Julie didn't seem the least bit disturbed by her brother's behavior. In fact she grinned widely. "Now you can read another chapter about Sherry Williams," she said brightly, and Brenna, feeling like a traitor, picked up the book.

A few minutes later she tucked Julie into bed and snapped off the light. She heard the steady rhythm of Warren's voice drifting into the hallway from Scotty's room. The door was slightly ajar and she peeked in to find Warren stretched out on Scotty's bed. One arm was draped over his son's small shoulders as he read softly about the war between the Robomonsters and Dino-clops. Scotty sighed and yawned, his mouth working over his thumb.

Sure, Brenna thought, half amused. *Sure, Warren Stone, you're real tough when it comes to your kids.*

She decided that if she were smart, she would leave now, but she couldn't. The door of the master bedroom was ajar and she could see the foot of the bed and a robe—a woman's robe, tossed haphazardly across the coverlet.

Her heartbeat accelerated. Was it Honor's robe—or another woman's? Had she been kidding herself? The thought that Warren had found someone else was chilling and her palms began to sweat. Maybe that's why he didn't want her here—the new woman would object.

Why, then, the shrine to Honor?

And why hadn't anyone, including Julie, mentioned that Warren was seeing someone?

Her throat went dry and she bit into her lower lip. Looking guiltily over her shoulder, she inched down the hall, her curiosity and dread leading her on. She knew that Warren would be furious if he caught her poking around in his bedroom—and rightfully so. Nonetheless, she pushed open the door, intending only to peek inside.

The silver-colored silk dressing gown was draped over a corner of the bed, as if it had been quickly flung aside. Brenna remembered the expensive wrapper as belonging to Honor—a gift from Warren. For a second she was relieved. Dealing with Honor's ghost was difficult enough; Brenna wasn't sure she could face Warren's interest in someone new.

So you still care! Gritting her teeth, she tried to ignore the obvious fact that her emotions for Warren still ran deep.

"Fool," she muttered, snatching the robe from the bed and glancing around the room Warren had shared with Honor. It was enormous. Cream-colored carpet stretched from a bay window at the front of the house to a balcony at the back. The king-sized brass bed occupied the center of the room and was covered in a thick comforter of silver and teal green. Matching chairs were scattered between a dressing table, bureau and chest of drawers in bleached oak.

Telling herself she should leave before Warren caught her, she folded the robe over her arm and walked quickly to the closet. She intended to find a hook or hanger, leave the robe and leave the room. But as she opened the closet door, the scent of cedar and lavender assailed her. Honor's clothes hung like forgotten memories. Full-length gowns, street dresses and sweaters in rich tones from rose to sapphire, forest green to khaki, crowned a row of shoes of every description: pumps, flats, heels and running shoes—even her white wedding slippers.

Honor's presence filled the closet as surely as if she'd been hiding among the gowns and jeans. Brenna could almost feel her sister in the tomblike closet and tears starred her lashes. Her fingers dug into the robe as she felt a pang of regret and grief for someone who was once so dear.

How could she blame Warren for loving Honor so, when she, herself, couldn't let go of the memory of her whimsical sister?

Battling tears, she hung the silvery wrapper on a peg, her fingers sliding down the soft cloth. It was obvious Warren hadn't been able to lay Honor to rest. The fact that she had died didn't alter the fact that Honor was still his wife.

And your sister—the mother of Warren's children.

The closet seemed suddenly claustrophobic and Brenna felt the urge to run, to leave this house—Honor's house—before she did something foolish. Yes, she wanted to help Julie, but deep down, she'd also hoped that she could help Warren. One of her reasons for returning to Oregon, she realized disgustedly, was purely selfish. She'd hoped that Warren would again stare into her eyes as he had that one summer evening in her mother's rose garden.

Sweating, she stepped out of the closet, quietly closed the door and turned, only to find Warren waiting for her. Sitting on the end of the bed, his eyes glittered angrily. "Find what you were looking for?" he asked.

Brenna closed her eyes, aching inside. "No—I wasn't looking for anything."

"Sure you were."

"I saw Honor's robe on the end of the bed and hung it up, that's all."

"Honor's robe?" he repeated.

Her eyes flew open. "Yes—it was right there." She pointed to the comforter, feeling his punishing gaze on her. Almost as if he didn't believe her.

"Her robe wasn't there."

"It was! The silver one! I—I thought you must have left it out...."

"Me?" His brows lifted dubiously and a smile, amused, twisted his thin lips. "I don't wear my wife's clothes."

"I know, but I thought maybe—" she shrugged "—you missed her, so you left her things around."

"That's ridiculous."

"Is it? Look at this house, for crying out loud! Honor's things are everywhere!"

Planting his hands at his sides, he pushed himself upright. "I don't give a damn about her robe," he muttered. "Maybe Julie had it out. She still plays dress-up."

"Oh." Of course—it sounded so logical. And she'd thought he'd been with another woman! Embarrassed, she hoped to avoid his eyes, but couldn't. His angry gaze was too magnetic.

He advanced slowly upon her and her heart began to pound with dread. Why, oh, why, had she felt compelled to linger in Honor's closet?

"You can have anything you want."

"What?"

"Honor's things—her clothes, perfume, whatever. You can have it all."

"No. Oh, no," she replied, breathing rapidly and trying to ease to the door. "Really, there's nothing…"

"Then why?" He was close to her now. So close she could see the pinpoints of furious light in his sea-blue eyes. She wanted to step backward, but couldn't; her shoulders and hips were already pressed to the cool panels of the closet door. "Why didn't you just hang up the robe and leave?"

Though she was dying inside, she inched her chin upward and met the fury in his gaze. "I just wanted to know what was going on in your head," she said. "Julie's worried about you." It wasn't really a lie, she reasoned—the child was concerned.

"Bull—"

"To put it as she did, 'Dad's a basket case.'"

His eyes flickered a little. She noticed the shadow of

his beard darkening his jaw and felt the angry bursts of his breath against her face. "All I am is furious. With you," he drawled slowly. "You have no right—"

"They're Honor's children. She was my sister. My only sister. I have the right to try and help them."

"Honor's children and mine," he corrected. "And I don't see how you expect to help anyone by sneaking into *my* bedroom and searching through the closets."

"I wasn't searching for anything," she argued. "I just want to know why, when Honor's been gone for four months, this house is…is still a shrine to her!"

Anguish twisted his features. "She was my wife."

Dear God, he was hurting so much! She reached upward and, with trembling fingers, touched his jaw. "I'm sorry, Warren," she whispered, her voice suddenly thick. "I miss her, too."

"You don't understand," he rasped, closing his eyes shut tight—guilt contorting his features. "No one can."

"You have to go on. We all do."

He drew in a shaky breath and placed his hands on the panels of the door, imprisoning her. "If you only knew," he whispered.

"I understand—"

He tensed. "I don't think you do," he said, blinking to stare at her. "You never did."

"Oh, Warren—"

The cords of his neck stretched taut. "I don't want your pity, Brenna."

"It's not pity," she whispered, the nearness of him causing her head to spin. She had trouble thinking and noticed the painful lines near his mouth. Heart pounding, she stroked his cheek. "I—I care about you, Warren. I always have."

"Don't, Brenna—" His tortured gaze locked with hers

for an instant before he turned his face in her hand and pressed his mouth against her palm.

The pressure caused her every nerve ending to leap to life and her heart hammered recklessly. His lips were hot and moist against her palm. Brenna's throat constricted. Was this what she'd wanted, what she'd hoped for? To be locked in an intimate embrace with Honor's husband—a man who had scoffed at her vows of love before? "Oh, God," she moaned, knees weak as his mouth moved slowly to the inside of her wrist and she felt the damp impression of his tongue on the heel of her hand. "Warren—"

"Why did you come back?" he asked, his voice hoarse and filled with torment.

The room began to spin.

"I just...I just want to help you—" she whispered weakly.

"And nothing else?"

"I—I don't know—"

He lifted his head to stare into her wide eyes. "Oh, Brenna," he groaned. His lips crashed down on hers so hungrily she gasped. So deep was the kiss, so filled with unleashed passion, she couldn't think beyond the power of his body against hers, the electricity sizzling between them. She was hot and cold and could do nothing but re-spond. When his tongue parted her lips, she complied, al-most eagerly, not daring to think that this man had been her sister's husband, the father of Honor's children, a man driven with the love of his wife to the point that this house was still filled with her essence.

Thoughts of Honor made guilt spread through her breast. But Honor was dead and Warren was still alive and here. *Love me,* she cried mutely, her arms winding around his neck as his weight slowly dragged them both downward. Her blouse slid against the painted panels of the door as her knees buckled, her fingers catching in the thick strands of his dark hair.

She didn't protest when he touched her breast, the flat of his hand molding over one soft mound. Silk rustled beneath his fingertips, and deep within her rib cage her heart was slamming wildly against her chest, her blood screaming through her veins, flaming with foolhardy abandon.

Her blouse was pulled from the waistband of her skirt, inching upward over her flat abdomen, and Warren's fingertips were in stealthy pursuit. One leg slung across her, his lips throbbing against her mouth. Moaning, he moved convulsively as his fingers delved inside her bra to touch a budding nipple.

"Daddy?" Julie knocked on the door.

The ecstasy of the moment was shattered.

Warren stiffened and raised his head, dark hair falling over his brow. With a sound of disgust he rolled away from Brenna and onto his feet. Brenna flushed, embarrassed to tears. She straightened her clothes with trembling fingers. How could she have let things get so out of hand? Her lips felt swollen and her breasts still ached.

"Daddy?"

"Just a minute, sweetheart," he said, his voice strained as he tucked the tails of his shirt into his slacks.

"I just wanted to say good-night."

"I'll be right there."

"Okay."

Cringing inside, her breathing still rapid and shallow, Brenna listened as Julie's small footsteps padded softly down the hall. The door hadn't been locked. What if Julie had just walked in and found her and Warren groping around on the floor like a couple of lusty teenagers? Dear God, she wanted to die. It didn't help that Warren was staring at her as if the entire incident were her fault.

"Damn it!" Warren said, shoving his hair out of his eyes.

She felt the need to apologize, but didn't. She hadn't been any more to blame than he.

"I—I'd better go," she whispered, adjusting the buttons of her blouse and feeling like an utter fool. "This—this wasn't such a good idea."

"Wasn't it?" he mocked, his mouth curving in frustration. "Wasn't it exactly what you expected?"

"No—I…"

"Then what the hell were you doing in *my* bedroom, Brenna?" he hissed. "If this wasn't a seduction—a replay of the past—"

"Seduction?" she repeated, stricken, her cheeks flaming again. "Is that what you think?"

"Frankly I don't know what to think," he admitted. "All I know is that you've insisted on bulldozing your way back into my house and my life, already playing mom to the kids and sneaking down the halls to my bedroom."

"I didn't sneak! And I'm here because *Julie and Scotty* need me. And don't try to blame me—you were pretty involved yourself."

"Maybe that's because I haven't been with a woman in a long time," he said, cutting her to the bone.

Though wounded, she held her voice steady. "I don't believe that any more than you do. If you'd really wanted a woman, I'm sure there are plenty available."

He stared at her in disbelief.

"But that's not the point," she hurried on, afraid she might lose her nerve or that he would contradict her again.

"And what is, Brenna?" he asked, tossing an arm in the air. "Just what the hell is?"

"This house is falling apart, Warren, whether you know it or not. Your daughter is worried sick that you're cracking up and I don't blame her! This place—" she gestured wildly "—is more like a mausoleum than a house. Where's the laughter, Warren? Where's the fun? Those kids are crying out for a little happiness."

His lips curled sarcastically. "All this profound professional psychiatric advice after only being here one afternoon."

"It's been long enough to see that you—all three of you—need help."

His eyes glittered angrily. "Aren't we lucky that you showed up to lead us to salvation?" he mocked.

"Go to hell."

He bit back a quick response.

Brenna walked to the door, her spine as straight as her pride would allow. There was no point in arguing. "Your daughter is waiting," she reminded him, then forced a cold smile. "And I've changed my mind. I won't be needing this." Tossing Honor's car key at him, she yanked open the door only to have it slammed shut by the flat of his hand. The key fell to the floor.

"Slow down a minute," he said, obviously straining to get a rein on his emotions. "I didn't mean—"

"You meant everything you said, Warren. Now, please, if you'll excuse me, I'd like to leave."

"Take the car."

Brenna was exasperated and wounded and she couldn't control her tongue. "No way. You might misconstrue it and think I wanted *Honor's* Audi. Well, I don't. And I'm not trying to steal her husband or mother her kids. As for this house," she said, her smile hard, "you know what you can do with it."

She shoved his stiff arm aside and marched down the hall, past the sounds of contented snoring from Scotty's room, to stop at Julie's door.

"You're still here?" Julie asked from her darkened bedroom.

Brenna smiled and sat on the edge of her niece's bed. "I've got to leave now," she whispered.

"Th-thanks for coming."

"I'm glad I did," she said, though she was still burning from her confrontation with Warren. Without thinking, Brenna leaned forward and kissed Julie's crown.

"Will you come back tomorrow?"

That was the sixty-four-thousand-dollar question, Brenna thought, frowning.

"Please. It's Scotty's birthday. I want to bake a cake!"

Brenna had completely forgotten that Scotty was about to turn six. "I thought you hated him."

"Only sometimes. Please, Aunt Bren?" Julie's small fingers wrapped over Brenna's arm.

"If it's all right with your dad."

"He won't care!"

I wouldn't bet on it, Brenna thought, sensing Warren's presence in the doorway. Obviously, he'd heard the entire conversation. He coughed quietly and Julie turned to the door.

"Dad?" Julie asked. "It's okay, isn't it? We can invite Grandpa, too!"

Brenna stiffened at the mention of her father. She hadn't seen him since the funeral.

"Grandpa's out of town," Warren said softly.

"He is? But he knew I was coming," Brenna said.

"His sister called. He'll be in Boise for a few days," he explained, his eyes still dark. "Olivia needed some help with some estate planning."

Julie sighed loudly and Warren turned to her. "But we'll see him in a couple of days. He said he'd call when he gets in." His eyes narrowed harshly on Brenna. "Maybe he couldn't reach you. Your phone's been disconnected."

"Maybe," she mused.

"But you'll come to the party, won't you?" Julie insisted, turning back to Brenna, her wide eyes reflecting the light from the hall.

"I'll try."

"Promise!" Julie demanded.

"Okay, okay. I promise."

"Good!" Julie clapped her hands together. "It'll be a surprise party!" she exclaimed.

"I'll see you then," Brenna whispered, squeezing Julie's hand. She couldn't read Warren's expression in the darkness, didn't know if he was furious or pleased, and she didn't dare hazard a guess. Tomorrow was her nephew's birthday and the least she could do was buy him a gift and bake him a cake. Warren couldn't object to that!

Leaving father and daughter, she hurried down the curving staircase and walked quickly into the kitchen. Her fingers were shaking as she flipped through the pages of the telephone book and dialed the number of the first cab company listed in the yellow pages.

"A car will be by in fifteen minutes," she was told, and she knew the next quarter of an hour would be the longest of her life. Running trembling hands through her hair, she tried to regain some of her composure as she heard Warren's heavy tread on the stairs.

She braced herself as he walked into the kitchen. "I'm sorry," he said without emotion as he glanced out the window at the dusky night. "When I found you in Honor's closet, I overreacted. I was, er, out of line."

"Again."

"Yes, again."

"Way out of line," she pointed out, then sighed. "But I probably was, too. I didn't mean to snoop. Really."

His mouth tightened.

"It's just that when I put the robe back in the closet, I felt almost as if Honor were there." She sighed. "Crazy, huh?" When he didn't respond, she added, "I didn't mean to pry."

His broad shoulders lifted. "Right. Look—I—I just really don't know how to deal with you, Brenna. You came barging into my life out of the blue and marched right into a hornet's nest. You act as if you want to move here for me and the kids and in the next breath you claim that you're going to work for a newspaper that would like to see me tarred and feathered."

"You're exaggerating again."

He didn't reply, just stared out the window to the glittering lights of Portland in the distance.

She couldn't help pushing. "And you're worse than a chameleon, you know—one minute this way, the next, another."

"Maybe I've never thought straight around you."

"And maybe you're still wallowing in your grief," she said. "Well, we all miss her, you know. Me, the kids and my dad. But we pick up the pieces and go on."

"I don't need a lecture," he said testily.

"Good, 'cause I'm not about to give you one." A horn honked and she realized the cab was waiting. "Good night, Warren," she whispered, then ran to the front hall, snatched her jacket off the hall tree and grabbed her purse. She could feel Warren's eyes on her, but she didn't look back, just opened the front door and closed it softly behind her. She wouldn't give him the satisfaction of knowing that she was still unnerved. Nor would she admit just how desperately she wished he would take her in his arms again. No sir. The next time, should there be one, she wouldn't let passion or faded memories cloud her judgment. If Warren Stone ever kissed her again, she'd be as cold as a North Sea wind.

WARREN DIDN'T MOVE. Through the tall windows near the door, he saw her dash down the path to the front gate and slide into the backseat of the cab. Headlights flashed through the windows as the car turned around to speed down the hill. The sound of the thrumming engine slowly disappeared.

He jammed his hands into his pockets and strode into his study. So what if she'd returned? What did he care that she was back in Portland? He couldn't get involved with his wife's sister, for God's sake.

Scowling, he opened a cupboard door, found a new bottle of Scotch and cracked the seal. Despite how he felt for Brenna, he had to remember that she was off limits. He had to. Not only for his own peace of mind, but because he had to protect his children. Thanks to Len Patterson and the shoddy reporting in the *Willamette Examiner*, there had been enough of a scandal when Honor had died. The whole mess had affected the kids as well as his job. Warren couldn't afford any more fuel for the fires of gossip.

Nope, he decided again, he couldn't let Brenna get to him. He splashed some liquor into a glass and tossed it down, then he resolutely recapped the bottle and switched off the light.

Glancing through the window, he looked past the yawning black hillside to the flickering lights of Portland in the distance. Somehow, some way, he told himself, he'd have to pretend that Brenna was nothing more than Honor's sister. And he could never allow another mistake—like the scene in his bedroom—to happen again.

So how will you stop it? a voice in his mind taunted. *How, when right this very minute, you can't help thinking about what would have happened if Julie hadn't knocked....*

Heat rose from his loins and thundered through his veins. It had been a long time since he'd been with a woman—too long. His sense of morality had kept him monogamous for the past ten years. Never once had he betrayed Honor. Not while she was living—not since her death.

But now, Brenna was back, stirring up old emotions and trouble.

Sick with disgust, he realized that it would only be a matter of time before he tried to make love to her. Even now he could envision her laughing hazel eyes, wisping auburn hair and secretive smile.

The ache deep within burned hotter and he tossed back his drink to drive away the humiliating urge to chase after her. The drink didn't help. It settled warm and cozy in his stomach but didn't push away the overwhelming feeling that he was about to make a huge mistake.

"Isn't one enough?" he muttered unkindly as he stared at the bottle and considered the last few years of his marriage to Honor. Frowning, he pondered another drink, then shoved the fifth back into the cupboard. Muscles knotted with tension, he trudged upstairs to face the stinging needles of an ice-cold shower.

CHAPTER FOUR

BRENNA'S STOMACH WAS in knots. She sat across from Len Patterson, editor of the *Willamette Examiner*, and waited as he studied her résumé and letter of recommendation. A tall, lanky man with thinning red hair and a pair of sharp brown eyes that constantly darted around the room, he'd talked with her for more than an hour. Though she felt the interview had gone well, her nerves were stretched to the breaking point.

"To be honest with you, Miss Douglass—"

"Brenna," she interjected.

He smiled. "Brenna. We're looking for someone with a little more experience reporting hard news. You've spent most of your time in the women's section." He frowned and picked up several articles she'd written for the *City Weekly*. "But your work is good—very good. And Stan Gladstone seems to think you can walk on water."

"Not quite," she replied.

Rubbing his chin, he obviously wrestled with his decision as he lifted her résumé from his desk. "Douglass?" he said as if turning her name over in his mind. He pulled pensively on his lower lip. "You wouldn't have been related to Honor Douglass Stone, would you?"

Brenna wanted to lie. The hairs on the back of her neck bristled. "She was my sister," she said simply.

"A tragedy," Len whispered. His high, freckled forehead wrinkled. "I'm sorry."

"So am I." Her throat felt hot.

He coughed then and let her résumé drift back to his desk. "How would you feel about a column twice a week like the one you wrote in San Francisco as well as pinch-hitting for our regular news team? You would probably have to cover a news story once, maybe a couple of times a week."

It sounded like heaven. "I'm sure I can handle it," she said without a trace of the nervousness invading her stomach. She thought fleetingly of Warren and how he would react, but decided that her career was no concern of his.

"Then it looks like we've got a deal. The job is yours, if you want it."

"I do," she said, relieved.

"Good, good. Glad to have you on the team." He pressed his palms against his desk and straightened before reaching across his desk to shake Brenna's hand. "I think you're just what the *Examiner* needs."

"I hope so."

"So your first day on the job will be May 17," he said, relinquishing her hand to thumb through his desk calendar. "Karla and Tammy will show you the ropes then—but you'll report directly to me."

"Good."

"See you then."

"Right," she agreed, eyeing his neat office. Not a paper was out of place. His pens were at attention in a coffee mug with big red letters spelling The Buck Stops Here. The prints on his walls, pastel watercolors of sailboats and sea gulls, were perfectly hung, and a copy of this morning's edition of the *Examiner* was neatly folded on a corner of his oversized desk. "Thank you, Mr. Patterson."

"Call me Len," he insisted. "It makes things simpler."

"Fair enough." As she walked out of his office, she exhaled. She'd crossed one hurdle, but not the most difficult. Now she had to face Warren with the news.

"Good luck," she whispered under her breath as she stepped through the revolving glass door of the *Examiner*'s lobby and into the late afternoon sunshine. Horns blared as cars and pedestrians vied for street space, but high overhead the sky was blue, only a few tattered white clouds blocking the sun.

"It's now or never," she told herself, hailing a cab and climbing into the worn backseat.

"Where to?" the driver asked, glancing in the rearview mirror as he guided the car into thick afternoon traffic.

Brenna reeled off Warren's address and the cabby's dark brows rose a fraction. "The heights," he murmured, cranking the wheel toward the forested hills surrounding the downtown area.

"Visiting friends?" the driver asked.

"Family," she said, not really thinking. "My brother-in-law, Warren Stone."

"The D.A.?"

Brenna smiled faintly. "Yes."

The cabdriver's dark eyes flashed in the mirror. "So you're related to him? He can't keep his name out of the papers, that one."

Brenna didn't comment and stared out the window, but she cringed inside. She wondered about the cab driver's remark as well as Len Patterson's immediate association between her and Honor. What if Warren was right about the *Examiner*?

Too late, she decided as she paid the driver and stepped out of the cab. She had landed the job at the newspaper and she intended to make the most of it.

She knocked once on the front door and heard the scramble of feet inside before it flew open. "I knew you'd come!" Julie cried, throwing her arms around Brenna's waist.

"I promised, didn't I?"

"I know. But Scotty bet me you wouldn't show up."

Brenna grinned. "I hope he didn't gamble away his life savings."

"Fifty bucks!" Julie said, her eyes gleaming.

"Did not!" From the upper landing Scotty threw a plastic dinosaur and it landed with a thud a few feet from his sister.

"You did, too, you little twerp!"

"Enough, enough," Brenna whispered, then glanced up at her nephew. "Happy birthday, Scotty."

His lower lip protruded. "Did you bring me a present?"

"I sure did."

His blue eyes twinkled and he edged toward the stairs. "Can I have it now?"

"Not yet, stupid," Julie said, her eyebrows drawing downward. "You have to wait until we have cake and ice cream and you blow out the candles." She rolled her eyes at Brenna. "He doesn't really understand."

"Let's give him a little time," Brenna suggested.

"Okay. But I wouldn't let Mrs. Beatty make the cake until you got here! Come on."

Wiping her hands on her apron, Mary Beatty rounded the corner from the kitchen. "Who was at the door?" she asked before catching sight of Brenna. "Thank God you're here," she said emphatically. "This one—" she gestured toward Julie "—has been on pins and needles since she got home from school."

"Well, we'd better take care of that right now."

"I've got everything ready for you and I'll just get out of the way, if you don't mind watching the kids until Warren gets home."

Brenna's heart did a stupid little flip and she blushed but managed to say, "No problem."

"And remind him that he told me not to cook—that

he was taking Scotty out for his birthday. I don't want to hear any complaints about the refrigerator being empty."

"I'll give him the word," Brenna promised.

"About time someone did," Mary muttered. Then, failing to smother a knowing smile, Mary grabbed her raincoat from the front closet, reminded the children to be on their best behavior and hurried outside. Once the housekeeper was through the door, Brenna glanced up, past the chandelier and through the balusters to Scotty on the top step. "You want to help?" she asked.

"He can't! The cake's for him!" Julie protested.

"Can, too!" Scotty insisted.

"But—"

"Of course he can. Come on Scotty—but wash your hands first!" She pushed Julie in the direction of the kitchen.

"Boys don't cook!" Julie said angrily.

"Sure they do—if someone gives them a chance."

"But this was supposed to be just for you and me!"

Brenna's brows lifted but she knelt beside her niece. "We'll do something alone later. Just the two of us. But right now, let's include Scotty."

"He'll just ruin it!"

"Will not!" Scotty ran into the room, shoved a chair next to the sink and climbed onto its seat. "See my loose tooth?" he asked proudly, opening his mouth to show a top front tooth dangling by a small fiber.

"Oh! Gross! Tell him he *can't* cook like that."

"Come on, Julie, be a sport," Brenna chided. "You've lost a few yourself."

Shrugging as if she were bored to tears, Julie reluctantly agreed and, with Brenna's help, measured the flour. Scotty promptly dumped one cup onto the tile floor and spent the next twenty minutes pushing his cars through the "snow."

"I told you," Julie whispered to Brenna.

"Let him play, he's not hurting anything."

"Mommy would have had a fit!"

Brenna was tired of being compared with Honor. "Probably," she admitted. "But I'm not your mom. As long as Scotty doesn't track it into the other rooms, we can clean it up."

"Not me!" Julie vowed.

"I will!" Scotty's face, hair and clothes were covered with a fine white powder, but for the first time since she'd arrived, Brenna saw a grin spread from one side of his face to the other. "And I want to lick the bowl!"

"I do!"

"I'm sure there's enough for both of you," Brenna said, feeling more like a referee than an aunt. She helped Scotty back onto his chair. "We'll lick beaters and bowl, *after* we clean up. Here, you can help pour the batter." Brenna helped Scotty with the bowl. He readily complied, carefully spooning the yellow mix into three layer pans before Brenna shoved them into the oven.

While the cake baked, they worked together to clean the mess, fortunately with minimal bickering. Julie began washing dishes, Scotty tried to dry and Brenna tackled the floor. She was sweeping Scotty's snow city into the dustpan when the back door creaked open and Warren strode in.

"Daddy!" Scotty scrambled out of his chair, knocking over a measuring pitcher, which Brenna caught before it crashed to the floor.

Warren lifted his son over his head and surveyed the counters, sink and floor. "This looks more like a battle zone than a kitchen."

"Maybe, but it'll be worth the mess," Brenna declared, wiping a smudge of flour from her cheeks just as the timer buzzed.

Julie took the layers carefully from the oven. "Don't they smell good?"

"Delicious."

"Did you bring me a present?" Scotty asked as Warren placed him back on the floor.

"What do you think?"

"Aunt Brenna did!"

"She did, did she?" Warren glanced at Brenna and she felt her pulse jump. Just one look from his blue, blue eyes and her wayward heart was racing.

"She says so!" Scotty insisted.

Warren winked at his son. "Well, so did I. Why don't you take a look outside?"

Both Scotty and Julie scrambled for the back door, running to the porch and squealing excitedly. "A bike! A bike!" Scotty cried, still jumping up and down when Brenna walked through the door. "Look, Aunt Brenna!"

"It's great." Brenna eyed the small silver bike with its heavy-treaded tires as Scotty climbed onto the seat and wobbled off the porch. The bike touched ground and Scotty pedaled faster to the cement of the driveway before nearly crashing into a rhododendron bush.

"He still needs training wheels," Julie whispered before dashing into the garage and reappearing on her own two-wheeler.

Resting her hip against a pillar supporting the roof of the porch, Brenna watched the children, though she was aware of Warren standing next to her. He was so near she could feel the heat of his body, hear the shallow whisper of his breath. "I think he likes it," she said, nodding toward Scotty.

Warren snorted. "He's been badgering me for weeks."

"It worked, didn't it?"

One side of Warren's mouth lifted. "Yep. I guess I'm

just a pushover. Just don't let the constituents know it. If the word gets out, I could lose my job."

Brenna's eyes sparkled. "No one, Mr. Stone, Mr. D.A. sir, would ever have the nerve to call you a pushover, believe me."

"Is that right?" Pressing his forearm on the post over her head, he leaned forward, his face so close to hers she could see the darker ring of blue around his irises as he gazed into her eyes. Slowly, he lifted a strand of her hair and studied the red streaks in her auburn curls. The scent of pine and lilac wafted through the air and warm rays of afternoon sunshine slanted through the branches of the trees near the porch.

"I—I think so."

"Hmm. You know, I remember this one girl who used to goad me into doing things I usually didn't." His thin lips twitched at the memory.

Good Lord, he was so close! Brenna had trouble finding her breath.

His eyes narrowed thoughtfully. "She talked me into climbing Rooster Rock, shooting the rapids of the Deschutes, riding bareback on the wildest horse on her father's farm—that sort of thing. But the trouble was, I just thought she was a crazy kid."

Brenna's cheeks grew hot.

"But she talked me into things I normally wouldn't have done—showed me things I'd never seen. And you know what?" he asked, his voice low.

"Wh-what?" Her heart was crashing against her chest.

"I don't think I ever thanked her."

Swallowing back a huge lump in her throat, she glanced away. "I don't think she expected it."

"Maybe not." His thumb touched the underside of her chin, forced her eyes back to his. "But she deserved it." Warren's face was sober and unlined, his eyes filled with the warmth she remembered and hadn't seen in ten long years. "I've made a lot of mistakes, Bren," he said, his voice low and gruff, his lips near hers. "And I've had my share of regrets, believe me. But I know, and I suppose I've always known, that you…you helped me through a lot of rough times."

"You don't have to say all this."

"Sure, I do. I should have said it a long time ago."

"Warren—"

"Shh." He pressed a finger to her lips and his gaze locked with hers. "I was an ass when you offered to help me at the funeral. I know you just wanted to help and I shouldn't have been so hard on you." The finger beneath her chin stroked softly and she turned liquid inside. "It was just all so difficult to deal with," he whispered. "There were things that happened between Honor and me before her death…things I hadn't sorted out."

"Are they sorted out now?"

"I don't know." He glanced past her shoulder to the yard, and the brackets near his lips deepened. "But, believe it or not, I'm glad you're here." His eyes searched hers. "I've missed you, Bren."

"Hey, Aunt Brenna! Look!" Scotty's voice rang through the lilac-scented air.

Warren stiffened and Brenna turned just in time to see her nephew riding his new bike with his hands high in the air. "Oh, Scotty, don't—"

Too late. The front wheel wobbled and the silver bicycle skidded into the door of the garage. Scotty slammed into the ground and started to scream.

Warren was down the steps and across the small stretch of grass in seconds. Brenna was on his heels.

"Hold on a minute," Warren whispered quietly, disentangling his son from the whirling spokes and greasy chain.

Scotty's jeans had split at the knee and tears rolled down his cheeks.

"Is he gonna be okay?" Julie asked as she jumped off her bike at the scene of the disaster.

"I think so." Warren hoisted Scotty into his arms and wiped the tears from his eyes. "Just a skinned knee and a bruised ego."

"He was showing off!" Julie pointed out.

"I think he knows that now," Brenna whispered, watching Warren hold his son as the boy's sobs slowly quieted. "I'll get the bandages and antiseptic."

"Then maybe we'd better get out of here, before someone really gets hurt," Warren decided as Brenna ran back into the house for the medical supplies.

By the time she returned, Warren had propped Scotty up on the rail of the porch, stripped off his jeans and washed his knee. Scotty was still sniffling as Warren sprayed his scrape with antiseptic and covered his knee with bandages. "Maybe you were right," he muttered to Brenna as he lifted Scotty to his feet, "I should have been a doctor. Come on, sport," he said to his son. "Let's go upstairs and change, then I'll buy you dinner." He glanced at Brenna. "You're invited, you know."

Shaking her head, Brenna whispered, "This is your time with your kids. I don't want to intrude—"

Warren touched the back of her neck and his expression was gentle. "Please," he insisted. "I want you with us. So do the kids."

"Yes, come on, Aunt Bren," Julie cried, and even Scotty tugged on her blouse.

"Okay, okay," she replied, unable to resist.

While Warren was helping Scotty into clean clothes and Julie was changing, Brenna frosted the cake. A few nagging doubts entered her mind, telling her that she was making a big mistake, reminding her of how cruel and cold Warren could be, telling her that he would be furious when he found out about her job at the paper.

Nonetheless, she finished decorating the cake and placing it in a box just as Warren returned. "All set?" he asked as Scotty and Julie flew through the kitchen and outside.

"I guess so." She found her purse and gift for Scotty. "If you're sure this is okay. I don't want to be accused of butting in later."

His eyes flashed for just a second, then he sighed. "Believe me," he mocked. "I'd be honored." With a sweeping gesture, he held open the back door.

Rather than toss back a hot retort, she swept through the door and climbed into the front seat of his car.

"Where are we going?" Scotty asked the minute Warren slid behind the wheel.

"Guess!"

"The Circus!" Julie and Scotty chimed.

"That's right." Warren grinned and winked at Brenna as he flicked on the ignition and shoved the gearshift into reverse. "Don't expect a gourmet meal."

"I won't."

The Circus, a restaurant in the shape of a huge tent, was a madhouse. Warren had reserved a table in "ring three," an enormous room with slides and carousel animals in vibrant colors of red, yellow and blue. Scotty and Julie ran through a fun house, stuck their faces through cutouts in the wall and slid down the circular slide while Brenna and Warren waited for their pizza.

"You come here often?" she asked, eyeing the children and parents, helium balloons and video games.

"As seldom as possible."

"I can't imagine why," she quipped, just as a huge pepperoni and sausage pizza was placed between them by a waiter in striped overalls. Warren waved his children to the table and for the next fifteen minutes they ate, battling with the stringy cheese and leaving crusts on their plates.

"Is that for me?" Scotty asked, eyeing the yellow package Brenna had propped against his chair.

"You bet."

"What is it?"

"Why don't you find out?"

Scotty didn't need any further invitation. He tore into the yellow paper and discarded the blue ribbon to uncover the latest book in the Dino-clops series and a matching movable plastic toy, a miniature of one of the robotlike dinosaurs. Scotty grinned from ear to ear and offered her a gap-toothed smile. "Thanks."

"You're wel—what happened to your front tooth?" Brenna asked.

Scotty's smile disappeared and he felt the hole between his teeth with his tongue before his face fell into an expression of complete misery. "It's gone!" he wailed. "Now the tooth fairy won't come!"

"You don't know where it is?" Julia asked.

"Maybe we'll find it," Warren said.

Brenna didn't see how. In the past few hours, Scotty had crashed on a bicycle, slid head first down a whirling slide, felt his way through a fun house and run in circles through a labyrinthine restaurant.

"We'll *never* find it!" Julie predicted. "I guess you just won't get a quarter."

Scotty withered into a stream of fresh tears.

"Oh, you don't know," Brenna replied. "I lost a whole mouthful of teeth and got paid for every one of them— even the ones I lost out on Grandpa's farm."

"Really?" Julie wasn't convinced, but Scotty was on the edge of his seat.

"Really," Brenna proclaimed, viewing Warren in the

corner of her eye. She gave him a kick under the table. "You remember, don't you?"

"Oh—uh, sure," he said unconvincingly.

"So, don't worry about it." She removed the cake from the box and set it in front of Scotty. "Come on, I'll light the candles, we'll sing and Scotty can make a wish."

"I wish I had my tooth!"

Brenna ignored that and lit the candles and within minutes the tooth was forgotten and she served everyone a slice of cake. "You did a great job on this," she said to Julie.

"Thanks—ooh—" Julie bit down and then pressed her napkin to her face. Sputtering, she spit the remains of her mouthful onto her plate and there, in the middle of mushed cake crumbs, was Scotty's baby tooth. "Yuk! Oh, gross! Oh, ick!"

"My tooth!" Scotty cried triumphantly, picking up the tiny white piece of enamel and stuffing it quickly in his pocket.

"How did it get in there?" Julie whispered, looking as if she were about to throw up. "You little dwork. You did this on purpose!"

"Did not!"

"Dad!"

"I think it's time to go," Warren said quickly, and Brenna forced herself to smother a smile as she gathered their things and headed, a sick-looking Julie in tow, to the car.

A few hours later, as Julie was washing her face, she glanced at Brenna in the mirror. "I'll probably die from Scotty's germs!" she pronounced.

"I don't think so."

Julie shuddered. "He's just so...so gross!"

Brenna smiled. "That's *exactly* what your mother used to say about me."

"She did?"

"Sure—it's all part of the big sister, little sister, or brother, routine. And it wasn't true. Just like it's not true with Scotty. Now, come on, finish up and climb into bed." She followed Julie into her room and felt warm inside, almost as if she could, someday, truly be a part of this small family—Honor's family.

"Will you be here tomorrow?" Julie asked as she snuggled under the covers. "It's Saturday."

"I don't think so," Brenna hedged. "I have to find a place to live."

"But, afterward—"

"I'll think about it," Brenna promised as she snapped off the light. "Good night."

"'Night," Julie mumbled into her pillow.

"Do think about it," Warren suggested in the hall.

"You were eavesdropping!" Brenna accused.

Warren lifted one shoulder. "Maybe a little."

She couldn't hide her smile as she reached for the banister. "I don't know—"

Warren's large hand folded over hers. "I thought I made myself clear on the porch," he said, and her pulse quickened at his touch.

The hall was shadowed, the only illumination a faint shaft of moonlight filtering through a two-story window in the foyer, and Warren's face, more angular in the halflight, was intense.

"You might change your mind," she whispered as he glanced to the hollow of her throat. "Your mood swings have been pretty noticeable."

His sensual lips tightened. "I don't think so." His thumb traced the cords in the back of her wrist, making it all the more difficult for her to tell him about her job with the newspaper.

"What if—what if I were to tell you that I landed the

job at the *Examiner*?" she asked, and he froze, his thumb motionless over her pulse.

"You didn't."

It was a flat, cold statement and it chilled her to the bone. "I start on the seventeenth."

In the darkness, she could see Warren's eyes narrow. "Did Len Patterson tell you why he hired you?"

"Yes. Because of Stan's recommendation and samples of my work."

"Humph."

Tossing her hair over her shoulder, she pinned him with her gaze. "Whether you believe it or not, Warren, I'm a good reporter. I *can* make a career for myself without any help from you—on my own merit."

"I wasn't questioning your ability," he said slowly. "I'm just not sure I trust Len Patterson's motives."

"Has anyone ever told you you're too suspicious?"

One corner of his mouth twitched. "A few people," he admitted.

"Well, they're right, every last one of them." Because she knew the conversation could only deteriorate, she hastened down the stairs and marched into the den. As she picked up the phone to call a cab, she noticed a copy of a rival newspaper lying open on the desk. The headline screamed up at her:

KIDNAPPING CASE IN QUESTION

She snatched the paper with shaking fingers only to read that Charlie Saxton's case could be thrown out because of a report by the *Examiner* in which Charlie was named a kidnapper rather than an *alleged* kidnapper.

"That's a prime example of what the *Examiner* calls reporting," Warren said just as the operator answered.

Brenna dropped the paper as if it were hot and requested

a car. Fortunately, there was a cab in the area. Replacing the receiver in its cradle, she met the fire in Warren's eyes.

"I only hope you realize what could happen at that rag," he warned ominously. "That reputation you're so proud of just might get tarnished."

"I'll be careful," she vowed, her chin inching steadily upward. "Don't worry."

"That's the problem, Brenna," he whispered. "I always do with you."

A horn blasted outside. Brenna brushed past Warren and through the front door, barely daring to breathe. Her heart was racing, her hair flying behind her as she dashed to the cab and crawled inside.

"Where to?" the cabdriver asked as he pulled away.

"Anywhere," she murmured under her breath as she leaned back in the seat. "Anywhere."

CHAPTER FIVE

BRENNA HANDED THE landlady a check for the first month's rent and security deposit.

"You'll love it here," Mrs. Thompson predicted.

"I hope so." Leaning over the curved rail of the balcony, Brenna wondered if she were making a huge mistake. Only five blocks west, across a deep ravine, was Warren's house. From her small fourth-story loft, she could see the ivy-covered brick chimneys rising above the trees.

"It's got everything you need," Mrs. Thompson pointed out. "*If* the stairs don't bother you."

"The exercise won't hurt me," Brenna replied as she walked Evelyn Thompson to the door and accepted the key.

"I'll have this place cleaned this afternoon. You can move in next week."

"I'll be here." As the landlady climbed down the stairs, Brenna eyed the single-bedroom apartment. With dormered windows and sloped ceilings, the cozy three rooms had once been servants' quarters to the family of a timber baron. The family had lived in the lower three floors at the turn of the century. In the late 1940s the house had been cut into four individual apartments and this one, on the uppermost story, reminded Brenna of her little loft in San Francisco. She locked the French doors and glanced again across the narrow ravine to Warren's house. Smoke curled from the tall brick chimney and morning sun reflected jewel-like on the leaded windows of his home. Brenna wondered what he and the children were doing just then and how he would react when he found out she lived within walking distance of him.

"Who knows?" she murmured as she crossed the apartment, walked onto the landing and locked the door behind her. Warren's moods were too mercurial and unpredictable for her to hazard a guess at his reaction. "Time will tell," she told herself and hurried downstairs.

THE OLD FARMHOUSE hadn't changed much. Still in need of a coat of paint, with rusted downspouts and a moss-covered roof, it stood as it had for nearly a hundred years on the banks of the Willamette.

Dixie, a golden lab who had replaced Ulysses years before, ran barking and wagging her tail as Brenna arrived. Cutting the engine of her rented car, Brenna braced herself for her reunion with her father. They hadn't seen each other since the funeral, though they'd spoken on the phone often enough. Snatching up her purse, she climbed out of the Ford and stopped to pat the dog, who pawed and whined for more attention.

"And I missed you, too," Brenna said, scratching Dixie behind her ears. With the dog bounding ahead, she strode through what remained of the rose garden to the back porch.

"Brenna!" James Douglass's voice boomed through the kitchen and he flung open the door. Wearing striped overalls and a dusty cap, he appeared older than she remembered. His face, wrinkled and ruddy, split with a wide grin. "About time you showed up!"

"Hi, Dad," she said, feeling his strong arms wrap around her. He smelled of earth and tobacco—familiar, childhood scents. A thick lump formed in Brenna's throat. "Sorry I'm late, I got held up looking for apartments today. But I didn't think you'd mind. Warren said you just got home last night."

"Yep—and the plane was late. I swear I'll never visit Liv again."

"And she'll skin you alive if you don't," Brenna said with a fond glint in her eye. Aunt Olivia resided in Boise and James had always complained about visiting his eldest sister.

"So—did ya find a place to live?"

She nodded. "A one-bedroom walk-up in the heights."

"Near Warren's house?"

"A stone's throw," she admitted, frowning.

His old face brightened. "How does he like that?"

"He doesn't know about it yet."

"He will. Soon enough," James decided. "Now, tell me, how've ya been?" he asked, holding her at arm's length and studying her with a practiced eye. "Not puttin' on any weight, are ya?"

"I hope not."

"Humph. You always were a skinny thing," he muttered, then clapped her on the back. "Well, come on in, I've been waitin' all mornin' to catch up. I guess if you're lookin' for an apartment, that means you got the job."

"Looks that way," she admitted, relieved that some of the tension between them had eased. She'd worried that her father might be distant, but she couldn't have been more wrong. He seemed genuinely glad to see her.

"This calls for a celebration, don't you think?" He reached high into a cupboard and pulled out two chipped cups, then hung his faded baseball cap on a rack near the back door.

"I guess."

"Well, sit down and act as if you're gonna stay awhile," he insisted as he poured them each a cup of coffee from a tin pot perking on one burner of the wood stove. The kitchen smelled of burning wood, bacon grease and tobacco. Cobwebs hung from the high ceiling and the linoleum floor was stained and cracked. The painted cabinets were chipped and dingy and the entire room looked like it could use a ceiling-to-floor douse of Lysol.

Nonetheless, it felt good to be home.

She sat in one of the cane-back chairs, careful that the woven seat of the chair she chose was still intact. "I am— staying awhile, that is."

"Good, good, now where is that…?" he mumbled, searching through a tall cabinet once used for his hunting rifles. "Here we go!" Grinning, he withdrew a dusty bottle of Irish whiskey. "Join me?" he asked, pouring a stiff shot into one coffee cup and holding the open bottle over the other.

"Don't you think it's a little early?"

He glanced at his watch. "Nope. It's already afternoon." After lacing the second cup with a healthy dose, he offered it to her. "It's not every day you blow into town."

"It has been a while," she admitted, sipping from the strong brew and watching as Dixie circled before plopping next to the stove.

"Well, I'm glad you're back, believe me," he said. "I just wish you could've picked a better rag to work for."

"Rag?" Brenna repeated, bristling. Had Warren already called and complained to James?

"Well, you know, the *Willamette Examiner* isn't the most popular paper in town."

Brenna stared at her father. "I think it is. The paper has a circulation of—"

"Oh, I know it sells well. But it's not too popular with me." His eyes grew dark and serious. "Several times they've done a hatchet job on Warren," he said, nearly under his breath, then forced a smile. "You've already seen him?" he asked, blue eyes questioning as he sat in his favorite chair, his back to the warmth of the stove.

Brenna swirled the coffee in her cup. "I think maybe

we should talk about that," she said. "Yes, I saw him—yesterday and the day before."

"You celebrate Scotty's birthday?"

"Yes." Her brow creasing, she added, "When I got here I was surprised that you hadn't told him I'd be visiting. He didn't have any idea that I was moving up. Apparently Julie didn't tell him about it until the day I arrived and you somehow neglected to mention it."

James's lower lip protruded thoughtfully. "I didn't see any reason to tell him."

"Why?"

He lifted one broad shoulder. "Oh, you know Warren, he's always had…a difficult time dealing with you."

"Someone should have warned him."

"And how would you have liked it if I'd told him, hmm? Wouldn't you have accused me of meddling?"

"Maybe," she admitted.

"Nope," he decided. "I was best out of it. Let the two of you battle like you always have."

"We don't—"

He held up a hand. "Let's not argue, okay? Besides, Warren and the kids will be here soon." He forced a smile and fished in the pocket of his shirt for a crumpled pack of cigarettes.

"They'll be here?" she asked in confusion. "Why?"

"I invited them—"

"Whoa. Slow down a minute. *You* invited Warren and his family out here when you knew I'd be here?"

"Right." He struck a match over the top of the stove and lit his cigarette.

"So what was with all the questions—you must have already talked everything over with Warren," she accused.

"All I did was ask the family out for a late celebration of Scotty's birthday. No harm in that."

"And Warren agreed?"

"Seemed to like the idea," he said, in a stream of blue smoke as he waved out the match.

"I don't believe it!"

"Look, Brenna, we've had enough trouble in this family and I've been as much to blame as anyone." His eyes grew dark. "You've been in California for nearly ten years and the times you did come to visit, it was always strained around here. Now that Honor's gone, rest her soul, we've got to try our best to pull what little family we have together."

He seemed so sincere and his face had lost some of its animation. His hands were folded over the table and he squinted through the smoke from his cigarette as it curled to the yellowed ceiling.

Brenna was flabbergasted. "Ten years ago you did everything in your power to keep me away from Warren."

"That was then," he said flatly.

"So what's changed?"

His old lips thinned. "You know what. Honor's dead. Her children don't have a mother and Warren—well, he's about as useful as a cougar without claws."

Brenna nearly choked on her coffee. "You don't expect me to just come up here and step into Honor's shoes?" she asked, wounded all over again. Didn't her father understand she was her own person?

"Of course not, Brenna," he said on a sigh. Stubbing out his cigarette, he snorted. "Maybe I'm just tryin' to make up for past mistakes. Lord knows I've made more than my share, 'specially where you're concerned."

"What's that supposed to mean?"

"Only that I didn't do right by you. Because I thought you were stronger than Honor—"

"But I wasn't!"

"Sure you were. Oh, I know she held us all together when your mama died, but she was still weak—inexperienced, maybe, when it came to practical matters such as a job or men. Good God, she almost threw Warren over for some no-good creep in debt to his neck."

"Jeff Prentice," Brenna said.

"Right. Crazy bastard, that one."

"Jeff was okay," she murmured, wondering why she felt the need to defend someone she'd never liked.

"Barely." Then he caught the look in her eye. "Oh, he turned out all right," James allowed. "But back then he was hell on wheels and *not* the man for your sister, believe me. She, of course, didn't know it." He lifted his hands and flexed his fingers, as if pleading with her to understand. "You, on the other hand, always knew what you wanted and had the grades and ambition to get it. From the first time you were able to read the funny papers, you wanted to be a writer—and look, you've done it."

"But Honor—"

"Had her head in the clouds. Thought she'd be a model, you know."

"She could have been."

"What kind of a job is that?"

"A good one, Dad. And Honor could have made it!"

"Bah—that's no life."

"Maybe not for you. But it was what Honor wanted," Brenna said, remembering all the times Honor had whispered her dreams to her sister. "And she was so…beautiful."

"Oh, she had the looks, all right," her father agreed, his eyes growing wistful. "I'm not denyin' that. But she didn't have any street smarts—no savvy. She always thought with her heart instead of her head and she had no drive— no determination. It was modelin' one week, becoming a stewardess or flight attendant or whatever they're called the next. She even had the crazy notion that she could become an actress, for cryin' out loud!" He shook his head and a shock of white hair fell over his eyes. "Warren Stone was the best thing that ever happened to her. I knew she'd never make it on her own—she needed a steady man."

"You just didn't want her to leave," Brenna thought aloud, remembering how much her father had loved Honor.

"That's part of it, I suppose," he allowed, frowning. "I always felt I had to protect her—point her down the right path." He rubbed a weary hand over his forehead. "I miss her, Brenna. She was just so special—like your ma."

Brenna didn't know what to say. Honor was gone—all of her dreams gone with her. Fingering the handle of her cup, Brenna whispered, "Honor had the right to live her own life, Dad."

"I know, I know." He stood, his back creaking as he straightened. "I suppose I shouldn't have interfered, but I thought I was doing right." Glancing guiltily in her direction, he squared his old Dodgers cap on his head. "Hindsight isn't always such a good thing."

He smiled. "Come on, now, let me show you what I've done in the orchard."

Dixie scrambled to her feet and stretched. Yawning, she ambled to the door, her claws scraping loudly on the old floor. Brenna shoved her chair back and followed her father onto the porch. They walked together through an overgrown path to the side of the barn where ancient apple, pear, plum and cherry trees grew. Blossoms of pink and white scented the air and bees hummed in the branches overhead. Dixie lifted her nose, whined and then took off to bark angrily at a stack of mossy oak piled against the weathered siding of the barn.

"Gray digger," James remarked, fishing in his pocket for his cigarettes again. "She'll probably go out of her mind until I tear the woodpile apart for her. By then the gray digger will be long gone."

"You've been working," she said, ignoring Dixie and eyeing some younger trees.

"About all I do these days," he admitted, stuffing his hands into his back pockets. "This and raise a few head of beef. Can't handle much more. I rent most of the farm to Craig Matthews."

"Do you?" She couldn't help but smile. Despite his anger on the night they'd broken up because of Warren, Craig had remained her friend. She'd attended his wedding and was glad when he'd finally found someone to love him. Though Brenna seldom saw him, she always sent a Christmas card and had received one back, until the past holiday season. "That's great. How is he? I haven't heard from him in nearly a year."

"He and his wife divorced," James said with a frown. "Don't know why—I never asked."

Brenna felt a pang of regret. "That's too bad."

"Well, it happened almost a year ago—he seems to have picked up the pieces pretty well."

"Aunt Bren!" Julie's voice sang through the fields. "Grandpa!"

Brenna turned and saw her young niece, blond hair rippling behind her as she ran down the path, Scotty on her heels.

"How's my dumplin'?" James asked, bending down and gathering a squealing Julie in his arms.

"Me, too!" Scotty demanded.

"Of course you, too." James hoisted Scotty in one arm and then balanced both children on the top rail of the fence. "'Bout time you showed up!"

"Dad had work," Julie complained. "He always has work."

"And I lost a tooth! Look!" Scotty opened his mouth as wide as possible.

James laughed. "So you did. And as for your father

working, that's a good enough excuse for me. Someone in the family's got to earn a living and I don't think it's gonna be either of you two." He tickled them and they laughed merrily.

But Brenna barely heard. Her eyes were on Warren, who, dressed in faded jeans and a pullover sweater, was sauntering toward the orchard.

"Fancy meeting you here," he said with a crooked grin as he leaned over the fence.

She melted inside. His gaze was warm and blue when it fell upon her. "Hi."

"Come on, Grandpa, take us on a ride!" Scotty cried excitedly.

"What ride?" Brenna asked.

"Just a couple of turns around the pasture on Ignatius," he said, chuckling as he carried his grandchildren into the barn.

"Ignatius?" she repeated.

"An old pony he picked up at auction last spring," Warren explained. "He was selling a couple of steers and saw Ignatius. The pony was lame, but your dad bought him for the kids." Warren climbed the fence and sat on the top rail. His jeans stretched tight over his hips and gaped away from his sweater, exposing the dark-skinned muscles of his lower back. "You can see better from here," he explained.

Brenna held her denim skirt in one hand and climbed the rails to sit beside him. The sun was warm, the sky over the blossomed trees cerulean, the wind gently whispering through branches overhead. White and pink petals drifted to the grass-covered knoll.

Brenna watched as her father led a chestnut-colored pony around a nearby field. Scotty wobbled on Ignatius's shoulders, and Julie, followed by Dixie, who had reluctantly given up her quarry in the woodpile, trailed behind.

"Your father's at it again," Warren finally said. The

breeze lifted his hair and his gaze was narrowed on the tiny entourage at the far side of the field.

"Doing what?"

"Meddling." But he said the word fondly, without the sarcasm that usually edged his tone.

"He claims he's sworn off."

"Don't believe him."

Brenna smiled. Rays from the sun warmed her back and the breeze carried the scent of apple blossoms and Warren—clean and masculine and close to her nostrils. His knee brushed hers as he shifted on the fence and her pulse quickened. "Dad's changed," she finally said. "He's mellowed."

"I doubt it." Glancing at her from the corner of his eye, he frowned a little. "Your dad will never change, Brenna." Then, looking up again, he hopped off the fence. "My turn to take them around."

As Scotty slid off Ignatius, Julie climbed on. The pony shied, but Warren steadied him and soon he was leading Julie on Ignatius while carrying Scotty on his shoulders. This time Dixie ran ahead, barking and bounding at the scent of a rabbit in the brambles over the old fence.

"He's missed you," James said, cocking his head in Warren's direction as he approached.

"What're you talking about?" she demanded, incredulous.

"Since Honor's death," James said quietly. "He hasn't been the same."

"Has anyone?"

"I guess not."

Observing Warren with the children and pony, his smile flashing bright in the afternoon sun, Brenna felt her heart swell. "So what makes you think that Warren missed me? I'm not his wife and he made it abundantly clear that he didn't want me around the other night."

"Give him time. He'll change his mind."

"That's part of the problem—he has. Or sometimes. I don't know where I stand with him."

"Maybe he feels the same way," James thought aloud.

"I doubt it."

Her father's jaw slid to the side, the way it sometimes did when he was wrestling with a decision. "Warren's always thought you were special, Brenna. It's made him crazy at times."

She climbed off the fence and dusted her hands together. "He has a funny way of showing it. He nearly insisted that I turn down the job at the *Examiner* and go back to San Francisco where I belonged."

"As I said, he's not too crazy about the *Examiner*."

"Or me returning to Portland," she said with a faint smile.

"But he's changed his mind?" James asked.

"For the time being. But that isn't cast in stone—he's been so…moody."

"He has been ever since Honor's death." James glanced at her from the corner of his eye. "He did love her, you know. It was a terrible blow."

"I know. We've, uh, all had some trouble adjusting."

James's lips pursed together and his eyes glistened.

Rather than fall into that well of pain again, Brenna cleared her throat and gestured toward the small horse. "Don't you have a bridle for Ignatius?"

"Just the halter."

"You sure?"

He nodded. "It's been years since I've had a horse on this place. I sold all the tack to Craig Matthews two or three years ago."

"Even Shorty's old bridle?"

James's eyebrows quirked and his face clouded. "I

haven't thought about your mother's Shetland for twenty years, Bren."

Needing a chance to escape from her thoughts of Warren and Honor, Brenna said suddenly, "I'll go take a look in the barn. Maybe I can come up with something."

"I doubt it."

She ducked inside the barn, where the smell of dust and dry hay and cattle brought back vivid memories of her youth. She and Honor had loved to play in the shadowed stalls and storage bins within the barn. They had balanced along the top of the manger, pretending it was a high wire, and had constructed forts within the hayloft itself—creating secret places where they could hide and read books banned by the school library with the aid of a flashlight. They hadn't minded the itch from the scratchy bales, nor the dust that had clogged their nostrils.

"That was a long time ago," she said, walking past the bins of oats and corn. She heard a mouse scurry across the floor as she reached the ladder to the loft and climbed upward. She didn't really understand her sudden need to return to a spot she'd cherished as a child, and when she reached the top and stood on the packed bales of hay, she wondered why she'd bothered. The hayloft was dark. Only a few brave rays of sun pierced through the grimy circular window high overhead.

"Brenna?"

She nearly jumped out of her skin as she recognized Warren's voice and heard the scrape of a boot below. "Up here," she called down, peeking over the edge of the loft and spying his dark hair.

"What're you doing?"

"Thinking back, I guess," she admitted, listening as his boots clanged against the rungs of the ladder.

His head poked over the edge and his eyes moved slowly

up her legs and skirt before his gaze locked on hers. "To when?"

"A long time ago. When we—er, I was a kid." Forcing a smile, she sat on the edge of a bale that had split.

"Lots of memories here?"

Too many, she thought. "Enough. Honor and I, we used to come up here and make forts and secret passageways—that sort of thing."

"I know. She told me."

Brenna's heart ached. She missed Honor—she really did. They'd shared so much. Unfortunately that sharing had included love for this one man.

With a powerful lift, Warren pushed himself over the final step and landed squarely on the bale next to hers. "Your dad sent me for you," he said, as if reading the sadness in her eyes.

"Oh?"

"He thought you might like to ride into town with him and the kids."

"Why's he going to town?"

"Ice cream. For Scotty's birthday."

"Maybe we both should go with them." She started to reach for the ladder, but he caught her wrist, spinning her around.

"Let him go, Bren. There's not enough room in the pickup for all of us."

"So why did he invite me?"

Warren's eyes grew dark. "Don't you see? He's trying his damnedest to make up to you for all those years he favored Honor."

Brenna blinked, stunned. Though it had been obvious within the family that Honor was James's favorite child, she had hoped that no one else realized that painful truth. "You—you knew?"

"Everyone did," he said flatly, but when his eyes found

hers, she saw a tenderness she hadn't expected. His fingers were still closed over her wrist and she felt her pulse jumping erratically.

In the distance, she heard the sound of an old truck's engine coughing and sputtering before finally turning over. Children laughed and squealed and then the sound of the engine faded.

"I guess we missed our ride," he said, one corner of his mouth lifting in crooked satisfaction. His gaze centered on her suddenly dry lips.

She resisted the urge to lick the rim of her mouth and nodded mutely. If only she could snatch her arm away from him, if only she could step away, break the magic spell he was weaving under the cobweb-draped rafters. But her heart was thudding, her quickened pulse leaping in her throat. She felt paralyzed.

"I'm sorry about last night and the night before," he said, swallowing. "I was—"

"Just being a bastard?"

His grin lengthened, stretching over his face in a bright gleam of white teeth. "I was going to say that I was in no position to criticize."

"I am a good reporter," she said, trying to pull away. *Please God, give me the strength to walk out of here,* she thought desperately. But no matter how she tried, she couldn't glance away from the mesmerizing seduction in his eyes.

"I know. I didn't mean half the things I said."

"Then you shouldn't have said them."

In the shadows of the barn, his face seemed more hollow and gaunt than before and his smug grin faded. "I wanted to drive you away," he admitted, finally releasing her wrist. Sighing, he pushed his hair out of his eyes. "I thought if you left, it would be easier for all of us. Especially me. But last night—after you'd gone—I changed my mind."

Her heart was thumping so loudly she was sure he could hear its erratic beat. "Why?"

"Because of the kids, mostly," he said, his voice low. "But that's only part of it." Gazing deep in her eyes, his hands resting gently on her shoulders, he let his thumbs touch the underside of her jaw.

Brenna's chest was so tight she could barely breathe.

"I want you to stay for me," he finally admitted, his face as tortured as she'd ever seen it.

How long had she waited to hear just those words? And now that they had been said, she found herself fumbling for an answer. But Warren rushed ahead of her.

"I was wrong at the funeral—and I was wrong the last couple of nights. I need help, Bren. We all do." A sad smile touched the edges of his mouth. "I'm just glad you had the sense to realize it."

"What changed your mind?" she asked, not daring to believe him—not trusting her own willing heart.

"A long night of soul-searching." Without any further explanation, he folded her into his arms and kissed her crown, his lips moving slowly against her hair.

Brenna knew that she shouldn't trust him—that she should pull out of his seductive embrace—but she couldn't. His arms around her felt so strong and protective, his clean, woodsy smell, so much like she remembered, heightened her senses. She was aware of nothing save the heat of his body pressed hard against hers and the answering flush warming her skin.

Though she knew she was playing with fire, she tilted her head back, lips eager to meet his. When his mouth slanted over hers and he gently parted her lips, she felt weak and trembling, anxious to be loved by him.

Alarms screamed inside her head—warning her that kissing him, exposing herself to all his pain again, would only hurt her in the end, but she couldn't stop the wickedly enticing sensations running rampant through her blood, nor ignore the burst of passion that curled and throbbed deep within her middle.

Her breathing was shallow, her protests only whispered when he wrapped his arms around her and dragged her to her knees, still kissing, still holding her tight as his fingers worked the buttons of her blouse through their openings.

She lay back, her fingers twined in his hair, her lips melded to his. His tongue darted and probed, exploring every inch of her and he shuddered from the sheer torture of holding his emotions under rein.

"I promised myself I wouldn't let this happen again," he whispered, but his fingers wound in her dark curls and his lips brushed lazily over hers.

Her blouse parted, exposing her white skin and lacy bra. "I—I told myself that I would stay away from you," she admitted. Her breath was ragged, her voice low and husky.

"So why haven't you?"

One hand slid past her neck to rest on the flat of her abdomen and she sucked in a swift breath. "You make it impossible."

"Oh, Brenna," he groaned, rolling over her. Though they were both fully clothed, he moved suggestively against her, rubbing and stoking fires deep in her soul. His tongue rimmed her lips, flicked against her teeth, then plundered more deeply.

She couldn't think straight and didn't want to. In the darkness of the barn, her senses were on fire, her fingers clutching his shoulders, feeling strident muscles through the soft fabric of his sweater.

Inching down her body, his mouth whispered sweet promises against her throat. He pushed her blouse past her shoulders. His breath was warm as it fanned her breast, and beneath the pink silk of her bra her nipple ached for his touch.

He placed his mouth over the silk-draped peak and his tongue stroked through the soft fabric.

Closing her eyes, Brenna cradled his head close to her, wanting more of him, not caring what she would feel or think later. The doubts that lingered in her mind were quickly consumed by the desire that stole so easily and hot through her blood.

She felt him unclasp her bra. Cool air touched her wet breast before his hand gently covered the proud peak, petting it until his lips brushed the nipple. Burning inside, she writhed beneath him, wanting more. She found the hem of his sweater and tugged. Warren lifted his head long enough for her to strip the sweater from him.

He was as she remembered. His skin still tanned, the whorling hair over his chest black against flat, rippling muscles now dewy with sweat.

As she stared up at him she reached forward, tracing the line of his breastbone, and lower, to his navel and the waistband of his jeans.

Closing his eyes, he shuddered. "Brenna, please—"

"Please what?"

"Oh, God. If we don't stop now, I won't be able to." He looked down on her again and his eyes were smoky blue. His gaze lingered in hers before drifting to her breasts, white and proud, crested with stiff dark peaks. Groaning, he rolled to his side, but folded her into his arms.

"Warren, I—"

"Shh. Don't say it. Don't say anything." He kissed the top of her head tenderly and rubbed against her. She could feel the urgency of his desire, hard beneath his jeans. "I—I think we should wait," he said, his voice trembling as much as she was deep inside.

"Why?"

"We—we both need time."

"Ten years isn't enough?"

"No, but—"

"Or are you saying this is all a mistake?" she asked between labored breaths. She struggled to pull away but his arms only tightened. How could she have let herself get so carried away? Just last night she'd promised herself never to trust herself with him again!

"Just listen," he rasped. He held her so close that his chest flattened her breasts and she could feel the coiled tension in his muscles. "I've done a lot of thinking," he admitted hoarsely. "If you only knew. I barely slept the last couple nights thinking about you and what you do to me."

She could hear the hammering of his heart, knew the pounding was answered by the rapid beat of her own. "Let me up," she whispered.

"Not yet, Bren, because I want you to understand."

She opened her eyes. "Understand what? That you're playing with me—seeing just how far I'll go and then pulling back?"

He seemed incredulous. "You just don't have a clue, do you?"

"A clue to what?" she asked hotly.

"Of just how much you mean to me."

"Oh, Warren, don't—"

The muscles of his face were so rigid his skin stretched taut over his cheekbones. "I'm not playing with you or using you or any of those trite, stupid, high-school games, Brenna. But I am trying, and it's damned hard, to use my head." Exasperated, he exhaled on a long sigh. "What we have to do is take one step at a time—we can't rush things. You only arrived here the other day, for crying out loud!" His lips brushed over her forehead and he picked a piece of straw from her hair. "I don't want to make another mistake with you."

"You mean like you almost did a few minutes ago?" she asked, though her heart was soaring at the depth of emotion in his words. She hardly dared believe that he really cared for her.

"I mean like ten years ago," he admitted.

"What's that supposed to mean?"

"Just that I didn't think with you—or with Honor. And I trapped myself, and hurt you."

"And Honor?"

His eyes darkened angrily. "It wasn't fair to her, either."

"But you loved her."

Swallowing hard, he nodded. "Too much maybe."

Aching, she fought tears. She wouldn't cry for Warren Stone. Not again!

"But that was the problem, Bren. I loved her so much, or thought I did—" His lips thinned. "Oh, hell, I was just a kid." Then, as if disgusted with himself, he found her blouse and draped it over her shoulders, still holding her close. "We all were."

Brenna tried to scoot away from him. "Maybe we shouldn't talk about this. It was a long time ago. It doesn't matter anymore."

"Doesn't it?"

She shoved her arms through the sleeves of her blouse, then saw her bra lying on a nearby bale. Embarrassed, she stuffed it in the pocket of her skirt. "I'm not Honor, Warren," she said. "I never will be—and, despite what you so obviously think, I don't want to be."

She tried to stand, but he reached up, grabbed hold of her forearm and tugged. She toppled in a mortified heap into his lap. "I know who you are, Brenna," he said, his skin stretched taut over the angles of his face, "I just don't know what to do about you."

"Nothing. You don't have to do anything!" Again she attempted to stand and was pulled back for her efforts.

His eyes glinted with a mocking light. "So I should just forget what happened between us?"

"Nothing did! Let go of me!"

"And what about last night and the night before?" he asked huskily, his arms encircling her waist to hold her against him.

"Just mistakes. Remember? Nothing happened!" Why, oh why, did she always feel like a child around him?

His lips twitched and he laughed so loudly the rich sound rumbled through the dusty barn. Blue eyes glinting, he growled into her ear, "If nothing happens between us—no sparks fly—I'd like to know why I was awake for two damned nights lying in sweaty sheets; why I couldn't wait to drive out here and try to corner you alone somewhere like this?"

"Ooh—you're absolutely insufferable!" Her fists balled and she wanted to pummel them against his bare chest.

"Go ahead—" he invited, and she flexed, but dropped her hands, counting slowly until her urge to strike him faded.

"No one can make me as angry as you can," she declared, kicking at a nearby bale. Dust swirled around into the air.

"I hope not!" With a self-assured grin, he released her and yanked his shirt over his head.

"You are the most infuriating—" Brenna stopped short. She heard the sound of her father's truck in the drive and was grateful for a chance to escape. Being alone with Warren was much too dangerous and maddening! She was always out of control, on the verge of killing him or making love to him.

Young voices pierced the quiet.

"Sounds like your brood has arrived," she said, quickly buttoning her blouse and combing the tangles from her hair with her fingers before climbing down the ladder.

Warren swung from one of the rafters and landed lithely on a pile of cut hay on the barn floor.

"Show-off," she accused, her anger dissolving at the flash of his smile as he caught up with her.

Footsteps pounded on the ramp and slowly the main door creaked open, letting in a stream of light, fresh air and two impish children. "Lookie what Grandpa got me!" Scotty cried, waving a huge candy bar in one hand and a kite in the other.

"Oh, boy."

"He said you could fly the kite for me."

"I'll just bet he did," Warren said, his lips twisting in amusement as he glanced at Julie. "And what about you— did you get something or did Grandpa forget you?"

"She already ate her treat!" Scotty tattled.

Ignoring Scotty's jab, Julie waved a book of paper dolls over her head. "Grandpa said you used to have some of these," she said to Brenna.

"Mmm." Brenna glanced down at the book of dolls with pink hair, miniskirts and jean jackets. "They were a little different," she said dryly. "No designer stuff."

"Too bad," Julie said.

"I survived."

They walked outside and Warren placed his arm familiarly across Brenna's shoulders. For the first time in ten years she wondered if there was a chance, even a slim one, that he would fall in love with her.

Or was she just a handy replacement? Did he finally realize that raising children alone was difficult and he needed someone to fill Honor's shoes?

White clouds gathered in the sky and Brenna shivered.

"Cold?" Warren asked, drawing her close.

"Not really." She glanced at him through a fringe of dark lashes. His face was set as he watched his children racing ahead, and Brenna wished she could read his thoughts. If only she knew how he really felt. Could she dare believe his caring words whispered in the throes of passion; or was he toying with her?

"Well, come on in and eat, before it gets cold," her father scolded from the doorway.

"Ice cream is supposed to be cold."

"Not just ice cream," James said. "The kids seemed to think I owed them a meal." He held up two white paper bags. "We visited the Colonel. The rest is already in the house."

"You need a microwave, Dad," Brenna suggested.

"I don't want one of them fool things in this house—a waste of money—that's what they are!"

She stepped into the kitchen. The scent of fried chicken and biscuits mingled with the smell of burning wood and tobacco assailed her nostrils.

"Aunt Bren, you sit by me, okay?" Julie asked eagerly, tugging on her free hand and leading her into the dining room. "I set the table."

"And it looks great," she said, eyeing the place mats and chipped dishes scattered haphazardly around the old oak table. "Just let me help Grandpa in the kitchen." She leaned over and whispered conspiratorially into Julie's ear, "Just between you and me, I don't trust him to warm up the chicken. He might burn it."

"I heard that!" her father grumbled from the kitchen, but he chuckled just the same.

"I'll help!" Julie said, her eyes gleaming.

"Good."

Ten minutes later, they were seated around the table and Brenna ended up on the chair next to Warren's. He seemed relaxed and comfortable, but as the minutes ticked by, Brenna felt uneasy and realized she was sitting in the chair that had been reserved for Honor.

As the family talked, she became more quiet, sensing that she really didn't belong. This was Honor's family, her children, her husband—a man with whom Brenna had nearly made love.

Julie's fork clanged against her plate. "This is just like it used to be," she said, attempting a smile, though her lower lip trembled.

Brenna's heart constricted. "I don't remember—"

"You weren't here," Warren said softly.

"Mama was!" Scotty announced, then slid off his chair. "I don't want no more. And it's *not* like it used to be!" He glared angrily over his shoulder at Brenna and his eyes reddened as he ran out of the room.

She scooted her chair back, but Warren put a hand on her arm. "This is *my* problem," he whispered. "I'll work it out."

Brenna felt miserable. She heard Warren take off after Scotty and felt her father's eyes on her.

"I'm not hungry, either," Julie said quietly, then bunched her napkin onto her plate and followed forlornly out of the room. Brenna pushed her plate aside.

The grandfather's clock ticked loudly from the hallway. Why had she been so stupid? How could she have thought for a minute that she could help Honor's children—provide them with the mothering they needed? Scotty outwardly despised her and Julie was confused.

"It'll take time," her father said, reading her thoughts.

She glanced up and saw him staring at her through the smoke from his cigarette. She hadn't even realized he'd finished with dinner.

"Maybe I shouldn't have moved up here," she thought aloud. Swallowing hard, she walked to one of the tall windows that faced the backyard. Looking through the panes, she could see Warren and the children in the field near the orchard. Warren was running, the kite streaming behind him, red and yellow against a brilliant blue sky. Scotty tagged after his father and Julie sat alone on a grassy knoll under a cherry tree, her knees tucked under her chin, her arms around her legs. Dixie was lying patiently at her side.

Brenna heard the floor squeak behind her and felt her father's gnarled hand on her shoulder.

"It's all gonna take time," he said softly.

"For what?"

"For us to be a family again."

"I'm not Honor and this—this isn't *my* family!" she said in despair. Her throat was swollen as she stared at Julie sitting with the dog in the field. Brenna knew how lonely the little girl felt, how confused. Remembering the first few months' after her own mother's death brought tears to Brenna's eyes. "I—I just want to help."

"You already have," her father said.

She didn't believe him. He was just a well-meaning old man hoping to mend the wounds of the past. But life didn't work that way.

Watching Warren run against the wind with the kite and Scotty trailing behind, Brenna realized she could never be a part of his family—not with Honor's shadow looming like a black cloud over them.

"Don't ever try to be Honor," her father said gruffly. "You remember who you are and I will, too." His fingers dug into her arm and when she glanced at him she noticed his eyes were red and misty.

Afraid she might break down altogether, she kissed him lightly on the cheek and found her purse. "I'd better check back with the landlady—find out if the apartment has been cleaned and whether I have a place to move into," she decided.

"Doesn't matter," her father said. "You can move back here."

"I—I don't think so. I'll call you later." Without a word of goodbye to Warren or the kids, she walked outside to the rental car, leaving the old farmhouse with its painful memories and lingering ghosts.

CHAPTER SIX

BRENNA BARELY RECOGNIZED her cozy little apartment in San Francisco. She'd spent the past two days packing boxes for her move to Portland, and every waking moment, her mind had strayed to Warren.

She hadn't heard from him since she'd left her father's house. From the farm, she'd driven directly to her hotel, called the airport and changed her reservation. She needed time alone to think, time away from Honor's town, Honor's children and Honor's life. She'd taken the first available seat on a flight back to San Francisco.

Now, two days later, she was still worried about moving to Portland, living so close to Warren, but able to face the challenge. "What's done is done," she told herself as she packed away the last of her kitchen plates and dusted her hands together. One way or another, she had to carve out her own life in Portland.

The doorbell rang and she peeked through the peephole, expecting the see the movers. Instead, she recognized Warren's handsome face through the small hole in the door. Good Lord, what was *he* doing here? Her traitorous heart slammed against her chest at the sight of his carved features and sky-blue eyes.

"Well, are you gonna let me in or are you going to leave me standing out here looking like an idiot?" he demanded, pounding on the door panels. "Brenna?"

Unable to hide a pleased smile, she unlocked the door and let it swing wide. He was pacing in the outer hallway, his hand pressed into the back pockets of his cords, furrows etched across his brow. "So you decided to let me in," he greeted, one dark eyebrow rising suspiciously.

"What're you doing here?"

"I thought I'd help you pack."

"Sure."

"Really."

She didn't believe him. Crossing her arms over her chest, she stepped away from the door, then motioned with one hand to the cartons, boxes and sacks littering the floor of the little apartment.

He surveyed the small room with its stacked furniture and a mound of clothes piled near the door. "I guess I waited too long."

"I guess so."

His gaze lingered on hers. "Then I'll just have to drive back with you."

She couldn't believe her ears. "What?"

"I said—"

"I know what you said, I just don't understand," she admitted, eyeing him skeptically. "You're not trying to convince me that you flew down here just to drive back."

"That's about it," he admitted.

"Why?"

"I thought we needed to talk—straighten out a few things. You left in kind of a hurry."

Suddenly, she felt nervous. "Don't you have a job or something," she said, changing the subject.

"I managed to swing a couple of days off."

"Just to follow me down here?"

His jaw worked and his lips became knife-blade thin. "If you remember, Brenna, you took off like the proverbial bat out of hell the other day. I called the hotel, but you'd already left and the phone company insisted you didn't have a working number down here."

He'd tried to call her? Her heart did a strange little flip. Maybe he did care. She glanced around the room, trying to gain her bearings. Warren was here for the express purpose of driving back with her? "I, uh, had the phone taken out before I flew to Portland."

"I remember," Warren said dryly. "I had hoped that it was just out of service, but since it wasn't...I decided to see you in person." He righted one upended bar stool and whistled. "How'd you cram all that—" he pointed to the mess "—into this place?"

"Careful planning." After closing the door to ensure their privacy, she balanced one hip against the corner of a big box. "The trick will be getting it into the new place."

"You have an apartment?"

"Yes."

Picking up a ceramic vase, he studied it and rolled it in his hand. "Near the house?"

"A few blocks," she admitted, feeling stupid. He probably thought she was trying to wedge herself into his life again.

"Julie will be ecstatic," he said.

And you, Warren? What about you? How will you feel if I'm just down the street? "How are the kids?"

He lifted one broad shoulder. "About the same."

"Who's taking care of them?"

"Mary promised to take them out to your Dad's for the weekend."

"So he knows you're here?" she asked, wondering at the conspiracy between her father and Warren. Years ago, they had worked against her; now, it seemed, they both were trying to mold her life—telling her where to live, whom to work for, how to handle the past—without regard to her feelings.

Sighing, Warren glanced to the ceiling high overhead. "It was his idea, I suppose."

Her heart fell to the floor. "So that's why you came—"

"No way." His mouth twisted cynically. "I've played it your dad's way before. This time, I'm calling the shots."

"This time?"

His eyes turned serious, a dark shade of blue that pierced her to her very soul. "I mean it, Bren. I'm not letting anyone, including your dad, tell me what to do. I think I made that clear to him the other day."

"I bet he liked that."

"Not much. But he accepted it." He studied the boxes again. "Your father and I have never really seen eye to eye."

"Is that so? Then why did I feel that the two of you had worked together ten years ago to push me away?"

"We didn't—"

"And now, now that Honor's...gone, you're both pulling and pushing again. But this time," she warned meaningfully, "I'm not eighteen. I know what I want from my life."

"And what is that, Bren?" he asked, rising from the stool and stepping quickly over the boxes that separated them. "Just what is it you want from life?"

You, her heart cried but she kept her secret buried. "What I've always wanted," she stated, tossing her head defiantly. "A career, husband, children—"

"In that order?"

She forced a cold smile. "Things just happened to work out that way."

His gaze narrowed on her lips. "You've got your work cut out for you," he said. "A job with the *Examiner* isn't going to be a bed of roses."

"So I've heard. Over and over again. And there's nothing you or Dad can do about it."

If he saw the challenge in her eyes, Warren ignored it and shrugged. "Okay, okay," he muttered, then added, "Since you're already packed and we don't have anything better to do, why don't we go out and cclcbratc?"

"Celebrate? Celebrate what?"

His eyes twinkled roguishly. "Certainly not your job—"

"I'm warning you!"

"So how about your move back to Portland?"

Her brows lifted and she felt better. "I thought you were against it."

"I told you—I did some soul-searching the other night." Clearing his throat, he hopped over a potted fern, side-stepped a packing crate of old records, then shoved open the French doors to the balcony. "So you've got a view of the bay."

"*Had* a view," she corrected, following him outside. A brisk breeze whipped her hair away from her face.

"This is a nice place," he said, almost to himself. His eyes were narrowed on the horizon, where ships churned slowly across the dark water. The air was clear and fresh and he breathed deeply. "Will you miss it?" he asked, cocking his head in the direction of the city.

"Part of it, I suppose." Leaning over the rail, goose bumps rising on her forearms, she watched a tugboat push a barge inland. "But I didn't have much choice, did I? The paper was sold and the new owners wanted changes. I just happened to be one."

Warren winced. "And there were no other jobs down here?"

She shook her head. "Nothing worked out."

"So you ended up with Len Patterson at the *Examiner*," he concluded, his mouth twisting down at the corners. "Seems like more than a coincidence."

"Why?" she asked. "Why are you so suspicious? It has to be more than this one case of kidnapping."

"A lot more," Warren allowed. He rubbed the back of his neck and glanced at her. "Len doesn't much like me."

"Seems as if the feeling's mutual."

Warren grimaced and a black cloud swept over his eyes.

"Len and the *Examiner* backed the other candidate in the last election."

"So?"

"So there's been some bad blood ever since." Stretching, he turned, leaning his back against the rail.

"You honestly think that Patterson hired me to get back at you?" A smile tugged at the corner of her lips when she saw the hint of defiance in his eyes, and she laughed, despite a cold chill at the memory of her interview and Patterson's questions about Honor. "Maybe you've been working too hard, counselor."

He shrugged and pulled thoughtfully on his lower lip. "I'd just feel better if you were with a different paper."

"Afraid it's too late for that." She was still trying to shake off the feeling that perhaps Warren was right when she heard someone banging on the front door. "I'm coming," she called, hurrying across the balcony, over the fern and through the stacked boxes.

As she gazed through the peephole, she recognized the coveralls of the moving company and yanked the door open. "Here it is," she said, gesturing grandly.

"It all goes?" asked the tall, lanky man whose name tag identified him as Rex Donahue.

"Everything."

"Okay, if you'll just look over these instructions, we'll get started."

Brenna read, signed and watched as the movers packed her belongings into a van double-parked on the street below. Within three hours, everything she owned was tucked neatly inside the van and heading northward on Interstate 5 to Portland.

"I guess that takes care of that," she said, glancing around the empty rooms for the last time and feeling nostalgic. This little crow's nest had been her home for so many years. Now, all that remained of her life in this city were the white marks on the wall where her pictures had once hung, her jacket still draped from a closet hanger and an oversize purse propped against the wall near the front door. "Empty, isn't it?" she whispered.

"Come on, I'll take you out to dinner," Warren said, as if sensing her case of the blues.

"Like this?" She glanced down at her faded jeans and pink sweatshirt.

"Looks perfect for a cable-car ride to the wharf." He grinned then, a white slash that was instantly infectious.

"Is *that* what you had in mind?" she asked.

"For starters. Come on." After swiping her jacket from the hanger, he hooked it over his shoulder. "When in Rome—"

"Not everyone in San Francisco rides cable cars."

"Prove it."

"Exactly what I would expect to hear from a district attorney," she teased. Feeling her dimple show despite her melancholy, she slid her arms through the sleeves of her wool jacket and hurried downstairs, where she deposited her key with her dour-faced manager, Mrs. Monroe. The woman barely grunted a goodbye as she opened the door and took the key in her outstretched palm.

From the interior of the dark apartment Brenna heard the familiar theme song from a popular soap opera before the door was slammed shut in her face.

"Nothing can tear Mrs. Monroe away from *Search for Love*," she whispered as they stepped outside. "Not even an earthquake measuring 7.5 on the Richter scale." She slipped her arm through Warren's and pointed out her car—an eight-year-old Volkswagen Rabbit, parked on a steep side street. Blocks beneath the front tires held the beat-up yellow car in place.

"You want me to drive?" he asked dubiously.

"Wouldn't dream of it." Her hair caught in the wind to

blow across her face. "I know these streets like the back of my hand." As if to prove her point, she picked up the blocks, tossed them in the backseat and climbed behind the wheel.

Warren crammed his long body inside and Brenna started the engine. She could feel the flush on her cheeks, knew that her eyes were sparkling green-gold, but didn't care. Just being with Warren in her city with nothing to remind her that he was once married to Honor helped her spirits soar.

"Why do I feel like I'm taking my life in my hands?" he asked as she rammed the car into gear and maneuvered through the congested traffic.

"Remember, you were the one who wanted a tour," she said, flashing him an impish grin as she cranked open the sunroof and wind screamed through the tiny car.

"I'll keep that in mind."

She drove toward Fisherman's Wharf and along the edge of the bay until she found a place to park a few blocks from the waterfront.

Warren, taking her hand in his, walked swiftly along the crowded sidewalk. Souvenir stands, craft shops and open fish markets lined the streets.

"You've been here before," she guessed.

"Once or twice," he admitted with a wink. Tugging on her hand, he led her through the shops and restaurants housed in Ghirardelli Square. The huge brick building, once a chocolate factory, was alive with tourists.

"Where are we going? I thought you wanted to ride the cable cars—"

"I do. But first—here we go." He shoved open a heavy oak and glass door to an authentic Irish bar. Smoke and laughter, shoe soles scraping, glasses clinking and the quiet hum of conversation filled the long, narrow room. Glasses and bottles of liquor shimmered against the backdrop of a ceiling-high mirror behind a mahogany and brass bar.

"Best Irish coffee in the world," he whispered in her ear. After ordering them each a drink from the barkeep, he located a quiet table near a corner window.

"Mmm. You may be right." Brenna sipped her drink and glanced outside to the pedestrians scurrying beneath the striped awnings. She felt warm inside, happy to be alone with Warren. As she swirled her drink and gazed into Warren's eyes, she was lulled into a sense of well-being. The past seemed just a faded memory; the future, inviting.

He sat across from her in the booth and the worry lines that had grooved his forehead disappeared. "So tell me why you never moved back before."

Didn't he know? Hadn't he sensed in the past ten years that she had never felt comfortable or welcome in Honor's town—his town? She cleared her throat and stared into her clouded coffee. "After college I landed a job at the *City Weekly*." Stirring her drink, she added, "I moved up until I had my own column, I liked the people I worked for, especially my boss. Why move?"

"I thought maybe you might have missed your family."

"I—I did."

He gazed at her thoughtfully. "I thought I might have been the reason."

Her heart slammed against her ribs. "You?"

"Because of what happened that night in the rose garden when Honor lied to me. Remember? You went out with Craig that night. Honor told me you were going to marry him."

Brenna's stomach twisted. "I never planned to marry Craig!" she said, wondering why Honor would lie.

"He carried a torch for a long time," Warren said, turning his empty cup in his fingers.

"For no reason."

"So what about you, Brenna? Did you carry a torch, too?"

"Craig was just a friend—"

"I wasn't talking about Craig." His eyes searched hers, delved past the barriers she had so carefully erected.

Oh, God! She was cornered and there was nothing she could do about it. "I suppose I did," she admitted, swallowing hard. The smoky atmosphere in the bar offered privacy and she was lost in the gentle blue of his gaze. "I didn't lie to you in the rose garden, Warren. I meant everything I said."

Laughter rippled from some men at the bar and Brenna imagined they were laughing at her and her stupid childish fantasy with her older sister's lover.

Warren's jaw tightened. He looked away to stare through the window. "I thought you were too young to know what love was all about."

"You were wrong."

"I guess I should have understood you weren't Honor. Even though you were two years younger, you knew your own mind."

Electricity sparked between them, the tension nearly visible, and the other sounds of the bar became muted. "I cared about you very much," she admitted.

"So you left because I was dating Honor."

"No! Not because you were going with Honor, but because you were planning to marry her. That was hard to deal with, Warren—very hard. I moved down here and tried not to look back."

"Did it work?" he asked.

She shrugged. "Most of the time." Clearing away the lump that had formed in her throat, she slung her strap over her shoulder. "If you want to ride on the cable car, we'd better go now," she said, hoping to turn the conversation before she was forced to admit that she had never stopped loving him, wanting him, caring about him all these years.

Warren touched her lightly on the cheek, then paid the check, and together they wended their way through the crowd of early afternoon customers to the front door.

Brenna wished she could read his mind—see past his sea-blue eyes and into his soul. She supposed she should have felt better about telling him the truth, but she didn't. Instead, she felt downright miserable. *What did you expect?* a nasty little voice in her mind nagged, *his confession of undying love?* "That would have been nice," she murmured.

"What?" Warren asked, bending so that he could hear her over the noise of the traffic.

"Nothing."

Fool! the horrid little voice accused as they crossed the street, dodging bicyclists and cars to stand in line for the next cable car. A few minutes later they were wedged with a throng of other people into a small, open-windowed vehicle that crawled steadily up the steep hills to Union Square. Warren clung to the side of the car and Brenna was at his side, her dark hair whipping across his face, her body pressed tightly against his. She had trouble watching the sights and ignoring the feel of his thigh against hers. As passengers jostled on and off the car at the stops, she was pressed tighter against him, felt the texture of his jacket against her cheek.

"This isn't half bad," Warren teased when two teenagers boarded and inadvertently shoved Brenna into him.

"If you don't mind being trampled to death."

"You're exaggerating," he whispered against her hair, but he folded his arms around her and she could feel his warm breath against her nape. The car jerked forward again before finally jolting to a halt at Union Square.

For the next hour they munched on pizza by the slice

and window-shopped before taking the cable car back to the wharf and eventually climbing into Brenna's hatchback.

"Well?" she asked, once she'd guided the Volkswagen out of congestion and away from the bay. "Are you satisfied that you've 'done' San Francisco?"

"At least part of it."

"And you're ready to drive all night in the car?" She glanced at her watch. It was after four. By the time they reached Portland it would be almost daylight.

"We'll drive up the coast and stop in Coos Bay or Florence," he drawled, glancing at her from the corner of his eye.

Brenna's hands tightened over the wheel. Spending a night driving alone with Warren would be difficult enough—she didn't want to think what might happen if they stopped at a beach cabin. "Don't you have to get back?"

"I'm off work till Wednesday and your dad told me to take my time." His lips twisted up at the corners. "You know, Bren, I think James has changed his mind about us. Ten years ago the thought that I might be interested in you made him see red."

"That was because he had already decided that Honor needed you," she muttered sarcastically. "At least she needed you more than I did."

Warren's face changed. His smile fell and he stared out the window to the city, with its tall skyscrapers, precipitous hills and gleaming water, as they drove rapidly northward. "I never should have listened to him," he murmured before lapsing into silence.

The miles slid past and Brenna, though her mind screamed against it, guided the car up the curving coast highway that followed the rugged edge of the sea. Through towering redwoods and pines the Pacific Ocean, gilded by the sun's slanting rays, flashed by in startling glimpses of aquamarine.

The air was fresh and clean, cool as it rushed through the little car. As they crossed into Oregon, the sun sank into the sea in a blaze of magenta and violet, streaking the sky and water with vibrant, shimmering rays.

Warren began to squirm in his seat. "How about a break?" he suggested. "I know a great restaurant not more than two hours ahead."

Brenna's stomach rumbled in response. "Two hours? I don't know if I can hold out."

"Neither do I," he admitted, rubbing his jaw.

"You wanted the scenic route, remember."

"Don't remind me."

Darkness had descended by the time Warren directed her to a weed-choked gravel parking lot next to a rustic restaurant with dimmed lights, burgundy shutters and weathered siding trimmed in dove gray. She parked near the front porch and gratefully climbed out of the car.

"This place doesn't change much," he said under his breath as he stretched his arms over his head and winced.

Mounting the plank steps, Brenna felt him behind her—so close they could touch. Inside, there were only a few patrons scattered at the polished oak tables. A large, friendly woman with flaming red hair smiled at Warren, called him by name and led them to a corner with a view of the ocean. A single candle flickered in the sconce on the table, its flame reflected in the pine-paneled walls. And far below the cliff on which the restaurant stood, illuminated by huge lights, a crescent of white sand separated the sheer rocks from the turbulent sea.

"Sorry to hear about your wife," the redhead said with a frown as Brenna sat in a captain's chair. She eyed Brenna as if she were an intruder.

The skin over Warren's face tightened and he didn't reply.

"Such a shame. How're the kids?"

"Fine," he replied quickly. "It's been a strain—but we're managing."

The waitress slid a wary glance at Brenna.

"This is Honor's sister," Warren said quickly. "Brenna Douglass."

Scrutinizing Brenna's face with disbelieving eyes, the waitress managed a thin smile. "Not much resemblance."

"No," Brenna said. "I take after my dad." Good Lord, why was she explaining herself?

After placing menus in front of them, the waitress scurried to another table.

"Who's she?" Brenna demanded.

"Connie something-or-other. I can't remember her last name, but she's worked here as long as I've known about this place. We—Honor, the kids and I used to eat here when we vacationed at the beach. Our cabin is...was just up the road."

"Was?"

"I sold it," he said flatly.

Brenna closed her eyes, realizing that Honor had been killed not far from these rocky shoals when the car she'd been driving had plunged through a guardrail and into the sea. Nervously, she fingered her water glass. "Why did you bring me here?"

"It was on the way," he said, shrugging, then rubbed his beard-stubbled chin. "I've never been back since the accident," he admitted. "Even when I sold the cabin, I had a real estate agent handle the whole thing. I signed the papers in Portland."

Stunned, Brenna glanced at her menu and somehow managed to order, but her thoughts were on Warren. His jaw was set, his expression stern, and he barely made small talk throughout the meal. He ate as if chained to the chair, his eyes shifting between the darkening night, Brenna's face and his plate.

Though she was hungry, Brenna barely tasted the fresh scallops and scallions or French bread. She was grateful when Connie appeared with their check and Warren left some bills on the table.

Outside the restaurant, she started for the car, but he slipped his arm around her shoulders. "Let's go down to the beach," he suggested.

"Here?" Glancing around the deserted parking lot, she shivered. The sky had turned inky, stars no longer visible, and the roar of the sea filled her ears.

"Follow me." He started down a sandy path on one side of the building.

Jamming her hands into the pockets of her jacket, she ran to catch up with him.

The path led through a thicket of berry vines. Brambles clawed at her jeans and the sleeves of her jacket, and thorns tore at her hair.

"Doesn't look like anyone uses this anymore," Warren said softly, his words barely audible over the thunder of waves crashing against rocks below.

The steps were steep and switched back and forth across the cliff face. The huge lights from above illuminated portions of the staircase. As Brenna inched her way down, she steadied herself by placing her hands on Warren's shoulders.

When they finally reached the sand-covered ground, he took her hand in his and walked north. Salt spray touched her cheeks and tangled her hair. "You used to come here often—you and Honor and the kids?" she finally asked.

He shook his head. "We did at first, but over the years— well, I guess we lost interest."

"How could you?" She felt so alive with the sound of the

pounding in her ears, the scent of salt in her nostrils, Warren's hand clasped possessively over hers. Brenna had always loved the ocean; had envied this little piece of heaven Honor had shared with Warren.

He glanced down at her and his fingers clenched more tightly over hers. "Things had changed between us," he admitted with a sigh.

Brenna's heart nearly stopped before kicking into a rapid double time when she saw the torment in his night-darkened eyes and sensed that she was about to hear a confession better left unsaid.

"You may as well know everything," he decided, frowning angrily. "Honor was divorcing me."

"No!" So stunned she couldn't walk, she pulled on his hand.

Warren spun and faced her. "It's true, Bren."

"But I didn't know—she would have told me—"

"Obviously not."

"Maybe I shouldn't hear this," she said, feeling as if she were prying into her sister's private life.

"You have to, Brenna. Just listen."

She didn't move. Couldn't. Why would Warren make up such a crazy story? Or could it be true?

The wind tossed his hair, and the lights above hardened the angles of his face. "Honor had come to the beach one last time to try and sort things out," he said, eyeing the foaming waves. "But it didn't work. She called me and told me that nothing would change her mind. She intended to take the kids and leave as soon as she returned to Portland."

"I don't believe this," Brenna whispered, shaken. She didn't want to hear that Honor was unhappy—nor that Warren, this caring man, had been so tormented. "Dad never said anything—"

"He didn't know. And even if he had known, he wouldn't have told you, Bren."

That much was true. Only since Honor's accident had she and her father grown at all close. She saw the pained expression in Warren's eyes and knew how much he ached inside. Numb, she finally believed him. "I'm sorry," she whispered, her voice thick.

He buried his face in the crook of her neck. Her hair, billowed by the wind, covered the back of his head in long, comforting waves. "So am I." He drew her close. "It's my fault, you know. I couldn't make her happy. And, if I'd been honest with myself ten years ago, Honor might still be alive."

"I don't understand—"

"Don't you, Brenna?" he charged, his tone growing harsh as he suddenly lifted his head. His face twisted into a mask of self-loathing.

Brenna didn't move.

"If I'd been honest with you—with her, maybe things would have been different." As quickly as he'd taken her into his arms, he released her.

She wasn't sure she wanted to hear whatever it was he had to say. "Maybe we should go back to the car."

"Not yet," he insisted. His breath fogged in the cold night air. "There was a reason I flew down to San Francisco this morning," he admitted, the brackets near his mouth deepening. "And it wasn't just to make sure you packed."

Dreading what he was about to say, she stepped back. "Warren, please—"

"I have a confession, Brenna."

"It's too late to—"

"I did love Honor when I married her. I swear to Almighty God that I did. But—" he took in a long, shuddering breath "—I loved you, too."

She shivered and huddled her arms around herself.

"It's true, Bren. I just didn't admit it to myself."

She didn't want to hear it—didn't want to think that in even some small way she'd come between him and her sister, the mother of his children. Sick with self-disgust, she started to run up the beach, away from the awful lies he was telling her.

Her feet pounded on the sand, echoing the horrid cadence in her heart. So long she'd wanted to hear that he had loved her and now—this, this *confession!* She felt dirty and angry and hurt, as if she had betrayed Honor.

She heard his footsteps, felt his arms close over her waist.

"Let me go, Warren," she cried, stumbling, feeling tears drizzle down her cheeks.

"Just listen, damn it!"

"No!" Tripping, she collapsed onto the cold sand. He tumbled over her, breaking his fall with his hands.

She was trapped beneath him and his flushed face was close over hers. His breath, short raspy bursts of air, fanned her face and chilled the tears in her eyes.

"I don't want to hear this!" She was breathless from her short sprint, gulping in air, her breasts heaving beneath him.

"You're going to listen whether you like it or not," he insisted. "Face it, Brenna. We've always been attracted to each other."

"No!"

"Ten years ago I didn't believe it, either. I thought you were going through a schoolgirl crush and that I was just reacting the same way any red-blooded American male would."

"Oh, God—"

"But, what I felt for you—how I wanted you—I convinced myself it wasn't real, that it was all just part of your fantasy. I was wrong."

"Warren, please—" She tried to squirm away but his face loomed over hers, his hands tight on her wrists, her back pressed into the sand.

"I didn't want to believe it, either. I wouldn't. God, I had a wife and kids! So I pretended that I didn't care for you at all. And everything I felt for you I buried so deep that I thought it would never surface again."

She remembered how cold he'd been at Honor's funeral; how furious he'd been when she'd announced she was moving back to Portland just last week.

"But then you came back," he said, angry all over again, a vein throbbing at his temple. "And I couldn't lie to myself any longer."

She wriggled fiercely, but he wouldn't let her go.

"That's why I fought you, Brenna, that's why I tried to shame you into leaving when I found you in Honor's closet."

"Don't do this, Warren," she begged.

"But I couldn't stop myself then," he said, "just like I couldn't resist you in the barn. And, damn it, I can't stop now." His lips crashed down on hers, and try as she might, she didn't have the strength to resist him.

Already breathless, she felt dizzy from his kiss. Wanton fires smoldered deep in her heart, igniting the flames of passion only he could fan. He touched her gently, his big hands soft and tender as they delved beneath her jacket to sculpt the contour of her breast.

She thought about Honor and felt as if she'd betrayed her sister, a sister who had raised her when their mother had died. Yet she couldn't stop loving Warren.

Moaning, her lips wet and anxious against his, she sobbed softly as she kissed him.

"Tell me you don't want me," he whispered, his breath as ragged as the jutting cliffs surrounding them.

"I—don't—"

"Tell me you don't love me."

His fingers trembled as they found the hem of her sweatshirt and touched the soft skin over her ribs. "I don't know—" Inching upward, one large palm slid beneath her bra. "I—oh—Warren—" She couldn't think, couldn't concentrate on anything but the gentle movement of his fingers against her breast. "This isn't fair," she protested as delicious sensations enveloped her. "I don't! I don't love you!"

"You do."

"Warren, *please!*" Desperate, she pushed at him, pummeled his chest with her fists until all the fight left her and she wound her arms around his neck.

"Just tell me you'll give us a chance, Brenna," he rasped, slowly extracting his hand. "Tell me we can try to get over the past."

"Is that what you want?" she asked, still dazed as she looked up at him. Her anger had faded and she was scared of the emotions racing through her blood. But as she stared up at him, she recognized him as the man she had loved most of her life. His black hair fell fetchingly over his forehead and his blue eyes were dark as the night.

"Yes," he vowed. "It took the other night when you walked out the door for me to realize that I couldn't lose you again."

She didn't know whether to laugh or cry. A few dark doubts lingered, warning her that everything was happening too quickly, but she cast aside her black thoughts and tangled her fingers in his hair. For too long, she'd loved him from afar.

"Trust, me, Brenna," he whispered.

And she did. With her whole heart, she believed in him.

Her smile trembled as she lifted her head and touched her lips to his, tasting the crystalline salt of her own tears.

"Be careful," he warned, his voice catching, "or I might lose control."

"Lose it," she whispered.

"Here? I don't think so." He glanced up at the restaurant perched high on the cliff. "I don't think we want to give Connie any more of a show than she's already seen."

"Spoilsport," Brenna teased, but didn't argue when he took her hands in his and pulled her to her feet. She shook the sand from her hair and dusted her jeans and coat.

Arms linked, they trudged through the sand to the staircase and Brenna rested her head against Warren's shoulder. Maybe, just maybe, he would love her as much as she loved him, and Honor would never come between them again, she thought. But part of her was disbelieving as Warren held the car door for her, then climbed behind the wheel.

"Rest," he whispered as she leaned against him, feeling his sweater next to her cheek, smelling the scent of salt air still clinging to his hair. She closed her eyes and sighed, more content than she had been in years. Honor's image filled her mind, but she steadfastly pushed it aside and forced herself to drift off.

BRENNA YAWNED, STRETCHED and felt a crick in her neck where she'd rested her head on Warren's shoulder. Blinking, she stared through the windshield and saw the lights of Portland glowing blue in the night.

"Awake?" Warren asked with a chuckle.

"Mmm. Barely." The car was warm and cozy and she never wanted this special time with him to end.

"You could stay with me," he suggested. His arm was draped familiarly over her shoulders. "Julie would love it." He kissed the top of her head. "And so would I."

Her heart squeezed and though she wanted to ignore the

doubts in her mind, she couldn't. How could she move into Honor's house? Honor's clothes still hung in the closet, her perfume still scented the bathroom, her jewelry filled her porcelain jewel box and her car was still parked in the garage. "Don't you think we're rushing things?" she asked.

His thin lips twisted cynically. "Maybe so," he admitted, "but it's your fault. You're the one who came back to Portland and stormed into my house, hell-bent to straighten out me and my children. You just barreled right into my life without really thinking things through."

"I had thought them through," she whispered.

Cocking a disbelieving brow, he maneuvered the car off the freeway and toward the west hills. "I don't think so. Don't get me wrong—I'm glad you returned," he said, his muscles relaxing and his fingers moving against her arm. "You made me face some things I hadn't been able to, but don't stop pushing now. Don't back off, Brenna."

"I'm not," she promised, snuggling closer again. "I just think we each need a little time and space." She glanced up at him, saw the protest forming in his eyes and touched his nose with her fingertip. "Don't argue," she said. "Just think about your kids. Julie might think I'm wonderful, but in Scotty's case the jury's still out. Maybe it always will be."

"No way," Warren chuckled. "One way or another, you'll worm your way into his heart."

"I wouldn't count on it. Maybe he doesn't out-and-out hate me, but he barely tolerates me."

"That'll change," Warren predicted, his eyes growing serious. "You know, in some respects he needs you more than Julie does."

The car climbed the steep hills and Warren parked at the curb in front of Brenna's apartment house. "I'll walk home," he said quickly as he pulled on the emergency brake.

"I'll drive you."

"It's only a couple of blocks, Brenna," he said, his gaze delving into hers. "And it won't hurt me to get a little exercise." His blue eyes glittered dangerously. "Besides, maybe you'll take pity on me and ask me to spend the night."

"Dreamer," she whispered, but her throat was thick as his lips brushed slowly over hers.

"Am I dreaming, Bren?" he asked hoarsely, but before she could answer he kissed her again. His lips were urgent and warm and her breath was trapped deep in her lungs. She circled his neck with her arms and pressed her eager mouth to his. Thoughtless of anything but the warmth invading her blood and the strong arms surrounding her, she moaned softly.

"Come home with me, Brenna. Please."

Dear God, how could she say no?

"I need you."

"And I need you, Warren," she replied, her thoughts as scattered as the stars winking in the midnight sky.

"Then spend the night with me."

"I want to," she admitted, her voice ragged. "But—I just want—to be sure."

"After ten years?"

She swallowed hard and drew away. "No—after four months," she whispered.

"I told you—"

"I know what you said, Warren, but I saw your house, *her* house— *her* things. And what's really hard to deal with is that Honor was my sister, Warren, not some woman I'd never met or known only briefly. She took care of me when Mom died and…and sometimes I feel like such a…a traitor."

He released her and swore under his breath. "Damn it, we've got to let her go. Both of us." Angrily ramming stiff fingers through his hair he exhaled a long, furious breath. His mouth was a tight line of disgust. "She's gone, Brenna.

But we keep acting as if she were alive, as if she could see or hear us, for God's sake." He yanked on the handle and shoved the car door open. "Come on, I'll walk you to the door." Then he glanced at the darkened Victorian house. "You're sure you want to stay here? Your furniture hasn't arrived and maybe the electricity hasn't been hooked up."

Brenna forced a smile. "I'll survive," she said dryly, though in the moonlight the tall house had taken on a sinister appearance.

"Right now that place looks like something right out of those Stalker horror movies."

"Home, sweet home," Brenna quipped.

"You're sure?"

"Absolutely," she lied, dreaming of how blissful it would be to spend the night in Warren's house, in Warren's bed, in Warren's arms. "Besides, I think I've got everything I need." Lips compressed in determination, she withdrew a sleeping bag, small athletic bag and flashlight. "This should do it." She patted the nylon bag and hoisted it over her shoulder. "I even packed my toothbrush."

"I guess I can't talk you out of this," Warren grumbled.

"Not tonight."

He grabbed the sleeping bag and flashlight. Together they walked up a concrete path to the front porch. "Thanks for flying down to San Francisco," she said, unlocking the door.

He tossed the sleeping bag into the foyer of the old manor. "My pleasure," he whispered, folding her into his arms and capturing her lips with his. "Believe me, it was all my pleasure."

She sighed and heard an answering groan from his throat. One of his hands splayed possessively across her back while the other twisted in the heavy strands of her hair, and all too eagerly she responded to him, kissing him hungrily.

"This is insane," Warren rasped, his chest heaving in counterpoint to hers as he released her. "Look, if you're not going to invite me in to share that—" he gestured quickly to her sleeping bag "—then I'd better leave now, while I still can." His palm slid down her cheek. "Believe me, I don't want to."

She almost asked him to stay, to spend a night with her alone. Before she could voice her change of mind, he turned on his heel, jumped down the three steps and disappeared into the dark night.

"It's for the best," she muttered to herself as she walked inside, dragging her meager belongings after her. "Take it slow." But as she looked around the inside of her new home, she felt an incredible shaft of loneliness pierce her heart.

STUFFING HIS HANDS into the front pockets of his jeans, Warren walked briskly. A misting rain fell from the sky and fog hung in the deeper clefts of the hills. The night air was cold but it helped cool his blood and clear his head. Scowling, he realized that Brenna was right. He was rushing things. But he couldn't help himself. Whenever he was around her he wanted to stay with her, possess her, claim her as his own. "Damned fool," he muttered, remembering it was just those crazy, hot-blooded emotions that had been the reason he'd married the wrong woman ten years before.

So here he was, ready to pursue Brenna as relentlessly as he had her older sister.

Warren groaned inwardly. Less than a week had passed since Brenna had announced she was returning to Portland, and he was already acting like a randy high-school kid. And that's exactly how he felt—as young and fevered as if he were nineteen.

He remembered the night she'd confessed her love. If

only he hadn't been so blinded by Honor. If only he'd believed Brenna old enough to be capable of love.

"Forget it, Stone. It's over and done with!"

The wind rustled through the oak trees overhead as he shoved open the front gate and walked into the house. It was quiet inside—too quiet. The children were still in West Linn with Brenna's father and all he could hear was the soft hum of the furnace and the steady tick of the grandfather clock near the stairs.

He kicked off his shoes and strode into the den where he reached for the first bottle he found: a nearly full fifth of brandy. But before he could pour himself a drink, he squinted through the window and into the dark night beyond. Through the windblown branches of nearby trees, he could see past the ravine and to the old Victorian house where Brenna now lived. One light blazed from an upper window and he smiled to himself. So the electricity had been turned on. Resting his shoulder against the sash, he imag- ined Brenna unrolling her sleeping bag, taking off her clothes, stepping into the shower with her dark hair falling in boundless curls past the soft, ivory-colored skin of her back....

"Boy, you've got it bad," he chided.

It didn't seem right that both he and Brenna were alone. He stared, hoping to catch a glimpse of her, but the apartment house was too far away and he turned his attention back to the bottle, seeking to quiet the restlessness that gnawed at him whenever he thought of her.

"Get a grip on yourself," he muttered, splashing brandy into a snifter and swirling the amber liquid. The phone rang and he grinned in satisfaction. Obviously Brenna missed him and had changed her mind. He snatched the receiver off the cradle. "Hello?"

"Stone?" a male voice asked gruffly. Warren recognized it as belonging to Robert Slater, one of his assistants.

He masked his disappointment and asked, "What's up?"

"Nothing good. But I thought you'd want to know. Charlie Saxton was released today—the judge threw his case out of court."

"He did *what?*" Warren said, rage welling up within him.

"Yep. Saxton's lawyer claimed he wouldn't get a fair trial in Portland what with all the press coverage—a jury would be prejudiced."

"I don't believe it," Warren muttered, feeling his face flush darkly.

"Believe it. And you can thank the *Willamette Examiner* for this one."

"I will," Warren vowed, his stomach wrenching violently. So Len Patterson and his group of hacks were at it again. He remembered the *Examiner*'s coverage of Honor's death and a bitter taste filled his mouth. "I'll thank Len Patterson personally."

CHAPTER SEVEN

THE OFFICES OF the *Willamette Examiner* hummed. As Brenna pushed through the main doors of the first floor of a high-rise brick complex just two blocks from Front Avenue, reporters and photographers were already huddled over desks, sipping coffee, munching on bagels and staring into computer screens.

She introduced herself to a smiling receptionist, who pointed out her desk and informed her that Len Patterson was waiting for her. "I'm Karla Meyers—just let me know if there's anything you need," she said as Brenna stuffed her purse into one of the drawers. "Len wants to talk to you once you get settled. Just knock on his door."

"I will. Thanks."

A few minutes later she was sitting in a chair opposite her new boss and scanning his notes.

"Those are some of the topics we'll want to cover in the home environment section this month," he said, gesturing to the pages in Brenna's hand. "See any problems?"

Brenna read the neatly typed sheet. The list included gardening tips, how to entertain children home from school in the summer, favorite local vacation spots, quality versus quantity time with children, and landscaping ideas. "Seems fine to me."

"What about the articles on marriage and children?" he asked. "You're single."

Brenna's muscles tightened. "I have a lot of married friends. Some even have children," she replied, trying to keep the sarcasm from her voice. Len did have a point, she thought grudgingly. He was just covering his bases.

"Not exactly firsthand experience."

"I'm very close with my niece and nephew. I plan to spend a lot of time with them."

"Warren Stone's children?"

She felt strangely protective. "Yes."

"You're close to them?"

"Very," she said, though she experienced a flicker of doubt. She hadn't heard from Warren or the kids in over a week. Ever since Warren had dropped her off at her apartment, she'd been alone. Not that she hadn't had more than her share of work cut out for her. The movers had deposited her belongings and she'd spent hours unpacking, arranging furniture, hanging pictures and arguing with the phone company about installing telephone service. She hadn't had time to walk over to Warren's house and she couldn't have called—but he, on the other hand, could have stopped by.

"Well, it's not the same as having kids of your own," Len said, bringing Brenna back to the here and now, "but it will have to do."

"I've written about kids before," she pointed out.

Thoughtfully, he drummed his fingers on the desk. "Then you're not afraid to tackle something like this?" He tapped the list with his index finger, indicating the topic of what to do with a child who is experiencing peer-pressure problems at school.

She almost laughed. "No."

He grinned then. "Good."

"Just last week I dealt with sibling rivalry, petty jealousy, the thrill of a first bicycle and the trauma of losing a front tooth in the batter of a birthday cake," she said, more confident. "And, believe it or not, it hasn't been that long for me. I can remember back to grade school."

"Okay, okay," Len said, holding up his hands but still grinning. "You're an expert."

"Almost."

Leaning back in his chair, he cradled his head in his hands. "Just make sure your articles are fresh and accurate and funny—above all else, let the humor of the situation shine through—just like you did for the *City Weekly*."

"I'll give it my best shot."

"Great." Apparently catching the defiant gleam in her eyes, he added, "I know, I know, don't say it: You're a professional, right?"

"Right."

"I didn't mean to come off like a drill sergeant." He rubbed his forehead and reached for a pack of cigarettes on the desk. "I just want to point out that Portland is a different market than San Francisco."

"I was born and raised around here."

"Okay. End of lecture. Show me what you've got." As Brenna stood, he added, "And you can check the files and go over the microfilm—just to acquaint yourself with the flavor of the home environment section and make sure you don't duplicate articles we've already printed."

"Will do."

He snapped his lighter over the end of a cigarette. "Good. These are just a few ideas to get you started, but if you come up with anything else, just ask me for approval." He offered her a wide smile. "I'm pretty open to new ideas."

"I'll remember that," she said as she left his office and realized for the first time that she was nervous. Len made her uneasy, but she told herself it was because she was new on the job and wanted desperately to make a good impression—her feelings had nothing to do with Warren and his reservations about the paper.

At her desk she scribbled a few notes to herself and considered possible angles for the stories Len had suggested. The ideas on parenting intrigued her and her thoughts drifted to Julie and Scotty. Frowning, she realized she missed them both and could even suffer their bickering to be with them. In a couple of weeks, they'd become very special. Tonight, she decided, she'd visit them...and Warren.

"Welcome aboard!"

Startled, Brenna glanced up to find a young woman with short strawberry-blond hair and a turned-up nose dusted with light freckles standing near her desk. She was wearing a denim skirt, oversize jewelry, a pink sweater and knee-high black boots. She held out her hand. "I'm Tammy Belding. I work in the entertainment section."

"I'm—"

"Oh, I know who you are," Tammy's bracelets jangled as she shook Brenna's hand and offered her a steaming Styrofoam cup of thick, black coffee. "And I took the liberty of scrounging up some coffee—if you can call it that. I hope you take it black. If not, there's sugar, cream and more of this sludge in the cafeteria."

"Black's fine," Brenna said gratefully. "Thanks."

"No problem." Tammy perched on the corner of Brenna's desk and crossed her legs as she took small sips from her cup. "Len showed me some of your work—clippings from the paper in San Francisco."

"He did?"

"Yeah. Your column in the *City Weekly* was great. It had style and humor. Just what this place needs." She glanced around the office, then lowered her head and whispered, "It's been like a tomb around here lately, everybody getting on each other's nerves. The owners of the paper are all upset about a couple of articles that have been printed."

"Oh." Brenna didn't know what to say to this sudden deluge of office gossip.

"Len's hoping your column will lighten things up a bit."

"I'll try."

"You'll do great. That boss of yours in San Francisco gave you a super recommendation and, as you've probably heard—" she glanced over her shoulder "—the *Examiner*'s in a little trouble."

"Trouble?" Brenna's heart sank.

"Oh, nothing financial. Not yet, anyway. Circulation's up and we have a great advertising section. But we've got some legal problems."

"Legal problems?"

Tammy shrugged. "It's not a secret, but some reports have gotten us into hot water with the district attorney's office."

"Oh?" Brenna's stomach knotted. So Warren hadn't been blowing things out of proportion.

"Yeah, like that fiasco with Charlie Saxton—the man accused of kidnapping his nephew. Boy, what a mess." She rolled her huge eyes. "I'm just glad my toughest assignment this week is a critique on a couple of new movies and a concert." She swallowed the last of her coffee then pointed a be-ringed finger at Brenna's computer terminal. "Just let me know if you have any trouble with that thing. It's been known to eat finished copy."

"I'll remember that."

"There should be a copy of the operating manual in your desk somewhere, but sometimes the hardware is touchy and you need more than a manual to fix it. If you do, just holler—I've got a sledgehammer in my desk."

"I'll let you know," Brenna promised as Tammy sauntered over to her desk and plopped into her chair.

Brenna spent the rest of the morning reading the most recent articles in the home environment section, then perused other stories as well. She had to admit that the society section seemed more gossipy than newsworthy, but the rest of the paper was accurate and concise.

Except for the Charlie Saxton story. Brenna had dug through the previous two weeks of papers and read all the articles relating to the Saxton case. There had been several errors in the original story and eventually the paper had all but tarred and feathered the man before the jury had been selected. Not that Charlie didn't deserve the bad press, she thought, but the objectivity of the paper had been compromised and Charlie's lawyer had found a way to have the case thrown out of court, at least in Portland.

She folded the paper and sighed. No wonder she hadn't heard from Warren. Charlie Saxton's case was only one of hundreds of cases from burglary to murder that Warren was responsible for. Her guilty conscience twinged and she reached for the phone. Maybe she should call him, or Julie. She paused. It was barely noon. Warren would be working, and the children were still in school. Disappointed, she decided she would have to wait.

After a quick lunch at a nearby deli, she returned to her desk, sketched out a story about the trauma of losing a front tooth and was surprised when she glanced at her watch and discovered it was after five. Half the staff had already disappeared, and the remaining reporters were slipping into coats, snapping briefcases shut or rummaging in their purses for keys.

"So, how'd it go?" Tammy asked, hefting her huge leather bag and pausing at Brenna's desk.

Brenna couldn't help but wonder if she really did carry a sledgehammer in the huge pouch. "Not bad." Brenna stretched and her back creaked. "But I'm ready to get out of here."

"You and me both." She grinned. "Tonight I'm going to the premiere of *The Stalker's Revenge, Part Seven.*"

"Lucky you," Brenna said, laughing.

"Don't suppose you want to join me?"

"I don't think so. Blood and guts aren't my thing."

Tammy shrugged. "Mine either, but I can't wait to see how they resurrect the Stalker. They killed him with an atomic bomb in *Part Six*. I thought that would be the end of him, but somehow he's come back and now he contaminates his victims with radiation before he does them in."

"Nice guy," Brenna murmured.

Tammy, jewelry clanking, waved and walked to the main door, then called over her shoulder, "I'll give you my personal review in the morning."

"I'll be on pins and needles," Brenna quipped, slipping her arms into her coat.

Outside, a May shower was in full force. Rain peppered the ground and ran down the streets to overflow the storm drains. Pedestrians, collars turned against the wind, hunched under umbrellas as they scurried through the clog of afternoon traffic.

Despite her raincoat and hood, Brenna was drenched by the time she found her car and climbed inside. She started the engine and rammed the hatchback into gear, slowly threading her way through the narrow streets and tall buildings near the river, then up the steep, wooded hills to her apartment house. She parked near the curb and dashed across the wet lawn and up the slick front steps.

As she passed the landlady's apartment, the elderly woman poked her head into the hallway. "The phone installation man was here."

Brenna sighed audibly and checked her watch. "I forgot all about him."

"Well, he was pretty steamed and said he couldn't wait. I talked him into coming back early in the morning."

"Thank you."

"He said he'd be here at eight o'clock. If that doesn't

work for you, you're supposed to call the telephone company."

"I will, and thanks," Brenna replied.

"Oh, and your brother-in-law stopped by."

Brenna's heart soared and she stopped dead in her tracks. She hadn't realized until this moment just how badly she'd missed him.

"He asked me to have you call him, once your phone was installed." She shrugged her slim shoulders. "But you can use mine."

"Thanks," Brenna said, "but I think I'll just drop by his house." Heart beating crazily, she climbed the stairs two at a time. Once inside her apartment, she stripped and flung her clothes onto the bed. Her thoughts were on Warren and the children. She couldn't wait to see them! Humming, she twisted the faucets in the shower and pinned up her hair as the old pipes clanged. Eventually, hot water began to steam the bathroom mirror and she stepped into the old, tiled stall.

The hot spray was little more than a thin stream of water, but it loosened her muscles and she closed her eyes, thinking of Warren. She ached to see him and the children again. It was a wonder, she thought, twisting off the water and reaching for a towel, how soon she'd grown attached to Honor's family.

The doorbell chimed impatiently and she flung on her fluffy forest-green bathrobe, cinched it tight and left a trail of water on the carpet as she ran to the door. "Who is it?"

"Take a wild guess."

Warren! Her pulse fluttered and she couldn't help but smile as she yanked open the door. He was wearing a navy suit, white shirt and loosened tie. His gaze slid from the falling knot of hair pinned loosely to her head, past her cheeks and neck to the cleft of her breasts, barely concealed by the overlapping lapels of her robe. "Looks like I got here just in time," he observed, eyes lifting to meet hers.

She could feel her face flush, but didn't care. It was so good to see him again. "Well, don't just stand out there, come in," she said, laughing as the twisted knot of hair slid down her back. She tried to repin it and failed. "Just give me a minute to change."

His lips twisted crookedly. "Don't bother on my account."

"I'm dripping all over—"

He stepped inside, kicked the door shut behind him and took her swiftly into his arms. "You look sensational," he whispered against her neck and she melted inside.

"What took you so long to get here?" she teased.

"Work. A few things came up."

"Such as the Charlie Saxton case?"

"Or lack thereof," he muttered, grimacing before holding her close. "But I've already dealt with that. In fact, I had a nice little chat with your boss."

"Len?"

"Helluva guy," he mocked. "I've never seen anyone backpedal so quickly."

"He—he's all right," she murmured, though it was impossible to think when she was so close to Warren, her body pressed intimately against his.

Her robe slid over one shoulder, baring her white skin. Warren's gaze lowered and he tugged at the few pins restraining her hair. The braid fell free, brushing her shoulder and settling against the soft skin just above her breast. Warren sucked in his breath and toyed with the curling auburn lock, the tip of his index finger grazing her skin and sending delicious sparks of desire running wantonly through her blood.

"Wh-where are the kids?" she asked, trying to control her spinning senses.

"Waiting," he said slowly, studying her lips.

"For what?"

"Us. I promised to take them to the rose garden in Washington Park for dinner and I thought you might want to come along."

"I'd love it," she admitted, then glanced to the window where drops of rain were streaking the glass. "But it's miserable weather."

His gaze drifted downward to the pulse jumping at her throat and the tiny drops of water still clinging to her neck. "We could postpone."

"No way," she said, though her heart pounded wildly as he pressed anxious lips to the base of her throat. Her knees felt suddenly too weak to support her. "I'm not going to disappoint Scotty. He's still not too sure if he likes me."

"He'll get over it."

Swallowing with difficulty, she shook her head. "He's too important. I can't let him down."

Warren's eyes had turned dark, but he released her and pressed his lips together. "Okay, okay. We won't disappoint the kids."

"That's more like it, *Dad*," she teased. Slipping quickly into the bedroom, she untied her robe, letting it fall to the floor as she stepped into a denim skirt and a cotton sweater. Her hair was still damp, so she clipped it away from her face, dabbed at her lipstick, slid into pumps and joined him.

"So have you got an alternate plan?" she asked, squinting through the wind to see water running off the eaves. She tugged her raincoat from a hall tree and frowned when she noticed it was still wet.

"Not yet." They walked downstairs and climbed into his car. A few minutes later he had parked in the garage and before Brenna had even stepped from the car, Julie burst through the door leading to the kitchen.

"Aunt Bren!" she said with a big smile.

"Hi, pumpkin."

The girl charged across the open garage floor and hugged her aunt before glancing up at her father. "Can we still have a picnic?" she asked. "Mary says it's too wet."

"Mary's probably right," Warren admitted, his eyes twinkling as he lifted his daughter off the cement floor. "But a promise is a promise—even if we have to eat in the car."

Inside, Mary Beatty was muttering under her breath as she stuffed checkered napkins into a huge wicker basket. "This is lunacy, that's what it is," she grumbled. "The children will catch their death out there."

"It's sixty degrees," Warren pointed out. "Besides, I thought people caught cold from other people, not the weather."

"Hogwash." But Mary smiled and closed the lid of the basket. "Just you make sure they wear their jackets. This one—" she hooked a thumb at Scotty "—doesn't believe in wearing anything to keep warm."

"I'll keep it in mind," Warren said dryly as Mary slid into her coat and scrounged in a kitchen cupboard for her umbrella and huge purse. "See you tomorrow."

Once the housekeeper had closed the door behind her, Warren snatched the heavy basket from the table and instructed the children to find their jackets.

"So how're you going to pull this one off?" Brenna asked.

"We'll ignore the storm."

Through the window, Brenna eyed the threatening sky. "I don't know how."

"We'll have the picnic in the covered area and then walk through the rose garden until the kids want to give up."

"Ready!" Julie announced, her boots clumping against tile as she raced back to the kitchen. Scotty was on her heels and a few minutes later they were all in Warren's car and driving toward the park.

"Daddy sold Mommy's car," Scotty announced. "Some lady bought it."

Brenna remembered the empty garage and her heart nearly stopped beating. At the time, it hadn't registered that Honor's car was missing. "What prompted that?" she asked, looking at Warren from the corner of her eye.

His lips tightened a little. "It was time."

"Oh."

"Mommy never liked the car anyway," Julie said, wiping the steam from a back window. "She wanted a Mercedes."

"Yeah, a silver one with a top that goes down!" Scotty agreed. "Daddy was supposed to buy her one for her birthday."

Brenna swallowed hard and her fingers clenched around the strap of her purse.

"She even talked to a salesman," Julie said, then her face crumpled. "I miss Mommy," she whispered, sighing.

Tears gathered in Scotty's eyes and his lower lip trembled, but he didn't say anything.

"I do, too," Brenna said, glancing over her shoulder to offer Julie an encouraging smile.

The rest of the ride was tense. No one said a word and Brenna's thoughts were tangled in a web of images: Honor the cheerleader, Honor sneaking around behind Warren's back, Honor whispering brokenly that everything would be all right when their mother had died, Honor's flushed face under a creamy-white veil as she'd married Warren and finally, the emptiness of that cold gray day when Honor had been buried. Julie and Scotty had been at the grave site, their faces ashen, their blue eyes rimmed in red. Warren had held Scotty in one arm and clung to Julie's little hand.

Blinking, Brenna cleared her throat. What was she

doing here? How could she possibly help Honor's children cope with their loss when she could barely handle her sister's death herself?

In San Francisco Honor's death hadn't seemed so real. In the past ten years there had been months when she hadn't seen or talked to her sister. But now, back in Portland, the lack of her presence—the emptiness—was oppressive.

Warren, too, seemed lost in thought. His brow was furrowed with deep grooves of introspection as he squinted through the windshield, the wipers slapping away the rain.

THE PARKING LOT was nearly empty, and steel-colored clouds threatened to let loose a downpour as Warren lifted the picnic basket from the trunk, then led Brenna and the children to a covered area on a hill overlooking the rose gardens. A few wet blossoms had burst into full bloom, offering solitary patches of yellow, orange, pink and red to the gloomy day.

"I'd forgotten how beautiful it could be up here," Brenna whispered, gazing past the gardens to the cloud-covered city beyond. Skyscrapers pierced the misting fog and the city sprawled gently from one side of the Willamette River to the other.

"It can be," Warren said.

"I'm hungry," Scotty cut in, not the least bit interested in the view, the roses or the supposed splendor of Portland.

"Me, too," Julie agreed.

Brenna helped Warren spread a cloth over the picnic table and offered sandwiches all around. They ate in silence, the glum day taking its toll. After munching apple sauce cupcakes, they walked through the rose garden in the rain and Scotty jumped in every puddle he could find. His pants were soaked.

Warren took Brenna's hand in his and buried them both

in his jacket pocket. "Maybe this wasn't such a great idea," he admitted, studying his children.

"You can't blame yourself for the weather."

"It's not the weather that's the problem."

Brenna glanced up to the ominous sky and felt raindrops pepper her cheeks. The storm was beginning again.

"Come on," Warren called as the wind picked up. Brenna packed the basket, then they all scurried down the trail to the parking lot and climbed into Warren's car. The rain was coming down in sheets by the time Warren drove through the winding streets and finally parked in the garage.

After building a fire in the den, Warren carried both children upstairs and bathed them. The water was still running as Brenna heated hot chocolate in the microwave and topped the steaming mugs with marshmallows. A few minutes later, Julie dashed down the stairs and slid to a stop near the table where Brenna had placed the cocoa.

"Wow!" Julie said, eyeing the cups. Her cheeks were freshly scrubbed and flushed from the bath, her hair tangled from a quick towel drying, her body snug in pale yellow pajamas. "Mom never did anything like this," she admitted.

Brenna wasn't about to fall to pieces at the mention of Honor. "I don't know why," she said. "Our mom used to make cocoa for us when she was alive."

Julie sat in one of the chairs, tasted the cocoa, then blew across her cup. "Did you miss her?" she asked.

"Who? Oh, my mother?"

Wide-eyed, Julie nodded.

"Of course I did. Sometimes, believe it or not, I still do. But I missed her the most right after she died," Brenna admitted. She took the chair next to Julie's, then selected a cup. Staring into the melting marshmallows, she frowned.

"But your mother helped me through that time. Even though she was hurting herself."

Julie considered. "You and Mom. You liked each other?"

"Most of the time."

"I hate Scotty."

"No, you don't." Brenna smiled sadly. "I'm sure there were times when Honor wanted to wring my neck."

"No."

"Oh, yes. Like the time she caught me in her new red sweater, or the time I 'borrowed' her lipstick on a really hot day and it melted, or when I was younger, when I smashed her bike—boy, she was really mad about that." Brenna stared at Julie's small face. How much she looked like Honor. The same big blue eyes, blond hair and tiny, rosebud-shaped lips. "But it worked both ways. Sometimes Honor did things I didn't approve of."

"Like what?"

Like lying to your father. Brenna shrugged, then walked to the window and stared out to the lights of the city, glittering far below. "She used to tease me a lot and she begged me to do her homework for her—type reports, give her the rundown on a book *she* was supposed to have read— used all the film in my camera. That sort of thing." Brenna thought back and sighed; she and Honor had shared so much and she missed her sister terribly at times. Right now, standing in the kitchen of the big old house, Brenna wished Honor were still alive.

"Did you?"

"Did I what?" Brenna asked, lost for a minute. "Oh— did I do her homework?"

Julie nodded.

"Not very often."

"I would *never* do any school things for Scotty."

"Careful, now. You might be surprised at what you'd do.

Sometimes you're so angry you feel like you really do hate him, but other times he's okay, isn't he?" Brenna prodded.

"Once in a while," Julie admitted grudgingly.

Brenna smiled, then set her cup on the windowsill. "Maybe I'd better comb your hair."

"No."

But Brenna was already behind Julie's chair and had found a comb in her purse. "I'll be careful," she promised.

Several times Julie cried out when the teeth of the comb caught on a tangle and Brenna felt all thumbs. Maybe she wasn't cut out for this, she thought, wincing, when Julie nearly jumped off the chair.

"That hurts," Julie whispered.

"I'm sorry." Eventually, thank God, she was finished. "There you go," she said, running the comb a final time through Julie's fine hair.

"Thanks—I guess."

"I don't suppose you want me to curl it?"

"Will it hurt?"

"No." Brenna held up two fingers. "Scout's honor."

Tilting her head back, Julie eyed her aunt. "Okay, but if it hurts, you'll stop."

"Fair enough," Brenna said. "Now, do you have any rollers?"

Julie shook her head. "I don't think so."

"Bobby pins?"

"Nope."

"How about something of your mother's? Maybe a curling iron or hair dryer?"

Julie's face fell. "Dad gave all her stuff away."

"He did?"

Julie nodded. "Just the other day. A big truck came and took away boxes and boxes of stuff. Dad said we had to get on with our lives, that we should still remember Mommy but that we had to clean out a few things."

"Like the car?" Shaken, Brenna tried to concentrate on the conversation. Why, now, had Warren suddenly emptied his house of Honor's things and sold Honor's car? Maybe he was truly trying to push his grief aside.

"And her hair stuff."

"I—I guess we'll just have to improvise," Brenna said quickly, trying to recover herself. "Ever heard of rag curls?"

Julie looked suspicious. "I don't think so. It sounds weird."

"Not weird, but simple. I braid your hair with rags and tomorrow morning you have wavy curls."

"You sure?"

"Absolutely! I've even done it before." Relieved that the conversation had turned from Honor, Brenna scrounged up an old sheet from the linen closet and tore it into long strips before twining sections of Julie's blond locks in tight braids. By the time Warren and Scotty entered the kitchen, Julie looked a little like Medusa.

"What's that?" Scotty wanted to know.

"A new fashion trend, er, old fashion trend. I think this is how my great-grandmother used to curl her hair," Brenna quipped as she reheated the cocoa, then plopped two new marshmallows into Scotty's cup.

"Looks funny," he declared. "Like a monster."

Warren glanced at his daughter and grinned. "Raggedy Ann," he quipped.

Brenna waved off their male opinions and poured water into the coffeemaker. "Just you wait until tomorrow. Julie will be gorgeous and you two will have to eat your words!"

Julie glowed but Scotty was outwardly skeptical. "She looks funny," he said again, then promptly drained his cup of cocoa before warily scrutinizing Brenna. "Will you read the new book?" he asked. "The one you bought me for my birthday?"

"I'd love to." Brenna warmed inside. This was the first time Scotty had asked for her help. A milestone. Grinning, she helped him out of his chair. "Come on, sport."

While she read to Scotty, Warren tucked Julie into bed.

Fifteen minutes later, the children were asleep and she and Warren were alone in the family room near the back of the house. The room was dark, except for the golden light from the fire.

Cradling a cup of coffee in both hands, Brenna sat on the wide ledge of a bay window while Warren stacked dry chunks of oak in the grate. Outside, wind buffeted the trees, and rain, catching the reflection from the fire and glowing amber, drizzled down the glass.

Brenna tucked her knees beneath her chin and watched as Warren leaned over to stoke the fire. She noted that his sweater stretched taut across his wide shoulders and his worn denim jeans fitted snugly over his buttocks and lean legs. The sweater gaped away from the waistband of his jeans, displaying dark skin and not an ounce of fat. His body was as lean and tight as he had been all those years before when, as a naive eighteen-year-old, she had surreptitiously studied him as he'd swum in the lake.

His stomach muscles had been flat, his chest sprinkled with dark hair, his shoulders strident and his legs long and muscular. His cutoff jeans had slung low over his hips— she'd been embarrassed at the sight of his navel—and, when he had leaned forward she'd glimpsed the dark line of his tan on his back. She'd been fascinated at eighteen, just as she was still. It didn't matter if Warren were wearing wet, low-slung cutoff jeans or a stuffy three-piece suit and starched white shirt, there was something earthy and sensual about him—something fierce and hungry beneath his cool blue eyes and controlled features.

Standing, he dusted the sawdust from his hands and reached for his cup, took a sip, then grimaced. "This seems to be lacking something," he said, before slashing her a knowing grin and searching in a cabinet near the fireplace. "And this is just what we need." With a flourish, he withdrew a bottle of Irish whiskey.

"I don't think—" she protested, but he was already pouring a shot of the liquor into her cup.

"Just like San Francisco," he said. "Remember?"

"How could I forget?"

He touched his cup to hers and asked, "How did the first day on the new job go?"

She shrugged. "It went."

"No problems?"

He was studying her face, scrutinizing her for a reaction. She thought about Tammy's gossip, but kept it to herself. No reason to inflame him any further with proof that the *Examiner* was just a gossipy, unprofessional rag. "Nothing serious. Len asked me if I knew anything about children and I told him about Scotty and Julie."

"Brenna, you didn't!" he roared, every muscle flexing.

She could have bitten her tongue. "It was nothing, really. He just wanted to know if I had any firsthand experience dealing with children and their problems."

"And you mentioned my kids?" he asked, the hard edge of his features harsh in the shadowy room.

"Yes." She felt foolish now, but couldn't undo what had already been said in the office.

Resting his hips against the back of a long couch, he didn't move a muscle. His lips were drawn tight and his eyes had become suspicious slits. "When you were interviewed for the job, did he ask you if you were related to me?" His voice was so low, it was barely audible over the pop and hiss of the fire.

"Not you directly. But he knew my maiden name—he guessed I was related to Honor."

"Son of a bitch," Warren whispered angrily. "Son of a goddamned—"

"He was just making conversation," she said, bristling. "He saw a connection, but I wasn't hired because I'm your sister-in-law." Eyes flashing, she sipped her coffee, watching as he paced in front of the fire. "You know, you seem to have some sort of witch-hunt going on with the *Examiner.*"

"Me? Hey, wait a minute. You've got things turned around. There's a witch-hunt going on all right, but not through my office. It's the stupid, irresponsible 'journalists' of the *Examiner* who're doing the hunting. The *Examiner* is always stirring up trouble." He took a long swallow and dashed the remains of his drink in the fire. The flames flickered and hissed.

She thought about everything Tammy had said and decided that Warren did have a point, though he was obviously exaggerating. However, she wasn't in the mood to argue. Besides, this particular conversation was a no-win situation. "I heard about the Charlie Saxton story," she admitted.

"I'll bet. As I said, I already talked to the esteemed Len Patterson."

She sipped her drink, regarding him silently over the lip of her cup.

"I thought he should know how I felt about Charlie's release and who I thought was directly responsible."

"I bet he liked that," she mocked.

"He pulled out all the old, worn phrases—freedom of the press and all that. But all in all, he never once admitted that he fouled up—just told me to call the legal firm for the paper. Yep, he's one great guy. I could just hear the wheels turning in his mind—as he tried to figure how the hell to cover his backside."

"People are human," she reminded him. "They do occasionally make mistakes."

"Unfortunately, it's not the first." His gaze grew distant as he stared at the fire. Shadows, orange and red, flickered across his features, deepening the angles of his face. "I just hope you don't get hurt, Bren."

"I won't." She tossed her hair over her shoulder and pushed her empty cup into a corner of the window ledge. "I'm a big girl now. Besides, I write about home and hearth and maybe the anxieties of balancing a career and children. Not exactly cloak-and-dagger stuff. Not even anything particularly controversial."

His mouth twisted wryly and he crossed back to the window. Resting his hands on her shoulders, he stared deep into her eyes. His thumbs stroked her throat and she shuddered, not from the cold, but in anticipation. Mellowed by the drink and the firelight, warmed with his touch, she could think of nothing but the mesmerizing way his fingertips moved in lazy circles over her pulse.

"Do you have everything all figured out?" he asked, curling a lock of mahogany-colored hair between his thumb and fingers and seeming entranced by the red highlights mingled with the dark strands.

"Not everything," she whispered.

"Neither have I."

Bending, lowering his head so that his lips just barely touched hers, he breathed into her mouth. "Don't say 'no.'" Then his mouth slanted over hers and his arms wrapped securely around her waist, drawing her up, her breasts and torso flat against the length of him as he swept her to her feet.

Light-headed, she could do nothing more than return the fever of his kiss. Her arms wrapped around his chest and even through his sweater she could feel the power of his muscles, the smooth skin of his back, the banded strength of his forearms. Entrapped, she saw the fire in his eyes, a reflection of her own. His hands tangled in her hair, drawing her down to the thick Oriental carpet, pressing her against the floor as his lips, hot and wet, slid hungrily over hers.

"Warren," she whispered, unable to quiet the thunderous beat of her heart or the ragged bursts of her breath. She kissed him and the fires of passion licked upward, raging out of control through her bloodstream.

"Make love to me," he whispered.

She could do little else. Drugged by the nearness of him, senseless with the feel of his hands on her skin, she could only move anxiously against him, unable to resist the power of his kiss.

Thoughts of Honor, dark guilty doubts, disappeared into the intimate corners of the room and she was alone with Warren, no one else. She could feel the weight of his chest crushing her breasts, hear the irregular beat of his heart and knew that this was their time.

His fingers slipped beneath the ribbing of her sweater, gently prodding the soft flesh of her abdomen before moving upward to touch, ever so lightly, the tip of her breast. She moaned, wanting more, savoring every sensation of liquid fire that crawled through her body as he lifted the sweater over her head.

She was aware of the rustle of burning flame and the faint smell of charred wood as his lips swept over her skin, rimming the circle of bones at her throat with his tongue until she moaned and melted inside, aching for him. She couldn't think, could only feel, and her hands moved upward along the strong muscles of his arms, tugging and pulling at the wretched sweater until his chest was bare and gleaming in the firelight. Dark hair whorled downward, covering his skin with a fine, black thatch that was soft in her fingers. She gazed at him in wonder, touching him gently, almost scared that the glorious sensations would somehow end.

Her breasts strained upward and he stroked them through the lacy silk of her bra before he nearly tore the scrap of cloth from her body and took one crested peak in his mouth. His tongue toyed with her nipple, suckling ravenously.

Moaning softly, she cradled his head in her hands. "Warren, oh, love," she whispered as he slid his hands along her back and forced her skirt over her hips. Cool air touched her bare skin as she lay naked on the carpet.

"Show me how much you want me," he murmured, one big hand kneading a breast while the other stroked her thigh.

She was dizzy and aroused and wanted more—all of him—everything he could give her. Licking her lips, she reached downward. Her fingers found the button of his jeans and she pushed the worn denim off his hips, her gaze traveling the sensual path her hands had taken. She'd never seen him naked before and couldn't help but smile as he kicked off his jeans and settled over her—long, lean muscles pressing erotically into her yielding counterparts.

"Are you sure about this?" he asked. Restraint pulled the corners of his mouth tight, but his hands trembled and sweat beaded his brow.

"Y-yes." Bewitched, she watched as he swallowed, his Adam's apple sliding provocatively inside his throat.

His hands were on her breasts again, kneading, circling, demanding until she thought she might go mad with the hot, wicked desire pumping through her veins. "P-please, Warren. I need you. All of you."

Closing glassy eyes, he moved over her, gently forcing her knees apart, pushing his way into her with a magical force that sent her skyward. He moved rhythmically, and she moved with him, slowly at first, then faster and faster until the corners of the room faded and she was spinning out of control, her fingers coiling in his black hair.

He groaned loudly, a primitive cry on his lips and a delicious explosion ripped through her body, sending ripple after ripple of warmth through her limbs. Tears gathered in her eyes and she clung to his glistening muscles. His skin glowed copperlike from the firelight and his eyes were squeezed shut.

She kissed his neck and he groaned.

"Honor…oh, lover," he rasped.

Brenna froze. Honor's name hung in the air and rang in her ears. "No," she whispered, unable to face the undeniable truth: Warren had pretended she was her sister! Wounded so bitterly that she felt sick inside, she tried to wither away from him.

His eyes flew open.

"Get off me," she whispered, scrabbling away.

But he didn't move. "Brenna, I don't—"

"Get off me!" She shoved with all her might and slithered away from him, snatching her sweater and skirt from the floor. "Oh, God," she cried. How could she have believed him. *How?*

"Hey, what's going on?"

"Don't you *know?*" she said, refusing to break down, though she was dying inside. Slowly, as surely as if he had thrust a knife into her heart, she was dying. "Can't you *remember?*"

"Remember what?" His utter amazement gave way to anger. "I know that we just made love and—"

"Did *we?* Or were you with Honor?" she flung out, burning with a revenge so intense she wanted desperately to hurt him as he'd scarred her.

"What are you talking about?" He shoved his rumpled hair from his eyes and she moaned.

Dear Lord, he was so incredibly handsome and male. She bit her tongue and threw her sweater over her head. "Get away from me."

But he advanced upon her slowly, his slitted eyes studying every angle of her face.

She wouldn't cry! She wouldn't! She'd never let him have the satisfaction of knowing how much she'd loved him, how much she'd been willing to give to him.

"Brenna, what the hell's going on?"

Moving backward, she stepped into her skirt. Then it hit her. "Oh, God, you really don't know, do you?" She swallowed the huge, acrid lump in her throat. "You called me by my sister's name, Warren. You called me Honor!"

His mouth twitched and his skin blanched.

"All this time you were kidding yourself." Her fingers fumbled as she struggled with her zipper. He tried to draw her into his arms. "You've never forgotten her—and neither have I!"

"No, Brenna, I swear—"

"I don't want to hear it." Without thinking, she slapped him so hard her palm stung.

He didn't move, just stared at her as a red welt appeared on his cheek.

She wanted to embrace him and apologize, but didn't. "Maybe this is just too much to deal with, Warren. Maybe you were right—I should never have moved back!"

He grabbed her then. He reached forward and yanked her so quickly that she spun backward and landed against the sheer strength of him. Completely naked, the shifting flames painting his hard muscles in rosy shadows, he held her tight against him. His eyes burned into hers. "You don't believe that."

"I do."

"She was my wife, damn it!"

"And *my* sister! Dear God, do you know how that makes me feel?" Her stomach quivered and she thought for a minute she might retch.

"Look, Brenna, I'm sorry."

"Sorry?" she cried, beside herself. "You're *sorry?* Well, so am I. For thinking that you and I could ever get away from Honor's shadow. She'll always be there, Warren, standing between us."

"It takes time. You said so yourself."

She wanted to sob and break down like a child. Didn't he understand? She'd given herself to him, thought that he loved her. And then, after the glorious instant when their bodies had fused, he'd called her by another woman's name. Her sister's name. His lover's name. "I—I've got to go," she whispered before she lost control and mortified herself further. Wrenching her arms away from him, she stumbled toward the door, ran through the kitchen and back porch, her bare feet scraping on the painted boards as she scrambled down the slick steps.

Rain was falling from the black sky, gurgling in the gutters and creating a sodden mess of the backyard. But she didn't care, didn't notice the drops streaming down her face or the wind tearing at her hair.

"Brenna!" Warren yelled, and she doubled her speed. But he vaulted over the porch rail and quickly outdistanced her. "Where do you think you're going?"

"Home!" She sidestepped, but he planted himself firmly in her path. Rain glistened in his dark hair and ran down his bare chest to disappear beneath his waistband. Lord, why did she still want him?

"Why?" He asked, snapping his pants closed.

"I told you why, Warren. I can't bear to make love to a man who pretends I'm someone else."

"I didn't."

"Don't lie, Warren," she said hotly, tears burning in her throat. "It doesn't become you."

This time when she tried to move past him, he grabbed hold of her waist and she was captured again.

"Let go of me, Warren!"

"Never," he vowed, his face lean and taut and uncompromising in the darkness. His eyes sizzled an electric blue. "I lost you once from sheer stupidity, and I'm not about to do it again!"

"I don't want to hear this." But her heart was beating double time and, pressed against his wet, bare chest, she could smell the warm, earthy scent of him, feel the corded anger in his stance.

"I love you, Brenna," he whispered.

"But back there—"

"I know what I said. It was automatic. I was married to her for ten years, Brenna. Ten years! I haven't been with another woman. Ever. Until tonight."

She felt her insides shredding. "Then that's the problem, isn't it?" she heard herself say. "I can't think of myself as 'another woman.'"

"You aren't," he vowed. "You're the only woman."

Except for Honor's ghost. Her throat clogged and rain streamed down her hair. Mud oozed between her toes. "I wish to Almighty God I could believe that you and I could put my sister to rest," she said, "but we can't. You can't and *I* can't."

His fingers tightened over her waist and the wind pushed his hair over his eyes in wild, coal-black locks. "You've just spent the past couple of weeks trying to convince me that we belong together and I believed you," he said, his mouth thinning with repressed fury. "I trusted you, even thought I could put away my guilt about having fantasies about my wife's sister."

"Don't—"

"I trusted you, Bren. Maybe too much. I remembered that young, idealistic girl, who wanted to set the world on fire, and I believed you when you said you could help Julie and Scotty."

"I can!"

"How? By being a stand-in mother from a distance? By working for a newspaper all day and offering some of your free time to them when it's convenient?"

Horrified, she tried to wrench free. "That's not the way it is. And don't turn this argument around, Warren! Don't play on my guilt with your children. I love them and I'll do what I can for them—but where I draw the line is I won't make love to their father so that he can go on pretending that his wife is still alive!"

As if she'd struck him again, he drew in a sharp breath and his hands clenched tighter over her waist. "Is that what you really think?" His nostrils flared and his jaw tightened, then, with a sound of disgust, he released her.

She nearly fell over. "I don't know what to think," she whispered. "But I should have realized that this would happen—that you would think I was Honor. Don't you understand, Warren?" she asked, nearly sobbing. "There is just no way, *no way* we can ever be together. She'll always be there!" Then, unable to look into his tortured eyes another second, she stumbled backward and started running as fast as her feet would carry her along the path, around the corner of the house and through the front gate. With the wind ripping through her hair, she sprinted under the blue glow of street lamps shimmering against the rain-drenched streets.

Down the hill, through the ravine and up again she raced, her breath burning in her lungs, her eyes smarting with tears. Warren used you, her mind screamed, *pretended you were Honor!*

The apartment house loomed ahead and she sprinted across the lawn and fumbled in the pocket of her skirt for the key before forcing open the lock and hurtling up the steps two at a time.

Her insides were churning as she slammed the door behind her and tore into the bathroom where she twisted on the hot water. How could she have trusted Warren? How could she have believed that he would love her and forget Honor, a woman he'd loved so long? She had been stupid and selfish. Of course he couldn't forget a woman he'd loved for more than ten years. Of course they had no chance to be together. She'd been a fool to expect their lovemaking to have turned out any differently.

Sick with herself, she stripped off her clothes, climbed into the shower and let the spray run over her in hot, steamy needles. Though her knees sagged, she didn't give in to the overpowering urge to drop to the floor of the stall and huddle in a corner like a wounded animal.

No, she decided, gritting her teeth against the emotions raging deep in her soul. No matter how much she loved Warren Stone, no matter how deeply she still cared, she would forget him—just as she should have ten years before!

CHAPTER EIGHT

WARREN DIDN'T FEEL the rain sliding down his chest. Hands planted firmly on his hips, he watched in silent fury as Brenna disappeared from sight. His fists were balled and he wanted to hit something, *anything,* just to release the tension that flexed his muscles so tightly they ached.

"You goddamned fool!" he swore at himself. He wanted to give chase, apologize, try to shake some sense into her, but he couldn't leave—not with the children alone in the house. Still swearing under his breath, he retraced his steps to the back of the house. Mud spattered his jeans and his feet were filthy. He didn't care. He took the back steps two at a time, then paused on the porch to slam his fist against a post supporting the roof. The entire porch shuddered and his hand throbbed painfully—stinging almost as much as his cheek. Scowling, he rubbed his chin, felt the hot spot where Brenna had slapped him then shoved open the door.

How could he have called Brenna Honor? Cringing at his own stupidity, he crossed the kitchen and stood dripping near the table.

He didn't even have a plan in mind when he picked up the phone, punching out Mary Beatty's number. It rang four times and Warren, a coiled mass of raw energy, drummed his fingers against the wall. "Come on, come on, be there."

She answered breathlessly on the sixth ring. "Hello?"

"Thank God you're home." He sagged against the wall. "Mr. Stone?"

"Look, I know it's after ten, but this is important," he said quickly. "Could you come over and watch the kids—stay the night?" he asked.

She paused. "Is something wrong?" she finally asked, her voice concerned. "Julie and Scotty—"

"They're fine," he said swiftly, then tried to come up with an explanation that didn't sound as if he'd gone off the deep end. He thought about lying, claiming problems at work, but said simply, "It's Brenna. I have to see her."

"I'll be right there." She hung up before he could explain.

Suddenly aware that his jeans were soggy and streaked with mud, he frowned at the mess on the floor, then strode into the family room. The fire still glowed scarlet, coffee cups were left on the windowsill and some of Brenna's clothing littered the floor. Scowling, he tucked her shoes and nylons under his arm, then mounted the stairs.

As he stripped, he could still see her in his mind's eye. Her image as he'd made love to her was still bright in his brain. He swallowed some whiskey and it burned the bottom of his stomach, but it didn't chase away his memory. Groaning, he thought of the way her fiery-streaked auburn hair had surrounded her face in a wild cloud, the trust in her hazel eyes, the rosy hue of her flushed cheeks. Her scent still filled his nostrils and he could remember the anxious sway of her body beneath his as he'd entered her. Their union had been passionate and glorious, filled with longing and love. *Until he'd whispered Honor's name.* Dear God, what had possessed him?

Furious with himself, he wiped the mud from his feet, walked through the shower and threw on clean Levi's and the first shirt he could find.

A few minutes later, he heard Mary knock and let herself in. "Mr. Stone?"

"I'll be right there," he called from his room. Stuffing the tails of his shirt into his jeans, he hurried down the stairs. Brenna's things were still on the landing in full view, but if Mary had seen them, she had the decency to hold her tongue as she pushed a mop across the kitchen floor.

"Leave it," he instructed. "I'll take care of this mess later."

"I'm almost finished." She eyed him curiously and leaned on her mop. "What happened? Is Brenna all right?"

"I hope so," he said, and decided Mary Beatty had the right to know what was going on. "We had a fight and she took off. She was…angry with me and forgot her purse and jacket."

"Humph."

"I thought I'd run them by."

She lifted a graying brow. "You'll be back later?"

"Yes."

Her face puckered and she swiped at a spot she'd missed on the floor. "Well, don't rush home on account of me. I'll spend the night in the guest room so you won't have to worry about the kids."

"Good." Carrying Brenna's things, he started for the door to the garage but sensed there was something more the housekeeper wanted to say. "What is it, Mary?" he asked, reaching for the doorknob, but glancing over his shoulder.

"Well, I don't suppose this is any of my business, and you just tell me if I'm out of line."

"I will."

"I've got eyes, you know. I can see what's happening here. Obviously Brenna cares about you and the children and not just because you're all related. And I know that you don't like that paper she works for, but that's her business." She sighed and her faded eyes pierced into Warren's. "This isn't an easy situation, what with her being Honor's sister and all, but don't do anything foolish and lose this girl. Your wife's gone, Warren. Julie and Scotty need a mother, and not just some woman off the street. They deserve a mother's love. If Brenna Douglass won't give them that love, no one will, because she's Honor's sister as well as a woman in her own right."

"Anything else?" he asked, his jaw so tight it ached.

"Yes. I know you sold your wife's car and moved out her things, but you've got to do more than that. *Honor's* got to leave this house—or stay where she belongs in the wedding albums and your memory." Then, as if realizing she was poking into a private area better left alone, she added, "I know you loved your wife, even with all the problems, but try to think of Brenna as a woman. Forget that she's Honor's sister. Now, go on, get out of here."

She shooed him with her hand and pushed the mop over the already-gleaming tile as Warren closed the door behind him and climbed into his car.

BRENNA WAS COMBING the tangles from her wet hair when the doorbell rang. She nearly dropped her comb and her heart somersaulted. She didn't have to guess who was ringing her bell. Obviously Warren was in the hall.

Steeling herself, she cinched the belt of her robe more tightly around her waist and was disgusted to feel her hands shaking.

She glanced through the peephole, then unlocked the door, but didn't move from the threshold. Warren's hair was neatly combed but raindrops still glittered in the thick black strands. His face was set, jaw rock hard, and his blue eyes were cool again.

"I thought you might need these," he said, offering her a bundle of purse, shoes, jacket and nylons.

"Thanks." She took her things and tried to shut the door.

She couldn't deal with him right now, her emotions were still too ragged and torn.

"Brenna—"

"It's late, Warren."

"I think we should talk."

Her eyes narrowed. "Don't you think you've said enough?" she whispered, then, seeing the shadow of regret darken his eyes, wished she'd held her tongue.

"You can't avoid me."

"Watch," she suggested, but her voice cracked.

"Oh, Bren, knock it off. This is childish."

"And that's how I feel, okay? Childish and hurt and furious at myself for ever thinking I could trust you."

"That does it," he muttered. Shouldering the door open, he grabbed one of her hands and drew her into the room.

"Warren, really, I don't think this is a good idea. What about the kids? You can't just leave them alone."

"I called Mary. She's at the house and prepared to stay the night if that's how long this takes."

"How long what takes?"

"Convincing you that I care."

Brenna's emotions tore at her soul, but her fists clenched. She couldn't trust him again, couldn't let herself believe him. "Go home, Warren."

"No way." He kicked the door shut and she jumped. "Just listen for a few minutes," he said, pushing her onto the couch. "I made a mistake, I admit it, and I'm sorry. But I can't promise you that it won't happen again."

"That's not good enough!"

"It has to be, damn it."

When she tried to get to her feet, he blocked her path and sat on the coffee table directly in front of her. His eyes wouldn't leave her face. "I don't think there's anything left to say," she said with an effort.

"I love you, Brenna."

Knowing that he was trying to be noble, she shrank inside. "You don't have to—"

"I love you! Aren't you listening to me?"

"Just because we made love—"

"And why do you think that happened?" he demanded. "Because I love you and I know you love me."

"No!" She'd just promised herself she wouldn't get tangled up in all those old, useless feelings of love. Pushing her hair from her eyes, she said as calmly as possible. "I don't love you, Warren. You were right. What I felt way back then—it's gone. It's over. It was just a stupid schoolgirl crush." Her heart was twisting, her soul black with the lie, but she held her chin upright and miraculously her eyes remained dry.

"You don't believe that any more than I do."

"It's over, Warren, before it really began."

The brackets around his mouth whitened in anger and every muscle in his face was strained tight. "I've denied what I felt for you for a long, long time," he admitted, his words filled with despair. "But I love you and I probably always have."

Brenna swallowed and whispered, "Honor was your wife."

"And I loved her, too, Bren." He moved to the couch and placed one arm solidly over her trembling shoulders. *Please, God, give me the strength to push him away!*

"Ten years ago, I was obsessed with her. She was beautiful and smart and special."

Brenna wanted to sink right through the couch and the floor. All of her determination seemed to seep away.

"I knew she was running around on me, but I wanted her, wanted to prove that I could have her. I loved her, Brenna, I won't deny it. And at first we were happy..." His voice trailed off. "I've already told you about that."

"You still love her," she said quietly. "And so do I."

"But she's gone, Brenna. We can't bring her back!" He leaned his head against the cushions of the couch, but his arm still rested firmly across her shoulders. "You were the one who told me just that, not too long ago."

"Maybe I was wrong."

But he wasn't listening. Caught in a painful tangle of memories, he said, "That night in the rose garden, at your father's house, you really threw me for a loop. If I hadn't been so bullheaded, maybe I would have been smarter. But my male pride was on the line and I had to prove that she cared about me.

"When I left you, I was confused," he said, staring at the ceiling. "You thought you loved me."

"I did," she said simply. She was shaking from the inside out and the tears she'd been fighting all night filled her eyes.

"I know that now, Bren," he whispered. "But I thought you were too young to know your own mind. You had all those dreams, Brenna, dreams of going away to school and being a journalist. You had a scholarship and a future as bright as the sun. I didn't want you to change all your plans for me and have you regret it all your life."

"I wouldn't have."

"You would have. Eventually. Even then, you knew what you wanted out of life and I was sure I couldn't be a part of it. Besides, you were only eighteen and I thought you were just going through a schoolgirl crush."

"You don't know how many times I wish it had been."

Tilting his head, he studied her, then drew her closer. She tried to resist, but couldn't. All of her pride and determination seemed to disappear whenever she was close to him.

"I was flattered," he admitted. "And I even had second thoughts about Honor, but when I found her with Jeff, I wanted to possess her again, prove that all those rumors about her were wrong. I didn't like playing the part of the cuckold—especially to Jeff Prentice. I guess I made one helluva mess," he said with a frown. "And now you and I are both paying for it."

She gathered every ounce of courage she could muster before she could be captivated all over again. "It's late, Warren," she said shakily. "I think you should leave."

"Is that what you want?"

Oh, God, no! "Yes."

His eyes hardened and he released her. "Okay, so maybe I made a mistake ten years ago and another one tonight. I've already apologized and, unfortunately, I can't change the past. But I think that you should give us another chance, Brenna."

"Why?"

"Haven't you heard a word I've said?" All the anger left his face to be replaced by awe as he smoothed her brow. His fingers quivered as he looked straight into her eyes. "I love you, Brenna. It's that simple."

If only it were. She swallowed back the hot lump in her throat and tried to break away from his searing blue gaze. At that moment she couldn't think straight. "I don't think we should see each other for a while," she whispered, feeling his fingers entwine with hers.

"Brenna, I want you to marry me."

"You *what?*" she whispered, astounded. Her heart hammered wildly, beating a wonderful, crazy cadence.

"I'm serious, Brenna. Tonight, when you walked out my door and I thought there was a chance I'd lose you again, I decided I wouldn't let it happen."

"But I've only been back—"

"We've known each other for over ten years. My children love you, they need you and so do I."

She didn't know whether to laugh or cry. She had fantasized about marrying Warren so many times long ago, but those girlhood dreams had faded when he'd married Honor. And in the past months, during her grief, she hadn't been able to deal with the fact that she loved him.

He touched the underside of her chin and it trembled. "This…this is too fast, Warren," she said, forcing her gaze to his. "There's too much to sort out. Not that long ago you accused me of trying to step into Honor's shoes and now you're asking me to do just that." She shook her head, feeling her hair brush against the back of her robe. "I—I don't think we're ready for marriage and I'm sure your children need time to accept me. At least Scotty does."

"Tell me you'll think about it." His thumb was stroking her neck, moving in lazy circles that caused Brenna's senses to reel.

"I'll consider it," she said, growing more determined. She loved him and wanted to be his wife, but couldn't stand the thought of being second to Honor—of trying to live up to Honor's image. "But I won't be able to marry you until I'm convinced that Honor won't hover between us, and I just don't know if that's possible."

Brows drawing downward, lips compressed thoughtfully, he sighed. "We'll just have to try, won't we?" Shoving impatient fingers through his still wet hair, he scowled. "I love you because you're not your sister, Brenna. Believe me, I don't expect you to become the person she was. In fact, I wouldn't want you to. I want to marry Brenna Douglass."

Sweeping a lock of burnished hair from her face, he leaned forward and brushed his lips over hers. "Trust me, Bren," he pleaded, before standing and staring down at her. "I've said what I have to say. I think the next move is yours." Without so much as a glance over his shoulder, he walked through the door and it shut with a loud click.

Brenna was left feeling empty and lost, wondering if she'd thrown away her most passionate dream: to love and be loved by Warren Stone.

"WRITER'S BLOCK?" TAMMY asked as she jangled past Brenna's desk. Her bracelets and chains were of tooled silver and her fingers were sprinkled with turquoise.

"That and a lot more," Brenna admitted. She twisted her neck and rubbed the knot at the base of her skull. She'd been huddled over the screen for hours, trying to come up with a new angle on an old story—balancing home and career.

"Want me to take a look at it?"

"Later—when I'm finished with the rough draft." Sighing, she reread the flickering screen and scowled. For the past week, she'd nearly lived at the office, reading old columns, coming up with new ideas and writing two articles. Len had been impressed, but she hadn't heard one word from Warren. Since he'd left her in her apartment he hadn't called or dropped by. But then he'd told her she had to make the next move. "Remember, that's what you wanted," she told herself, scowling at the bright green letters. So far, her story was about as bad and boring and trite as it could be.

"Pardon?" Tammy asked.

"Nothing—I was just thinking."

"Well, *I* think you need to get out of the office for a while. You act like you're chained to that damned computer."

Brenna laughed. "Heaven help us."

"Come on, let's go to lunch. I'll buy!"

Deciding she wasn't doing the paper or herself any favors, Brenna snapped off her machine. "Best offer I've had all day," she murmured, reaching for her purse.

The sky was a clear, vibrant blue as they walked three blocks to a small restaurant that was tucked into a corner of an old, renovated hotel and served the "most authentic Mexican food in the Northwest," or so the sign in the window claimed.

The floor was rust-colored Mexican tile and the arched ceilings were decorated with an Aztec-looking border and huge, lazy paddle fans.

"Try the deep-fried burritos," Tammy suggested, her gaze skating over the menu. "They're positively out of this world—or at least out of this country."

"Okay."

When a waitress in an off-the-shoulder dress appeared, Tammy ordered for them both, including an appetizer of super nachos with the two burritos.

"This is more food than I eat in a month," Brenna observed a few minutes later as a platter of nachos was placed between them on the table.

"Live a little." Tammy shoved a tortilla chip into the cheese and sour cream. "I always eat a big lunch because a lot of times I hit the earliest possible shows and miss dinner. In the past two weeks, I think I only ate dinner once and that was cold pizza at 10:30," she said, thinking aloud.

Brenna smiled. "So how was that horror flick last week?"

"Wonderful," Tammy said, grinning. "And guess what, even though the Stalker appears to be dead at the end of part seven, I think the producers are already planning a sequel."

"Just what this country needs," Brenna quipped.

"Hey—don't knock it. That kind of thing is my bread and butter. I'm checking out a new movie tonight—a romantic comedy—and tomorrow I've got front-row seats at a rock concert. Sunday I'll see a local production of last year's smash hit on Broadway and I'm waiting for a promo copy of a new album by my favorite group. I hope it's better than their last album. The entire record absolutely reeked! And that's my *professional* opinion."

Laughing, Brenna said, "I don't know how you have the energy."

"I love it! Even with all the deadlines and pressure I can't think of anything I'd rather do. Can you?"

Brenna mused, glancing out the window to the busy street and thinking about the mediocre story she had tucked away in the memory banks of her computer. "Not really—except on days like today."

"Don't be so hard on yourself. Your first two articles were great! Len was practically dancing on the ceiling."

"Thank God." She bit into her burrito and wondered if Warren had read her column. The first had been a humorous account of "coming of age" by losing a first baby tooth. The second had been more serious, a woman's view on a controversial new bill before the state legislature.

"Len's back is against the wall," Tammy said. "The owners of the paper are worried. There's talk of a lawsuit over this Charlie Saxton thing and Len's taking all the heat from them as well as the local district attorney's office."

Brenna nearly choked. "The D.A.'s office called Len again?"

Tammy shrugged. "I guess so. Anyway, this isn't the first time the *Examiner*'s been on the bad side of the district attorney. It's no secret that Len kind of has it in for Warren Stone."

"Is—is that right?" Brenna asked, sipping from her water glass and trying to appear calm.

"Yeah. There was a big stink when Stone's wife died and Len made the most of it." Tammy attacked her burrito with a vengeance. "Hey, aren't you hungry? This is great." She jabbed a big piece of her burrito with her fork.

Brenna's appetite had waned and she toyed with the food on her plate, shoving it from one side to the other. "I think maybe there's something I should tell you," she said quietly, knowing that Tammy would eventually figure out her connection with Warren. Since Tammy was becoming a friend, she decided to be honest with her.

"Yeah? What's that?"

"Warren Stone's my brother-in-law."

"Your…" Tammy's voice trailed off in astonishment and she dropped her fork into the remains of her burrito.

"Honor Stone was my sister."

"Oh, God." Tammy turned about three shades of red. "Look, I didn't know. I'm really sorry."

"It's all right," Brenna assured her with a shrug.

"I can't believe it! Does Len know this?" She took one look at Brenna and her lips thinned. "Of course he does. That creep! He probably hired you just to get the inside information on Warren Stone." Then, shaking her short, spiky hair, she pushed her plate aside.

"You think he would do that?"

"I don't know. Look, Len's all right. Just a little slimy around the edges sometimes. But I don't think he'd hire someone for revenge. His job is too important to him. You've seen that cup on his desk?"

Brenna nodded, remembering the mug with The Buck Stops Here emblazoned in bold red letters across the white ceramic.

"Well, he means it. He'll back up any reporter on the staff. That's why he's in such hot water over the Charlie Saxton thing. By rights, he should have fired Karla."

"The receptionist?"

"That's *why* she's the receptionist. She's a reporter and she covered the Saxton story. If you ask me, she blew it. Anyway, Len wouldn't fire her, just reined her in a little. He claims that it was his responsibility as editor to catch her mistake."

"That doesn't sound like a guy who's 'slimy around the edges.'"

Tammy sighed and placed her elbows on the table. "I know, I know. I just have a bone to pick with him, I guess. He, uh, came on to me when I was first hired—and he was still married at the time. When I told him I wasn't inter-ested, he pushed it, but he finally got the message." Tammy glanced ruefully at Brenna. "I guess I should forgive him, huh? It's been nearly two years. He hasn't bothered me since and now he's divorced. Fortunately, he's found some-one other than myself to keep his interest. Guess who?"

"I couldn't."

"Karla."

Brenna gasped.

"Yeah, maybe that's why he stuck his neck out that far for her. Who knows and who cares?" She plucked the check from the table and pushed back her chair. "I hate to say it but it's time to go back to the salt mines."

"Thanks," Brenna said as they walked back to the of-fice in the bright sunlight. "Next time lunch is on me."

"It's a deal," Tammy replied, flashing Brenna a grin as she scurried to her desk.

Brenna spent the next four hours in the newspaper's library, finished her rough draft, let Tammy have a copy, then left the office. She intended to drive straight home, but didn't.

The day was too good to spoil by holing up in her apart-ment. As she drove, sunlight streamed through the sur-rounding fir trees and a breeze, warm with the promise of summer, moved the branches. Brenna felt restless and more than a little twinge of guilt. Not only had she avoided Warren in the past several days, but she hadn't seen Julie or Scotty. She hadn't quite come to terms with Warren's proposal and therefore hadn't wanted to face him or the children.

Warren's house loomed ahead. On an impulse, she shifted down, wheeled into Warren's drive and parked. At the door, she hesitated, wondering what she would say, then rapped solidly on the dark panels.

"I'm coming," Mary called as she peered through the

window and pulled open the door. A smile as wide as her face stole over her chin. "Come in, come in, I was just wondering about you."

"You were?"

"Uh-huh. Julie's working on a writing assignment in school and I'm absolutely useless when it comes to putting words on paper."

"I know what you mean," Brenna said, thinking of her own block this afternoon.

"I was hoping you could help her, what with you being a reporter and all."

"I'll try."

"Thank goodness!" Mary ushered Brenna into the kitchen where Julie was sitting at the table. Her brow was puckered, her tongue wedged between her teeth as she struggled with her pencil, paper and eraser.

"How's it going?" Brenna asked, and Julie glanced up, her blue eyes bright.

"Aunt Bren!" she cried happily, then looked down at her eraser-smudged work. "It's going horrible!"

"Writer's block?"

"What?"

"That's what it's called when you have trouble creating. A friend of mine accused me of having it this afternoon."

"Then I've got it!"

"So maybe you need to take your mind off whatever it is you're writing for a while."

Julie's eyes twinkled and she glanced at Mary, who was obviously the taskmaster.

Brenna said, "Why don't we go out for French fries or a milk shake or an ice-cream cone?"

"Can we?" Julie asked, dropping her pencil. It rolled across the table and fell to the floor.

"Sure. We can even take Scotty."

Julie scowled, but Mary Beatty interjected, "He's not

here right now. He went over to a friend's house after kindergarten."

Brenna touched Julie's blond crown. "Then I guess it's just you and me."

"Is it okay?" Julie asked Mary.

"Of course it is. Just remember that this—" she tapped the paper with the tip of a broad finger "—won't go away. It'll be here when you get back."

"I know," Julie said, rolling her eyes as she dashed from the room.

"You wear a jacket," Mary called after her, but Julie had already yanked a sweatshirt from a peg near the back door and was running outside.

"We'll be back in a couple of hours," Brenna promised as the housekeeper closed the door behind them.

"Okay. Where to?" she asked as she climbed behind the steering wheel.

Julie was already strapped into the passenger seat. "Thirty-one flavors!"

"Thirty-one flavors it is!" Brenna backed out of the drive and guided the car down the hill. "You'll just have to tell me how to get there."

Within ten minutes, Julie had pointed the way, Brenna had parked and they were seated inside the small ice-cream shop licking double-dip cones.

"So tell me," Brenna said, "what do you have to write about?"

"Something boring!"

"Such as?"

"Such as what I'm going to do for summer vacation." Julie sighed and wiped a dribble of strawberry from her chin. "I don't even know *if* we're going anywhere."

"So why not ask your dad?"

"He'd just get mad. We were supposed to go to the beach…but that was before Mommy…" Her eyes grew sad. "Anyway, he already sold the cabin and I don't think we're going anywhere."

"When's the assignment due?"

"Monday." Julie munched some of her sugar cone and stared outside. "Cindy's going to Disneyland and Michelle's going to Hawaii," she said miserably with a drawn-out sigh. "Even Jamie Foster is going somewhere. Her aunt lives in Boise."

"Is that what you want? To go to Boise?"

Julie shrugged. "I guess not."

"Surely some of the kids in your class are staying around Portland."

Julie's lower lip protruded. "I don't have anything to write about."

"Maybe—maybe not," Brenna said. "There are lots of nice places around Portland, and if you ask, I'm sure your dad will plan some trips around the city. You could go to the zoo, Mount Hood, the children's museum or even the beach. It's only a little over an hour away."

"Dad said he'd never go to the beach again," Julie argued.

"I think he's changed his mind. He and I stopped at a restaurant on the coast when we were driving back from California. I just bet all you have to do is tell him you want to go to Seaside or Astoria and he'd take you there."

Julie studied the melted remains of her pink ice cream. "Will you ask him?" she asked.

"If you want me to."

"And if he says he'll take us to the beach, will you come?"

Brenna smiled, then blotted a strawberry smudge from her niece's cheek. "Wouldn't miss it for the world. Now, listen, I'd better take you home. Mary will have dinner on the table."

"I'm not hungry," Julie protested.

Brenna eyed the child's dripping cone. "Do me a favor and at least pretend to eat dinner, okay? Otherwise your dad and Mary will take turns skinning me alive."

"Dad won't. He likes you," Julie said, dropping her cone in a nearby trash can and pushing open the glass door of the little shop. "He likes you a lot."

"And I like him."

Julie slid into her seat and fiddled with her seat belt as Brenna jabbed the key into the ignition and the car's engine started with a roar.

Glancing over her shoulder, she guided the car out of the tight parking spot and eased onto the highway.

"Will you tell me something, Aunt Bren?" Julie asked softly.

The quaver in Julie's voice caught Brenna's attention. "Sure. What is it?" From the corner of her eye, Brenna could see Julie's hands twisting nervously in her lap.

"Are you gonna marry my dad?"

CHAPTER NINE

BRENNA STOOD ON the brakes and the car screeched to a stop. A car horn behind her blasted sharply.

"I just wanted to know if you planned on marrying Daddy," Julie repeated, more determinedly.

Shaking, Brenna stepped on the accelerator and the car moved forward. "I don't know," she admitted, wondering how Julie had become so perceptive. "Did your dad talk to you about this?"

"Oh, no." Julie shook her head vehemently. "He'd kill me if he found out I asked you. But, well, I think you should. Then you could live with us," Julie decided, crossing her arms and staring straight at Brenna. "It would just be a whole lot better. You could do things with us."

"We are doing something," Brenna pointed out. "Remember the ice cream?"

"I know, but I mean other things."

"Such as?"

"Such as coming to my class play?" Julie asked, her teeth digging into her lip anxiously. "It's later this week. Everybody's mother is coming."

"Oh." Brenna's heart twisted.

"Dad said he'd come, but he has to work." She glanced at Brenna from the corner of her eye. "He said you have to work, too."

"You already asked him about this?"

"Yeah." Julie slid down in her seat and turned to stare glumly out the window.

Brenna felt miserable. How many times had she wished her mother could watch her play powder-puff football or read her first published piece in the school paper or just be there to talk to when she had problems at school? She knew what Julie was going through and ached to help her.

"It's not as simple as just getting married," Brenna said.

"Why not? Don't you love daddy?"

"Of course I do, but…" Dear Lord, how could she possibly explain?

"If people love each other they should get married." Julie crossed her arms with all the authority of her nearly eight years.

"Okay, say I did marry your dad. How would Scotty feel?"

"Who cares?"

"I do. He'd be my stepson."

"Well, you're already his aunt."

"That's a little different." Brenna blew a strand of hair from her eyes as she headed the car up the steep hills. "This is already too complicated," she murmured under her breath.

Julie didn't say another word the rest of the way back to the house and Brenna grappled with her conscience. She loved Warren, wanted to marry him, but just wasn't convinced that they were ready to start a life without Honor's memory overshadowing them. Torn between being impetuously trusting and more reasonable, she still hadn't reached a decision by the time she parked her car in front of the huge stone house.

Warren's car was in the driveway and Brenna's heart nearly stopped. What would she say to him?

Julie dashed into the house with Brenna lagging about three steps behind.

Warren was in the kitchen. His palms flat against the

counter, he was leaning over and studying a cookbook spread open on the Formica top.

"Daddy!"

Glancing up, he caught sight of Julie and a proud smile slashed across his face. "Hey, pumpkin. How are ya?"

"Great!" Julie flung herself into his arms. "Aunt Bren bought me a double dip."

"Did she now?" he asked, rubbing her nose to his before settling her against his hip. His gaze strayed over his daughter's shoulder to Brenna. The warmth in his eyes faded and his smile froze. "If it isn't the *Examiner*'s answer to 'Dear Abby.'"

"And 'hello, how are you' to you, too," she mocked.

"It's been a while, hasn't it?" he replied. "But I guess you've been busy with your work."

"Have you bothered to read any of it?"

"Both columns."

"And?"

He set Julie on the floor and she scampered out of the room. When he looked at Brenna again, his gaze had softened and his smile appeared more genuine. "I guess it comes as no surprise that your column is the best thing in the entire paper. Although," he added, glancing to the open hallway to see that Julie wasn't playing nearby, "I wasn't too thrilled to see my family put under a microscope."

"I didn't—"

"Come on, Brenna. Your first article was about Scotty's tooth."

The screen door banged against the wall and Scotty, dirty from head to foot, asked, "My tooth was in the paper?" He grimaced, showing off the gap in question.

"Your dad's exaggerating," Brenna said, then winked at Scotty. "You can't trust him all the time, you know. Lawyers sometimes twist the facts to make their point."

Scotty blinked and his brows drew quizzically over round blue eyes. "Dad never lies."

"A credit to the prosecution."

"Thanks for your insight on the legal profession," Warren chided, but his lips curved into a smile. "Stay for dinner?" he asked casually just as Julie sauntered back into the kitchen.

"I really should visit Dad."

"Can't it wait until tomorrow?"

She couldn't resist. "I suppose."

"Please stay," Julie begged, tugging at her sleeve.

"Okay—if you finish your homework."

Julie made a face but walked to the table and picked up her assignment. "I'll do it in my room."

"And I'll ride my bike. I don't have homework!" Scotty said, needling Julie as she walked up the stairs. Before Brenna could blink, he was through the back door, down the steps and struggling to climb onto his new bike.

"I'm glad all that's settled," Warren admitted. Once assured they were alone again, he slipped his arms around her waist and drew her near. She felt his fingers lock at the small of her back, but didn't protest. For the past few days she'd thought of nothing but being with him again.

"So am I," she admitted.

His gaze moved slowly over her face and Brenna's pulse jumped. "We've missed you," he said simply, and her heartbeat quickened as his breath fanned her face. "I thought you might not show up for a while."

"I—uh, thought about it," she admitted.

"What changed your mind?" His eyes delved deep into hers.

"A lot of things. But I felt guilty about the kids."

"Is that all?"

She tried to lie, but couldn't. "Of course not," she murmured, leaning against him. "I'm probably the biggest fool in the Pacific Northwest, but I missed you, too." She listened to the steady beat of his heart and felt his fingers move slowly upward to press against her shoulder blades.

"How much, Brenna?" he asked, his hands moving sensually against her back.

"Too much." Swallowing hard, she tilted back her head, offering her mouth to his.

He claimed it quickly, his warm lips moving anxiously against her own. "I was afraid you'd changed your mind," he admitted, his arms around her tightening. "I thought I'd chased you away."

"It takes more than one slipup," she said, though the wound still burned deep in her heart.

"Good." He kissed her nose and eyes and was about to kiss her again, when he heard Scotty outside. With a groan he released her and he leaned against the counter for support. "I don't know how much more of this I can stand," he muttered, his breath ragged.

"That makes two of us." Her lips felt swollen and heated and she wanted more of him than this small sample. She stepped back a pace and noticed that Warren's serious expression had faded. He slapped her playfully on the behind. "Now that we understand each other, let's get down to the business at hand." He gestured impatiently at the open cookbook. "How would you like to make dinner?"

"Me?"

"Scotty wants some concoction Honor used to make and I can't find it in any of these books." Frowning, he reached into a basket of fruit and absently polished an apple with the tail of his shirt.

"Concoction?" she repeated. He'd said Honor's name so casually, as if she were still alive, just in the next room. *Calm down, Brenna, you've got to learn to deal with this. If you love him, you'll accept that he was married to Honor.*

"Some sort of goulash," Julie explained as she waltzed

into the kitchen, plucked a banana from the basket and breezed out the back door. "Homework's done," she said as she stepped onto the porch.

"Goulash? That was probably a recipe my mother used to make. Honor must have kept it in her head."

"Do you know it?" Warren asked, biting into the apple and studying her.

"I think so," she said shakily. She couldn't believe they were discussing her sister so easily, and she could sense that there was more he had to say.

"Good. Let me know if you need any ingredients. Scotty and I will run to the store."

"Whoa—hold on a minute. I thought *you* invited me for dinner."

"Come on, Bren. I read your column. You're just a whiz in the kitchen, aren't you?" Though he smiled, there was a sarcastic edge to his words.

"I'm a writer, not a gourmet cook."

"Look, Honor wasn't exactly Julia Child, but occasionally she did give it a shot. Besides, you need the practice of cooking for a family of four."

"Do I?" Her heart somersaulted and her gaze locked with his. His lips had thinned, his eyes growing steely blue.

"I haven't changed my mind. But you said you needed time and space."

"So that's why I didn't hear from you?"

"One reason."

"And the others?"

His brows drew together and he rubbed the back of his neck. Staring out the window, he watched as Scotty rode his bike in circles in front of the garage. "To be honest with you, I didn't like your first article. I saw my kids being used to sell copies of that damned paper and I was furious."

She started to protest, but he held up his hand. "But

then I got smart, Bren. I knew you wouldn't intentionally hurt my children or me."

"I wouldn't."

"You'd better not," he warned, then shoved his hair from his eyes. "Also, I'm going to quit apologizing for being married to your sister. It's a fact and I have the children to prove it. For over ten years, she was a part of my life and since you've been back, I've been trying to deny it." He took another bite of his apple. "But I'm not going to anymore. Honor was my wife, the mother of my children and your sister. Some of the time, at least in the beginning, we had a pretty good life and I can't change that or apologize for it. I want you to marry me, Brenna, but I'm not going to try and sweep the past ten years of my life under the carpet. Neither am I going to glorify it or act as if Honor were a saint." Releasing a deep sigh, he tossed his apple core into a nearby wastebasket. "I'm asking you to accept me—all of me, including my past with your sister." He closed the distance between them and stood near enough that she could feel the heat from his body, see the shots of silver in his eyes. "If you can't deal with the fact that Honor and I were married, then maybe we shouldn't see each other anymore."

Her heart felt as if it would drop to the floor. "But—"

"Like it or not, Brenna, I was married to your sister, I loved her and I made love to her as often as I could!"

Brenna had to sit down. She nearly fell into the chair Julie had recently vacated. Her stomach was shaking nervously and her head was spinning. He sounded so logical, so detached. She had the feeling she'd just witnessed a very clever show—a show usually reserved for the courtroom.

"You can't strip Honor and what we had together from me."

"I—I wouldn't want to."

He cocked a disbelieving brow. "There's a lot I want

to tell you about her," he admitted, his gaze shifting from the hall and then to the open door of the back porch. "But I think we should wait until we're alone."

"Why?"

"Because," he said tightly. "I want you to know everything about my marriage to your sister. The good and the bad."

"It's not necessary. Really."

"Maybe not. But I want all the cards on the table—no surprises after we start our life together."

She could tell that he wasn't about to change his mind, though she didn't want to know all the intimate details of his relationship with Honor. It seemed sacrilege to dredge up the problems now, when Honor was gone.

Brenna's throat was dry, but she wanted desperately to change the subject. "So—uh, you don't mind my articles about the children?" she asked weakly.

"Oh, I mind them, but I can't tell you what to write any more than Honor could tell me what career choices I should have made." The skin over his face drew taut as if a bitter memory had surfaced. "Don't get me wrong about the *Willamette Examiner*. I don't like that rag any more than I ever did. But I trust you. And that's what it all boils down to, doesn't it? Trust? Besides, when you marry me, you'll quit."

"Don't count on it," she murmured. "I know you don't like the paper but I love my job."

"And what about the children?"

"You don't think I'll take care of them?" she demanded sharply. "Aren't you the one who accused me of trying to mother them? Of stepping into Honor's shoes?" Standing, she thrust an angry finger in his chest. "I can balance career and homemaking and if you don't believe me, read my next article!"

To her surprise, he laughed.

"You think this is funny?" she charged.

"Don't you?" His face split into a wide, affectionate grin. "You're telling me to read about you in the *Examiner*?"

"Well, I guess—"

He wrapped his arms around her waist and placed his forehead squarely against hers. "I can see that living with you is going to be a challenge, Ms. Douglass."

"You'll never get bored," she quipped.

"That I believe. Now, about those articles about home and hearth—you know the ones—in which my children are the prime examples of how you deal with life? Just promise that you won't use any names. As long as the kids and I are anonymous or not humiliatingly comical, I won't object."

"That's pretty diplomatic of you."

"I just hope I don't end up regretting this."

"You won't," she promised, wrapping her arms around his chest and kissing him lightly. "Now, about this goulash?"

He groaned and his lips moved lazily over hers, causing her pulse to leap expectantly. "We could go out—later," he suggested, drawing her close.

"No way," she said, breathing erratically as she stepped out of his embrace. "You already promised Scotty!"

"My mistake."

His eyes were a slumberous shade of blue and it was all she could do to keep her thoughts on dinner. "I'll need beef, onions, catsup and brown sugar to start with," she said, backing away from him. When her heart had quit clamoring, she opened the pantry and scrounged through the shelves for the rest of the ingredients.

"Spoilsport," Warren muttered.

"Get out of here," she teased.

While Warren adjusted the seat of Scotty's bike, Brenna worked in the kitchen adding ingredients as they came to mind. She knew her goulash wouldn't taste like Honor's, but she hoped it would be a fair imitation. *Just like me,* she thought unhappily, then gave herself a swift mental kick. She wasn't going to compare herself with Honor any longer.

As the sauce was simmering and the pasta boiling, she set the table, then watched Warren through the window. The sky was dusky as he bent over the silver bike. Sweat had dampened the back of his shirt and his black hair fell in wavy, disobedient locks over his forehead. She could hardly believe that he wanted her to be a part of his family, to share his life with him. If only she could! If only Honor's memory were truly just that—fond recollections of a sister and wife.

"This is your problem," she told herself as the timer buzzed over the stove. "He seems to have handled it." *Do you really believe that? He called you by her name,* a horrid little voice in her head reminded her. *After he made love to you.* Furious with herself, she started pouring the sauce into a serving dish and reminded herself that Warren had vowed that he loved her for who she was, not because she was Honor's sister, and she was going to trust him. If it killed her.

FROM THE HALLWAY, Warren heard the regular sound of Scotty's breathing and a cough from Julie's room. He poked his head inside his daughter's bedroom and watched as Julie moved her lips and snuggled more deeply into her pillow. Moonlight streamed through an open window and glistened silver in her pale hair. How much she looked like Honor, he thought with a sad smile. A soft breeze caught in the lacy curtains, billowing them from the sash, and the scent of roses hung heavy in the air, reminding him of that summer so many years before—a summer in which he'd been consumed with Honor and blind to her younger sister. He'd been stupid, impetuous and unwittingly cruel to a girl who had truly believed she'd loved him.

Feeling suddenly old, he sat on the edge of Julie's bed, his weight sagging the mattress as he pushed her hair off her cheeks.

"Daddy?" she whispered, blinking.

"Right here, pumpkin."

Julie yawned, and mumbled, "I want Aunt Brenna to marry you."

"I want that, too," he whispered, stroking her forehead before standing and stretching. He was tired and his neck ached. The pressures of work as well as his anger with himself still ate at him as it had from the time he'd called out Honor's name.

Mentally, he'd beaten himself up all week, wishing there were some way he could make up for his gaff to Brenna. He'd been tense as a coiled spring, but had decided to play it safe. Rather than push her into a commitment, he would wait—give her the time and space she needed, though it was killing him.

"Did she leave?" Julie asked.

"Fifteen minutes ago."

Julie's long sigh wafted through the room. "I wish she never had to leave, Daddy."

"Me, too." Leaning over, he kissed Julie's forehead. "I'm working on it, sweetheart," he vowed, but his daughter was already asleep.

He crossed the room and hurried down the stairs. Brenna's scent still hung in the house along with the spicy odor of the mouth-watering goulash. He wished he had asked her to stay. But after the meal had been finished and the dishes stacked neatly in the dishwasher, Brenna had said she had to visit her father.

Warren hadn't argued, even though for a moment he'd

thought she'd seemed disappointed. But he had to wait. Even though she'd visited him on her own initiative, the next move was still hers.

THE WINDOWS OF the farmhouse glowed yellow in the night as Brenna pulled into the driveway of her father's farm. She parked behind a truck she didn't recognize and walked up the familiar path to the back porch.

Dixie growled, then thumped her tail against the battered floorboards as Brenna approached. "How are you?" she asked, bending to scratch the old dog behind her ears.

Dixie stretched and stood, her tongue lopping to one side of her mouth.

"Is Dad home?" Brenna asked, before knocking sharply and letting herself in through the unlocked screen door. "Dad?" she called as Dixie bounded through the kitchen toward the living room.

"Oh, Brenna, come on in," James called from his favorite easy chair. His stockinged feet were propped on a worn old ottoman as he sat smoking in front of the television. He moved one hand. "Look who's here."

Brenna's gaze swung to the couch where Craig Matthews was lounging. His hair was still blond but had thinned over the years. His skin was tanned and leathery from too many hours of hard work in the sun.

Craig took one look at her and straightened. "I heard you were back in town," he said, flashing her a grin. "I wondered when I'd see you."

"I guess right now," she said.

"Well, come on in and stay awhile," her father insisted, reaching into a shabby chair next to his and scooping up a disorganized stack of newspapers that had been scattered on the frayed cushion.

"If you're watching the game—" she protested, eyeing

the baseball game on the TV screen. A lanky batter was approaching home plate.

"Who needs it? It's the bottom of the eighth and the Dodgers are down nine runs. I doubt if they'll pull it together in half an inning." With a sound of disgust, James pointed the remote control at the screen and clicked the television off. "Hope you don't mind, Craig."

"Nope," Craig stretched and stood. "I'm really not that much of a baseball fan."

"He thinks he needs to keep me company," James explained with a wink.

"I think you've got it all turned around," Craig replied, and Brenna remembered his divorce. "Maybe I should be going anyway," he said, edging toward the door.

"Hogwash. Just 'cause I shut off the game—"

"That's not it," Craig replied. "I thought you and Brenna had some catching up to do."

"Can't we catch up with you around?" James asked. "I've got a fresh pot of coffee on the stove, so just hold on to your horses." He stood slowly and ambled toward the kitchen.

"Don't you know yet that you can't boss Dad around?" Brenna asked.

Craig shrugged and settled back onto the couch. "I guess I forgot for a minute." Then he glanced at Brenna and gave her an embarrassed smile. "Just like I forgot what it's like when you're around. He—" Craig cocked a thumb toward the kitchen "—is a changed man."

"I hadn't noticed."

"Oh, yeah," Craig whispered. "He wasn't kidding when he said I came over to keep him company. I did at first. What with the divorce and all, I needed to get out, and James, here, was having a rough time coming to grips with your sister's death. It really tore him up."

"It was a blow," Brenna admitted. "For everyone."

His eyes were kind. "I'm sorry about Honor," he said slowly. "I know you and she were pretty close when you were kids."

"That we were." Sighing, she chased the painful memories away. She didn't want to dwell on her grief. She'd promised herself to put Honor's death behind her and she intended to do just that. "Now it's my turn," she said. "I'm sorry to hear about you and your wife," she said.

"Me, too," Craig admitted, a shadow of sadness stealing across his even features. "I guess she wasn't interested in being married to a farmer. I knew it all along, I suppose, but I thought maybe she would change. I was wrong. Some women are willing to change for a man—others aren't. I shouldn't have expected it from her."

Brenna was about to point out that no one should have to change for someone else, but decided to hold her tongue. Obviously Craig was still hurting and there was no reason to rub salt in his wound.

James returned with coffee and instructed Brenna to hunt up some cookies in the cupboard. All she could find were a few dry store-bought snickerdoodles, but neither her father nor Craig seemed to mind. They chomped them down easily and she decided that the next time she visited her father, she'd bring something for his sweet tooth.

"I been cuttin' out all your articles," James announced, lighting a cigarette.

For the first time Brenna realized that the newspapers that were now lying on the floor were pages of the *Willamette Examiner*. "You have?"

"Yep, I renewed my subscription when they hired you. Decided to let bygones be bygones."

"I don't understand."

"I've got all the clippings hung on a bulletin board in the den."

"Is that right?" She grinned.

"Sure—up there beside those articles you wrote from the paper in San Francisco."

"You subscribed to the *City Weekly*?" Brenna asked, surprised.

He shook his head and frowned. "Nope. But Honor did. She clipped out the column and gave it to me."

"I—I didn't know," Brenna whispered, stunned.

"She was very proud of you," her father replied. His weathered face was suddenly serious. "So was I. Still am, even though you're working for the *Examiner*. The way I figure it, you're improving that paper, pulling it out of the gutter."

"Out of the gutter?" she repeated. "Because of all the hubbub about Charlie Saxton?"

"Hell, no! What's he got to do with anything? For once I agreed with the *Examiner*. Far as I'm concerned, that kidnapping bastard can rot in the state pen! I hope Warren nails that SOB, the jury throws him in prison and they lose the key."

"I—I don't understand. What were you talking about? What were all those accusations against the *Examiner*?"

Craig shifted uncomfortably on the couch. "He's still angry with the way they handled Honor's death."

"Oh?" She remembered then that her father had said something earlier, the first time she'd visited him.

"I don't want to talk about it," James said quickly, his eyes bright. "Brenna works at the *Examiner* now and that's that."

Obviously, as far as he was concerned, the subject was closed.

Later, when the coffee cups were drained and conversation had dwindled, Craig stood. "I'd better be shoving off," he said. "I have a date with a roll of barbed wire and about forty fence posts in the morning."

Brenna glimpsed the clock over the mantel and scowled. "I should leave, too," she admitted.

"Already?" her father asked.

"It's nearly eleven."

"So it is." He tugged on his lower lip. "You going to the cemetery this weekend?" he asked as she reached for her purse. "It's Memorial Day, y'know."

"I—I hadn't thought about it."

"We always visited your ma's grave on Memorial Day," he reminded her, "and I could use the company."

Guiltily, she met his faded eyes. "Of course. We'll cut roses from the garden, just like before."

"Good, good," he muttered as he walked her and Craig to the door.

Outside the moon was high in the sky, illuminating the surrounding fields with an iridescent silvery glow. Brenna's shoes crunched on the gravel as Craig walked her to the drive. He paused near his pickup. "You're good for him, y'know," he murmured, tilting his head toward the house. "It's good you moved back."

"I'm glad to be here."

Resting a hip against the dented fender of his truck, he asked cautiously, "I suppose you've seen Warren?"

She nodded.

"Good. That's good." He glanced across the rolling fields and frowned. "From what I hear, he's been throwing himself into his work, feeling guilty as hell about her death."

"Guilty?" How would Craig know about Warren's feelings?

Craig shrugged. "Just gossip," he said quickly, then cleared his throat. "He could use a strong woman to lean on about now."

"Don't tell me—you've been talking to Dad."

"Not about this," he said, then explained, "I just remember how it was, Brenna. Ten years ago, you were crazy in love with Warren and since you've never married, I'd guess you still care."

"You knew?" she gasped.

"Of course I did." His teeth gleamed white in the night. "Everyone did. Except Honor and Warren. They were so caught up in their own problems, they probably never guessed. But the rest of us, including your old man, could see it. You were pretty transparent about your feelings."

Brenna felt her cheeks singe.

"It wasn't too hard to figure out why you ran so fast to California—scholarship or no scholarship."

"So much for keeping up false pretenses," she murmured.

"No reason to. The way I see it, Warren Stone is one lucky man to have you still interested." He yanked open the door of his truck. "I'll see you later."

"Sure." As she slid behind the steering wheel of her car, she noticed that her hands were shaking. She forced the car into gear, backed out of the drive and wished she didn't feel pulled in so many directions. "It doesn't matter," she told herself as she snapped on the radio. "It doesn't matter what Dad or Craig or anyone else thinks. All that matters is that you love Warren and he loves you."

The thought was so wonderful, she almost convinced herself.

CHAPTER TEN

THE NEWSPAPER OFFICE was nearly empty. Only a few reporters still sat at their desks, glaring at their computers or typing frantically.

Brenna swallowed the last dregs of her cold coffee, grimacing at the bitter taste. She should go home, she thought. Her muscles ached from sitting at the computer all day. Glancing at her watch, she groaned. It was nearly six and though she didn't have any firm plans, she had intended to call Warren or his children. She smiled at the irony of it. Scotty and Julie probably hadn't missed her at all, but, oh, how she longed to see them again.

"Idiot," she told herself.

"Better call it a day," Tammy suggested from the desk behind.

"I'd love to, but I need some more information." She swung her chair around to face Tammy's. "Len wants me to write a travel piece and I wondered if anyone has ever done any stories about Multnomah Falls."

"In the Gorge?" Tammy asked, balancing her hip on the corner of Brenna's desk.

"Right."

"I don't know." Tammy rubbed her chin with a silver-ringed hand thoughtfully. "I think there was something, just last winter. We had that awful freeze and some guys were climbing the frozen falls."

"Doing what?" Brenna asked, certain she'd misunderstood.

Tammy grinned, her eyes sparkling with amusement. "Don't you know about it? Oh, it's a great story! Well, you know how every once in a great while, we have a cold winter—I mean *really* cold? The Columbia Gorge gets the worst of it. When the weather stays below freezing for weeks, Multnomah Falls ices up. It's really gorgeous. All this cascading water is actually frozen in motion as it spills over the cliff."

"Go on," Brenna urged.

"Eventually, if the temperature is below freezing for long enough the giant icicles reach the entire length of the drop. That's when these guys—mountain climbers, I suppose—go out and scale the ice."

"That's crazy!"

"Maybe."

"Why do they do it?"

"Because it's there," Tammy said with a laugh.

Brenna's mouth dropped open.

"Anyway, if you check the files in December or January, I'm sure you'll find some information about the falls."

"I will. Thanks."

"No problem. I'm on my way to the jazz festival. I'll give you a report in the morning." She waved, then bustled out of the office, only the ankle chains around her boots clanking.

"I guess it's now or never," Brenna told herself as she stretched.

In the file room, she located the appropriate microfiche and placed it on the viewer. She glanced through the headlines of each day in December, briefly scanning the pages, searching for any information on the frozen falls.

In fifteen minutes she'd viewed nearly two weeks' worth, when a headline, bold and glaring, stopped her short. Her hand quit moving and her heart nearly stopped.

There, on page one of the City section of the paper, under Karla's byline, was a story on Honor's death:

> Honor Douglass Stone, wife of District Attorney Warren Stone, was killed last night when the car she was driving plunged over a cliff just north of Florence this morning. The single-car accident occurred at approximately 2:15.
>
> Mrs. Stone was pronounced dead on arrival at Memorial Park Hospital. Her blood-alcohol level exceeded the legal limitations and the last person to see her alive, Mr. Elroy Ballard, who claims to have been her modeling agent, admitted that she had spent the evening in a local restaurant and lounge and had been drinking heavily.
>
> Mrs. Stone was rumored to have been considering divorcing her husband. Recently she had been escorted to various social functions by Mr. Ballard.
>
> Mr. Ballard claims his relationship with Mrs. Stone was strictly professional and that she was attempting to revive a modeling and acting career that she had put on hold to marry Stone some nine years ago.
>
> She is survived by her husband, two children, her father, James Douglass, and a sister, Miss Brenna Douglass of San Francisco.

The article continued by explaining where the funeral services would be held.

Brenna was shaking with fury by the time she was finished reading Karla's report. No wonder Warren hated the *Examiner*.

She skimmed the following day's paper. There was another article, even worse than the first. This one, written again by Karla, brought up Honor's drinking and unhappy marriage and suggested that Warren had been more wrapped up in his work than interested in the welfare of his family.

The first two stories were just the tip of the iceberg. In a series of articles "examining the personal lives of elected officials," Warren's life was put under a microscope. Honor's drinking was blamed on dissatisfaction with her life as the wife of the district attorney and Warren was painted as being an uncaring husband dedicated to his job to the point of obsession. Other officials were mentioned, but, in Brenna's opinion, this series of columns was a hatchet job on Warren and his family. Fortunately, the children were barely mentioned.

By the time Brenna had finished reading the last of the series, her eyes swam with images of her sister.

She wanted to take all the microfiche, throw it in the nearest waste can and burn it. Injustice ran hot through her veins as she copied each page that mentioned Honor and carefully folded the damning sheets with trembling fingers.

She drove straight to Len Patterson's apartment and knocked loudly on his door. No answer. She waited, pressing his doorbell furiously until she was convinced he wasn't there.

Then, still seething, she drove home. Though the evening sky was overcast, she kept the windows rolled down, letting the cool air brush over her cheeks and through her hair as she thought about her sister and how much Honor had done for her.

"It's not fair," she cried, echoing the sentiments her niece and nephew so often voiced. "Damn it! It's not fair!" She slammed her fist against the wheel and her horn blasted, startling her.

She was almost home and couldn't remember the ride. Nor had she realized that she'd been crying. Her cheeks were wet and stained, her throat so clogged, she had trouble breathing as she parked at her apartment house.

She went through the motions of wrenching on the emergency brake and cutting the engine without knowing what she was doing. And it was only as she ran up the path to the front door and she heard her name that she realized Warren was leaning against a pillar supporting the porch.

"Brenna?"

She froze, her fingers clutched around her purse.

"Is something wrong?" He was walking toward her, slowly, his gaze trained on her face. His eyes were sober, his expression kind, and she wanted to cry all over again. "Come on," he said, meeting her on the path as night descended. "I was going to take you to dinner, but maybe you want to clean up."

She tried to force a wavering smile, but couldn't. When he placed his arm around her shoulders, she felt as if she'd finally come home. "Come on, Bren. Whatever it is, it can't be that bad," he said tenderly as he helped her up the stairs and shoved open the door.

"I'm fine," she whispered, trying to still the rage burning bright in her heart.

"Sure you are."

In her apartment, he drew her into the circle of his arms and placed his chin on her head. "You want to talk about it?" he asked so tenderly she thought her heart would break.

"In—in a minute. Just give me a little time," she said, wanting to control her flaming emotions before she talked with him.

"Whatever you need."

He dropped his arms and she walked quickly to the bathroom. Leaning over the sink, she caught sight of her reflection in the mirror and cringed. Her face was red, her makeup smeared and running from her eyes, her hair a tangled mess from the wind. After splashing water over her eyes and cheeks, she repaired the damage and braced herself.

When she emerged from the bathroom, she found Warren sitting on the edge of the couch, his hands on his knees. A single glass of wine sat on the coffee table. "I thought you might need this," he explained, motioning to the rosé.

"I don't think wine will help."

"Want to talk about it?" he asked again, his eyes following her as she sat across from him on the hearth.

The bricks were cold and Brenna shivered, rubbing her arms.

Warren's face hardened. "Something happened at work," he guessed. "You're late."

"Yes."

"It's Patterson, isn't it?" he charged, his lips pulling tight over his teeth. "If that bastard's hurt you, I'll go down to that office personally and beat the living daylights out of him."

"Don't worry, I'll take care of him," Brenna said, surprised at her own need for revenge. No, not revenge, *justice!* "It's nothing to do with me," she said slowly.

Thick brows drew over his eyes. "I don't understand."

"Neither did I," she admitted, "until this afternoon. I was going through some files for background on a piece I'm working on and I ran across these." She reached for her purse, opened it, withdrew the photocopies and scooted the gray pages across the coffee table.

"What's this?" he asked, then his voice faded and he sucked in a swift breath. The lines around his mouth turned white as he took the pages and crumpled every last one in his fist. "Damn!" he swore. "Damn! Damn! Damn!" Eyes glittering, he tossed the wrinkled sheets back at her and they fell, still wadded together, to the floor. "No thanks. I've read them too many times to count."

"I didn't understand," she whispered. "I didn't know why you hated the *Examiner* so much."

"So now you do."

"I'm sorry."

"It's not your fault, Brenna. I just hate to think of you throwing in with that lot." He clasped his hands together and gritted his teeth. "It's not just me, you know. The *Examiner* takes potshots at everyone. Some people claim that the bad press comes with the territory—part of being a public figure."

"But that—" she pointed an accusing finger at the papers "—was beyond the limit of common decency."

"It sells papers, Bren. Just because Honor was your sister doesn't matter. Just dollars and cents."

She wasn't convinced. "More than that—these stories were wicked. Vicious. Sure, Karla brought up other people, but for the most part, you were singled out."

"Last December I was an easy target." The muscles under his jacket were flexed so tight that the fabric of his suit jacket was stretched taut across his shoulders. Ramming his hand through his hair in frustration, he stepped over the coffee table to sit next to her. "I told you I was going to explain about Honor—everything," he said finally. "Maybe now is the right time."

Already cold, Brenna felt a shiver dart down her spine. She didn't want to hear any more about her sister. "There's no reason to dredge all this up again."

"It's time, Brenna. And I want to start over with you, so just listen." He took one of her hands in his, then leaned the back of his head against the bricks. The same guilty look she'd come to recognize clouded his features. "Sometimes I wonder if Honor's death was my fault," he said.

"No."

He closed his eyes, squeezing them tight—as if to block

out a scene too horrible to watch. "I still have questions," he said raggedly. "And I wonder if she committed suicide."

"What? Warren, no!" Brenna insisted, shaking her head vehemently. "No, Warren, no way. Honor loved life!" But Warren's fingers had grown cold in hers.

"You don't understand, Brenna. Honor wasn't happy. She hadn't been for a long time. When Julie told you Honor wanted me to be a doctor, she wasn't kidding."

"But you were a lawyer when she married you," Brenna protested.

"Right. And she expected me to go into corporate law, climb the ladder in a big firm in town, become a social bigwig. I did try it for a while, but I couldn't stand it. I'd always intended to work in criminal law, but I guess Honor thought she could change my mind.

"And it's not that we needed the money. I'd inherited from my folks and I'd always been careful. So over her protests I quit my job at Henning, Foxworth and Marshall and started working for the city."

"But if that's what you wanted…"

"It wasn't what *she* wanted—or had expected. Honor thought working in the district attorney's office was a big comedown. She didn't see that I had to work on something more real and interesting than corporate tax laws, mergers and civil lawsuits."

Brenna fought the urge to argue with him. No, she told herself, glancing to their entwined fingers, his dark and clenched, hers smaller and shaking, he had to speak.

"As the years passed she became dissatisfied. Being married to the district attorney wasn't exciting. She was always reading the society columns, dreaming of what her life could have been had she been the wife of one of the prominent attorneys in town.

"She did her best to climb the social ladder and she was accepted, always going to charity functions and the like. Because of my work, I couldn't always go with her," he admitted. "That was one mistake. One on a long list."

"But you can't blame yourself for what happened."

"Can't I?" His fingers flexed over hers. "The writing was all over the wall and I ignored it. I told myself that given enough time she'd come around, see things my way."

"But she didn't," Brenna guessed.

"If anything, she became more intolerant and she started to drink, Brenna. A lot. I caught her a couple of times when I'd come home late. She'd either been out or stayed home alone, but she'd been drinking.

"For a while she denied it, but I eventually got through to her. She promised me that if I let her start modeling or acting or whatever the hell she wanted to do, she'd get help and we'd go to a marriage counselor."

"Did you ever see someone?"

He shook his head. "We didn't get that far. She hooked up with Ballard, her agent. He told her not to worry about her age. She was beautiful and had star quality or some such malarkey."

"And she believed him."

"Implicitly." His face slackened. "She felt her life had become so dreary and ordinary that she needed some kind of excitement and glory, I guess. Ballard said he could deliver, so she signed on the dotted line, then promptly told me that she was filing for divorce."

Brenna could barely breathe. Honor had once said something to make her think that her marriage wasn't rock solid, but Brenna had dismissed her sister's unhappiness to one of her moods. "I thought you told me she went to the beach to think things over."

"That's what I believed. But things didn't quite turn out that way. She and Ballard got drunk and she left the bar in a huff."

Brenna asked, "They fought?"

"Yes. But Ballard never said what it was all about," Warren said, his jaw working. "I don't think they were lovers. I bought the story that their relationship was purely business, but I don't really know and now it doesn't matter. My guess is that he told her he'd changed his mind about her career. Right after the accident, he packed his bags and moved to L.A."

"And that's why you think her death was suicide?" Brenna asked, disbelieving.

"I just don't know."

"Oh, Warren," Brenna whispered, her heart filled with sadness. "You never really knew her, did you? She would never have ended her life intentionally. When Mom died, she was the strong one for me and Dad. And whenever the going got tough at home, she was always the one who looked on the bright side. I won't believe it," she said emphatically. "Honor may have had her problems, and she was probably unhappy, but she wasn't one to give up." Taking his face between her palms, she forced him to stare into her eyes. "It was an accident, Warren," she said, her voice tight as she read the guilt in his eyes.

"I've tried to believe that."

Stroking the hair from his eyes, she wanted to weep. "Don't torture yourself. It wasn't your fault."

"How can you be sure?"

"Because I know you, Warren. You would never have hurt her, not intentionally." Swallowing a huge lump, she leaned forward and pressed her lips to his, brushing them slowly across his cool mouth. "You're the kindest man I've ever known," she admitted, linking her arms around his neck.

"You didn't think so the other night," he reminded her.

"And I was wrong. Dear Lord, Warren, I was wrong." She tilted her face to his, eagerly parting her lips, and he couldn't resist. With a groan, he lifted her off the hearth and carried her deftly into the bedroom.

She didn't protest when he laid her across the bed, but welcomed him with loving arms. Kissing her fiercely, he tumbled onto the mattress with her, his lips searching, his tongue probing.

While lying across her, he slowly disrobed her, his fingers trembling as he removed her skirt and blouse and grazed the soft skin of her abdomen.

The waning light of early evening shadowed her room as she removed his clothes, until at last they were naked, lying together, entwined as lovers as he kissed her over and over again. "I love you, Brenna," he whispered against the wild cloud of her hair and kissed her with such a tenderness she thought her heart might break.

"I love you, too," she admitted, the words tumbling free as she wound her arms around his neck and moved with him, feeling his body join with hers, hearing the rough sound of his voice as he whispered her name.

"Brenna. Oh, Brenna…"

CHAPTER ELEVEN

THE FOLLOWING MORNING Brenna marched into Len Patterson's office. Still furious from her discovery the previous evening, she was bound and determined to have it out with her boss. "Do you have a minute?" she asked, her voice firm, though deep inside she was still seething.

He glanced up from his desk and smiled. "Looks serious."

"It is."

"Have a seat." Waving her into a side chair he added, "But before you get into anything too heavy, these are for you." He shoved a stack of six or seven envelopes across his desk to her.

"What are they?"

"My guess is fan mail."

"Thanks." Brenna glanced through the envelopes, but didn't recognize any of the return addresses. Nor did she care.

"Thank *you*," Len said. "I know I gave you a hard time on your first day. Now it looks like you didn't need any pep talk. The owners of the paper are pleased with your work. Keep it up."

"Good. Because there's a bone I want to pick with you."

Toying with a pencil, he said, "Shoot."

"It's about my sister."

"What about her?"

"I read all the articles that were printed about her death."

"I see." He leaned back in his chair and flipped his pencil back and forth.

"They were libelous."

"No—"

"Bull!" She could feel the color in her cheeks, the fire in her eyes. "Look, when I took this job, I got a lot of flack from my family—my father and brother-in-law. I didn't really understand why. But after I read those articles, I was furious! There was no reason to print all those stupid, unfounded rumors about Honor!"

Len shifted uncomfortably in his chair. "The rumors weren't unfounded, Brenna. We checked several sources."

"At the very least your articles were inflammatory."

"Maybe. But it was news. Warren Stone is an elected official. He's newsworthy."

Brenna's gaze narrowed. "He has two children. My sister's children, for God's sake. The children I use when I want to refer to some domestic scene—for the same paper that tore their mother's reputation to shreds! Fortunately, they're too young to read and understand."

Len's mouth grew hard. "I'm backing up everything we've printed, Brenna. The same way I'll back you up if you ever become embroiled in some controversy. And you may as well get this straight: Just because Warren Stone is your brother-in-law doesn't mean he gets any favors. However, and this isn't to go outside this room, the paper's taken some heat, so we're trying to clean it up a little. Not that we ever printed anything that wasn't substantiated by two sources, mind you. But the pressure's on. So if it's any consolation, I'll apologize to you right now for any grief the paper caused your family."

"I want a written apology and retraction."

"No way." He looked directly into her eyes. "I'm sorry, Brenna. But your sister's story is ancient history. All I can promise is more responsible journalism in the future. If that's not good enough—" he shrugged "—then so be it."

"It's not good enough," she said.

"Then it's your decision whether you want to continue working on the paper or not. As I said, we're trying to clean up our act. You've helped. I won't lie. I hope you'll stay. The paper needs you. But I can't twist your arm, Brenna. You can stick around and try to help make the *Examiner* better, or you can throw in the towel."

"I'll think about it," she said, rising to walk to her desk. Still seething, she didn't even bother to glance at the letters in her hand, just flipped them against her open palm. She tried to calm down, think rationally. Though she was still angry, she grudgingly realized that dredging up all the old pain would do more harm than good, and after fifteen minutes of arguing with herself, she decided that quitting would be the coward's way out. She had committed herself to the *Examiner*, and now she'd help it climb out of the mire.

Taking in a bracing breath, she walked back to Len's office, rapped on his door and, still clutching the mail he'd given her earlier, dropped into the chair she had so recently vacated.

"I don't want to leave," she admitted, knowing she'd pushed as hard as she could. Len wasn't about to budge. "I just had to get it off my chest."

He seemed relieved. "Good."

"But there is one thing," she said, remembering her promise to Julie.

"I suspected as much. What?"

"I want to take off early today."

One sandy eyebrow raised.

"How early?"

"After lunch. Just think of it as research for an upcoming article. My niece has a part in a class play and her father can't attend."

"Go ahead—just make sure you write a blockbuster story about it," Len replied, already reaching for his phone. The interview was over.

As she walked back to her desk, Brenna felt as if a horrid weight had been lifted from her shoulders. Though Honor's name hadn't been vindicated and Brenna hadn't received the satisfaction of a retraction, at least she had been able to stand up for her sister. Maybe that was enough. And maybe Len would turn the paper around. Maybe she *could* be the difference....

"You look just like you could spit bullets," Tammy observed from her desk. She was wearing plastic today—a rainbow of bracelets crawled up her arm and huge red hoops dangled from her ears.

"Do I?"

"What happened?"

Brenna explained about her discovery the night before and her confrontation with Len.

Tammy's bright eyes squinted. "There's more to it than that, though," she said. "I can understand why you're upset, but you've been sensitive every time Warren Stone's name is mentioned. Have you got a thing going with him?"

Brenna grinned. "A thing?"

"That's it, isn't it? You're in love with him!"

"Shh!" But Brenna couldn't lie to the one person in the office she considered her friend. Not after last night, when Warren had held her in his arms and vowed that he loved her. Unfortunately, he'd had to leave early to pick up Julie and Scotty at Mary Beatty's, and Brenna had spent the rest of the night alone. "Maybe I am."

"Well, I'll be," Tammy said, but smiled. "That's great. The way I see it, those two little kids need a mother more than an aunt."

"I'm not so sure they both think so. But I'm trying," Brenna admitted. "Which reminds me. You'd better watch out or I might take over your job."

"Oh?"

"Yep. Today I'm going to review a new revival of *Snow White* as performed by Mrs. Stevens's second-grade class at Hamilton Elementary! Want to join me?"

Tammy grinned, but shook her moussed locks. "Thanks, but I'll wait for the big-screen version."

"That's already been done," Brenna reminded her.

"Just the same, I'll take a rain check."

"Your loss." Brenna read through the letters, then covered her first news story: an angry debate between protesters and members of the city council concerning the site of a proposed chemical plant.

After organizing her notes and sketching out her story, she drove to the school and sat in a desk meant for a seven-year-old, as Julie, who played one of the seven dwarfs, and the rest of her class performed. Julie's eyes glimmered with excitement when she caught sight of Brenna and she almost fumbled her one line.

Afterward, Brenna met Julie's teacher and sipped punch with a group of mothers clustered around a small table in the shape of a half-moon. "This is the reading table," Julie explained, then pointed out a hamster, gerbil, two parakeets and a family of rats, all housed in cages in the corners of the room. The walls and windows were decorated with artwork the children had created. Paper sailing ships hung from the ceiling, a finger-painted poster of animals in the sea adorned one wall, and on the desks were workbooks with pictures the children had drawn throughout the year.

"You don't want to look at that," Julie said suddenly when Brenna started thumbing through her folder.

"Sure I do, hon. I'm proud of what you do."

The book fell open to a page reserved for a picture of

the family. Julie made a strangled sound as a crayon drawing of Warren, Scotty, herself and Honor fluttered open. The date on the work was November, one month before Honor's death.

Brenna's throat clogged as she read the look in Julie's eyes. "This is a beautiful picture," she said quietly.

Julie grabbed the booklet and shoved it into her backpack. "It's dumb."

"No, Julie. It's very nice."

"But it's a lie!" Julie whispered harshly, tears standing in her Honor-blue eyes. "I don't have a mother anymore." Red-faced, she dashed from the room.

Brenna rushed after her. "Julie—Julie, wait."

But Julie wasn't listening. She shoved open the glass doors and with her blond hair streaming behind, sprinted between the parked buses to wait, sobbing, at Brenna's car.

"I'm sorry," Brenna said, once she'd caught up with the girl. "I didn't mean to pry."

Sniffing, Julie stared up at the white clouds floating lazily against a cerulean sky. "Can we just go?" she demanded.

"In a minute. I want to pick up your jacket and Scotty."

"He's not here. He goes to morning kindergarten. Remember?"

Thank God, Brenna thought. "Then I'll be back in a minute." She unlocked the passenger door. "Here—you wait inside, okay?"

Still fighting tears, Julie nodded mutely.

Mrs. Stevens had just dismissed the class. "Is she all right?" she asked as the children filed out of the room behind another teacher.

"I think so."

"It's hard for her," Anne Stevens remarked, thinking. "And Memorial Day is just around the corner. Believe it or not, she's the only child in the class who doesn't have both parents. Several children have parents who are divorced, but they still have contact with both their mother and father as well as stepparents."

"Is there anything I can do?"

"You did a lot just showing up today. I was afraid that Julie would be the only child without someone here to watch her debut. Even the working mothers usually ask an aunt or friend to stop in. Sometimes it doesn't work out, but this year, we've been lucky."

Anne found Julie's jacket and handed it to Brenna. "She's talked an awful lot about you, you know."

"Is it confidential?"

The teacher smiled. "I don't think so. She seems to think a lot of you."

"She's a very special little girl," Brenna admitted, surprised at the new depth of her feelings for Honor's first-born. "And the loss of her mother has been a difficult adjustment for her." She couldn't help but think back to her own loss. She'd been much older than Julie, but still the pain of her mother's death had been excruciating. For months afterward, Brenna had cried herself to sleep each night. "Please, let me know if she's having any problems at school."

"So far, she's holding her own. We talked to Julie's father a couple of times after his wife's death, but until today, Julie seemed to be handling everything I've assigned her, although she was pretty vocal against one writing assignment."

Brenna sighed. "I know."

The teacher extended her hand. "Thanks for coming."

"My pleasure." Carrying Julie's jacket over her arm, Brenna threaded her way through the crowded, noisy halls to the front door, then picked a path between the parked buses and cars to her little Rabbit.

Julie was sitting in the passenger seat, slumped down so far that the top of her head was barely visible.

"How about an ice cream?" Brenna asked.

"No thanks."

"We could go to the park."

"I just want to go home," Julie mumbled.

Wishing there were some way she could comfort her niece, Brenna drove away from the school. "Look, Julie, I know that this is a difficult time for you—"

"I don't want to talk about it!" Julie cried, her face red and twisted against tears. "Just—just leave me alone."

"Okay," Brenna whispered. "But if you change your mind, just let me know."

Julie didn't answer. Her small shoulder was turned away from Brenna in an attempt at ostracizing her aunt and Brenna didn't press. Sometimes, she reasoned, even children have to work through their grief and despair. "You don't understand," Julie muttered. "No one does."

"Maybe you're wrong about that." Fingers clenched around the steering wheel, she added, "I remember how much it hurt when your grandma died. And the pain didn't go away overnight. But it does get better, honey. Really." She reached forward and smoothed Julie's blond hair.

Julie sobbed loudly. "So why won't you marry Daddy and make everything all right?"

Brenna swallowed hard. "Even if I do marry your father, it won't be the same as it was. It'll be different."

Julie shook her hand aside and jerked open the door. Feet flying, she raced up the front walk with Brenna chasing after her. She nearly ran into Mary Beatty in the front hall.

"What the devil?" Mary asked as Julie, still crying, ran up the stairs.

"I'll handle this." Brushing past the housekeeper, Brenna flew after Julie only to have Julie's bedroom door slammed in her face. Holding on to her shattered nerves, Brenna knocked firmly on the door.

"Go 'way!"

"I just want to say one thing."

"Go away! Daddy was right! I should never have written you!"

Ignoring her niece's pleas and the prick of her conscience, she opened the door to find Julie, her shoulders shaking, her little back stiff with pride, staring out the window.

"Julie?"

"Leave me alone!" she cried, swiping at her nose with the back of her sleeve and not even glancing in Brenna's direction.

Brenna closed the door and leaned against it. "All I wanted to tell you," she said softly, her voice hoarse with the emotions that were ripping her apart, "is that I love you, Julie. Very much. I might have come here because you wrote me and asked me to, but I couldn't leave if I tried. You're too important to me, sweetheart."

Julie made a little choking sound.

"I'm sorry if I hurt you and I'll try not to let it happen again. Because I'm staying, Julie. I'm staying in this town with you and Scotty and whether I marry your father or not won't change the fact that I love you as I would my own child, with all of my heart. That will never, ever change."

Julie didn't move and Brenna had to blink against the storm of tears that threatened her eyes. Shaking, she left Julie's room and walked down the stairs on trembling legs. She felt drained inside and experienced the sinking sensation that she wasn't cut out to be a mother—at least not the mother of a grief-stricken seven- and six-year-old.

After explaining quickly to Mary about the episode at school, Brenna spent a few minutes with Scotty and was surprised that he seemed glad to see her. He offered to show her his bug and rock collections and even favored her with a toothless grin.

"One step forward, two steps back," she told herself as she drove home. "It just takes time." Smiling through unshed tears, she thought about Warren, their lovemaking and how much she cared for him. Despite her problems at the paper, despite the struggles with the children or any lingering doubts about Honor, she loved Warren Stone as fervently as she had all those years ago.

As she parked the car and strode up the path to the old apartment house, she silently vowed that she'd pull everything together to be with Warren and she didn't care if she had to move heaven and earth to do it!

AT NINE THIRTY the phone rang and Warren's weary voice echoed over the wires. "I just wanted to thank you for playing mother today," he said.

"I don't think I did a very good job."

He sighed audibly. "Mary told me everything and the way I see it, Julie owes you an apology."

"Don't worry about it. Let's just get through this miserable holiday," she suggested, hating the thought. "I think I'll spend some time with Dad—maybe even stay the night out at the farm for the holiday."

"Does that mean there won't be any time left for me?"

She chuckled deep in her throat. "There's always time for you, counselor," she said, surprised at her own boldness as she heard him groan on the other end of the wire.

"I could be there in three minutes."

"And what about the kids?"

He laughed. "They'd be with me."

"Maybe you three just need some time alone," she said.

"You're probably right, but I hate it." He hesitated a moment. "You know, Julie and Scotty are out of school next week. What do you think about taking a trip to the mountains?"

"I—I don't know. I'll have to clear it with Len."

"That shouldn't be too tough. We'll leave Friday and you can report for work bright and early Monday morning. I have a friend who owes me a favor and he owns a cabin just out of Sisters."

"It sounds perfect," she murmured, leaning against the wall.

"Not quite. I want us to go up as man and wife."

"Oh, Warren—there're so many things to straighten out," she protested, though her heart was soaring.

"Nothing we can't handle together. Think it over, Brenna. I'm serious." Without waiting for a reply, he hung up and Brenna was left dreaming about spending a weekend alone with him and his children. If only she could get through the next three days.

MEMORIAL DAY DAWNED in a blanket of fog. Brenna stared from the window of her bedroom to the weed-choked grass below. Long before, she'd stood at this very window, watching as Honor dashed across the dry lawn to meet Jeff Prentice.

Before she could get too wrapped up in her sad memories, she changed from her nightgown into a long skirt and blouse, clipped her hair away from her face and bustled down the stairs.

She found her mother's old clippers on the back porch and, with Dixie frolicking playfully at her side, snipped the first scarlet, pink and yellow buds from the old rosebushes. The petals were wet with early morning dew, the thorns hidden beneath shiny green leaves. More than once she pricked her finger, but she smiled as she placed the blossoms in a wet paper towel.

"That about does it," she murmured to the dog as she

bundled the flowers with rubber bands and carried them into the kitchen. After placing the fragrant blooms in a water-filled quart jar, she started coffee, then dug through the refrigerator.

By the time her father ambled down the stairs, the coffee was perked, bacon was sizzling in a frying pan and she was ready to crack eggs into the leftover grease.

"Up with the chickens," her father observed.

"Why not?"

He grinned slowly and poured himself a cup of coffee. "No reason I guess, except that we don't have chickens anymore."

"Good. They were a mess. Always fighting, squawking and leaving droppings and feathers all over the ground. You're better off buying your eggs at the store."

"If you say so."

Taking a seat at the table, James lit a cigarette and sipped his coffee. Brenna could feel his gaze on her as she moved from the old stove to the refrigerator and back again.

"This place is fallin' apart," he mused as if he'd never noticed before.

"It just needs a little work."

"A lot of work."

From the corner of her eye she could see him glance at the cobweb-dusted ceiling to the split linoleum and scratched cupboards. "All it needs is a handyman, a woman's touch and about ten gallons of paint."

"That all?" he mocked.

"Well maybe some disinfectant and flooring and—"

"Enough already." He waved her words aside. "It's good enough for me."

"Dad?" she asked as a sudden thought struck her.

"Hmm?"

Forking the bacon onto a napkin-covered plate, she asked, "Why didn't you ever remarry?"

"Obvious reasons." He frowned through the smoke. "At first I didn't think any woman would want to be saddled with two headstrong teenagers like you and your sister."

"Were we that bad?"

He lifted a shoulder and stubbed out his cigarette as she placed a platter of toast and eggs in front of him. "'Course you weren't. Best two damned daughters in the county."

"Sure," she mocked.

"Well, to tell ya the truth I just never met anyone who could fill your mother's shoes. She was one special lady," he said, his eyes fading in fond remembrance.

"But don't you ever get lonely?"

"I suppose so. But I don't dwell on it. No reason." He jabbed a piece of bacon with his fork and dropped the hot meat onto his plate.

After they finished breakfast and the dishes were cleared, James drove his old pickup up a winding road leading to the cemetery.

A few pale rays of sun pierced through the fog and dew clung to the grass. Silvery-green leaves fluttered in the branches of old oak trees as Brenna followed after her father, picking her way through the marble tombstones before stopping at her mother's grave.

"She was a good woman," James whispered. He placed several heavy blossoms in a small vase. "Things would have been different had she lived. So much different." He frowned and gazed across the valley, past the rolling acres of farmland.

Brenna shuddered. Though the day promised warmth, she was cold to the bone, as cold as she had been on the day of Honor's funeral. Unhappily, she placed the cut blooms over her mother's grave, then walked the short distance to the plot where Honor was buried.

A beautiful wreath of white carnations, salmon-colored rosebuds and fir bows adorned the grave. Obviously, Warren and the children had already visited. A pang of sorrow cut through Brenna's heart and she realized how much she missed his children. How was Julie since her traumatic day at school, and Scotty—was he even old enough to understand this macabre ritual of decorating graves?

Swallowing a thick lump in her throat, she placed roses from the garden across Honor's grave. A breeze blew her hair away from her face and chilled her cheeks. She glanced up to find her father dabbing at his eyes with a handkerchief.

"Oh, Honor," she whispered quietly as she arranged the fragrant blossoms, "why did you have to die?" Then, coughing, she straightened and helped her father back to his truck. He seemed suddenly old and tired.

"I don't know why you put yourself through this torture," Brenna said, once he'd let out the parking brake and they were rolling through the wrought-iron gates at the entrance of the cemetery.

"It's simple. I don't want to forget my wife and daughter."

"You wouldn't." She glanced at him ruefully. "You could have remarried, you know. Mom would have understood."

Frowning, he reached into his pocket, found a crumpled pack of cigarettes and shook one out. "I just never felt right about seein' other women," he admitted, striking a match and inhaling deeply. The cab of the truck was filled with smoke and he cracked his window. "Besides, my time has come and gone." He chuckled and the sound rattled in his chest. "Even my sister, Olivia, is busy working out her will—all caught up in putting her effects in order, just in case the Lord calls early. Nope. I don't need another wife. It's too late for me."

"That's certainly a defeatist attitude," Brenna pointed out. "You're never too old."

He shifted gears and the old truck leaped forward. "Maybe you should take that advice yourself."

"Me?"

"You've been here nearly a month, Brenna. I know you've been seein' Warren. So what's keeping you apart?"

Leaning against the passenger window, she leveled a suspicious eye at her father. "Don't play matchmaker, Dad."

"Don't have to. I've got eyes, don't I? I've seen you two together and I already told you that I probably made a mistake way back when. I heard you tell Warren you loved him then and my bet is, you still do."

"Oh, Dad."

"You denyin' it?"

Crossing her arms over her chest, she frowned. "It's complicated."

He chuckled again. "You just findin' that out? I don't think so. 'Sides, complications never stopped you before. You've always gone after what you wanted."

"This is different."

He stubbed his cigarette in an already overflowing tray. "No different. You're just scared, that's all. Afraid he's going to hurt you like before."

"Maybe."

James cranked on the wheel and the truck bounced into the two uneven ruts of the drive. "I guess I've got a confession to make," he said, pulling up at the house and rubbing a tired hand around his neck.

"You, too."

"Yep. Warren came to me back then. Right before you took off for school."

"He did?" Brenna had her hand on the door, but stopped and faced her father.

"Yep. We had a talk, a long talk."

Brenna's heart began to pound.

"He admitted that he was confused—that he loved Honor, but that he'd kissed you and had feelings for you as well." James sighed long and hard. "I guess I'd seen it coming all summer long, but I didn't want to believe it."

Brenna could barely breathe.

"I told him that you were just going through a phase, that you were too young to really know what you wanted. Then I told him about your scholarship and that if you didn't accept it, I wouldn't be able to afford to send you to college."

"You did *what?*" Brenna cried, disbelieving.

"I'm not proud of it. I know I would have scrounged up the money someplace, but I thought it would be best for you to go to Berkeley. Before you fell in love with Warren you talked of nothing but going away to school—a good school, an expensive school—and becoming a writer. I didn't want you to blow that. Not for Warren Stone. Not when he could help straighten out Honor."

Her insides twisted. "Oh, Dad," she whispered, wondering what course her life would have run if her father hadn't interfered. "Why didn't Warren tell me?"

"I asked him to keep it between us. He's a man of his word." He glanced at his gnarled hands before meeting her eyes again. "I'm not proud of what I've done, Brenna. But believe me, at the time I thought I was doing what was best for you and Honor. Maybe if your ma would have lived…" Frowning, he yanked open the door. "I guess we can't think about might-have-beens. But you, you can start over."

She climbed out of the pickup shakily, then followed her father into the old house.

"You're right," he said, squinting at the dingy walls and cracked floor. "It's time I either sold this place or put some money into it. I guess I've been a fool. I didn't want to take down anything or change it. This was the way your ma kept the place."

"Mom's been gone a long time," Brenna whispered.

"I know. And I guess it's time to do something."

"Don't sell it, Dad," she said suddenly, her thoughts still tangled with the past. "What would you do in a condominium in town?"

"Beats me." He bent over and scratched Dixie behind her ears.

Brenna touched his arm. "Don't do anything rash," she said. "I'll help you clean it up this summer and I bet you could rent most of the acreage to Craig, maybe even pay him to make some of the repairs. Believe it or not, I can paint and hang wallpaper."

His smile faltered. "It's good to have you back, Bren," he admitted, voice cracking.

She threw her arms around his neck and felt tears well in her throat. "It's good to be back, Dad. So good. Even though I should run you out of town on a rail for butting into my life ten years ago."

"Are you so unhappy?"

She thought about it and held him at arm's length. "No," she admitted. "Not anymore. But I think I have a few things to straighten out with the local D.A." Smiling through unshed tears, she raced upstairs, packed her things, then kissed her father goodbye. This time, she was going to ask Warren to marry her—and she wasn't about to take no for an answer!

CHAPTER TWELVE

WITHOUT HESITATION, BRENNA drove straight to Warren's house. Sun peeked through the misting clouds high overhead, and on impulse, Brenna let the top of her convertible down. The old Rabbit chugged up the winding roads of the west hills, through the thick stands of fir and maple.

Brenna's heartbeat was racing as fast as the engine of her little car by the time Warren's house was in sight. She licked her lips, told herself this day above all else he had the right to his privacy, then promptly turned into the drive. As far as she was concerned it was now or never. Either she was part of this family or not. Today she would find out.

Mary Beatty answered the door and her mouth stretched into a wide smile at the sight of Brenna. "So, look who's here! And just in time!" she said.

"In time for what?" Brenna asked, glancing past Mary to the stairs where Warren paused, halfway down. Brenna felt her eyes sparkle at the sight of him. In brushed gray cords and a loose-fitting sweater, his hands thrust into his pockets and his hair falling over his brow, he didn't move, just stared at her with interested blue eyes.

"I thought the children would like a picnic, but old spoilsport here claims he has to work." Mary winked broadly as she stepped out of the door. "Maybe you can change his mind."

"It's a holiday," Brenna said, but Warren's mouth twisted downward as he descended.

"Doesn't matter. I have to go into the office."

"The Charlie Saxton case?" she asked, already knowing the answer.

"There are a couple of cases that have to be reviewed—a couple more important than the Saxton case. And as far as Charlie Saxton goes, it looks like we just might get a break. He may be tried in Washington County. That's good enough."

Brenna nodded. Washington County was part of the tri-county area that served Portland, though Warren was the district attorney for Multnomah County.

"Saxton's lawyer is calling foul of course, but I think the judge isn't going to listen this time."

Brenna was relieved.

"I know the D.A. and he's agreed to work with me. We just have to iron out a few details."

"Work, work, work," Mary grumbled. "And what about your children, huh?"

"I'll take them on a picnic," Brenna offered. "Maybe Warren can join us later." She glanced at Warren for support, but his expression didn't change."

"You don't have to."

"I *want* to. Besides, I need to talk to you."

His eyes glimmered. "Good news or bad?"

"I'll let you be the judge of that."

Mary shot Warren a knowing glance. "Okay, I'll fix a basket."

"Don't bother, I'm sure Julie, Scotty and I can handle it."

Nodding, Mary said, "I suppose you can. But I promised the children they could spend the night with me. Julie's begging me to teach her how to make popcorn balls."

"No problem. I'll drop them off late this afternoon."

"Don't I have any say in this?" Warren asked, but a smile twitched at the corners of his mouth.

"None whatsoever," Mary chided. "That's what you get

for working on a holiday." She reached for her coat, waved to them both and breezed out the door.

Brenna crossed her arms and arched one brow. "Any arguments, counselor?"

"Not for the moment," he said, but his gaze searched her face. "I wondered when you'd show up again."

"I was going to leave you alone today," she admitted. "I thought maybe you and the children would want to…"

"Mope around and grieve?"

"I guess." She lifted one shoulder. "I saw the wreath on Honor's grave."

"It's one thing to remember. Another to wallow in self-pity," he said. "I don't see what good it would do to spend the day grieving. It's over."

Brenna heard the back door open, then bang shut. A minute later Julie peeked around the corner from the kitchen. "Aunt Bren?" she asked softly.

"Hi, pumpkin."

"Are you mad at me?" Julie asked, her lip caught between her teeth as she approached.

"Of course not."

"I mean about the other day. At school."

"It's forgotten, okay?" Brenna said, kneeling to look her niece straight in the eye. "We all have bad days."

Julie stared at the floor. "Dad says I owe you an apology." She glanced at Warren from the corner of her eye. "I—I'm sorry."

Brenna kissed Julie's forehead and she nearly cried when Julie's little arms surrounded her neck. "Forgiven and forgotten, okay? Now, why don't you start scrounging around in the kitchen for something to take on a picnic."

Julie's head snapped up and her face brightened. "We get to go?" she asked her father.

"I still have to work. But Aunt Bren will take you and Scotty."

Julie's face fell a little, but she managed to square her shoulders.

"I'll try to make it later, okay?" Warren suggested. "You could have the picnic at the creek at Grandpa's farm and I'll try to meet you there in about three hours."

"Okay," Julie said grudgingly.

"Why don't you spread the good news to your brother?"

Julie, calling Scotty's name, charged through the kitchen and out the back door. "I appreciate this, Bren," he said once they were alone. "The kids were really disappointed."

"No problem," she quipped, and gasped when he suddenly drew her into his arms.

"I've missed you," he admitted, smiling as he kissed her forehead. The strength of his embrace, the glint of blue fire in his eyes and the feel of his body next to hers was intoxicating. "We all have."

"Me, too," she whispered, leaning against him for a moment and drinking in his scent—a woodsy masculine smell that she'd come to recognize. Her cheek rubbed against the soft fabric of his sweater and he groaned from deep in his throat. "You can't imagine just how much."

"Show me," he murmured, his lips brushing the hair on the top of her head. "Later. When we're alone."

Brenna's pulse fluttered. "After we set a few things straight," she said.

Pounding footsteps clattered through the kitchen and the children rounded the corner just as Warren released her.

"You leaving?" Scotty asked.

"'Fraid I have to. Aunt Bren will be here."

Scotty's lip protruded, but he didn't argue as Warren scooped both Julie and him into his arms and kissed them on the cheeks. "I'll meet you at the farm," he said. "Save a sandwich for me!"

"Peanut butter and jelly?"

Warren groaned. "Whatever," he replied, setting both children onto the floor. "Good luck," he called to Brenna as he reached for his jacket and walked out the front door.

"Okay, you guys," Brenna said, winking at Julie and Scotty. "Your dad left me in charge. That means just about anything goes. So—what should we have on the picnic?"

"Candy bars!" Scotty cried.

"And pop!" Julie added.

"And ice cream!"

Brenna laughed. "I think I'll have to draw the line at ice cream. It'll melt."

"We have a cooler," Julie insisted.

"I doubt if it will work, but we'll give it a shot," Brenna decided. "I want to go home and change into jeans, so let's get started!"

THE SHADED CREEK, protected by saplings and young fir, twisted and glittered silver where shafts of afternoon sunlight filtered through the branches as it wound crookedly down the hill to the river.

Balancing the cooler in both hands, Brenna picked her way across the flat stones to a perfect picnic spot beneath the spreading branches of an old maple tree.

"I can't make it!" Scotty pouted as Julie carefully crossed the rushing water.

"Sure you can. I'll help."

Brenna crossed again, took Scotty's hand and helped him ford the stream. He slipped once, but she caught him. Unfortunately one high-topped basketball shoe was dunked in the frigid water. He shrieked, clutched her hand more tightly, and they both nearly toppled into the stream.

"Here you go, sport," Brenna said as they finally touched solid ground on the far shore.

"Why'd we have to come here?" Scotty asked.

"Because right over there is the best crawdad hole on the entire farm."

"The what?" Julie asked.

"Crawdads, er, crayfish. You know, like tiny little freshwater lobsters?"

Julie wrinkled her nose but Scotty seemed intrigued.

"Your mom and I used to do this when we were kids," Brenna explained. "Just wait and I'll be back with the poles."

A few minutes later she had deposited the picnic basket and some willow branches on a blanket. "I'll show you how this works."

"How come Grandpa isn't fishing with us?" Scotty asked, watching as Brenna tied a string around one whittled end of a smooth branch, then carefully threaded a safety pin to the loose end of the string.

"He had a few chores to do. He'll be here in time to eat, believe me."

Julie's forehead furrowed. "I don't get it," she said, but even her skepticism faded as Brenna stuck a small piece of bacon on the pin and cast the line into the water.

"Now what?" Scotty asked.

"We wait and watch. Come on, I'll fix a pole for you." She worked on the two extra poles and Scotty couldn't leave well enough alone. He dangled his string in and out of the water, the bacon plopping, dunking and surfacing as James, wearing fishing boots, crossed the creek.

"How's it going?" he asked, eyeing his grandchildren fondly.

"Pretty good."

"I got one!" Scotty said, jerking his string out of the water. Attached to the end, one claw around the strip of bacon, was a small crayfish, clinging for its life.

Brenna was on her feet in an instant. "Scotty, be careful!"

But it was too late. The crawdad dropped onto the ground and scooted backward, claws lifted, toward the creek. Fearlessly Scotty reached down to pick up his catch.

"Ow!" he yelped as one tooth-edged claw cut into his finger.

"You have to be careful." Brenna tried to pick up the crayfish from behind, but the red-brown crustacean reached the water's edge and backed beneath the surface to hide in the rocks.

"Ooh!" Scotty moaned. "He's gone."

"Come here, son." James reached for the boy, but Scotty turned to Brenna, stretching out his hands for her. Brenna had to smother a smile. This was the first time he'd shown any sign of accepting her.

Blood dripped from Scotty's finger and big tears of humiliation filled his eyes.

"Here you go," Brenna said, quickly grabbing a clean paper napkin and wrapping his hand. "Hold it high while I find some bandages."

Sniffling, Scotty did as he was told just as Julie whooped in delight. "I've got one! I've got one!"

"Just a minute," Brenna said as she dashed to her car, found her first-aid kit and returned.

"I'll handle this," James said. "I've caught a few in my day, y'know."

While Brenna cleaned and taped Scotty's wound, Julie landed the first crayfish and plopped the snapping animal into a bucket of water.

Still sniffling, Scotty peered into the bucket. Then, not to be outdone by his older sister, he picked up his pole again. Within the hour they'd caught nine crayfish and the bucket was full.

"I think we'd better eat now," Brenna suggested as she placed sandwiches, bananas, cookies and cans of pop on the blanket.

But Scotty hurled his line into the shallow water again. "Can we keep 'em?" Scotty asked.

"I don't think so—" She heard a car's engine rumbling down the rutted road through the fields and smiled when she recognized the glint of metallic silver through the trees. "I tell you what, why don't you ask your dad?"

Scotty didn't wait. He plowed through the shallow water, missing the stepping stones. On the opposite bank, he took off, black hair flying, pole still clutched in one chubby bandaged hand just as Warren climbed out of the car.

Brenna couldn't hear their exchange, but saw Scotty point to the creek, his wounded finger, then to her.

His teeth gleaming in the afternoon sun, Warren lifted Scotty onto his shoulders and carried him back to the picnic spot. "I hear you've already had one casualty."

"So far," Brenna admitted.

Warren's eyes gleamed mischievously. "Scotty claims you've made quite a haul."

"We caught a few."

"Can we keep 'em? Please?" Scotty begged.

"Yeah, Dad, can we?" Julie chimed in. "I'd like to take one to school for show-and-tell."

"Just what your room needs," Brenna said with a smile. "Another critter."

"Mrs. Stevens would love it!"

"She probably would," Brenna agreed, thinking of Brenna's young teacher.

Warren peered into the bucket. "I suppose it would be all right. *If* you promise to let the rest of them go. And after you've taken the crawdad to school, we'll bring it back here and release it."

"Oh, Dad," Julie complained.

"That's the deal. Take it or leave it. Same goes for you, sport," Warren said to Scotty.

"I'll take it," Julie said grudgingly.

"Good. Now, show me what you brought. I'm starved."

Scotty eyed the blanket. "Where's the ice cream?"

"Ice cream?" Warren repeated.

Brenna grinned. "I left it in Grandpa's freezer. We can have some before we leave."

"But you promised—"

"I know I did," Brenna said. "But it was already mushy when we got here. I didn't think you wanted to drink it."

Warren settled onto the blanket and ate while Julie and Scotty reluctantly released the captured crayfish. "I want ice cream," Scotty said.

James winked knowingly at Brenna. "I'll take them back to the house. You can pick them up later." He helped the children cross the creek and guided them into his old truck.

"Alone at last," Warren whispered. Stretched out on the blanket, leaning against the rough bark of the old maple tree, he looped his arm over Brenna's shoulders, pulling her back against his chest, his chin resting on her hair as they watched James's pickup bounce down the rutted lane, then disappear from view. "Now, if I remember correctly, you seemed hell-bent to talk to me earlier," Warren said, kissing her crown. "Any particular reason?"

"Nothing all that important," she teased, though her heart was hammering so loudly she was sure he could hear it. "I just thought you should know that I've decided to accept your proposal."

His lips moved against her hair. "You're sure?"

"Positive."

"Good, because I'm not about to let you change your mind."

"Never," she promised as she sighed contentedly. Half lying on the blanket, she watched a few rays of afternoon sun dapple the water. The creek lapped at their feet, gurgling noisily as it cut a lazy path down the hill and through the thicket of firs. Overhead, bees hummed and birds chattered.

Warren twisted his fingers in her hair, lifting it from her nape before he kissed her. Shivers of desire darted beneath her skin. "I've always loved you, Brenna," he admitted roughly.

"And I you."

"Promise me you'll never leave."

"You couldn't get rid of me if you tried." Twisting in his arms, she stared straight into his eyes. "I love you," she vowed. "I always will!"

"Good, you can spend the night showing me since the kids will be at Mary's."

Brenna grinned, a warm happiness glowing from deep within. "Gladly, counselor."

Without another word, he held her face between his hands and kissed her with trembling lips.

She closed her eyes, almost feeling the weight of Honor's shadow being lifted from her shoulders. Finally, Brenna felt as if she'd come home. And this time, she vowed, kissing Warren fervently, she'd never leave.

* * * * *

Look for the pulse-pounding new thriller from

ELIZABETH HEITER

Eighteen years ago, FBI profiler Evelyn Baine's best friend, Cassie Byers, disappeared, the third in a series of unsolved abductions. Only a macabre nursery rhyme was left at the scene, claiming Evelyn was also an intended victim. After all these years of silence, another girl has gone missing, and the Nursery Rhyme Killer is taking credit. Is Cassie's abductor back, or is there a copycat at work?

Evelyn has waited eighteen years for a chance to investigate, but when she returns to Rose Bay, she finds a dark side to the seemingly idyllic town. As the place erupts in violence and the kidnapper strikes again, Evelyn knows this is her last chance. If she doesn't figure out what happened to Cassie eighteen years ago, it may be Evelyn's turn to vanish without a trace.

Available now, wherever books are sold!

Be sure to connect with us at:
Harlequin.com/Newsletters
Facebook.com/HarlequinBooks
Twitter.com/HarlequinBooks

www.MIRABooks.com

MEH1738

REQUEST YOUR FREE BOOKS!

2 FREE NOVELS
FROM THE SUSPENSE COLLECTION
PLUS 2 FREE GIFTS!

YES! Please send me 2 FREE novels from the Suspense Collection and my 2 FREE gifts (gifts are worth about $10). After receiving them, if I don't wish to receive any more books, I can return the shipping statement marked "cancel." If I don't cancel, I will receive 4 brand-new novels every month and be billed just $6.24 per book in the U.S. or $6.74 per book in Canada. That's a savings of at least 22% off the cover price. It's quite a bargain! Shipping and handling is just 50¢ per book in the U.S. and 75¢ per book in Canada.* I understand that accepting the 2 free books and gifts places me under no obligation to buy anything. I can always return a shipment and cancel at any time. Even if I never buy another book, the two free books and gifts are mine to keep forever.

191/391 MDN F4XN

Name	(PLEASE PRINT)	
Address		Apt. #
City	State/Prov.	Zip/Postal Code

Signature (if under 18, a parent or guardian must sign)

Mail to the **Harlequin®** Reader Service:
IN U.S.A.: P.O. Box 1867, Buffalo, NY 14240-1867
IN CANADA: P.O. Box 609, Fort Erie, Ontario L2A 5X3

Want to try two free books from another line?
Call 1-800-873-8635 or visit www.ReaderService.com.

* Terms and prices subject to change without notice. Prices do not include applicable taxes. Sales tax applicable in N.Y. Canadian residents will be charged applicable taxes. Offer not valid in Quebec. This offer is limited to one order per household. Not valid for current subscribers to the Suspense Collection or the Romance/Suspense Collection. All orders subject to credit approval. Credit or debit balances in a customer's account(s) may be offset by any other outstanding balance owed by or to the customer. Please allow 4 to 6 weeks for delivery. Offer available while quantities last.

Your Privacy—The Harlequin® Reader Service is committed to protecting your privacy. Our Privacy Policy is available online at www.ReaderService.com or upon request from the Harlequin Reader Service.

We make a portion of our mailing list available to reputable third parties that offer products we believe may interest you. If you prefer that we not exchange your name with third parties, or if you wish to clarify or modify your communication preferences, please visit us at www.ReaderService.com/consumerschoice or write to us at Harlequin Reader Service Preference Service, P.O. Box 9062, Buffalo, NY 14269. Include your complete name and address.

SUS13R

LISA JACKSON

77877	PROOF OF INNOCENCE	__ $7.99 U.S.	__ $8.99 CAN.
77876	MEMORIES	__ $7.99 U.S.	__ $8.99 CAN.
77728	CONFESSIONS	__ $7.99 U.S.	__ $9.99 CAN.
77578	STRANGERS	__ $7.99 U.S.	__ $9.99 CAN.

(limited quantities available)

TOTAL AMOUNT	$ _____
POSTAGE & HANDLING	$ _____
($1.00 FOR 1 BOOK, 50¢ for each additional)	
APPLICABLE TAXES*	$ _____
TOTAL PAYABLE	$ _____

(check or money order—please do not send cash)

To order, complete this form and send it, along with a check or money order for the total above, payable to Harlequin HQN, to: **In the U.S.:** 3010 Walden Avenue, P.O. Box 9077, Buffalo, NY 14269-9077; **In Canada:** P.O. Box 636, Fort Erie, Ontario, L2A 5X3.

Name: _____
Address: _____ City: _____
State/Prov.: _____ Zip/Postal Code: _____
Account Number (if applicable): _____
075 CSAS

*New York residents remit applicable sales taxes.
*Canadian residents remit applicable GST and provincial taxes.

HQN™

www.HQNBooks.com

PHLJ0115BL